who do i talk to?

Other Novels by Neta Jackson Include:

The Yada Yada Prayer Group Series

The Yada Yada Prayer Group
The Yada Yada Prayer Group Gets Down
The Yada Yada Prayer Gets Real
The Yada Yada Prayer Gets Tough
The Yada Yada Prayer Gets Caught
The Yada Yada Prayer Gets Rolling
The Yada Yada Prayer Gets Decked Out

The Yada Yada House of Hope Series

Where Do I Go?

who do i talk to?

BOOK 2

A
yadayada
HOUSE *of* HOPE
Novel

NETA JACKSON

THOMAS NELSON
Since 1798

NASHVILLE   DALLAS   MEXICO CITY   RIO DE JANEIRO   BEIJING

Published in Nashville, Tennessee by Thomas Nelson. Thomas Nelson is a trademark of Thomas Nelson Inc.

Thomas Nelson, Inc., titles may be purchased in bulk for educational, business, fund-raising, or sales promotional use. For information, e-mail SpecialMarkets@ThomasNelson.com.

Published in association with the literary agency of Alive Communications, Inc., 7680 Goddard Street, Suite 200, Colorado Springs, CO 80920, www.alivecommunications.com.

Scripture quotations are taken from the following: the HOLY BIBLE, NEW INTERNATIONAL VERSION®. Copyright © 1973, 1978, 1984 by International Bible Society. Used by permission of Zondervan Publishing House. All rights reserved.

The *Holy Bible*, New Living Translation, copyright © 1996. Used by permission of Tyndale House Publishers, Inc., Wheaton, Illinois 60189. All rights reserved.

THE NEW KING JAMES VERSION®. Copyright © 1982 by Thomas Nelson, Inc. Used by permission. All rights reserved.

The KING JAMES VERSION of the Bible. Public domain.

"I Go to the Rock," words and music by Dottie Rambo. © 1977 New Spring, Inc. (ASCAP). Administered by Brentwood-Benson Music Publishing, Inc. Used by permission.

"Lord, Prepare Me," words and music by John W. Thompson and Randy Scruggs. © 1982 Whole Armor Publishing Co. Administered by The Kruger Organisation, Inc. (TKO). All rights reserved. International copyright secured.

"'Tis So Sweet to Trust in Jesus," words by William Kirkpatrick, 1883–1921. Public domain.

"I'll Fly Away," words and music by Albert Edward Brumley, 1905–1977. © 1932 in *Wonderful Message* by Hartford Music Co. Renewed 1960 by Albert E. Brumley & Sons/SESAC (admin. by ICG). All rights reserved. Used by permission.

This novel is a work of fiction. Any references to real events, businesses, organizations, and locales are intended only to give the fiction a sense of reality and authenticity. Any resemblance to actual persons, living or dead, is entirely coincidental.

Library of Congress Cataloging-in-Publication Data

Jackson, Neta.
  Who do I talk to? / Neta Jackson.
      p. cm. — (A Yada Yada house of hope novel ; bk. 2)
  ISBN 978-1-59554-524-4 (pbk.)
  1. Christian women—Fiction. 2. Shelters for the homeless—Fiction. 3. Chicago (Ill.)—Fiction.
  I. Title.
PS3560.A2415W48 2009
813'.54—dc22   2009024971

Printed in the United States of America

09 10 11 12 RRD 6 5 4 3 2 1

To Brenda Williams,
outreach coordinator at the Joshua Center in Chicago,
who dispenses no-nonsense help, hope, and love
to women both on and off the street . . .
"Because," as she says, "I've been there."

prologue

Springs protested in the darkness as a lumpy body turned over on the bottom bunk. From another bunk—one of four lining the walls of the small bedroom—a pair of nearsighted eyes peered anxiously into the shadows, making out the dim outline of her roommate trying to get comfortable on the narrow mattress.

"Lucy?" The voice was tremulous, a cracked whisper. "Are you awake?"

"Mmph." The springs groaned again.

For several moments all was quiet. Then—

"Lucy?"

A long sigh. "Whatchu *want*, Miz Martha? It's late."

"Is Gabrielle asleep?" The anxious whisper poked the darkness.

"Fuzz Top? Think so. Ain't heard nothin' from her bunk. But if you don' stop talkin', you gonna wake her up."

"But she was crying. I could tell. A mother knows."

"Well."

"Why was she crying?"

A snort from the other bunk. "She got her reasons."

"But . . ." The unsteady whisper trailed off. The elderly woman reached a hand out from under the blankets provided by the homeless shelter until she touched thick doggy hair, newly washed and silky. A rough tongue licked her fingers. Now the voice choked up. "I was just so happy you and Gabrielle found Dandy, I didn't ask why she's sleeping at the shelter tonight with me. Shouldn't she be home with her boys?"

"Well."

The woman named Martha slipped her hand back under the covers, pulled them up under her chin, and closed her eyes. Her slight body made only a small ripple under the blankets. It was her first overnight at Manna House. She felt a little strange—but her daughter had come to stay with her a night or two, that's what she said. Martha was glad, even though she didn't know why Gabrielle was sad. And her new friend Lucy was "sleeping over," too, just like a slumber party.

Martha giggled. A homeless shelter! Noble would roll over in his grave if he knew where she'd ended up. But she wasn't lonely here, not like she'd been in the big old house in Minot. And Dandy was asleep on the little rug by her bed, just like always. He'd been lost all day . . . but she couldn't remember exactly why. Had he run away? No, Dandy never ran away. Well, it didn't matter. He was safe now, snoring gently beside the bunk bed. But . . .

Her eyes flew open, staring at the bottom of the upper bunk overhead. Somebody had said, *"What's that dog doing here? Manna House don't allow no dogs!"*

Oh dear. Would the shelter let her keep Dandy? Oh, she couldn't stay another day if Dandy wasn't welcome.

She rose up on one elbow. "Lucy! You still awake? Do you think—?"

"Miz Martha! If you don' shut up and go to sleep, I'm gonna come over there and bop you one." Martha's roommate flopped over, turned her back, and the springs groaned once more. "Wonkers!" The gravelly voice settled into a mutter. "I get more sleep out on th' street than I do in a roomful of talky wimmin."

chapter 1

A lawn mower rumbled through my dream, shredding it beyond remembering.

Semiconsciousness rose to the level of my eyelids, and they fluttered in the dim light. *Uh-uh. Not a lawn mower. Snoring.* Philip was snoring and popping like a car with no muffler. I reached out to roll him over onto his side—

My hand hit a wall. No Philip in the bed. Something was wrong. What was it? A heavy grief sat on my chest, like someone had died. *Had* someone died?

I struggled to come to full consciousness and half-opened my eyes. Above me, all I could make out in the dim light was a rough board. I stared, trying to make sense of it. Why was I lying underneath a wooden board? Was *I* the one who died? Was I inside a wooden coffin?

Coffin?! A surge of panic sent me bolt upright. "Ow!" I cracked my head on the board, and the snoring stopped. Rubbing the tender spot, I squinted into dimly lit space and made out three bunk beds, one against each wall of a small room.

Mine was the fourth.

No coffin.

Blowing out my relief, I swung my feet over the side of the lower bunk but was startled as a hairy face pushed its cold nose against my bare leg with a soft whine. I reached out and touched the familiar floppy ears. *Dandy.* My mother's dog . . .

And suddenly all the cracked pieces of my life came into focus.

I'd just spent the night at Manna House, a homeless shelter for women, where, until yesterday, I'd been on staff as program director.

The small lump in the bunk across from me was my mother.

The bigger lump in the bunk next to her, producing the high-decibel racket, was Lucy, a veteran "bag lady," who for some odd reason had befriended my frail mother.

Mom and I were "homeless" because yesterday my husband had kicked both of us *and* the dog out of our penthouse condo along Chicago's Lake Shore Drive, changed the locks, and skipped town . . . taking my two sons, P. J. and Paul, with him.

As reality flooded my brain, I fell back onto the bunk, bracing for the tears I knew should follow. But the well was dry. I'd cried every drop the evening before and long into the night. Now raw grief had settled behind my eyes and into every cavity of my spirit.

I must have dozed off again, because the next thing I heard was a ringing handbell and several raps on the door. "Wake up, ladies! Six o'clock! Morning devotions at six forty-five sharp,

breakfast at seven. People with jobs get first dibs on the showers."
The footsteps moved on to another door. "Wake up, ladies! . . ."

I groaned and sat up, being careful not to hit my noggin
again on the bottom of the top bunk. Should have gotten up
when I first awoke and jumped in the shower then. No telling
when they'd be free now.

My mother was stirring on the bunk next to mine, but Lucy's
bunk was empty. "Mom, you okay? Do you need help getting to
the bathroom?" I pulled on the same slacks I'd been wearing the
night before.

"I'm all right." She gingerly got out of bed, attired in a pair
of baggy, clean-but-used flannel pajamas the shelter had provided, then carefully spread out the sheets and blankets. "But I
don't have my clothes. Where are my clothes? I have to take
Dandy out."

Dandy! A quick glance confirmed that the dog was not in the
room. But neither was Lucy. "Don't worry, Mom. I think Lucy
took him out. Wasn't that nice? You can put on the slacks and top
you wore yesterday. Mr. Bentley said he'd bring our things when
he got off work last night." The doorman at Richmond Towers
had kindly offered to load his own car with the piles of bags and
suitcases my husband had unceremoniously dumped outside our
penthouse door, but Mr. Bentley didn't get off until ten o'clock
and still hadn't arrived when we'd gone to bed. Who knew how
long it had taken him to get all that stuff down the elevator from
the thirty-second floor!

But if there was one person in the world I could count on, it
was Mr. Bentley. Our stuff would be downstairs . . . if we ever got
there.

Clutching the shelter-issued "Personal Pak"—toothbrush,

toothpaste, soap, deodorant, comb—my mother managed to navigate the crowded bathroom with me hovering right behind her. She even smiled as several of the young residents called out, "'Mornin', Gramma Shep! How'd ya sleep?" and "Hey! Nice of Miz Gabby ta stay over with ya."

I wanted to die right there. If they only knew.

Good thing I had no time to linger in front of the mirror after brushing my teeth. I looked a fright. My hazel eyes were red rimmed and my frowsy, reddish-brown curls a snarly mess, and would probably stay that way until I got a chance to wash my hair and use some conditioner.

Back in the bunk room, I tried not to show my impatience as my mother slowly dressed. *Is it too early to try calling the boys?* I had to talk to them! It was already seven thirty in Virginia. I fumbled for my cell phone. *Not in Service* blinked at me.

I groaned. *Right.* I forgot. Philip had canceled my cell.

Okay, I'd use my office phone . . . wait, I needed to get a phone card first. Shelter phones had local call service only. "Mom, come *on*. You ready?"

My mother looked at me reproachfully. "Always in a hurry. Hurry, hurry . . ." But she put up her chin and headed out the door.

The night manager had told us last night we could use the service elevator—not available to most residents, but they made an exception for my seventy-two-year-old mother. But Mom had taken one look at the small cubicle and said she'd rather take the stairs, so this morning we went down, one step at a time, to the multipurpose room on the main floor, where the residents were gathering somewhat reluctantly for morning devotions. I realized that even though I'd been working at the shelter for two months,

I had no clue what the morning routine was like before 9 or 10 a.m. when I had usually arrived. "Guess I'm going to find out," I murmured, pouring two ceramic cups of steaming coffee from the big carafes on a side table, added powdered cream, and settled down beside my mother in one of the overstuffed love seats.

"*Buongiorno, signores!* Who will read our psalm this morning?" The same booming voice that had woken us up with a thick Italian accent, packaged in a sturdy body about five foot four, black hair pulled back into a knot, waved her Bible and "volunteered" the first person who made eye contact.

I'd met the night manager briefly at our Fun Night several weeks ago and again last night, but for the life of me I couldn't remember her real name. Everybody just referred to her as "Sarge." I'd been told she was a God-fearing ex-marine sergeant, just the sort of tough love needed on night duty at a homeless shelter. She knew my mother had been put on the bed list, but Lucy's and my arrival last night with a muddy mutt in tow had thrown her into a conniption. She and Lucy had gone nose to nose for a few minutes, but with my mother crying tears of joy over the return of her lost dog, to the cheers of half the residents, Sarge had the presence of mind to call the Manna House director to ask what to do with the shelter's former program director who'd just turned up with a muddy dog, distraught and needing shelter.

I could only imagine what Mabel Turner thought. How many times had the director graciously made exceptions for me in the two months I'd been on staff? I'd lost count.

But somehow Dandy had gotten a temporary reprieve, and we both got a bed.

But . . . *Oh God? Now what?*

"'. . . Better the little that the righteous have than the wealth of many wicked,'" one of the residents was reading. The psalm got my attention. "'. . . for the power of the wicked will be broken, but the Lord upholds the righteous.' Psalm 37, readin' verse 1 through—"

"Humph!" growled a gravelly voice coming up behind me. "Ain't seen it happen *yet*."

"Ha. That's 'cause ya gotta be *righteous*, Lucy," the reader shot back. Snickers skipped around the circle.

"Sit *down*, Lucy," Sarge barked. "If you are going to be late, at least do not interrupt. All right, who has a prayer request for today? Any job interviews? Wanda, did you get your state ID yet? . . . *Va bene*, we will pray about that. Anything else?"

Behind me, Lucy leaned over the back of the couch and whispered in my ear, "I put Dandy in your ol' office downstairs after he did his bizness, thinkin' it might be best ta keep him outta the way this mornin'. But there ain't much room for him in that ol' broom closet. It's all full of your stuff that Mr. Bentley musta brought last night. Suitcases an' boxes an' stuff."

I gave her a grateful nod over my shoulder. "Good idea, Lucy," I whispered back. "Thanks for taking him out this morning." It *was* a good idea. The familiar smell of our belongings would probably keep the dog pacified for a while. "And thanks for giving him a bath last night. Sorry I didn't say something earlier. I was a bit of a wreck."

"Humph. You *still* a wreck, missy. Didja look in a mirror this mornin'?"

I rolled my eyes and didn't care if she noticed. As if *Lucy* had a leg to stand on, in her mismatched layers of clothes, most of which could use a good wash. Better yet, tossed out for good. And her matted gray hair looked like she cut it herself . . .

A hairstylist. That's what we need at Manna House! I wonder if anyone knows a beautician who'd be willing to volunteer, come in a couple of times a month—

I caught myself. What in the world was I doing, thinking like a program director? *You quit yesterday, remember?* I reminded myself. And I had bigger problems to deal with.

Much bigger.

I was pacing back and forth in Mabel Turner's office when the director arrived that morning.

The attractive African-American woman, every hair of her straightened bob in place, opened the door and stopped, hand on the doorknob, her eyebrows arching at me like twin question marks. "Gabby Fairbanks."

"Um, Angela let me wait in your office." I jerked a thumb across the foyer where the receptionist busied herself behind the glassed-in cubby. "I'm sorry, Mabel. I just couldn't wait out there in the multipurpose room with people all around. I—" I flopped down on a folding chair and buried my face in my hands.

Mabel shut the door, dropped her purse on the desk, and squatted down beside me. "Gabby, what in the world happened?"

I thought the well had gone dry, but the concern in her rich-brown eyes tapped another reservoir of tears, and it took me half a box of tissues to get through the whole sorry mess. *Locked out. Put out. Boys gone. No place to go but here.*

"I-I didn't even g-get to tell Philip I quit my job here like h-he wanted me to, or—or that Mom was going to stay here at Manna House and be out of his hair . . ." I stopped and blew my nose for the fourth time. "B-but he was so *mad*, Mabel, 'cause I accidentally passed on a message from his business partner, you know, when he and the boys were out on a sailboat with one of his clients last weekend, and it caused him to lose that client. He blamed me, said I didn't want his business to succeed—but that isn't true, Mabel! He—"

"I know, I know." The shelter director patted my knee, stood up, and got her desk chair, pulling it around so she could sit next to me. "But he just locked you out? I mean, he can't do that! Go talk to the building management. Today. If both your names are on the purchase contract, he can't just change the locks and kick you out. That's your home too! And he can't just take the boys either. You have rights, Gabby. You—"

I held up my hand to stop her, staring at her face. *Both our names?* I felt confused. Had I ever signed anything to purchase the penthouse? I tried to think. Philip had come to Chicago four months ago to finalize things with his new business partner and find a place for us to live . . . and then we just moved.

"I . . . never signed anything," I croaked.

"But they require both spouses on a joint account to—"

"We don't have joint accounts." I swallowed. "I never really questioned it. Philip was always generous. I had his credit cards and a household account in my name . . . It never seemed important."

Mabel looked at me for a long minute. "Do you have *any* money, Gabby?"

I winced. "Probably a couple hundred in my household account. And I should have a week's salary coming from Manna

House still." Which we both knew wasn't much. The job had never been about the money.

I jumped out of my chair and began to pace once more. "I don't want to talk about money, Mabel. Or even the penthouse. Good riddance, as far as I'm concerned. It's the boys! I need to get my sons back!" My voice got fierce. "He . . . he just up and took them back to their grandparents in Virginia! I never even got to say good-bye." I shook a finger in her face. "I'm their mother! You said it yourself—I've got rights!"

Mabel grabbed my wrist. "Gabby . . . Gabby, stop a minute and listen to me. Sit."

I pulled my hand from her grasp and glared at her because I didn't have anyone else to glare at. But I sat.

She took a big breath . . . but her voice was gentle. "Gabby, you do have rights. But you need to understand something. No court is going to rule in your favor if you don't even have a place to live."

chapter 2

I wept and railed in Mabel's office for a good hour. It took that long for the full weight of my overnight calamity to sink in. She was right. By now the boys were probably cozily ensconced at their grandparents' home in Petersburg. Who in their right mind would ask them to come back to Chicago and sack out at a homeless shelter just to be with Mom?

Fury at Philip fought with gut-wrenching loss. How could my own husband *do* this to me?!

Mabel mostly listened. But once I was out of steam, my former boss gently but firmly insisted I needed to work on a plan. "Be realistic, Gabby. One step at a time. What do you need to do *today*?"

We made a list. Buy a phone card until I could get a pay-as-you-go cell phone. Call the boys to make sure they were all right. Go to the closest ATM and find out if my credit cards were still good. (Fat chance.) Use my debit card to assess exactly how much money I had in my personal checking account. Go back to

Richmond Towers and talk to the manager. What were my legal rights concerning the penthouse?

"Are you going to call Philip, Gabby? Maybe he got angry and just overreacted. He might be having second thoughts about what he did."

Oh yes. I'd love to call Philip and curse him to his face. But I shook my head. "Tried that already this morning from my office. He didn't answer. And I can almost guarantee he's not having second thoughts. The whole thing was too calculated. Deliberately losing the dog. Packing up all my stuff, and Mom's too, and clearing us out. Canceling my cell phone. Changing the locks. Taking the boys on a trip—probably back to Virginia."

"Then find a lawyer, Gabby."

"Oh yeah. And pay attorney fees with what money?" I stood up to go.

"Wait a moment. Two more things . . . no, three." Mabel went behind her desk, pulled a form from a stacker, and handed it to me. "First, fill this out when you can."

I glanced at the paper. *Intake Form for Manna House Bed List.* The questions were standard: "Are you currently using drugs? Alcohol? . . . Cause of homelessness? . . . Previous living situation? (Prison? Public housing? Non-housing/Street/Car?)" . . . I looked up at Mabel. "You've got to be kidding."

"Not kidding. Sorry. Just do it, Gabby. Second . . ." She reached for a file folder, pulled out a sheet of paper, and held it up facing toward me. I recognized the resignation letter I'd turned in yesterday. With a sly smile she tore it in half, crumpled the pieces, and tossed them into the wastebasket. "I'm giving you your job back. Also not kidding." The smile rounded her smooth, nutmeg cheeks and crinkled the corners of her eyes.

My throat caught, and I had to clear it a couple of times. "Thanks," I finally croaked. "And the third thing?"

She came around the desk and took my hands. "Let's pray, Gabby. All of this looks like a mighty big mountain, but the God I know is in the mountain-moving business."

I slipped through the multipurpose room, grateful to see my mother dozing in an overstuffed chair near a group of shelter residents gossiping loudly about who was the hottest guy on *Survivor*. She was fine for the moment. I headed for the stairs to the lower floor, which housed the shelter's kitchen, dining room, recreation room, and my office—a former broom closet. Literally.

I needed to check on Dandy and then get out of there. Get that phone card. Call the boys. It was frustrating that I couldn't just pick up my office phone, but I understood why all the shelter phones were "local calls only."

At the bottom of the stairs, I peeked around the corner, hoping Estelle Williams—the shelter's weekday lunch cook—hadn't come in yet. The fifty-something African-American woman had offered to stay overnight with my mom her first night, but when I showed up unannounced, offering the lame excuse that "Lucy and I found my mother's dog, so I thought I'd just stay the night," she decided to go on home.

"No sense all of us smotherin' your mama," she'd muttered. She didn't ask any questions but had given me a funny look. It was hard to hide anything from Estelle. The woman could read my face like an open book.

I heard pots banging. So much for Estelle coming in late. But her back was turned. Maybe I could just slip into the tiny office, get Dandy, and—

"If you're lookin' for a certain yellow dog, Gabby Fairbanks, Lucy already took him out." Estelle's voice stopped me before I even had my hand on the doorknob. I turned. The big-boned woman was coming around the wide counter that separated kitchen and dining room, a puffy, white hairnet perched on her head and a white apron covering one of the loose, handmade caftans she usually wore. She made a beeline for me and without ceremony gathered me into her arms. "Oh, baby. You don't have to pretend with me. I know all about it."

My eyes burned hot but stayed dry. "You know? How—?" My voice was muffled against her broad bosom.

"Mm-mm. I was still here when Harry showed up last night with his car crammed front to back with your suitcases and boxes. I helped him shoehorn all that stuff into this lame excuse for an office."

Harry Bentley. Estelle's new love. "He—he told you?"

"Humph. Not Harry. But, honey, I already knew your man kicked out the *dog*. Already knew he gave your *mama* an ultimatum. Why else is Gramma Shep here? When Harry showed up with all your stuff . . . It ain't exactly rocket science, Gabby." The woman held me at arm's length. "You want to talk about it, baby?"

I shook my head. "I will, though. I promise." Estelle meant well, but I had to get out of there! "I've got to find my boys. Know the closest place to get a phone card?"

She gave me another funny look, as if adding up all the bits and pieces. Without a word, she moved to the counter, grabbed her oversize bag, rummaged in it, and pulled out her own cell phone. "Take it. Use it. No fussin' at me either. Girl, you don't have *time* to go lookin' for someplace 'round here that sells phone cards."

Hunched over Estelle's cell phone on the front steps of the shelter, I punched in my in-laws' home phone number. I didn't know it by heart—we'd always had their number on speed dial—but I still had juice in my defunct cell phone, thank God, and was able to access my phone book. *I need to write down all the phone numbers before my battery's totally gone*, I told myself, as the phone rang in my ear.

One ring . . . two . . . three . . . four . . . and then the answering machine picked up. *"Y'all have reached Mike and Marlene Fairbanks—"* I flipped the cell phone shut. No way was I going to leave a whimpering message on their answering machine.

My spirit sagged. Were they out? Just not answering their phone? *Oh God! I need to talk to my boys!*

An elevated train squealed and screeched over the trestle that crossed the street a block away. I sat on the wide front steps for several more minutes, trying to think what to do. It was a perfect Chicago day, temperatures in the seventies, sunny blue sky above . . . well, somewhere up there above the three-story apartment buildings and storefronts that rose all around me. I closed my eyes. A breeze off Chicago's lakefront somehow found its way into the narrow streets of this tiny neighborhood just north of Wrigley Field, home of the Cubs. As much as I'd disliked living up on the thirty-second floor of a luxury high-rise along Lake Shore Drive, I missed the sweeping view of Lake Michigan. Today the water would be sparkling blue.

Maybe I *should* call Philip's cell again . . . No. I'd call his office. If he was there, he *had* to answer his office phone. And if he wasn't, maybe Henry Fenchel would answer. Philip would've told his business partner where he was, wouldn't he?

I flipped open my cell phone to get my husband's office number. The battery was already getting low! I let myself into the front door of the shelter with my staff key. "Angela, quick. I need paper and pen." I grabbed the pad and pencil the young Asian receptionist offered me and ran back outside—bumping straight into a woman coming in the door, wearing her baby in a sling on her hip.

"Edesa!" A sense of déjà vu swept over me. Edesa—a young black woman from Central America—and her husband, Josh Baxter, a white, still-in-college kid with gray eyes and a great grin, had been the first people I'd met on these very steps the first time I'd visited Manna House. It seemed years ago, but it had only been a little more than two months.

Edesa Baxter shifted the dark-haired baby on her hip, her wide, beautiful smile greeting me. "Gabby? I didn't expect to see you here today! I thought . . . I mean . . ."

I held up my hand. "Can't explain now. I'm sorry, Edesa." Feeling terrible at brushing her off, I scurried down the steps and ran to the building next door, which housed a twenty-four-hour Laundromat on the corner. I dropped into one of the ugly, molded-plastic chairs, flipped open my fading cell phone, called up the phone book, and scribbled down as many numbers as I thought I'd need right away: Philip's office; Philip's cell; Philip's parents; Philip's partner, Henry Fenchel. My aunt Mercy in Minot, North Dakota; my mom's home phone back in Minot, even though nobody was there. The Manna House number, Mabel's cell, Estelle's cell . . .

I finally flipped the phone closed. Maybe I could borrow a charger from somebody who had a phone like mine and get the rest. But I still had to find my kids.

A bald-headed dude, wearing a dingy sleeveless undershirt that showed off the tattoos covering both arms from shoulders to wrists, pulled a huge wad of wet clothes from a front-loading washing machine and stuffed the whole caboodle—jeans, a sweater, a bunch of whites, plaid boxers—into one of the humongous dryers and set it on High. *Huh. Who cares if he fries his clothes.* I turned my back and punched the office number of Fairbanks and Fenchel into Estelle's phone.

Someone picked up on the first ring. "Fairbanks and Fenchel, Henry speaking."

My mouth suddenly went dry, and my heart thudded so hard I could feel the pulse in my ears. "Uh, hi, Henry. It's Gabby. Is, uh, Philip there?"

"Philip?" Henry sounded surprised. "No. Aren't you—?" He seemed to catch himself. "Uh, Philip left a message for me yesterday that something came up, he had to take the boys somewhere and wouldn't be back till Wednesday. I just assumed you . . ." His voice drifted off.

I felt as if I couldn't breathe. Henry didn't know any more than I did. Less. He probably had no idea Philip had kicked me out.

I gulped some air and decided not to play around. "Henry, Philip left me. Locked me out, actually. And I have no idea where he is or where he's taken the boys. I *need* to find P. J. and Paul. If you know *anything*, or hear from Philip, please call me at . . . uh, my work number." I rattled off the Manna House number.

There was a long moment of silence on the other end of the

phone. "I'm real sorry, Gabrielle. I don't know what's going on. But, uh, I can't get involved in personal stuff between you and Philip."

"No, no, of course not, but—"

"I mean, he's my business partner. We've got a lot invested in this venture."

"I know. I'm sorry. It's just that . . . the boys—"

"I don't know anything about the boys, Gabrielle. Look, I need to go." The phone went dead in my ear.

I flipped Estelle's phone closed and pressed it to my forehead, feeling like a fool. Why was I apologizing? Why was I *always* apologizing?

And what was *up* with Philip's partner, anyway?! Henry and his snobby wife, Mona, had acted like best buddies when we first arrived in Chicago, getting tickets to the Blue Man Group, going out to dinner, all of us spending a day sailing with one of their clients. Now, suddenly, he was all business. Even my given name.

Tattoo guy looked over at me with a leer. I turned my back.

What now? I'd been assuming Philip had taken the boys back to their grandparents in Petersburg, Virginia. When Philip and I had moved to Chicago in April, leaving the boys in boarding school, P. J. and Paul had spent weekends with their grandparents until P. J.'s eighth-grade graduation. Both Philip and his parents talked as though the boys would go back to Virginia for their next school year—"*After all, Fairbanks boys have always gone to George Washington Prep*"—though I'd been contacting prep schools and magnet schools all over Chicago. And Philip had threatened to send the boys back when summer sailing camp fell through—which wasn't *my* fault, but Philip made it seem that way since I'd taken the job at the shelter and couldn't immediately pick up the slack.

But . . . what if he hadn't?

chapter 3

Panic flickered in my chest. My breath shortened. I was going to hyperventilate if I wasn't careful. *Breathe in slowly, Gabby . . . breathe out . . .*

As my heart rate slowed, I could almost hear Mabel's firm voice in my head. *"Be realistic, Gabby. One step at a time. Do what you need to do today. And pray. You can't do this on your own."*

Pray. Seemed like all my prayers were of the "Help!" variety lately. Before I came to Chicago, my prayers had gotten pretty rusty. But the staff at Manna House all seemed to be on a first-name basis with the Almighty, talking to God like He really cared about the mundane problems of homeless women. Mabel had even said *I* was an answer to their prayers for a program director and that God had a purpose for bringing me to Manna House after tripping over Lucy in the park that rainy day.

And the worship teams from different churches that came to the shelter each weekend to lead Sunday evening praise acted like worshipping God and studying the Bible were more exciting than . . . than watching the Cubs hit a homer.

The last two months had brought back a lot of what I'd been taught by my parents and our little community church growing up in North Dakota. A faith I'd pretty much tossed out when my starry-eyed marriage right out of high school hit the skids after only two years. In fact, meeting the charming Philip Fairbanks on a summer jaunt through Europe had all the earmarks of a "happily ever after" fairy tale, so why bother to pray?

That was before everything started to fall apart between Philip and me, and the only firm ground I had to stand on was my job at Manna House Women's Shelter, and the people there who made me feel that I *mattered*.

I stuck Estelle's cell phone in my shoulder bag, left the Laundromat—tattoo guy was still smirking at me—and started walking the few blocks toward the Sheridan El Station. "God," I whispered, "it's me, Gabby. Thanks for . . ." *Good grief, what do I have to be thankful for?* Well, lots, come to think of it. ". . . for a roof over our heads last night for both Mom and me. That Lucy found Dandy after Philip let him run loose all night and he got lost. That Mabel gave me my job back, so I'll have some income." I smiled to myself in spite of my predicament. Three whole sentences and I hadn't yelled "Help!" yet. But I was getting there. "But I really do need help, Lord. Please, please help me find out where P. J. and Paul are so I'll know they're okay."

Realizing I'd left the shelter without checking out or telling anyone, even my mother, where I was going—against shelter rules—I fished out Estelle's phone again and called. "Angela? It's Gabby. I forgot to sign out. I have some errands to do. Could you tell my mother I'll be back soon? . . . I don't know, maybe a couple of hours . . . Thanks. Oh! If you see Lucy, would you ask her if she can take care of Dandy? I'll make it up to her, promise."

The El tracks loomed overhead where the Red Line stopped at Sheridan Road. I crossed the street and pushed open the door of the convenience store that sat next to the station. Did they have phone cards? What about an ATM machine? The clerk, who looked Indian or Pakistani under a cap of straight, black hair, pointed to a circular rack of prepaid phone cards, then jerked a thumb out the door. "Bank! You have to go bank for ATM machine."

I quickly bought a twenty-dollar phone card with my debit card, knowing I had at least that much in my household account, and scurried out the door, looking up the street beyond the El station. Bank? I hadn't realized there was a bank close by, probably because I'd always walked straight from the El station to the shelter, going the other direction. But sure enough, a small bank sat on the corner half a block north—probably a branch of some big bank I'd never heard of.

An old man was using the ATM inside, and I fidgeted while he fumbled with his card and the push buttons. But finally he stuffed his money, card, and receipt in his pants pocket and shuffled out the door, tipping his hat at me on the way out. I was in such a hurry to find out the bad news, I had stuck my Visa card into the machine before his polite gesture even registered on my scrambled brain. And I hadn't acknowledged it.

Guilt joined the puddle of self-pity I was wallowing in. Would life ever be normal again? Would I ever wake up again with my children safely under the same roof, my husband in my bed—huh! Not that I wanted him there right now, maybe never—looking forward to an ordinary day, happily greeting the people who came across my path? After fifteen years of not having to think about money, was I now destined to live from paycheck to paycheck, counting every dime?

Get a grip, Gabby. I shook off the maudlin thoughts, tapped my PIN number on the pad, and tried to make a "credit loan" of a hundred dollars. The card came spitting out at me. The readout said, *Card Rejected.*

I tried my American Express. *Card rejected.* The only other credit cards I had were for Bloomingdale's and Lord & Taylor, and I was pretty sure what would happen if I walked into one of those stores and tried to use them.

The slimeball! Philip had canceled them all—which, frankly, was what I'd expected, though I'd hoped . . .

I had one last card, the debit card to my household account. I stuck it into the slot, tapped in my PIN number, and withdrew twenty dollars. A moment later, a twenty-dollar bill, my debit card, and the receipt whirred out of their slots. I focused on the receipt. How much was left?

The faded blue ink at the bottom said, *Balance: $187.23.*

Someone else came into the foyer and stood behind me, wanting to use the ATM. I stuffed the twenty, the debit card, and the receipt into my shoulder bag and stumbled out the door of the bank. That was it? That was all the money I had in this world?

The rich aroma of fresh coffee lured me into the Emerald City Coffee Shop under the El tracks. I flopped down in a chair at one of the small tables near the front window. A cup of coffee, that's what I needed to steady my nerves . . .

Wait. Could I afford a cup of coffee? My hands shaking, I grabbed a napkin and pulled a pen from my purse. Thirty dollars in my wallet—no, make that twenty after I paid for the cab last night that brought Lucy, me, and a bedraggled Dandy to the shelter. Add twenty that I just took out of my account, that's forty. One-eighty-seven still in the account, plus forty cash . . .

I had roughly $220 to my name. Plus a twenty-dollar phone card.

That was it.

So much for a mocha latte at three dollars a pop.

Wait . . . My last two-week paycheck from Manna House should come by Friday. I suddenly felt like laughing. I was rich! Well, maybe not rich. Not enough to live on, not enough to rent an apartment yet. But at least I could afford one cup of coffee.

I was relishing each sip of a medium regular coffee with cream when I heard a cell phone ringing close by. Didn't recognize the ring, so I ignored it—until I realized the ringing was coming from my shoulder bag. Estelle's phone! Was she calling me? Or was someone else calling her? Should I answer it?

I grabbed the phone, flipped it open, and looked at the caller ID. *Harry Bentley.* Eagerly I pushed the Talk button. "Mr. Bentley? It's me, Gabby!"

"Uh . . . Mrs. Fairbanks? Uh, I thought . . ."

"Oh, Mr. Bentley, I'm sorry. You were calling Estelle. She loaned me her cell phone." I felt guilty, as if I'd intercepted a note between two lovers. Shouldn't have answered the phone. "But she's still at Manna House. You could call the main number."

"Mm. That's all right. I'll catch her later. But . . . just a minute. Can you hold?" Without waiting for an answer, I heard Mr. Bentley turn from the phone and say something to someone in his polite doorman voice. "All right, all right. You have a nice day,

Mrs. Pearson, you hear?" His voice came back on, though speaking low as if not wanting others to hear. "Mrs. Fairbanks, are you still there?"

"I'm here, Mr. Bentley."

"Just wanting to know . . . are you all right?"

The kindness in the older man's voice nearly turned on the faucet again. I fished for a tissue. "Um, still in shock, I guess. Trying to sort things out . . . you know."

"Did you get hold of your boys? Don't mean to pry, but . . ."

"That's all right, Mr. Bentley." I had to swallow hard a couple of times. "I appreciate your concern. Haven't talked to them yet. No one answers at my in-laws'."

I heard the doorman mutter something on the other end that I didn't catch. But then he said, "Well, don't worry, Mrs. Fairbanks. I know you're upset—you've got a right to be—but I'm sure your boys are all right. Bad as it is, they're with their dad."

My reply came out in a choked whisper. "I know. Thanks."

"Well, now. Don't know if you plan on comin' back to Richmond Towers today or not, but thought I'd let you know I haven't seen Mr. Fairbanks, and I've been on duty since six this mornin'. Don't think he's come back. The manager is in the office, though. You might want to come up here and, well, you know, see what can be done about getting you back into your penthouse."

I sat up. That's right. That was still on my list of things I needed to do today. "Thanks, Mr. Bentley. I'm coming now. See you in thirty minutes."

I grabbed the napkin with the total of all my worldly finances scribbled on it and headed out the door of the coffee shop for the turnstile in the El station. That's when I remembered one other asset that was going to come in handy. I had a transit card in my wallet I'd bought just last week with twenty-five dollars in fares on it.

Should last me awhile—especially since the "commute" to my job from bedroom to office was now just down the stairs.

chapter 4

I rode the Red Line north to my usual stop, followed the other passengers down to street level, and started walking the few blocks to Richmond Towers. But when I turned the corner and saw the glass-and-steel building rising into the sky just ahead, I suddenly couldn't breathe. My hands started to shake.

I can't do this! Was it just yesterday that I'd come home from work, ready to tell Philip that I'd found a place for my mom to stay until I found something better? Ready to tell him I'd quit my job, just like he wanted, so I could supervise the boys this summer? Thinking these efforts would make everything all right that had gone wrong between us? Making a sacrifice worth the price of selling my soul.

Only to find that my sons were missing and I was out on the street . . .

The shock and rage of those first few hours threatened to boil up once again. *Steady, Gabby. Don't lose it right here on the street.* Besides, I encouraged myself, the first person I'd see when I walked through those doors would be Mr. Bentley. I forced myself to walk the last two blocks, each step a prayer for courage.

I pushed through the street-side revolving doors into the spacious lobby of the luxury high-rise, quiet and empty of building residents in the noontime lull. I'd always felt like an imposter pushing through those doors—as if someone would find out I was just a small-town girl from North Dakota—and today even more so. But like a familiar Chicago landmark, Mr. Bentley sat behind the half-moon desk, uniform cap tossed aside, bald head glistening like a brown bowling ball, and spearing what looked like Chinese takeout with a plastic fork. The knot in my spirit loosened a hitch.

I cleared my throat. "Mr. B."

Mr. Bentley jumped as if I'd said, "Boo!" spilling some of his lunch. "Don't sneak up on a body like that, Mrs. Fairbanks." He grabbed a napkin and dabbed at his pants.

"I'm sorry. Didn't mean to scare you." Hard to believe he hadn't heard me come through the revolving door. Mr. Bentley was usually aware of every squeak and puff of air that went through that foyer. "That must be some takeout you've got there."

"Humph. Nothin' special. I was just thinkin' about somethin'. . ." He grabbed his cap with the gold braid, buttoned his coat, and came around the desk. "You all right? I was afraid the manager might go out before you got here. But he's still here. You go on." The doorman gave me a push toward the glass door marked Building Personnel Only. "I'll buzz you in."

What I really wanted to do was hang out with Mr. Bentley for five or ten minutes before going in, but he was already leaning on the buzzer to the glass door across the foyer. I hurried over and pulled it open. "All right, all right!" I hissed over my shoulder. The doorman gave me an encouraging nod and flicked his hand as if shooing me in.

Several doors lined the short corridor: Sales Office. Lock Boxes. Security. Restroom—Staff Only. I stopped in front of the door marked Building Management, which was slightly ajar. What in the world was I going to say that wouldn't make me—or Philip, for that matter—look like a fool in front of a total stranger?

I knocked and peeked in. "Excuse me?" A fortyish white man in shirt sleeves and a loosened tie sat at his computer, papers spread over the desk. The nameplate on his desk said Walter Martin. "Mr. Martin? Do you have a moment?"

The man looked up. "Uh, certainly. Did you have an appointment, Miss . . . ?" He fished for his appointment book and frowned at it, as if wondering if he'd forgotten.

"Mrs. Fairbanks. Penthouse, thirty-second floor." Just saying the little refrain made me feel bolder, though I wished I'd found a dress and heels to wear and paid more attention to my hair and makeup. My head of natural red curls—though it had darkened to a chestnut color in recent years—had a tendency to get frowsy in humid weather.

"Fairbanks," he murmured. "Oh yes, your husband left a phone message on my answering machine. I'm sorry, I've been so busy I haven't called him back yet. Is that why you're here?"

I tried not to stutter. "Phone message?"

"Mm, yes. Something about canceling the penthouse lease early, needing to move suddenly. Said he'd have everything out by the end of the month. Of course, unless he can get someone to sublet, he will be responsible . . ."

I didn't hear the rest. My mouth went dry, my brain stuck on "lease . . . move . . . end of the month." *Lease?* I thought Philip had bought a condo! And he was moving out?

I tried to clear my brain. "Excuse me."

The man stopped his spiel. "Yes?"

"Could I see a copy of the contract?"

"Of course." The man rolled his chair, opened a file drawer, and after a moment of pawing through its contents, pulled out a file. He opened it, scanned the contents—then looked up at me. "I'm sorry. This is awkward. But only Mr. Fairbanks's name is on the lease. If you are his wife, of course you have a right to see it, but . . . do you have any identification?"

My cheeks flamed. What did he think I was, some hussy trying to pull a con? But my better sense told me to stay calm, play the game. He had to do what he had to do.

"Of course." I pulled out my wallet and slid my driver's license toward him. Still a Virginia license.

"I see. Do you have any identification with your current address? Or a current utility bill with both your and your husband's names on it?"

I flinched. We'd been in Chicago for barely three months. I hadn't applied for a new driver's license yet. The bills came in Philip's name—not that I had a copy of any of the utility bills on me anyway. The manager was probably wondering why I didn't just run upstairs and get a copy of the electric bill, or our marriage license, or something! But everything like that was on the thirty-second floor in Philip's study, behind a front door with a new lock, and my key did not fit that lock.

"Mr. Martin—" I hesitated. How much should I say? Should I just leave? But something inside me rebelled against rolling over and playing dead. "Mr. Martin, my husband left me yesterday and took our children. Not only that, but I can't get any of the ID you need because he changed the locks, so I can't get into my own home. I came here because I need to know what my rights are respective to—"

"Changed the locks? Did you say Mr. Fairbanks—?"

I nodded. "Yes, and—"

"But he can't do that! Not on leased property. Management needs to have a key to leased units in case of emergency."

I didn't know whether to laugh hysterically or scream bloody murder. I tried to keep my voice steady, but the sarcasm leaked anyway. "Maybe he *can't*. But he *did*. And this *is* an emergency, Mr. Martin. *My* emergency. I came here to ask what you can do about it."

Mr. Martin slumped back against his executive chair. He ran a hand over his military-short haircut, avoiding eye contact. Finally he picked up the file folder and busied himself putting it back. "I'm sorry, Mrs., uh, Fairbanks. My hands are tied. It is against Richmond Towers policy to get involved in domestic affairs. If you had some ID proving you have a spousal right to enter the penthouse . . ." He shrugged. "I'm sorry."

Again I had to fight the urge to get hysterical. Wordlessly, I retrieved my driver's license, put it back in my wallet, and stood up. I didn't trust myself to say anything, so I simply turned and left.

"Should sic Mr. Bentley on him," I muttered to myself, yanking open the glass door at the end of the corridor. "He'd vouch for me, tell Mr. Martin what he saw with his own eyes last night." But when I came out into the foyer, Mr. Bentley had the desk phone cradled in his ear, scribbling a message. *Forget it, Gabby. Don't drag Mr. Bentley into your mess. This is his job, remember?*

I was pretty sure he didn't see me as I slipped out the revolving door.

Barely noticing the squeals, rattles, and bumps of the El heading back to the Wrigleyville North neighborhood, I pressed my forehead against the cool window. *A lawyer. That's what I need.* Obviously I wasn't going to get anywhere trying to navigate the land mines of my situation by myself. I wasn't even sure I cared about getting back into the penthouse. Did I want to be someplace where I wasn't wanted? Not if my boys weren't there. I didn't even care that much about the furniture and stuff that filled the place, though there were personal things I did care about—photo albums, the boys' baby books, household items that had been wedding gifts from my parents . . .

But even those things seemed unimportant right now. Not until I talked to my sons and knew they were all right. And then . . .

"I'll get my boys back. Whatever it takes, Philip Fairbanks! You wait and see," I muttered, leaving steam on the window. In the window reflection, I saw the woman next to me give me a strange look. She got up and moved across the aisle as the train slowed.

So what? Let her think I was nuts. This was my stop.

I strode briskly the few blocks to Manna House. More focused now, I tried the number for Philip's parents again before I went inside the shelter. Still no answer. But this time I left a message. "Mike and Marlene, this is Gabrielle. If P. J. and Paul are there, tell them I need to speak with them as soon as possible. *Today,* not tomorrow. My cell phone is not working. They can call this number or . . ." and I rattled off the number for Manna House.

I felt proud of myself for not screaming or blubbering at my in-laws. I was firm. Clear. Concise. Surely they'd see I was a reasonable person and let the boys call.

Unless . . .

My stomach felt weak. What if Philip hadn't taken them back to Virginia?

I had to call Philip. No way around it. What was I afraid of? What more could he do to me that he hadn't already done?

Leaning against one of the double oak doors of Manna House, shaped to resemble the doors of the old church that had once housed the shelter before it was rebuilt, I dialed my husband's cell number on Estelle's phone. It went right to voice mail. "Fairbanks. I'm not available right now. Please leave a message . . . *Beep.*"

Just hearing his voice sucked the confidence out of me. But I tried. "Philip, it's Gabby. I need to know where you've taken the boys. I need to talk to them. Please." My voice started to crack. "Please. That's all. Just let me talk to my kids." I repeated the Manna House number and hung up.

I bent over, hands on my knees. "Oh God, please . . ."

The door beside me opened. "Sister Gabby? Oh, *mi amiga,* I am so glad you are back. Your mother is worried about you."

I recognized Edesa Baxter's voice but didn't look up. I remained bent over, just shaking my head. The next moment I felt the young woman's arms go around me. "I heard what happened, *mi amiga.* Mabel told me," she whispered in my ear. "God knows. He will help you be strong. We will all help you."

I was picking at the chicken stir-fry and rice that volunteers from a local church had brought for the evening meal, trying to shut out the constant fussing of two-year-old Bam Bam, whose mother had just signed up for the bed list, when Wanda motioned to me, waving the kitchen extension. She pointed to my office. "Better take it in dere!" she yelled over the general hubbub.

My chair tipped over in my haste to get to my broom-closet office. I set it upright so fast, it wobbled and almost toppled the other direction, but I didn't wait to see if it fell again. I tried to open the office door, but my mother's dog was standing in the way, trying to get out of his prison. "Dandy!" I hissed. "Back, back!" Finally closing the door behind me, I snatched up my office extension. "Hello? Gabby speaking!"

Silence. At first I thought the call was lost. Then I heard a small voice. "Mom?"

The room seemed to spin. I squeezed my eyes shut and sank into the desk chair. "Paul! Yes, yes, it's me. Are you okay, honey? Where are you?"

"I'm . . . we're at Nana and Grandad's house. Didn't Daddy tell you?"

"Well . . . sure, sure, I knew you'd be there." My brain scrambled, searching for the right words. How much did the kids know? What should I tell them? "Just asked 'cause I called earlier and you weren't there, thought maybe you were still out."

"Oh. Nana took us shopping for some shorts and stuff. But . . . Mom?"

The jealous monster squeezing my heart nearly cut off my breath. *I* should be taking my boys shopping for shorts and T-shirts, not Marlene Fairbanks! I took a deep breath. "What, honey?"

"What's wrong with Grandma? How come you hafta stay with her instead of us?"

I fought for control. "Is that what Daddy said?"

"Yeah. He said Grandma needed you real bad and you couldn't take care of us right now, so we had to go back to Virginia right away. He told us you and Grandma were movin' out, and we had to pack your stuff. But . . ." I heard Paul start to cry. "Why didn't you come say good-bye to us? I tried to call your cell, but you didn't even answer!"

chapter 5

I HATE you, Philip Fairbanks!

My emotions seethed as I tossed in my bunk that night, unable to sleep, listening to Lucy's heavy breathing across the room. How could the man I'd just spent fifteen-plus years of my life with let my kids think *I* was the one who wanted to move out so fast, I didn't even have time to tell them good-bye? Let them think I just wasn't answering my cell phone? Had them actually help pack up my things because Mom and Grandma were moving out?

You pig! I slugged the pillow I'd been clutching, wishing it was his face. *You slimy snake!* I threw in a few other dirty names, punching the pillow with each one.

I finally fell back, blowing out the dregs of tension. At least . . . at least Philip had said their grandma needed me "real bad" right now—not that I didn't love them anymore, or something equally devastating.

Still!

Lucy's heavy breathing hiked up a couple of notches into a rumbling snore. I flopped over on the skinny bunk and smashed the pillow over my ears. In the dark cocoon I created, the phone call with my sons played over and over again in my head . . .

Philip Jr.'s voice had been guarded. "Hey, Mom."

"Hey there, kiddo." It was *so* tempting to blurt out that their father had *stolen* them from me, and I was going to bring them back the very next day! But . . . back to what? I needed time!—time to figure out my options, to make a plan.

"Is Paul still there? Listen, both of you. I want to tell you something. Your dad and I . . . there's been a misunderstanding. I found a place for Grandma to stay, but your dad didn't know that. But I want *you* to know that I *never, ever* meant for you to go back to Virginia so suddenly, especially without saying good-bye. I—I want to be with you so bad." My voice caught, and I had to stop.

Paul jumped in. "Why can't Grandma and Dandy just live with us, Mom? I don't mind sleeping in P. J.'s room."

"Says you," his brother shot back. "I want my room back. I'm almost fourteen, you turkey."

"So? We have to share a room here at Nana's. Why not—"

"Boys!" I had interrupted. "It's . . . it's not possible for Grandma and Dandy to live with us right now." *Because your dad's a selfish pig,* I'd wanted to add, but bit it off. "But I want to get you back home with me as soon as possible."

"Gee, wish you guys would make up your mind!" P. J. had stormed. "Granddad just said he could sign me up for a summer lacrosse league! I'd be sure to make the spring team when I go back to GW if I could play this summer." GW . . . George Washington Prep, "where all the Fairbanks boys" had gone to school.

"So? Go ahead and stay here. I'll go back with Dad, and we'll *both* have our own rooms!"

"Stupid. Dad just left for the airport."

That news had hit me like cold water in the face. So Philip was on his way back to Chicago. Well, Henry Fenchel had said he'd be back in the office on Wednesday. *Tomorrow* . . .

I rolled out of the bunk. Rehearsing the phone call with my kids would never let me sleep. Usually when I couldn't sleep, I'd get up, make some chamomile tea, and read something for a while. What did one do in a homeless shelter?

Dandy popped up from his rug beside my mother's bunk and tried to follow me. "Stay, boy," I whispered. "Lie down. Stay." I squeezed out the door, shut it behind me, and padded quietly down the stairs. Or so I thought.

Sarge met me at the bottom step on the main floor. *"Mi scusi!* Back upstairs now—oh. It is you, Mrs. Fairbanks." The night manager folded her arms across her chest. "So, you do not abide by resident rules, no? And I know you still have that dog upstairs. Against *all* kind of rules, if you ask me."

I thought fast. "Uh, I need to go to my office for a minute. Sorry I disturbed you." I hustled down the next flight of stairs to the lower level, made my way by the dim EXIT-sign glow to my office, and flipped on its light. *Maybe I should do some work, give me something else to think about. Mabel rehired me, after all. Better start earning my keep—*

That's when I noticed the envelope propped against the computer, my name on the outside. Easing myself into the desk chair, I pulled a sheet of paper from the envelope. Edesa's handwriting . . .

Dear Sister Gabby,

My heart breaks for you, mi amiga, to have your children taken away so fast. But you are not forgotten! My Yada Yada sisters gave me this precious word from the Lord when it looked as if we might lose our Gracie:

"Can a mother forget the baby at her breast and have no compassion on the child she has borne? Though she may forget, I will not forget you! See, I have engraved you on the palms of my hands; your walls are ever before me. Your sons hasten back, and those who laid you waste depart from you." (From Isaiah 49. There's more. You might want to look it up!)

Dear Gabrielle, your parents gave you the right name! Live it!

¡Te amo!

Edesa Reyes Baxter

My heart beat faster as I read the note. I read the Bible verse again, and then again. "*. . . Your sons hasten back . . .*" Was this a promise for me? But it was from the Old Testament! Written thousands of years ago. How could it . . . ?

I pressed the note to my chest, turned out the light, and schlepped up the two flights of stairs to the bunk rooms, strangely comforted. *"Your sons hasten back . . ."*

Lucy was still snoring when I opened the door to the room we shared. Tiptoeing to her bunk, I felt for the old woman's body, put both hands under her side, and rolled. With a grunt and a groan, the "bag lady" heaved over onto her side, smacking her lips in her sleep. I waited, holding my breath.

Sweet silence.

Crawling into my own bunk, I slid Edesa's note under the pillow. As I drifted off to sleep, I wondered, what did she mean about *living* my name?

The six o'clock wake-up call grated on my nerves after my short night. Didn't homeless women *ever* get to sleep in? On the other hand, breakfast was ready at seven, prepared by the night staff— oatmeal and toast this morning—and the coffee was hot. I needed at least two cups to pry my eyelids awake.

I had just finished telling my mother I would get the rest of her clothes and personal things situated up in our bunk room, when Sarge rang the big handbell for attention. "Listen up, *signore*! Here is the chore list for today. Wanda and Gabby, breakfast dishes. Martha Shepherd and Tanya, wipe tables and sweep. Lunch . . ."

Drat! I'd forgotten about the chore list. How was I supposed to take care of my mother, put in my hours as program director, and start the uphill battle to get my kids back while washing dishes for thirty-some people? I sighed. Couldn't very well complain. All the residents helped with the daily chores in one way or another. At least my mother hadn't been saddled with heavy duty, like the dishes.

"Hey!" Lucy's crusty voice broke into my thoughts. "What if I don' wanna *be* here at lunchtime! Cheese Louise. A body's got things to do, places to go. Can't hang around all day just 'cause you put my name up there to push a broom after lunch."

"Trade with someone, then," Sarge shot back. "Just so it gets done."

Which was just as well, because Lucy ended up trading chores with Tanya, who had a nine o'clock interview at one of the housing agencies and wanted to get out of there. That put Lucy and my mom working together, so I just left them to it, while Wanda tried to teach me the ins and outs of the huge industrial dishwasher—though her Jamaican accent was so thick, I had a hard time understanding half of what she said.

"No problem, Sistah Gabby! You spray off de food, mi stack de dishes in de trays, slide dem in dis way, slide down de door, push dat button . . . see? All dere is to it!"

Except there was no such thing as "spraying off" cold oatmeal stuck inside the multiple bowls, which meant I did a lot of scraping and scrubbing before Wanda could load the trays.

By the time I'd dried and stacked the heavy coffee cups that came out hot and steaming from the dishwasher, my curly hair had frizzed up like a Brillo pad under the required white hairnet, and my hands were beet red. Delores Enriques, the nurse from the county hospital who came in once a week on Wednesday, was already setting up her makeshift nurse's station in a corner of the dining room. I gave her a wave as I hurried upstairs to check on my mom. She was sitting in a far corner of the multipurpose room chatting with Carolyn, the shelter's self-appointed "book maven," who'd been trying to set up a library with donated books. To my surprise, Dandy sat on his haunches, pressed close to my mother's knees, her hand lightly stroking his head.

I looked nervously about. "Mom! I don't think Dandy should—"

Carolyn put a conspiratorial finger to her lips. "Shh. We saw Sarge leave, so Lucy brought Dandy up. Nobody's gonna care for a few minutes." The middle-aged resident, who wore her long, brownish-gray hair slicked back from her pallid face in a straggly ponytail, grinned at me. "Say, Gramma Shep is the first person I've met at Manna House who's also read Robert Browning's poems. How come you never told me that?"

Just then Estelle breezed through the double doors from the foyer, loose orange caftan flying, carrying two bulging bags with yarn and needles sticking out of the top. Without breaking stride she called out, "Mornin', ladies! It's Wednesday—knitting club gonna be startin' up in a few minutes. Sure could use your help again, Gramma Shep." The colorful black woman disappeared down the stairs to the lower level.

I grinned. Looked like the knitting club I'd suggested Estelle pioneer was off and running for its second week, giving women something to do while waiting for the nurse to see those who signed up. Pleased, my mother struggled up out of the over-stuffed chair to follow. I started to help her, but Carolyn got there first. "Nah, let me. I'll get your mom downstairs and put the dog in your office. Just don't ask me to take him out and pick up his poopies. No sir. That's where I draw the line."

I tried not to laugh. "Thanks, Carolyn." I knew Lucy had already taken Dandy out once, and with Mom busy for the next hour or two, I should be able to get a few things done. First stop, Mabel's office.

As briefly as I could, I brought the director of Manna House up to speed on my visit to Richmond Towers yesterday, the status of my finances, and the phone call with my children, including the fact that Philip was probably back in town and expected at his office. "At least I know where to find him," I said wryly. "But I need a lawyer, Mabel—someone who does family law. Problem is, I don't have any money."

Mabel flipped her old-fashioned Rolodex and wrote down a number. "Legal Aid. Ask for Lee Boyer. He's done work for some of the shelter residents before. He's a good man."

"Thanks. Oh, before I forget . . ." I handed my boss the intake form I'd filled out. "Never thought I'd be checking off any of those boxes. Pretty humbling. Always thought homeless people were, well, like Lucy, bag ladies or winos living out on the street for years. But now look at me." I shook my head.

Mabel arched an eyebrow, the only wrinkle in her maple-smooth skin. "You're not the only person with a college degree we have in here. Look at Carolyn. She's got a master's degree in literature! Had a string of bad luck financially, lost a lucrative job, didn't have any close family, got evicted for some reason—"

"Yeah. That's me. Evicted by my own husband." I knew I sounded sarcastic. I stood up quickly. "Thanks, Mabel. I'm going to call Legal Aid and then get to work."

"One more thing, Gabby."

I paused. "Yes?"

"Sarge says we have to do something about the dog. She's right. What if every resident wanted to bring her dog or cat into the shelter?"

I groaned. "I know, I know. It's just . . ." I dreaded telling my mother she couldn't keep Dandy. "What am I going to do? He's been Mom's constant companion since Dad died! I'd keep him myself if I had my own apartment, but . . ." I shook my head in frustration. Dandy wasn't the only reason I needed to find an apartment—soon!

"Well, maybe we can find a foster home for him. I'll start asking around." A slow smile spread over Mabel's normally business-like features. "Lucy sure seems to have taken a shine to him."

"I know! She took him out three times yesterday and again this morning. Don't know where they go—there aren't any parks close by that I know of."

I started to leave when she called me back again. "Gabby?"

Now what? I tried not to roll my eyes.

"Don't be thinking about showing up at Philip's office today."

I gave her a look. I'd been toying with that very thought. Oh, how I wanted to give that man a piece of my mind, and do it in front of his partner and any clients who happened to be there too!

She jabbed a finger at me. "See the lawyer first. Know your rights. Until then, you'll just be acting the fool, and he'll feel justified walking out on you."

Now I did roll my eyes, jerked open her door, and let it close—hard—behind me.

chapter 6

I couldn't get an appointment with the Legal Aid guy until Friday. "But this is urgent!" I protested.

"Honey, they're all urgent," said the woman on the other end of the phone. "Mr. Boyer can see you Friday at two o'clock. You want the appointment or not?"

Frustrated, I said yes and banged my office phone back onto its base. Friday was two days away! Yeah, Mabel had told me to get legal advice before I confronted Philip . . . but two days?!

Outside my office door, the dining room buzzed with women waiting to be called by the nurse. Everything from bunions caused by ill-fitting shoes to mysterious rashes to a variety of STDs needing medication. Maybe Delores Enriques, the pediatric nurse from the sprawling county hospital on Chicago's near south side, had something that'd help the headache spreading over my skull like a cracked egg . . . or maybe I just needed to *do* something.

Like a steam-driven engine, I hauled the rest of my mom's

and my stuff two flights up to the bunk room we'd been assigned, put our necessities in the small dresser drawers provided for each resident, and stuffed the rest of the suitcases and boxes under our bunks. Not exactly the beautiful walnut bedroom set that had been a wedding gift from Philip's parents—and definitely not the spacious walk-in closet in the penthouse. At the same time, the Lord & Taylor pantsuits I'd just stuffed under the bed would make me stand out here at the shelter like a gold front tooth.

It took five trips, but by the time I shut the door on the bee-hive going on around the makeshift nurse's station in one corner and the knitting club in another, my broom-closet office seemed five times bigger. Even Dandy seemed happy with the new arrangement, coming out from under my desk and stretching along the wall next to the file cabinet.

For the next hour, I tried to get back up to speed with plans for the activities program here at Manna House—after packing it up on Monday, thinking I wouldn't be back and someone else would have to take over as program director. I focused on the activities I'd already put in place:

An ESL class once a week . . . Tina, one of the residents, a big-boned Puerto Rican who was fluent in both Spanish and English, had agreed to try teaching English as a second language to Aida Menéndez, a young Latina who'd been bounced around in the foster system until she was eighteen and dropped out of school because of language problems. Tina was good for a few weeks anyway, until she lined up some resources for alternate housing or found a job, and then I'd need to find someone more perma-nent. Edesa and Josh Baxter had rustled up some ESL materials from Josh's mom, a third-grade teacher on the north side. *I'll have to sit in on Tina's weekly session, see how it's going,* I thought.

Typing . . . Josh's mom, Jodi Baxter, had also agreed to teach a typing class on Saturday morning for residents who wanted to improve their job skills. The shelter had a schoolroom with two computers, but Jodi had said three people showed up for the first class a few weeks ago. I made a mental note: *Ask the board for another computer.*

And the knitting club . . . that had been easy. When I first took on the job, I'd noticed Estelle knitting something blue and bulky while managing the signup list to see the nurse. Now five or six women were knitting and purling away on Wednesday mornings, watching simple winter scarves grow longer, if not exactly symmetrical.

I chewed the end of a pencil as I studied the list of possibilities for more "life skills" for these women with precious few resources. Now that Estelle had been hired on a part-time basis, she was the obvious resource for basic classes in cooking and sewing. That proposal was already on Mabel's desk. And Edesa's husband, Josh, had casually suggested a sports clinic for the shelter kids on the weekend . . . *Hmm.* His dad was the athletic director at Rogers Park High School. Possible resource there.

I grinned to myself. Might as well get the whole Baxter clan involved here! They'd supported the Fun Night that Precious McGill and I had cooked up last month. Precious, a former resident and now a volunteer with the after-school kids—couldn't exactly call it a "program" yet—had managed to get all the residents and most of the staff off their duffs that night, doing the Macarena . . .

Precious! I suddenly realized I hadn't seen the livewire volunteer *or* her teenage daughter, Sabrina, since I got back from North Dakota with my mother almost two weeks ago. I doubted she knew I'd resigned on Monday, much less became a "resident" that same night. What was up with *her*?

I reached for the phone and my staff directory.

And I thought I had problems.

The first time I tried the number I had for Precious, I got her voice mail. *"Can't talk now, but leave a number an' I'll call ya back—if Jesus don't come back first, and if He do, it ain't gonna matter!"* I was a little taken aback, but managed to leave my name and a brief "Call me at Manna House when you've got a minute."

When Estelle banged on a pan for lunch, I went out and asked if she'd seen Precious lately. She shook her head. "It's goin' down tough for her an' Sabrina lately. Not sure she's in town." The big woman flounced behind the counter. "Line up, ladies! Who wants to ask God to bless this food?"

Going down tough? What did that mean? I decided I'd try calling again later.

Thankfully, the knitting club was putting away their projects in a corner of the dining room, so I didn't have to look far for my mother. But when I went to get her, I noticed her pale eyes were wet. "Mom? What's wrong?"

"I c-can't do it anymore, Celeste." Her lip trembled.

Uh-oh. Calling me by my sister's name was always a red flag. I gently took her knitting needles and the lump of pale green knitting attached. Dropped stitches and erratic knots were hopelessly tangled. "Oh, Mom."

One of the other knitters, a heavy-chested black woman named Sheila, shrugged sympathetically. "Last week, Gramma Shep was helpin' alla us. Today . . . dunno."

"It's all right, Mom. Let's put it away for now. We'll fix it later." *As in, ask Estelle to knit a few rows with the green yarn and let Mom start over when she wasn't feeling confused.* Steering my mother into the lunch line, I helped fill her plate with the fixings for tacos and was getting her settled at a table when I noticed Tanya's eight-year-old son sitting by himself at the end of our table, poking at his food. His usual shelter playmates—Trina and Rufino, seven- and six-year-old siblings—were throwing food at one of the other tables.

"Your mom not back yet, Sammy?"

Poke, poke. "Nah. Diane s'posed ta be watchin' me." He jerked a thumb in the direction of a dark-skinned woman with a big, loose Afro, like a throwback to the sixties. "But she say she gotta go out after lunch, even if my mama not back."

That was strange. Tanya had said she had an appointment at nine o'clock and she'd be back before lunch. The pole-thin young woman with the flawless caramel skin barely looked old enough to have a kid Sammy's age, but she'd always seemed to keep an eye on him. "Well, I'm sure your mom will be back soon. Come on and eat with Gramma Shep and me."

Sammy moved down a few chairs and grinned. "Yeah. Can't wait till she get back. Mama say we gettin' our *own* place now."

But Tanya wasn't back by the time the dishwashers started cleanup—and Tanya had traded her breakfast chore for Lucy's lunch assignment. "Hey, come on, Sammy, help me wipe these tables, okay? You start there while I get Gramma Shep settled for a nap." I winked at him. "Babies and grammas need their naps, you know," I stage-whispered. He giggled.

I didn't dare take my mom up to the bunk room, in case she woke up and tried to come down the stairs by herself, so I helped her stretch out on a sofa in the multipurpose room before I went back to the dining area. She'd be fine. My mom could sleep with a party going on, and it was better if there were people around anyway.

Still no Tanya. "Do you like to draw, Sammy?" I asked as we dried the last table. A smile lit up his face. So I found some scratch paper and a bunch of markers left over from the ad hoc "after-school program" Precious had supervised and let him color on the floor of my once-again-crowded office. At first he was a little timid to have Dandy curled up on the floor, too, but the next time I looked, dog and boy were nose to nose as if consulting how best to paint the Sistine Chapel.

My throat caught. What were my boys doing today? Should I try calling them now? No, more likely to catch them around suppertime. I tried Precious again—and this time she answered.

"Hey. Whassup, Gabby." Her voice was flat, tired. Didn't sound like the Precious I knew, ready to jabber about whatever trivia had caught her fancy in the paper that day, or—even more likely—never missing an opportunity to rib die-hard football fans that her Carolina Panthers had "whupped" the Chicago Bears in the divisional play-offs last season.

I decided against unloading my melodrama up front. "That's why I'm calling *you*, Precious. Haven't seen you around since I got back from North Dakota." I knew I'd told her I was taking my boys to see their grandmother—though she probably didn't know I'd brought my increasingly confused mother back to Chicago with me. "Are you okay?"

A pause. "I ain't gonna be frontin' ya, Gabby. I'm all tore up."

"Precious, what's wrong?"

I heard a long sigh in my ear. "Sabrina got all mad 'cause I wouldn't let her go to the prom with some baggy-pants gangbanger. That girl up and went anyway—an' *I* got so amped, I showed up at the hotel and dragged her out." She snorted. "Wasn't a good scene, know what I'm sayin'?"

My eyes were so bugged out, all I could do was make a strangled noise I hoped sounded like "uh-huh."

"Anyway, she up an' ran off, jus' disappeared . . . Didn't nobody there tell you this, Gabby? Estelle and Edesa and they Yada Yada Prayer Group cooked up an all-night prayer meetin' a week or so ago, prayin' God to protect my girl! You wasn't there?"

I gulped. "Sorry, Precious. I must've still been out of town." I didn't say that when I got back a week and a half ago, things got "all tore up" at the Fairbanks household too. If someone at Manna House told me that Sabrina had run away, it definitely didn't penetrate the fog in my brain.

"Yeah, well. Girl, I was goin' outta my mind! Then I get a call from the state cops—they picked up Sabrina hitchhikin' with some no-good hustler 'bout a hundred miles outside a' Greenville. Still got a slew o' cousins here. Jesus, help me! Don' know what Sabrina was *thinkin'*—"

"Did you say 'here'? Where are you, Precious?"

"Greenville. South Carolina. Where I grew up, girl! Now Sabrina sayin' she don' wanna come home with me, wants to stay with the cousins. So I gotta stay here awhile till we get things worked out. But . . ." Her voice trailed off.

I waited a beat or two. "But what, Precious?"

Another long sigh. "That ain't the worst of it. She's pregnant."

I sat at my desk with my head in my hands for a long time. My heart ached for Precious. She was only thirty—which meant *she* had gotten pregnant at fourteen. I knew she wanted a different life for Sabrina. Look how far she'd come! Before the fire that had taken down the old Manna House building, Precious had been a resident here. Now look at her! She had a job waitressing—or did. No telling how long a restaurant would hold her job for a family emergency. She'd gotten her own apartment with a Section 8, worked the lunchroom at Sabrina's high school, *and* volunteered here at Manna House. And she was so smart! No telling how far she could go given half a chance.

Now this.

I felt a tug on my arm. "Miz Gabby? Is my mama back yet? I gotta go real bad."

"Oh, Sammy." I'd almost forgotten about the little boy. "Come on, I'll take you."

I stood outside the bathroom until he was finished, then sent him back in to wash his hands while I picked out a copy of *Curious George* from the bookcase in the rec room, which was usually noisy this time of day—or had been before school was out. The other four shelter kids must be out with their moms. "Come on, kiddo." We climbed the stairs to the multipurpose room on the main level. Good, my mother was awake, just sitting patiently on the couch, hands in her lap, watching people come and go.

"Mom, would you mind reading to Sammy? He's waiting for his mother."

She seemed delighted. But she crooked a finger at me. "Where's Dandy?" she whispered. "Does he need to go out?"

Oh brother. The dog had been shut in my office all day. How long had it been since he'd been out? The headache threatened to send tentacles snaking over my head again. But I assured Mom I'd take care of Dandy, then hurried into the foyer and knocked on Mabel's office door.

"Come in."

I poked my head in. "Um, we've got a situation. Tanya never came back from her nine o'clock housing appointment. My mom's reading to Sammy at the moment. But it's already two thirty. Should we be worried?"

chapter 7

Mabel pulled Tanya's file. "Hm. Stephanie's her case manager." Stephanie Cooper was a social worker who volunteered two mornings a week doing case management for Manna House. "Her housing sheet says . . . here it is. 'Deborah's Place, Wednesday, June 21, 9:00 a.m.'" The director looked up. "I'll make a call, see if she showed up for her appointment this morning. We don't normally go chasing after people, Gabby. If they're a no-show by curfew, their bed goes to someone else. But leaving Sammy here is a different story . . ."

I nodded and backed out. *Tanya better not be a no-show.* I had too much on my own plate to take her kid under my wing too. Slipping past my mother and Sammy, who were both giggling at *Curious George,* I headed back to my office. I really needed to get some work done . . . Oh, good grief! I'd just volunteered for dog duty too.

Except my office was empty. No Dandy. The door was shut . . . *How did he get out?!* I groaned. I did *not* have time to go looking for the dumb dog! And if he did his business somewhere in the shelter, that was *it*. I'd send him to the pound myself! I'd—

That's when I noticed that Dandy's leash was gone too.

I sank down into my desk chair. Lucy had probably taken him out. Or somebody. Right now, I didn't care who. I was too close to losing it. I needed to get a grip.

Pray. That's what Edesa and Mabel and Estelle always encouraged when the devil grabbed life by the tail. And I wasn't the only one with heartaches. Look at Precious! And Edesa nearly lost the baby she and Josh were trying to adopt when Gracie's ex-con daddy showed up. And Mabel's nephew who lived with her—the kid couldn't be more than fourteen years old—got so much ragging at school because of his small size and effeminate ways, he'd tried to commit suicide.

In every case, seemed like the first thing they did was get people together to "pray up a storm," as Precious put it. And God seemed to answer their prayers.

Why not mine?

Wish I had someone to talk to. To help me pray.

Somehow I managed to get through the rest of the afternoon, checking on my mother and Sammy from time to time. Caught them playing checkers. The next time I checked, they were watching *Jeopardy* in the TV room. Well. That was one small blessing, anyway. Seemed to be doing as much good for my mom as for Sammy. Not to mention it gave me time to do some research online into museum fees and events going on in Chicago that summer that might make good outings for the residents. Two measly day trips a month. Was that too much to ask?

Printing out my proposed "day trip budget"—which included a fifteen-passenger van—I looked at my watch. Five o'clock. Virginia was an hour ahead . . .

I picked up the phone, using the calling card I'd bought yesterday, and dialed Philip's parents in Petersburg.

"Fairbanks residence."

My stomach tightened. Philip's mother. Probably the last person I wanted to talk to right now. "Uh, hello, Marlene. This is Gabby. May I speak to P. J. and Paul, please?" *Ugh!* It galled me to even say *please.* The woman had never liked me, never thought I was good enough for her charming son. It wouldn't surprise me if she and Philip had engineered the whole debacle of getting me out of the penthouse and spiriting away my kids.

"I'm sorry, Gabrielle—"

Yeah, I'll bet.

"—The boys are out with their grandfather right now. I'll tell them you called." The phone went dead in my ear.

I held the receiver at arm's length and gaped at it. The nerve of that woman! She hung up on me! She had to know the boys were at her house without my permission. If she didn't, she would have been more gushy, more chatty, filling in the blanks with what a *glorious* time the boys were having.

My thoughts smoldered like old electrical wires on overload. *Kidnapped.* That's what it was. Could I file kidnapping charges against my husband and his parents? Taking my kids across state lines without my knowledge or permission? But I had to wait two whole days before I could even talk to a lawyer! Maybe I should've just called the police last night. Could still call them. But . . . would they just think I'm crazy?

Oh, God. I buried my head in my arms. *I don't know what to do.*

I feel so alone! But even as *kidnapped* and *police* and *crazy* settled like jagged glass shards into my spirit, I suddenly remembered the words Edesa had written in the note I'd found last night . . .

"I will not forget you."

I lifted my head. Where was that note? I searched my desk, then remembered I'd left it under my pillow in the bunk room. Didn't matter. I'd look it up . . . Isaiah, chapter 49. In fact, Edesa had said there was more I should read.

I reached for the Bible I'd found that morning when I sorted through all the stuff my husband had tossed out into the penthouse foyer. By the time I got done reading the chapter four or five times, I felt strangely comforted—and even vindicated.

If this chapter was meant for me, Philip should be worried. Very worried.

Lucy brought Dandy back just before supper, both of them soaked, caught in one of Chicago's late-afternoon thunderstorms. They'd been gone more than three hours, and Dandy wriggled his rear end like a rag mop on amphetamines when he saw my mom, leaving wet splatters everywhere and sending Sammy into giggles. When I casually asked Lucy where they'd been, the old woman gave me a look. "Out. Don't it look like it? Humph. Gotta get me some dry clothes. Here . . ." She tossed me a rag. "You can clean up the dog. An' if I was you, I'd put him up in the bunk room 'fore Sarge shows up."

Good point.

Supper came and went. I didn't feel like talking, but I sat with my mom and Sammy to be polite, picking at the tuna casserole on my plate. Tanya still hadn't shown up, and the shelter curfew was eight o'clock, unless a resident had prior permission. Sammy was getting very clingy with "Gramma Shep." Poor kid. If worse came to worst, I'd tell him he could sleep in our bunk room tonight.

When I still hadn't heard from P. J. and Paul by seven thirty, I slipped into my office and called again. This time P. J. answered.

"Oh, hi, honey. I'm glad I got you! Did Nana Marlene tell you I called earlier?"

"Uh, don't think so. Maybe she told Paul."

I doubted it. I tried to sound interested in what they'd done that day—trip to the pool, watching the baseball games at the local park—all the while trying to curb my jealousy that the Fairbanks had my sons.

P. J.'s voice got challenging. "So did you and Dad work out this 'misunderstanding' about where the heck we're supposed to be this summer? It's not fair, Mom! First we come to Chicago. Then Dad brings us back to Petersburg. Nana says we're staying here, but *you* say it's all a misunderstanding an' you want us back in Chicago. Will you guys just . . . just make up your stupid minds?"

It was all I could do not to rip the phone out of its jack and throw it against the wall. Fighting back tears, I managed, "I don't blame you for being upset, P. J. It *is* unfair. And it's not your fault. I . . . Dad and I need a few days to work some things out. Please be patient."

"Well, what about the summer lacrosse league? Can I sign up or not?"

A sense of foreboding came over me so strong, I could almost taste it. If P. J. signed up for that lacrosse team in Petersburg, my sons were as good as lost to me.

I finally pulled myself together and went back upstairs to the multipurpose room—where a tearful Tanya was arguing with the night manager.

"But I got here before curfew, Sarge! Look. It's only 7:57!"

"So? This is not a babysitting service, Tanya. *Capisce?*" The night manager slapped the side of her head. "What were you thinking, leaving Sammy alone here all day while you were out? Rules are rules, no?"

"I know! I shouldn't a' done that. It—it was j-just . . ." The skinny young woman started to hiccough with fresh sobs. Sammy plastered his face against her side, his arms hanging on tightly. My mother was standing off to one side, wringing her hands.

"Uh, Sarge?" I'm not sure where the guts came from to speak up. "Why don't we leave Tanya's case till tomorrow when Mabel can decide what to do? If you want, they can move to our bunk room tonight. I'll take responsibility for the decision."

"Humph. *Some people* sure do feel free to bend the rules, if you ask me." Sarge moved off, grumbling. "Like a certain *dog* that is not supposed to be here. No?"

"Don't worry, Sarge. Mabel's looking for a foster home for Dandy."

Sarge headed for the foyer to check in the last few curfew-beaters—including Lucy, who was just coming in with Dandy after his evening walk around the block. "The dog better be gone by *Sabato!*" she tossed over her shoulder.

Tanya grabbed a tissue from a nearby box and blew her nose. "Thanks."

I waited until the double doors had swung shut behind Sarge. "I'm not your case manager, Tanya, but I think you have some explaining to do." The TV room was full of *CSI* fans, so I led her into the toddler playroom, empty at this time of night. Sammy wasn't about to be separated from his mother, and *my* mother followed right on our heels. Well, so be it. We all deserved an explanation.

Tanya sat on a preschool chair, knees together, feet splayed out, tearing her used tissue into little shreds. "Well, I had a"—*hic*—"appointment at Deborah's Place this mornin', an' . . . an' I was so sure I was gonna get a place for me an' Sammy this time. A studio, one-bedroom—I didn't care. 'Long as it was just us. Miz Gabby, I been puttin' my name on lists for six months! We was in two other shelters 'fore we came to Manna House—one place was jus' one big room for about thirty wimmins plus they kids. Manna House been good to let me an' Sammy stay here together, an' the bunk room's better'n nothin'. But I want my own place! You understand, don'tcha? What kinda mother has her kid livin' in a *shelter*?" Tanya's face went dark. "But this mornin' they sayin' I don't qualify. Somethin' about gotta be in they drug program. But I ain't done no drugs!" The tears threatened again. "Man! I felt so bad, I wanted to hurt somebody! Or . . . or get drunk or *somethin'*! So I . . . I just walked around, and, yeah, I drank a few beers. But that's all. Honest! I didn't get high or nothin'. And I never meant to leave Sammy. Aw, come here, baby. Mama's sorry." The two wrapped their arms around each other and rocked.

I shut my eyes, her story too painful to process. Here I was, wallowing in my private pity party, and I'd been homeless for all of *two days*. I felt like the spoiled princess who complained because there was a pea under the mattress.

"Am I wrong, Miz Gabby?" Tanya's voice broke into my stupor. "Sammy an' me, we just need a place. But it's like a dead-end road. Can't get an apartment. Don't wanna raise my kid in a shelter. Am I wrong for needing a little help to get on my feet?"

"No, no. You're not wrong, Tanya." I sighed. *And you're not the only one.*

chapter 8

Tanya and Sammy took over the fourth bunk in our room—the more the merrier, as far as Dandy was concerned. Lucy, on the other hand, muttered her disapproval the whole time we were getting ready for bed. "Howza body s'posed ta sleep packed up in here like a bunch a' sardines . . . Too many lungs usin' up all the air . . . Humph. Dandy an' me gonna go sit inna lounge till you all go ta sleep . . ."

Well, fine with me. Maybe I could get to sleep before Lucy came to bed and started her engines.

And I'd guessed right about Mabel the next morning. Since Tanya had shown up by curfew and hadn't broken an actual *written* rule—though leaving your kids unsupervised was about to become one—Mabel gave Tanya another chance, but with a stern warning that she was on probation. Probably to soothe Sarge's prickled sense of protocol as much as anything. I had to grin inside. Mabel and Sarge were like two sides of a kitchen sponge, one side soaking up people's blunders and good intentions gone awry, the other scratchy and rough to deal with the tough cases.

Having to wait another whole day to talk to a lawyer, though, almost killed me. This was ridiculous! Three days ago my husband had kidnapped my children—yes, that was the word for it—leaving me homeless and broke, and I wasn't supposed to confront him until I had my *facts* lined up in a row?

Bunk the facts. He needed to get a load of my *feelings*.

Twice I picked up the phone, dialed his office, and then hung up after one ring. The third time I steeled myself to stay on the line. Someone picked up. "Fairbanks and Fenchel. May I help you?"

The female voice took me by surprise. Since when did Philip and Henry have a receptionist? Sounded young too.

Okay. I can play this game. "Philip Fairbanks, please."

"May I say who's calling?"

I thought fast. "CitiCorp Business Accounts." It was a bald-faced lie, but she probably had instructions not to send through any personal calls.

"One moment." The line went blank. But a moment later the woman came back on the line. "I'm sorry. He's in a meeting right now. Would you like me to put you through to his voice mail?"

I almost slammed the receiver down—but caught myself. "Yes. Thank you."

Two rings in my ear, then Philip's voice message, pleasant and professional. No hint that he was a monster in a business suit. I heard the beep. "Philip. This is Gabby. You'll be hearing from my lawyer, and I'll see you in court." I hit the Off button.

There. No hysterics. No crying. No pleading. But now he knew I wasn't rolling over and whimpering like a kicked puppy.

And I had every intention of showing up at his office in person as soon as I had my facts in hand.

Better yet, what if the *police* showed up at his office? With a wicked sense of vengeance, I picked up the phone again. Voices in my head said, *"Wait, Gabby."* But I felt driven by an insatiable need to *do* something, to make something happen.

I dialed 9-1-1.

"9-1-1. What is your emergency?"

"My—my children have been kidnapped!"

"Ma'am? Can you give me your name and location?" The questions kept coming—name and ages of my children . . . when did I discover they were missing . . .

"You say they turned up missing Monday night?"

"Yes! I came home from work, and the doorman said they'd left with my husband—and I haven't seen them since!"

"Your husband." The tone of voice changed. "Ma'am, if your *husband* took your children—"

"Without me knowing about it! He took them! He kidnapped them!"

"I see. Mrs. Fairbanks, that was three days ago. Why are you only reporting them missing now?"

"I . . . I . . ." My confidence drained away as though someone had pulled a plug. "Please. Help me. Please get my children back."

"So you don't know where they are."

"Well, yes, I do . . . but I didn't at first. He took them to his parents' in Virginia."

I could almost hear the silence on the other end laughing at me.

"Look, officer!" I was angry now. "My husband took my

children away from me, without my knowledge or permission. He took them *out of state*. That's a federal offense, isn't it?"

Another pause. "Ma'am, do you have reason to believe your children are in danger?"

I felt pinned to the wall. "No," I whispered. "No. They're . . . they're all right. But they—"

"So you've talked to them."

"Well . . . yes. But—!"

"Mrs. Fairbanks. We'll send an officer out to take a report, but this is really a civil matter. It will need to be settled in court."

"Uh . . . no, that's all right. You don't have to send anybody. I'll . . . I'll talk to a lawyer."

I sat at my desk, burning with embarrassment and frustration. I'd made a fool of myself. So much for the cops barging into Philip's office and dragging him away in handcuffs. But I still knew I was right. Philip had kidnapped our children. And I was going to get them back.

Somehow I made it through that Thursday, trying not to feel like a fool. Even had a chance to sit down with Estelle and pull together ideas for the basic cooking and sewing classes we'd talked about before. We decided on Monday afternoon for Basic Sewing—threading needles, sewing on buttons, making repairs, hemming a skirt—while I worked on getting some sewing machines for the next level.

Huh. I have a sewing machine just sitting up in the penthouse. Maybe I should fight to get my stuff back.

"—Basic Cooking?" Estelle was saying. "You know I don't use no recipes. It's all in here." The fifty-something woman tapped the side of her head. I noticed she was wearing her hair down more often, her silver-streaked hair falling in kinky waves to her shoulders. And was that glow on her cheeks natural or a touch of golden blush?

"So Harry Bentley likes your hair that way?" I tried to keep a straight face.

She gaped at me. "An' since when is that any of your business? Humph."

"Since I'm the one who introduced you two. As for recipes . . ." I moved right on without blinking. "Just start with simple stuff—different ways to fix chicken, season vegetables, some healthy soups and salads. You know, using the basic food groups to create a balanced diet, stuff like that."

Estelle wagged her head. "Girl, you know I'll be goin' up against Fast Food City! Lot of these women think protein means a McDonald's burger, veggies mean a bag of potato chips, and fruit means a bowl of Froot Loops." Estelle started to shake with silent chuckles.

I suddenly had a burst of inspiration. "Hey. Maybe we ought to ask Edesa to show up at your class to teach good nutrition—she's working on her degree in public health. Poor nutrition has to be a big factor in many of the health problems we see in here."

"Yeah, well, you better sneak that stuff in between fried chicken an' chocolate cake. Ain't nobody goin' to show up for a whole class on *nutrition*."

So it was settled. "Cooking with Estelle" on Thursday afternoon, served up with a sneaky side of "How to Eat Healthy and

Live Longer"—providing Edesa was available. But as Estelle got up to leave, she hesitated, looking me up and down. "How you doin', Gabby? I *know* you got more on your mind than cookin' an' sewin'."

It was so tempting to unload on Estelle, to bare the fragments of my heart, torn between wanting my sons back—*now*—and knowing I had nothing to offer. I needed somebody to tell me I wasn't a total fool for calling the police, for ignoring Mabel's advice and trying to contact Philip, but I knew if I opened my mouth, I'd be a wreck. I needed to keep going, keep working, keep my mind busy, or I'd never be able to hold on to this job. And I needed this job, for a lot of reasons.

I shrugged. "Hanging in there. I see a lawyer tomorrow at Legal Aid. Can't do much until then."

The older woman lifted an eyebrow, as if seeing right through my little charade. "Hm. Well, honey, seems to me one of these days you gonna want to do some screamin' at that man of yours. Just want you to know, I'd be glad to come with you so he don't bully you around. Might even do a little screamin' myself."

Friday. I woke up early, before the six o'clock wake-up bell by the ever-punctual night manager, and caught myself smiling at Estelle's offer. For some reason it made me feel good. It hadn't occurred to me to take someone with me when I did go see Philip with my facts. Well, if I did, Estelle would be the one. No one— not even Philip—would mess with her.

Sensing I was awake, Dandy padded over and nosed my arm. *Hmm. Why not take the dog for his morning walk?* Lucy saw me pulling on a pair of jeans and started to roll out of bed. "Let me," I whispered. "I need to get out. You can sleep in today. Where do you go—the cemetery?"

"Cemetery don't open till eight thirty," Lucy muttered. "Gotta go someplace else." She rolled over and was snoring again before I got Dandy's leash on, grabbed a couple of plastic grocery bags from her stash, and sneaked down the stairs. I heard someone—probably Sarge and her assistant—banging around in the kitchen, setting out breakfast. In the foyer, sunlight streamed in the stained-glass windows on either side of the oak doors, creating dancing prisms of colored light on the floor. I dutifully signed out, quietly opened the front doors, and slipped out.

Yes! Blue sky overhead. Cool, no hint of humidity. A beautiful day. I suddenly felt a pang of longing for the park and lakefront abutting Richmond Towers. I'd love to let Dandy run on the beach, kick off my sandals, and dig my toes in the sand. But here . . . I glanced up and down the neighborhood surrounding the shelter. Mostly two- and three-story apartment buildings. Brick, crowded together, several with storefronts on the ground level. The occasional Victorian house squeezed between them, with a six-foot wrought-iron fence in front as if holding the buildings on either side at arm's length with its iron bars.

How far was it to the lake? Maybe a mile. I quickly nixed that idea. Another time. Too bad Graceland Cemetery hadn't opened yet. Closest thing to a park I'd seen around here.

By the time we got back, morning devotions were just ending. Sarge hustled everyone downstairs for the usual weekday breakfast of cold cereal and milk, toast and jam, juice and coffee, giving Dandy and me the eye. "Saturday," was all she said.

I felt a flicker of panic. That was tomorrow. Had Mabel been asking around for a foster home for the dog? She hadn't said anything. And what about my mother? She was oblivious that Dandy's days were numbered.

But I determined not to let Dandy's fate get me down. Today was an important day. Today I had an appointment with a lawyer. Today I was going to get some answers.

chapter 9

A knock on my office door was followed immediately by a glowing brown face, brilliant blue headband, and bouncy hair twists. "Are you alone, *mi amiga*?" Without waiting for an answer, Edesa Baxter called over her shoulder in a stage whisper, "Coast is clear. Hurry!"

The next moment, Josh Baxter hustled into my office, carrying a large bakery sheet cake, followed by Edesa with Gracie on her hip. They shut the door behind them and stood there like the Three Bears, caught sneaking into Goldilocks's house instead.

"Can we hide this cake in here, Gabby? Josh, set it on top of the file cabinet, out of her way."

"Um . . . sure. What's going on?"

"Da-Da!" Gracie squealed, spying Dandy, who'd gotten up to sniff at our visitors.

"How d'ya like that?" Josh made a face as he carefully set the cake on top of the file cabinet. "She says 'Da-Da' and means 'doggy.'"

I had to smile. The young Baxter family made such an odd,

cute trio. The ten-month-old's creamy tan skin and loose, black curls made her look as if she could be their natural child—white daddy, black mommy—instead of a Latina child in the process of being adopted. "Are you going to tell me what all this hush-hush business is about?"

Edesa leaned forward, keeping her voice low. "*Sí! Sí!* It is Estelle's birthday today! But this is just the backup cake. Señor Harry is bringing—"

Oh no! Estelle's birthday! I slapped my forehead. "Drat! I forgot! I even mentioned it to Mr. Bentley last week, and then . . ." I shook my head. "With all that's happened this week, it totally slipped my mind. I don't have a card or a gift or—"

Edesa put a finger on my lips. "Hush, *mi amiga*. It's all right. Estelle thinks we've all forgotten. Which is good, since . . . why are you poking me, Josh?"

"Don't give it away, Edesa, my sweet. It's supposed to be a surprise, remember?"

"Sounds like a regular party." Had to admit my nose felt a little out of joint. Seems like somebody should have at least *told* the person in charge of shelter activities what was going on. But Edesa and Josh didn't seem to notice my little snit.

"*Sí!*" She giggled. "Estelle *might* guess that we'll celebrate her birthday Sunday night at Yada Yada, but she won't suspect anything today. Oh!" Edesa looked at her watch. "I've got to run. I'm teaching Bible study in ten minutes. Pray for me!" She handed the baby to her husband, blew them both a kiss, and disappeared out my door.

Yada Yada Sunday night. That was the prayer group Edesa and Estelle and Josh's mother, Jodi, were part of. Knowing each other so well, they celebrated birthdays . . .

I shook off my melancholy, aware that Josh and Gracie were still standing in my two-bit office. "Say, Josh, as long as you're here, I wanted to ask you about that sports clinic idea you once mentioned."

"Sure, Mrs. Fairbanks—I mean, Gabby—I'd be glad to talk about that. But . . ." The young man shifted the baby in his arms and cleared his throat. "Maybe it's none of my business, but Edesa said that you . . . uh, that your husband—"

"Josh. It's all right. Sit down." I indicated the metal folding chair leaning against the wall. As he flipped it open with his free hand, I went on. "If you mean, did my husband kick me out of our penthouse? Yes. That and he took the kids back to Virginia without my knowledge or permission. So . . ." I shrugged. "I'm staying here at Manna House for the time being. My mother too." For some reason, it was easier to be matter-of-fact with this young man than it was with Edesa or Estelle or Mabel. I even allowed a sardonic half smile. "Every staff person ought to be a resident of the shelter for a while. Gives one a whole new perspective."

Josh shook his head. "I'm so sorry, Gabby. I thought . . . well, guess I'd hoped Edesa and I could get to know you two better, you know, as an older couple who've been married a few years."

Now I did have to blink back a few tears. I nodded. "Yeah, I know. That's how it should be. But . . ." I bit my lip and glanced at my watch. Ten forty. Still three hours to go before I could meet with the lawyer. Philip and I were on a road I hoped Josh and Edesa never had to travel.

I'd intended to duck into Edesa's Bible study, but Josh and J ended up tossing around different ideas to meet the needs of kids who ended up at the shelter, while Gracie grabbed things off my desk. Now that his classes at UIC were over, he said, he'd have more time on the weekends. "Weekdays, though, I'll be working full-time for Peter Douglass till school starts again. He has his own business—Software Symphony. Edesa and I really need a bigger apartment, but that takes moola."

Huh. Takes moola to get one, period.

Currently, there weren't that many moms with kids at the shelter, but Josh talked about taking them to ball games this summer, finding a park where the preteens could shoot hoops and get some pointers, maybe starting a weekend league in this neighborhood for other kids. "My dad coaches some summer leagues. Maybe he could help us get started. We need a van, though. Can't keep borrowing the one from the church."

"Yeah, well, I just added a fifteen-passenger van to my program budget. We'll see if the board has a collective heart attack . . . Oh my. Is that the bell for lunch already?" Well, at least the rest of the morning had gone fairly quickly. Only two more hours . . .

Estelle had outdone herself on the lunch menu. A chicken pasta salad with walnuts and grapes and hot garlic bread. Maybe she was celebrating her own birthday by giving everybody a treat. She was certainly dressed brightly today—a long, blue tunic with silver filigree around neck and sleeves, worn over wide-legged pants, though the big white apron and food-worker's hairnet didn't do anything for the outfit. But nobody said anything about "birthday," so I kept mum, even when I went back for seconds.

While I was waiting my turn at the counter, I heard the doorbell ringing on the main floor . . . and then twice more, as if no one was around to answer. Darting up the stairs and through the multipurpose room, I reached the front door and pulled it open.

My friend from Richmond Towers and a young boy stood on the steps.

"Mr. Bentley! Mm. Don't tell me. You're here because—"

"Uh, you said this was Estelle's birthday, didn't you?"

I sighed. "Yeah, I did. But with everything that's happened this week, guess who forgot? Come on in." I held the door for them as they stepped inside, noticing the big, square box the youngster was carrying. "Who's your young helper here?"

Mr. Bentley grinned. "That's right, you two haven't met. This is my grandson, DeShawn. He's living with me now. DeShawn, this is Mrs. Fairbanks. She's, uh, from Richmond Towers, where I work. Here, let me take that." He took the cake so his grandson could shake hands.

The boy grinned at me. He looked about nine years old, recent haircut, caramel-colored skin, a tad lighter than Mr. B, firm handshake. "I didn't know you had a grandson." I felt like kicking myself. Why hadn't I ever asked Mr. Bentley if he had family? The boy was a little younger than Paul. If he'd just come to live with his grandfather, something must've happened to his mom and dad . . . like my boys, living with *their* grandparents now. But Mr. Bentley seemed tickled as all get-out. "I—I'm happy for you."

"You doin' okay? Your boys . . . ?"

"They're okay. Just trying to get them back is all." I managed a smile. "Look, you two can go on down. They've already started eating."

"Uh, is there a way I can sneak this in without Estelle seeing? We'd like it to be a surprise."

I peeked through the clear top of the cake box. Another cake—this one fat and round. "Wow. I guess we're gonna pig out on cake today. Here, let me carry it. She won't even notice what I'm carryin' when she sees you." I winked at Mr. B.

Sure enough, Estelle was so flustered to see Mr. Bentley, she didn't even notice me taking the cake box to the other end of the room. She filled two more plates of food and even sat down with her guests at one of the tables, seemingly delighted at the news that the boy had come to live with his grandfather. "Stu told me!" she exclaimed.

Stu? That's what she called her housemate, whose real name was Lily or Leslie Stuart or something like that. How did her housemate know Mr. Bentley? Now I was starting to feel left out. Everybody and their cousin seemed to know about Mr. Bentley's grandson except me. Wasn't he *my* friend first?

My disgruntled thoughts were interrupted by Mr. Bentley tapping a spoon on his glass for attention and announcing that this was a special day for a special lady—Estelle Williams's birthday. She tried to make him sit down, but everybody began singing "Happy Birthday" in two or three different keys while Mr. B brought the new cake and set it in front of Estelle.

Yells of "Make a wish!" . . . "Ohh, now, that's purty" . . . and "Cut it, Estelle! Don't wait all day!" greeted the end of the song. Mr. Bentley handed a kitchen knife to the "birthday girl" and sat down again.

"Oh, now. This cake is just too pretty to cut," Estelle protested sweetly, quickly taking off her apron and hairnet when Josh waved a camera.

"Cut it!" everyone yelled. I grinned. The residents were really enjoying this.

Estelle slid the knife through the frosting, thick with decorative pink and yellow sugar roses. Then she stopped, a puzzled frown pinching her forehead. She tried again in a different place. The knife only went one inch deep. "What?" she mumbled.

Behind Estelle, Edesa and Josh had hands over their mouths, trying to keep from laughing aloud. *What in the world?*

Estelle caught them. "Uh-huh. I get it now. " Turning back to the cake, she lifted the knife over her head in both hands and plunged it into the middle of the cake. This time the knife went in, though it took an extra push on Estelle's part. Then she lifted the knife and the whole cake came with it.

The entire dining room was gasping with laughter. "What is it?" . . . "What? No cake?"

Estelle lowered the cake to the table, the knife still plunged into its heart, then took a big swipe of the frosting with her finger until she reached the "cake." "Uh-huh. Just what I thought. Foam cushions." I'd never seen Mr. Bentley laugh so hard.

"Ah, he gotcha good!" Lucy yelled.

Estelle wagged her head. "Harry Bentley! I oughta throw this whole frosted pillow in your face, but I'm too . . . I'm too—" And forgetting decorum, she picked up the bogus cake and dumped it right on his bald head.

Mr. Bentley's grandson was hopping up and down, pointing at his grandpa.

With perfect timing, Josh and Edesa brought out the real sheet cake from my office, giving Mr. B a chance to wipe frosting off his face and talk Estelle into letting him give her a birthday hug. I wanted to squeeze in my own hug and wish Estelle a happy birthday, but I glanced at the clock above the kitchen counter. *Ten after one.* My appointment at Legal Aid was at two! I needed to get out of there.

The prank Estelle's friends had played on her—"It was all Mr. Bentley's idea," Josh had said—left me feeling strangely hopeful. Estelle had once been a resident at Manna House—though I still didn't know why—but now look at her. Laughter. Jokes. New friends. Even a new beau . . .

"Mrs. Fairbanks?"

I looked up from the magazine I'd been flipping through in the waiting area of the Legal Aid clinic to see a man standing in the doorway, looking at me expectantly. *Wait a minute.* I'd been expecting some freckle-faced, idealistic law student in his twenties. Or maybe a fatherly type, retired, rich, doing pro bono work on the side. But this man was late thirties, probably five-eleven, wire-rim specs, brown hair with blond flecks brushed neatly to one side, nice tan, open-necked shirt tucked into a pair of jeans. Could've been Bill Gates for all I knew. Sure of himself. Decidedly casual.

And boots. I smiled, feeling a surge of familiarity. Maybe it was my North Dakota blood, but Lee Boyer—if this was indeed Lee Boyer—could've walked right off a cattle ranch into my father's carpet store.

I followed the man back to a small cubicle office and sat in the chair facing the cluttered desk while he shut the door. On closer look, those flecks in his hair were more silver than gold. Okay, maybe forty-something.

"What can I do for you, Mrs. Fairbanks?"

My mouth went dry. For some reason I felt embarrassed to tell my sob story to this man, who looked like someone I might've gone to school with back at the University of ND. But that's why I was here. To his credit, the lawyer took copious notes. He asked a few more questions about my mother. Did I have power of attorney for her? If not, was she rational enough to sign over power of attorney?

I felt frustrated by the direction of his questions. "Mr. Boyer, it's my *kids*—"

"I understand, Mrs. Fairbanks. But the fact that you currently have responsibility for your mother, who seems to be suffering from some kind of dementia, definitely strengthens your case." He handed me a set of power of attorney forms to fill out. "Talk to your sisters and your mother and get these filled out, all right? It's important. Now . . ." He leaned back thoughtfully, making a tent with his fingers. "Let's start at the beginning. Your husband is in violation of both Family Law *and* the Landlord-Tenant Law by changing the locks of your apartment without a court order. It doesn't matter if your name is not on the lease. Your husband can't evict you without proper legal procedures, and you can get a court order to return to the apartment."

"A court order? How long would that take? He's given notice that he's breaking the lease and plans to move out by the end of the month. That's next week!"

"Hm. That's tight. We could try to hurry that along, but maybe the main question is, are you prepared to take over the lease if your husband bails?"

Take over the lease? I shook my head slowly. "No way could I afford the penthouse at Richmond Towers on my own. Even if I could, I don't want it. Not now. Please. Just get my kids back. That's all I care about."

He jotted another note. "All right. We'll come back to this later. Now, the kids . . . P. J. and Paul, you said. If there is no order giving your husband custody—"

"Absolutely not!"

"—and if he has hidden your children in another state, you can call the police on the in-laws for kidnapping—based on the grounds that he can move *with* them, but he cannot move the kids alone and leave them in the care and custody of another, without your consent or a valid court order."

"But I already called the police." I'd left that part out, hoping to get a different answer from the lawyer—or that the lawyer would call the police when he heard my story. But now I rehashed what happened when I'd called 9-1-1.

The lawyer pulled a law manual from a stack on his desk and flipped through it. A minute passed, then two. Then he nodded. "Well, that's right. Since the kids aren't being hidden, and you're able to talk with them by phone, there would be no charge for kidnapping." Lee Boyer leaned forward, hazel eyes behind the wire rims sympathetic. "But no judge is going to take kindly to what your husband has done, Mrs. Fairbanks. At this point, our options are to file an unlawful eviction case *and* a custody case, and we can merge these into one. And divorce. You definitely have grounds to file for divorce."

Divorce? "Uh, wait a minute. Can't I get my kids back without a divorce?"

"Of course. But you should know your rights, Mrs. Fairbanks. Your husband has left you virtually penniless. If you successfully file for divorce, you are entitled to half of your husband's estate."

My eyes widened. "Did you say . . . *half* of what my husband is worth?" I almost laughed aloud. Oh, wouldn't that news spin Philip's clock!

Lee Boyer nodded. "And you have a strong case, though you

should do what you can to make it even stronger. Prove you can support your children. Get a higher-paying job if necessary. For goodness' sake, get out of the shelter and find an apartment with adequate room for two young teens! I have to warn you, Mrs. Fairbanks. We are Legal Aid. We do what we can. But someone like your husband, with a high-powered job and the money to retain an expensive lawyer, can keep throwing legal hurdles in the way to make life difficult."

His eyes were kind. "Just so you know . . . this might take awhile."

chapter 10

My head was spinning. I needed to think! Or . . . or talk to someone. But who? It was all so confusing!

I wandered the unfamiliar streets, looking for a café or coffee shop, trying to keep the closest El station within my frame of reference. All I could find was a tiny restaurant called Joe's Eats, with "Breakfast Special—Grits, Ham or Bacon, 3 eggs, Toast, $4.99" painted in red right on the window. I sat in a booth with a Formica tabletop and ordered a cup of coffee. It came in a thick, white mug and looked so strong I added twice the amount of cream I normally used.

During the meeting, Lee Boyer had been very encouraging about my rights, everything from getting the boys returned to me, to hope that I wouldn't be permanently destitute. And Philip! The jerk was in *big* trouble. The lawyer didn't say what the consequences might be, but he did say what Philip had done was illegal. *And* that a judge wouldn't take kindly to his disappearing act with our kids, which would give me an edge in any court case.

But the words *"This might take awhile"* cut off my hope at the knees. What did that mean? I wanted my sons back now!

Grabbing a paper napkin, I pressed it to my eyes, hoping to stem the tears threatening to well up and explode, right there in Joe's Eats. *Oh God, Oh God, what am I going to do?!*

"Refill, miss?" A thick-waisted waitress with flabby arms hovered over my cup with a coffeepot. "Got some good lemon pie too."

I shook my head, blew my nose in the napkin, and reached for my purse. "Just the bill." I had to get out of there.

Standing outside Joe's Eats a few minutes later, I realized I had no idea where to go or what to do. In the back of my mind, I'd imagined taking the El to the Aon Center after my meeting and showing up in the offices of Fairbanks and Fenchel, confronting Philip with my legal facts. But I knew Philip would just put another black mark on his ledger of my "sins" if I confronted him at his office, "ruining his business."

Maybe Estelle was right. I should take someone with me, someone who could keep me from being mowed down by Philip's spin on everything.

Still! It galled me to wait even one more day before confronting Philip face-to-face! The man had kicked me out and disappeared with my kids *four days ago*—and so far hadn't heard a peep from me except the cryptic message I'd left on his phone. He was probably laughing into his Chardonnay, thinking, *What a wimp.*

Well. He had another thing coming.

Gripping my shoulder bag, I headed for the El station. I'd just go back to Richmond Towers and wait till he came home. Six o'clock . . . nine o'clock . . . midnight. Didn't matter. He had to come home sometime. After all, I still had my security ID card that would get me in. Or I *could* just show up early tomorrow morning, when he'd be sure to be home . . . On second thought, bad idea. He could just refuse to let me in. No, I had to be in the penthouse foyer when he got off the elevator—

"*Streetwise* paper, lady? One dollar." A *Streetwise* peddler waved a copy of the latest issue at me, a friendly smile showing off a couple of missing teeth. I started to pass by, but the man beamed happily. "Got my name in here, an' a picture too! *Streetwise* Salesperson of the Month! I'll autograph it for you."

I had to smile. What was one measly dollar? If Mr. Lee Boyer was correct, I had a whole lot of money sitting in Philip's bank account.

A few minutes later, standing on the northbound El platform with my "autographed" copy of *Streetwise*, I started having second thoughts about confronting Philip at the penthouse. No telling when he would get home on a Friday night. I could wait for hours. But more than that, when he got off that elevator, we'd be alone, and no matter what my resolve, in two seconds he'd twist anything I'd say to make it be my fault.

A northbound train squealed into the station. I stood rooted to the platform as passengers jostled past me, reason and rage wrestling in my gut. Maybe I should get on and just get off at the Sheridan station and go back to Manna House. Or ride farther north and take my chances at Richmond Towers. Wait till he showed up and let him have it, both barrels, come what may.

No. I was tired of waiting. Now or never.

The doors closed. The train pulled out. I watched as it rattled out of sight; then I headed back down the stairs and up to the southbound platform.

At least I had dressed up a bit for my appointment at Legal Aid—boot-cut black slacks with a belted jacket over a teal silk blouse and low, sling-back heels. A pit stop in the women's restroom on the first level of the Aon Center to repair my makeup and tame my curly mane gave me confidence that I looked attractive. Sane.

I stuffed the voice whispering, *"Should you be doing this, Gabby?"* I didn't care. I had to quit running. I had to face my demons—in this case, my husband. The office was the most likely place to find him. The most likely place to guarantee that neither one of us would make a scene. I was going to march in there and—

A young woman looked up from the reception desk when I opened the door marked Fairbanks and Fenchel—Commercial Development Corp. She looked to be in her twenties. Short brunette hair. Conservative lavender blouse. Small pearl earrings. Attractive, but no fashion model. She smiled. "May I help you?"

"Yes. I'd like to speak to Philip Fairbanks."

She reached for the phone. "Your name, please?"

"Gabrielle Fairbanks." Her eyebrows went up. I helped her out. "His wife."

She picked up the phone and turned slightly aside. A moment later, Philip's office door opened, and Henry Fenchel stepped into view. The man was in his early forties, same as Philip, but a bit fleshy in the face, thinning hair. Tended to be a good ol' boy. He stopped. "Gabby." He sounded startled.

"Hello, Henry." My voice was calm. I did not smile.

The receptionist hung up her phone. "Mr. Fairbanks will see you. Go on in."

I pushed past Philip's partner, stepped into Philip's office, and closed the door behind me. My husband was standing at the wide window with his back to me, suit coat off, looking tall and slim in his pale green shirt sleeves. I said nothing, just waited. It was probably only five seconds, but it felt like five minutes. He finally turned, coffee cup in hand, expression mild, dark eyes and lashes framed by his beautiful tan.

I wanted to groan. *Oh gosh.* Did he have to look so gorgeous?

"Gabrielle." He waved his coffee cup at the mahogany chair on my side of the desk. "Sit. Would you like coffee?"

Would I like—? "No." I had no intention of acting as if we were just having a friendly little chat. But I did sit down, crossing my legs to keep them from shaking. Philip casually pulled out his executive chair and leaned back. Another five seconds went by. I got an inquisitive look, as if he wondered what I was there for.

Just do it, Gabby.

"I saw a lawyer today. What you've done, Philip, is *illegal*. You can't just kick me out without a proper order of eviction. You can't just take my children away from me and deposit them with your parents in another state."

Philip's eye twitched, and the corner of his mouth curved ever so slightly. I got the message loud and clear: *"But I did, didn't I?"* The anger that I had so carefully repressed threatened to surge right out of my gut in a seismic eruption.

Don't, Gabby, don't!

I waited until I could speak without screaming and took a deep breath to steady my voice. "My lawyer is filing an unlawful eviction case *and* a custody case. There's no question a judge will rule in my favor."

"Your lawyer?" His shrug felt like a slap in the face. "Tell me something, Gabby. Exactly how do you plan to *pay* for a lawyer?"

I stared at him.

"Ah." He smiled. "Legal Aid. Of course."

A glass paperweight sat on his desk within arm's reach of me. Oh, how I wanted to snatch it up and throw it at that smug smile. Or right through his picture-perfect window overlooking the city skyline. But even as I imagined glass shattering everywhere, I knew in my gut Philip was goading me. *"Go ahead, Gabby. Do something crazy."*

A hysterical giggle nearly escaped the emotions churning under my skin. Right. With my luck, the falling glass would probably kill somebody on the street below and I'd get sued. Or dragged off to jail.

I'd lost my upper hand. "Philip . . . why?" I couldn't help it. My voice shook. "Why tear our family apart this way?"

His eyebrows shot up and he threw his hands open. "Me! *Me?* I seem to recall *you* were the one who took this do-gooder job that started screwing everything up! The one who just showed up with her mother and her mutt, turning our household upside down. Without considering me at all in your decisions, I might add. Oh yes, the one whose idea of taking care of our sons was to drag them to a homeless shelter and expose them to all sorts of riffraff all day."

"But . . . but, Philip. I was trying! I came home Monday to tell you I'd quit the job and that I'd even found a place for my mom."

His eyes narrowed. "What place?"

"Why, Manna House. The shelter. They said they'd take her in, and she seemed happy with . . . What?"

My husband had started to laugh. He shook his head, shoulders shaking. "Listen to yourself, Gabby. The shelter! The *shelter!*

You're like a broken record. If you weren't so pathetic, this would be funny—"

His phone rang. Still chuckling, he picked up. "Oh, sure. Put him through." He glanced at me, then swiveled his chair so that his back was to me. "Oh, hey, Bill! What's up? . . . Saturday? What time? . . . Yeah, yeah, sure, I could make that . . . No, no, that's good . . . Gotta dig out my clubs, though. We just moved, you know. I might be a little rusty . . ."

I stared at the back of his head. Hot tears stung my eyes. I was so close to a meltdown, I was afraid to move.

Afraid not to move. I had to get out of there or I'd go crazy!

Maybe I was already crazy.

Oh God, Oh God, Oh God . . . have You forgotten all about me?

I stood up on wobbly legs and somehow made it to the door as Philip chatted on the phone. But as I put my hand on the doorknob, a Voice seemed to be whispering in my ear: *Gabby. Gabby. Can a mother forget the baby at her breast? Though she may forget, I will not forget you!* I recognized the verses Edesa had written in her note. And there was more. Something about God engraving my name on the palms of His hands . . . and sending sons hastening back.

I couldn't remember it all word for word, but the turmoil surging through my veins suddenly lost steam, replaced with . . . what? A sudden stillness in my spirit. No hysterics. No hot anger. Just the return of a quiet confidence.

I lifted my head and waited at the door until Philip ended the call. He seemed surprised that I was till there. "My things," I said. My voice was steady. "I want the rest of my things. Like my sewing machine. I need it for a class at the shelter. I need to know when I can come get it."

chapter 11

Mabel had already gone home by the time I signed in at Manna House at five forty. *Rats.* Was she gone for the whole weekend already? I had to talk to somebody before next Monday! Mabel was the one who'd steered me to the lawyer at Legal Aid. I wanted to debrief what Lee Boyer had told me and figure out what my next step should be.

Didn't immediately see my mom, so I headed upstairs to change out of my pantsuit. Actually, what I really needed to do was think through what had happened at Philip's office. Already I was kicking myself for barging ahead. What had I accomplished? Nothing—except a flippant promise to let me pick up my sewing machine sometime next week. We didn't talk about the boys, about what he'd told them when they left, or how they felt about being jerked back to Virginia so suddenly. Didn't talk about when P. J. and Paul were coming back, or what was best for them in the middle of our mess. The hundred and one important questions.

I wiggled out of my pantsuit. *Ugh!* I didn't even get the satis-
faction of making Philip squirm. Evidently, my husband was
missing the squirm gene. Probably incompatible with the
Fairbanks DNA, always right, always top dog—

Dog. Oh good grief. Dandy! Had Mabel found a foster home
for Dandy? . . . No, of course not, or I'd have heard about it by
now.

Quickly pulling on a pair of jeans, I scurried downstairs. What
in the world was I going to do? Sarge usually showed up at seven,
and she would no doubt ask when I'd have Dandy out of there.
This weekend . . . I'd just have to work on that this weekend.

Several women in orange-and-black Manna House volunteer
T-shirts—some church group, no doubt—were bustling around
the kitchen, setting big pans of covered hot food into the steam
table section of the kitchen counter. I found my mother and
Carolyn sitting at one of the tables, sorting clean flatware from a
dishwasher rack into their appropriate buckets—forks, knives,
spoons. It was a good thing Carolyn was working with my
mother, or she'd be there till midnight at the rate she was going.
I peeked into my office . . . no Dandy.

"He's out with Lucy, if you're wondering," Carolyn called
out. "Been gone most of the afternoon. Speaking of gone . . . I'm
here filling in for you. You're supposed to be on setup with your
mama here."

"Oh, Carolyn. I'm sorry. I had an appointment right after
lunch and didn't even look at the chore list."

The book lady smirked. "Works for me. I just traded with
you. You got my spot on supper dishes."

Oh great. That's when I usually tried to call P. J. and Paul.
Maybe I should try during supper.

After making sure my mother was settled at a table with a plate of food, all the proper utensils, and Aida Menéndez nearby to look after "Gramma Shep," I took my own plate of sliced ham, scalloped potatoes, and chopped salad into my office. Using my phone card, I dialed the Virginia number for Philip's parents.

"Fairbanks residence." Male voice. Philip's father.

"Hello, Mike. It's Gabby."

"Oh. Hi there, Gabrielle." He sounded uncomfortable. Maybe at least one Fairbanks male had the squirm gene. "Guess you want to speak to the boys. They're outside riding their bikes right now. Can you call back, maybe an hour?"

I fought with my disappointment. "All right. Sure. But . . . Mike? Can I talk to you a minute?"

"Uh, sure."

"Mike, you know Philip brought the boys there without my knowledge and without my permission, right?"

His silence definitely squirmed. Then, "Yeah, yeah. I pretty much figured. But Philip told his mother you two are having some marriage problems. Maybe it's better if the boys are here right now, instead of, you know, in the middle."

The bald truth of it hit me square between the eyes. I shook off his words. "But that's kidnapping, Mike. Across state lines, no less." Not exactly true, but I wasn't ready to give up ground yet. "I don't want to press charges if I can get my sons back."

Now the silence at the other end stretched long and deep. Finally a heavy sigh. "Gabrielle, I don't want to get in the middle of stuff with you and Philip. You know I didn't approve of him moving up there to Chicago in the first place. As far as I'm concerned, the boys are Virginia born and bred and belong here. But I'm not their parent. What do you want? You want me to put the boys on a plane back to Chicago? You feel okay with them traveling by themselves? Just say the word and I'll do it."

Now it was my turn to be speechless. Did I hear right? I could have my sons back, just like that? Mike Fairbanks would go around his son on my say-so?

"Mike, I . . . I appreciate that. But I don't have any money for plane tickets right now. Long story."

"Don't worry about that. I'll pay for it, and you can pay me back whenever."

My heart was beating so fast, I felt as if I'd just sprinted the quarter-mile. This weekend?! I could have the boys back with me by this weekend?

And then what, Gabby?

I finally found words. "Mike . . . thank you. But you're right. It's not simple. Can I call you back? I need to think it through."

"All right. But call me tonight, or first thing tomorrow morning. If you decide to leave them here, P. J.'s chomping at the bit to sign up for lacrosse summer camp the four weeks of July. Tomorrow's the last day to get his name on the list."

My hand was shaking as I hung up the phone. *"If you decide to leave them here . . ."* The decision was in my lap.

I joined the cleanup crew after supper in a daze. The church group volunteers put away leftovers and took the trash bags out the side utility door that accessed the gangway between buildings, and then they were gone—scuttling back to their own homes and families somewhere in the 'burbs. Hannah the Bored—my private name for the gum-chewing girl who was forever doing her nails—elected to wipe tables and sweep the floor, the easiest after-meal cleanup. That put me on dishes with two of the new residents, which meant I had to show them how to run the monster industrial dishwasher, leaving me no time to *think*.

I finally escaped into a sink full of large serving pans that needed scrubbing. A one-woman job. My mind spun around Mike Fairbanks's offer with every swirl of the scrub brush. On one hand, a no-brainer! Of course! Send the boys back! I'd take the Blue Line out to O'Hare Airport and meet them myself.

And then what, Gabby? Bring them here to Manna House? That was the rub. Even if the boys were willing to stay here—big *if*—it wasn't even possible. The shelter only allowed mothers with boys up to age eleven, and P. J. was almost fourteen. *Well, what about someone else taking them until I find an apartment—but who? The only people I know here in Chicago I met here at the shelter . . . Wait.* An idea danced in my brain as I sloshed suds in the sink. Josh's parents—Jodi and Denny Baxter—had taken Lucy for a few days when she had that cough. Josh said they had extra bedrooms now that he and his sister were out of the house. Would they—?

This is ridiculous! Even if the Baxters agreed, would my boys? Leave their grandparents to stay with total strangers? Not a chance. And Philip would have a fit.

Oh God, what am I going to do?

I glanced at the kitchen wall clock. *Quarter to eight.* An hour later in Virginia. I had to call Mike back, soon! The rest of the cleanup crew had already finished. Draining the sink, I took off my apron, flipped off the kitchen lights, and started for my office—when I noticed my mother standing in the middle of the dimly lit dining room, wringing her hands. "Mom! You okay?"

"Dandy." Her lip trembled. "I can't find him."

"Oh, Mom. Lucy took him out." *Like hours ago.* "I'm sure

they'll be back soon. You know Lucy!" Yeah, but if "soon" wasn't the next few minutes, Sarge would lock the doors at eight, and that would be it.

As if on cue, we heard a commotion on the main level and a sharp bark. I gave my mother a hug. "See? There he is! Come on, let's go see him." I tried not to show my impatience. I needed to call the boys' grandfather—and I still had no idea what I was going to say. All I knew was that I wanted my boys back, *now*.

In her haste, my mother stumbled a bit going up the stairs, and I had to slow her down. But as we came into the multi-purpose room, she was rewarded with a dynamo of yellow hair jumping all around her, whimpering happily. "Oh, Dandy, good boy, good doggy. Are you hungry? You are? Oh, look at your red bandanna. Look, Gabby, Lucy dressed him up! . . . Yes, yes, good doggy. I missed you too."

But I was looking at Lucy's purple knit hat squaring off in the middle of the room with the night manager. Lucy planted her fists on her lumpy hips. Sarge folded her muscular arms across her bosom as the two women went nose-to-nose.

"That dog ain't goin' ta no pound," I heard Lucy say.

"Rules are rules, Lucy Tucker. No pets at the shelter. *Capisce?*"

"This ain't the army, and you ain't commander in chief."

"And this ain't no pet hotel. The dog goes—tomorrow."

Lucy shook a finger in Sarge's face. "Dandy's *family*. Miz Martha's family. Her mean ol' son-in-law already kicked the dog an' Miz Martha out. Ya gonna do it again? Huh? Huh?"

"'Course not. Miss Martha can stay. But the dog gotta go. *Sabato.*"

"Humph!" Lucy waved her hand in disgust and stormed past

us, heading for the stairs to the bunk rooms. "Over my dead body," she muttered.

My mother tugged on my arm. "Celeste? Celeste? What does the night lady mean, the dog has to go? Not Dandy. She's not talking about Dandy, is she?"

By the time I calmed my mother down, gave Sarge a piece of my mind for talking about the dog in front of her, and got my mom upstairs and ready for bed, it was almost ten o'clock. Eleven in Virginia! Was it too late to call? I ran down to my office and picked up the phone . . . and then put it back in its cradle.

What was I going to say?

Early tomorrow. Mike said I could call early in the morning. All right. I'd sleep on it and call first thing in the morning.

Except . . . I couldn't sleep. The bunk room felt stuffy and crowded. Tanya and Sammy took up the fourth bunk. Lucy's snoring grated on my raw nerves. And seeing Mom's tears as she'd hugged Dandy good night before crawling into her bunk was about the last straw. The next day loomed like a hangman's noose outside my prison cell. I had to decide one way or another about the boys . . . had to find a foster home for Dandy before the Battle Ax called the pound . . . and it was the weekend! No Mabel to talk to. Would Estelle be in to cook lunch? I had no idea. Edesa and Josh had no reason to come in, unless Josh just happened to drop by to hang out with the kids. Even Harry Bentley didn't work at Richmond Towers on the weekend.

Wait. Jodi Baxter was scheduled to teach a Saturday typing class at eleven. Maybe I could talk to her! Except . . . eleven o'clock would be too late.

I needed to talk to someone *now*. But who?

"Come to me . . . all you who are burdened and carrying heavy loads . . ."

I remembered the Voice in my spirit and the verse I'd read in Matthew's gospel. That left God. I'd have to talk to God.

Slipping quietly out of bed, I tiptoed to the door, opened it, and listened. All was quiet. Maybe I could sit in the tiny lounge here on this floor if no one was sleeping out there, which sometimes happened. As I slipped out, Dandy squeezed out right behind me. "No, no, go back, Dandy," I hissed, trying to shove him back into the bunk room. But he wouldn't budge. I sighed. "Oh, all right," I whispered. "But if you alert Sarge, your name is mud."

The lounge was empty. Just a few stuffed chairs covered with cotton throws, a futon that had seen better days, and a table lamp. I wished I had my Bible, but it was downstairs in my office. Well, just as well. I'd keep the light off and just pray.

Curling up on a chair, I pulled the cotton throw around my shoulders. Dandy stretched out at my feet. *God,* I prayed silently, *You've been calling me to come to You. But it seems like I keep getting kicked off the path! Please . . . please lead me down the right path. I don't know what to do!*

My prayer drifted into rehearsing the options I'd already discarded. The boys couldn't stay at the shelter—and probably wouldn't want to. Probably wouldn't want to stay with the Baxters either, even if they were invited. Well then . . . the boys could stay with Philip! Except . . . he was moving out of the penthouse next week. But where? Would he have room for the boys? Or would he take them right back to Virginia?

God! I'm going in circles here!

And then the answer dropped into my spirit, like a flashing road sign. *Leave the boys in Virginia for the month of July.* I'd resisted the idea with every fiber of my being. It felt like I'd be giving in, letting Philip win! But . . . if I asked myself, *What's best for the boys right now?* given that I was living in a shelter and didn't know how soon I could get an apartment, or how quickly Lee Boyer could push through the custody petition—the answer was clear. Don't keep jerking Paul and P. J. around. Let them stay with their grand-parents. One month wasn't the end of the story. I still had two months to get them back here in time for school. And P. J. could go to lacrosse camp, like he wanted—

A low growl broke my concentration. "Dandy! Hush!" I hissed, kicking at the dog with a bare foot. But he was already on his feet, nose pointed toward the stairwell. I reached for him and felt his body tense. The rumble in his throat persisted, and he padded silently toward the stairwell.

Scrambling out of the chair, I tried to stop him. He probably heard Sarge or the other night assistant—a social work intern from a local college—doing their rounds. But I was too late. Dandy had already disappeared down the stairwell.

I followed as quickly as I could. *Good grief!* Just what I needed, for Dandy to tangle with Sarge in the middle of the night. Animal Control would be here at daybreak.

Aha . . . there he was, crouched at the staircase leading down to the lower level. One good grab and—

I stopped. Muffled noises and several thumps from below was followed by a voice snarling, "Shut up." My heart triple-timed. A *man's* voice!

At that instant, Dandy scrabbled down the staircase like a cougar after its prey. I tried to scream, "Dandy! Come back!"—

but nothing came out of my mouth. Instead I heard Dandy barking fiercely, and then—

"Call him off! . . . Umph!" *A man's voice!* "Get that dog off me—Ow! Ow! My hand! You—" A string of gutter words filled my ears as I stood frozen on the stairs. "Call him off, I tell you, or I'll cut him!"

And then a yelp of pain.

Dandy!

chapter 12

Without thinking, I burst into the open dining area in time to see a dark shape flying through the air and drop to the floor with another yelp as though in pain. "Dandy!" I screeched—and that's when I saw a stocky, dark figure whirl toward me.

"Watch out!" a woman's voice yelled. "He's got a knife!"

The dim room came into focus, as though time had stopped. Dandy lying on the floor . . . Sarge jerking her body back and forth on a chair . . . the blade of a kitchen knife gleaming in the glow of the EXIT sign . . .

But as the dark figure suddenly lunged toward me, Dandy scrambled to life and leaped, grabbing the man's wrist in his mouth. The man yelled. Man and dog fell to the floor. I heard, rather than saw, the knife clatter to the floor, skidding toward me.

"Grab the knife, Fairbanks!" Sarge yelled. "And untie me—now!" Adrenaline pulsing, I snatched up the knife.

Dandy still had the man's wrist gripped in his teeth, shaking it and holding on even as the man flailed about on the floor, hitting the dog with his other hand, trying to shake him off. A few feet away, Sarge half rose from the chair she was sitting in, but it came with her. That's when I saw that her hands were tied to the back of the chair with what looked like a dish towel.

"Fairbanks!" Sarge snapped. "Now!" Coming to life, I dropped the knife at her feet and loosened the clumsy knots. In two seconds Sarge was free. She snatched up the knife, breathing heavily. "Call 9-1-1. I've got it now."

I ran for my office phone. As I punched in the emergency numbers, I heard the man yell, "Call off the dog! He's tearing my hand off!"

"Lie still, buster. Then we'll call off the dog."

I quickly told the emergency operator we had an intruder with a knife at the Manna House Women's Shelter and gave the address. "Keep the line open," the operator said. "Cars are on the way. Do you need an ambulance?"

"No . . . yes!" *Oh God, what if Dandy really hurt that guy?*

Still clutching the phone, I stepped back out into the dining room. The night assistant clattered down the stairs, followed by Tina carrying a kid's plastic bat and several other residents who'd heard the commotion.

"Turn the lights on!" Sarge ordered. She had the knife pointed at the guy's chest. Even with the light on I couldn't tell his race or age beneath the scruffy, week-old beard and knit hat pulled low. He was moaning, wide eyes darting between his captor and Dandy, who crouched on the floor, mouth still locked on the man's wrist.

"Somebody tie his free hand to that table leg there. Tie his feet too. Get those dish towels or an extension cord—anything!"

Still holding the phone, I grabbed the dish towels the man had used to tie Sarge to the chair, and between the three of us—me, the college intern, and Tina, looking like a Puerto Rican Amazon carrying that plastic bat—we got the man's ankles tied and his free hand "handcuffed" to a table leg.

"Okay, Fairbanks. Call the dog off—and we better wrap something around this sucker's wrist. There's a lot of blood there."

I knelt down, my whole body shaking from the trauma of the past few minutes. "Let go, Dandy. Good boy . . . it's okay." Dandy let loose of the man's wrist, still crouching by his side. "Good boy. Come on, now . . . here, boy."

Dandy tried to rise, but let out a whine and sank back to the floor. Then, with an effort, he crawled away a few feet, using only his back legs and one of his front paws.

A wide smear of blood followed in his wake.

"No!" I cried, falling to my knees beside him. "He's hurt! Dandy's hurt!"

A dizzy hour later, I found myself pacing in the waiting room of a twenty-four-hour animal hospital, while somewhere behind closed doors a vet worked on the slashing knife wounds on Dandy's shoulder and chest. Lucy had appeared in baggy flannel pajamas just as the police were hauling the intruder to the ambulance outside, and she insisted on coming along when a nice young policeman offered to drive Dandy and me to the vet. He even put the siren on and raced through half a dozen red lights.

I barely remembered running upstairs to shed my bloody silk pajamas, pulling on a pair of jeans and a T-shirt, and grabbing bath towels to wrap Dandy in. Thankfully, my mother had slept through the whole thing.

In the police car, Lucy had held Dandy's head in her lap,

stroking his ears gently and murmuring encouraging words. But now she sat huddled in a corner, eyes streaming beneath the purple knit hat jammed on her head and swiping her nose with the back of her hand. I finally got a wad of toilet paper from a bathroom and stuffed it into her hand.

Before leaving us at the vet, the police officer—his name tag said Krakowski—had taken my statement of what happened. But the streetlights had dimmed and early morning fingers of light were tapping the rooftops by the time the vet came out. The good news was, the knife had not punctured any vital organs. The bad news was that the wound had torn muscles and tendons in the shoulder and chest, and might affect how well Dandy could walk in the future. The vet had to do about fifty internal stitches and twice that many external stitches. Did we want to leave him there for a day or two to rest?

Lucy emphatically shook her head. "Ain't gonna let that dog outta my sight. Miz Martha gonna want to see him, too, or she's gonna be mighty upset."

To my surprise, Officer Krakowski showed up to take us back to the shelter. "He's a hero, you know," the officer said, carrying a doped-up Dandy to the squad car and laying him carefully on the backseat. "The whole precinct is talking about him."

Lucy scrambled into the back from the other side, so I ended up in the front seat. "So, uh, the intruder guy," I ventured. "Was he hurt very bad?"

Officer Krakowski laughed. "The perp? Could've been worse. He's got some scratches and bites on his wrist, but if Dandy had been serious, his teeth could have punctured an artery. They got the guy patched up in the ER, and they're booking him down at the precinct."

Thank You, God. The way he'd been yelling, I was afraid Dandy had done serious damage, and, intruder or not, the guy would probably have sued us.

Officer Krakowski glanced sideways at me. "Just one thing. Dandy's up to date on all his shots, right? The hospital wanted to know."

Good grief! How would I know? My mom was so forgetful. I twisted in my seat belt. "Lucy. Does Dandy have a rabies tag on his collar?"

"Yeah. Somethin' like that."

"What's it say?"

Silence in the backseat. I twisted further. Lucy was glowering at me. "Can't see so good back here," she finally muttered.

"Don't worry about it," the police officer said. "We'll check it when we get him inside."

I glanced at my watch as we turned the corner by the Laundromat. Almost six thirty. I hadn't slept a wink all night. My eyes were so heavy I could barely keep them open. But it would be awhile before I got a chance to catch a nap. First thing I had to do was make a call to Virginia . . .

"See? What did I tell you? This city loves a hero." Officer Krakowski was grinning.

The squad car had pulled up in front of Manna House, and immediately we were surrounded by a flock of reporters and cameramen. Microphones were shoved in my face as we got out of the car. "Mrs. Fairbanks! Can you tell us what happened?" . . . "How badly is the dog hurt? How many times was he shot?" . . . "Why was the dog at the shelter? Is he homeless?"

I looked frantically at our police escort, but he was carefully lifting Dandy out of the car. Cameras clicked like little cap guns.

Dodging microphones and cameras as best I could, I scurried up the steps and rang the door buzzer, wishing I had my key—but of course I'd forgotten my purse, wallet, ID, keys. As soon as the door opened, I held it until Lucy and the officer had Dandy safely inside, then turned around to face the vultures.

"Uh, hi folks. It's been a stressful night, as you can all imagine. I'm sure Manna House will issue a statement as soon as possible. Please be patient." With what I hoped was a friendly smile, I escaped inside, pulling the big oak door shut behind me until I heard the lock click.

But inside the multipurpose room, another contingent crowded around Lucy and Officer Krakowski as the policeman gently laid Dandy on the closest couch. Even Mabel was there. No surprise. Sarge probably called her while the detectives were still taking statements. The excited residents in various stages of dress and undress were all talking at once. "Is he okay?" . . . "Aw, look, they shaved off all his purty hair on that side" . . . "How come I didn't hear nuthin'?" . . . "I wanna see!"

"All right, all right, back off, everybody," Sarge barked. "Let Miss Martha have a minute—it's her dog." The night manager ushered my mother, still in her nightgown, to the couch and got her settled beside Dandy, making sure she was comfortable.

I saw Mabel speak to Officer Krakowski, frown and nod; then the two of them headed in my direction. The officer handed me a card. "Checked the tag. The dog's good. Call me if you need anything." He jerked his head toward the front doors that held the media at bay and smiled. "Good luck. You're going to need it."

Mabel saw him out.

"Fairbanks?" The night manager showed up at my elbow. "You okay? Here—bet you could use some *caffe*, no? Just made it."

Sarge handed me a steaming Styrofoam cup. "Got someplace quiet you want to put Dandy so he can rest? Just say the word—I'll take him there."

If I wasn't so tired, I would have guffawed. Was this the same Sarge who'd been breathing threats about sending Dandy to the pound today?

"Thanks, Sarge." I took a sip of the hot coffee. Black, no cream. *Oh well.* "Guess my office is the best place for now, out of the way, if we can find some soft blankets or something. But first I need to—"

"Not to worry. Leave it to me." Sarge marched off on her search-and-recover mission.

My head ached. I wanted to go to my mother, who seemed bewildered by all the commotion. I really wanted to go to bed. But instead I made my way down to my office, flipped on the light, and pulled the pad with the Fairbanks' number on it toward me. I picked up the phone and dialed.

One ring . . . two . . . three . . . four—

"Mike? . . . It's Gabby. Sorry I didn't call last night. I needed time to decide what's best for the boys and . . ." I pressed my fingers against my eyes, willing the ache in my head and my heart to go away. "Anyway, I want to thank you for offering to send the boys back. But I've decided"—I had to push the words out—"I've decided they should stay there for the next few weeks. Let P. J. go to lacrosse summer camp. When camp is done, maybe things will be different here."

A moment later I hung up the phone, laid my head down on my arms, and wept.

chapter 13

A knock at the door made me grab for a wad of tissues and blow my nose. Lucy marched in with a tattered comforter that had seen better days, followed by Sarge carrying Dandy. Hovering behind them in the doorway, Tanya had an arm around my mother, who was still in her nightgown. "Tried to take her back upstairs to get dressed," Tanya whispered to me, "but she don't wanna leave the dog."

"That's okay." I slipped out of the tiny office so my mother could get in and supervise.

"He needs fresh water," she fussed. "And food in his bowl."

"Yeah, yeah," Lucy muttered, and marched out with the water bowl. We all knew Dandy wouldn't be eating or drinking anytime soon, but none of us were inclined to argue.

Sarge was next to leave. "Oh, Fairbanks, Mabel wants to see both of us soon as you get things squared away down here." She looked at her watch. "Breakfast stuff is on the counter. But I'd like to get out of here by eight if you—"

I nodded. "It's okay. I'm not hungry. Just let me get my mother settled and I'll be right up." If I didn't fall over first.

Tanya promised to get my mother fed and dressed when she was ready. Sammy eagerly said he'd "dog-sit," and I was surprised when my mother agreed. A lump caught in my throat. If my Paul knew that Dandy had been injured while protecting the shelter, he'd want to be the one sitting by the dog's "bedside."

Oh God! Did I make the right decision? Maybe I should have told the boys' grandfather to send them back here anyway and let the chips fall where they may!

Couldn't go there. I needed sleep. I needed . . . uhh, I was supposed to talk to Mabel. After pouring another cup of coffee from the carafe as I hustled through the multipurpose room, I knocked on Mabel's door and peeked in. Sarge was already hunkered on a chair, elbows on her knees. Mabel got up and gave me a quick hug. "Are you all right, Gabby?"

I offered a weak smile. "Been better. But I'll be okay." I sat down before my legs betrayed me.

Unlike her usual careful outfits, Mabel looked like she'd grabbed clothes off the floor without bothering to fix her face—a black silk headwrap still covered her hair—which wasn't surprising after getting a call from the shelter in the middle of the night. "We're all tired," she admitted, "so I don't want this to take long. Sarge already gave me a brief overview, but I'd like to hear again what happened from both of you, to get our facts straight." She jerked her head in the direction of the melee we knew was waiting outside. "I suppose we'll have to make a statement to the media before they'll go away."

I wagged my head. "How did they even know about this? We didn't call them!"

Sarge grunted. "Police scanners. Some reporters chase police stories like lawyers chase ambulances. If one of our residents had got cut up by the perp? The media couldn't care less. But a dog playing hero?"

My hackles rose. "Dandy wasn't playing! He knew something was wrong. I've never seen him act like that. He's usually a teddy bear!"

Sarge patted the air with her hand. "*D'accordo, d'accordo.* I am not blaming the dog. He saved my life, for all I know."

I stared at her. Frankly, I hadn't given much thought to what Sarge had endured during the night. "How . . . I mean, what happened before Dandy got there?"

"All right," Mabel interrupted. "Let's back up. Sarge, tell me again what happened."

The night manager shrugged. "The kid and I—Susan what's-her-face—"

"Susan McCall, your assistant," Mabel said.

"*Sí,* the kid. Anyway, we did rounds at midnight, everything was okay, *capisce*? Susan sacked out on a couch for a few z's, not a problem. I might have dozed . . . then I heard a sound downstairs. Didn't think much about it. Fairbanks, here, sometimes bends the rules and goes to her office in the middle of the night—"

I flushed but held my tongue.

"—but I decided to check. Made my way downstairs, and some tomfool is in the kitchen, rummaging around in the fridge. I thought it was one of the residents, helping herself to a midnight snack. So I yell, 'Hey!' Somebody turns out to be this big dude. He grabbed a knife—"

"Grabbed it?" Mabel asked. "He didn't have it with him?"

Sarge shook her head. "Saw him grab it out of the knife block. Definitely a Manna House knife. Then it happened so fast—that dude jumped over the counter and had that knife at my throat. Uh-uh, no way baby, not going to argue with a knife. Saw too many slit throats in Iraq . . ."

I gaped at her. I'd been so wrapped up in my own personal drama, I'd never given a thought to what Sarge had experienced in the military.

"Anyway, the perp found some dish towels and tied me to one of those plastic chairs. He was just about to stuff a gag in my mouth when"—Sarge broke into a laugh—"when all hell broke loose in the stairwell. Next thing I knew, that fur ball charges into the room, barking and snapping. It was dark, you know, so I am not sure exactly what happened. But the guy must have grabbed up the knife and cut him—kicked him too—because the dog yelped and went flying. That's when Fairbanks, here, showed up screaming bloody murder." Sarge volleyed the verbal ball at me. "Your turn."

I was so tired my memory felt blurry. But I admitted I couldn't sleep last night, so Dandy and I had been in the lounge upstairs. "Praying," I added. "Dandy heard something. I tried to stop him, but he was off like a shot . . ." I filled in the rest of the story as best I could.

Mabel had been listening intently and taking notes. When I finished, she jumped in. "Two questions. How did the intruder get in? And what did he want? Police said the side door off the gangway was unlocked when they arrived."

Sarge got defensive. "That door's always locked, except for deliveries. We don't let residents use it for any reason."

"Yes," Mabel shot back, "but it's your responsibility as night manager to check that *all* doors are locked every evening."

Ha. Part of me would have loved to let Sarge squirm after all the grief she'd given me about Dandy. But the night's events had been traumatic for her too—confronting the intruder alone, finding a knife at her throat, getting tied up.

"Uh, Mabel. I'm partly to blame as well. I saw the supper volunteers take trash bags out that side door and didn't think anything about it. I was on cleanup, the last one to leave, and I should have checked that door. But I had big problems on my mind and just wasn't thinking."

To my surprise, Sarge shot me a look that seemed almost . . . grateful.

Mabel finally leaned back. "Well, obviously, we need to tighten the security. When something like this happens, we all have to learn from it. We can't afford to make mistakes. We were fortunate this time. It could have been worse . . ."

I zoned out, impatient to talk to my mom, get some sleep, call the boys to tell them about Dandy, ask how they felt about staying another month in Virginia. But I tried to focus.

". . . a lot to be thankful for. We need to give God some serious praise around here! And no doubt about it, Dandy's the hero of the day. I'm so sorry he got hurt, Gabby. How's your mother taking it?"

I shook my head. "Haven't really talked to her. I'm not sure she understands. She gets confused when things get stressful. But I think she's doing all right for now. I just hope those reporters don't find out Dandy is her dog and shove those microphones in her face. She'd freak."

"Good point. Right now I think they assume Dandy is your dog, Gabby. Let's keep it that way."

Not that I wanted any microphones in my face either. "Uh, I

kind of promised we'd give them a statement soon, just so they'd let us get in the door." I looked at Mabel hopefully. "Would you . . . ?"

Mabel made a face. "All right. Hopefully, this will blow over soon. Most of our guests don't want—or need—media spotlight. Guess we should call a meeting of all the residents and make sure everybody has the straight story so we don't start a lot of rumors."

The three of us worked on a statement we hoped would satisfy the diehards still waiting outside. Finally Mabel stood up. "All right, while I'm giving our statement, would you two gather the residents in the multipurpose room? Sarge, can you stay a bit longer? Gabby, do we have anything scheduled this morning?"

I squeezed my eyes shut, trying to think. "Uh, yes, Jodi Baxter is coming to teach a typing class at eleven." I groaned inwardly. I'd had every intention of trying to talk with Jodi when she came this morning, thinking Mabel wouldn't be here. I still needed help sorting out the options the Legal Aid lawyer had presented to me. But now, all I could think of was sleep.

"Fine. We'll be done by then." Mabel started out of her office, then caught her reflection in the glass windows around the receptionist's cubby. "Oh, Lord, help me. You sure do have ways of keeping me humble." Our shelter director gave a short laugh, then gave a shrug and marched toward the front doors, crowned with her bedtime hair wrap.

I had to smile. Was that a prayer? Mabel talked to God like He was just another person sitting in on our conversation.

While Mabel was out facing the cameras, Sarge started rounding up the residents and I checked on Dandy—stretched out on his comforter, eyes closed, the bandages wrapped around his shaved chest and shoulder rising and falling with each labored breath. Eight-year-old Sammy sat patiently nearby.

"You okay, Sammy? You want a book to read? Or here . . ." I grabbed some blank paper and colored markers from my desk. "Would you like to draw?"

Tanya's boy nodded eagerly, took the paper and markers, and scrunched down on the floor. Then he looked up. "Some a' the other kids wanted ta come in, but I told 'em nobody s'posed ta be in your office but me. Ain't that right, Miz Gabby?"

"That's right, Sammy. For now, anyway." Smiling at his loyalty, I scurried back upstairs to the main floor, where residents were gathering just as Mabel came back through the double doors into the multipurpose room. I was glad to see my mother dressed in navy blue slacks and a clean—though wrinkled—white blouse, and her hair brushed. I slipped up to her, gave her a hug, and pulled a folding chair close.

Done with her statement, Mabel marched into the multipurpose room and clapped her hands. "Everybody here? Good. Ladies, quiet down . . . Hello! Ladies! We need to brief you about what happened last night, and—"

"'Scuse me, Miz Mabel!" Lucy's hand shot up.

"We'll have time for questions later, Lucy. First—"

"'Scuse me, Miz Mabel. We got somethin' ta say first, right, ladies?"

Murmurs all around. Mabel sighed. "All right, Lucy. What is it?"

Lucy poked Carolyn. "You go. They gonna listen to you, 'cause you got all that book learnin'."

"She would, *si te callaras la boca*, Lucy!" Tina hollered. Everybody laughed.

"Ladies, please . . ." Mabel looked frustrated.

Carolyn stood up. "Sorry, Mabel. We don't mean to joke. We've been talking—all the ladies here—about what happened last night, and we have a proposition to make."

Heads nodded all around the room. "That's right" . . . "*Sí*" . . . "Uh-huh" . . .

Lucy poked Carolyn again. "Get on with it."

"Lucy, if you poke me one more time, I'm—!" Snickers from the residents. "Anyway, we all know Dandy's been living here on borrowed time. Sarge has been saying he's got to be out of here by this weekend."

Sarge threw up her hands. "Well, not *today*. The dog's hurt."

"Exactly. Gramma Shep's dog got injured protecting all of us from an intruder. Hurt bad. So all of us here agree we owe him somethin'. We took a vote—"

Mabel's eyebrow went up.

"—and we all agree that Dandy should be made a resident of Manna House Women's Shelter as official watchdog."

The room erupted with cheers and claps from the residents, even Sheila, the big-chested woman who'd screeched like a banshee the first time I brought Dandy and my mom to the shelter for a visit. Carolyn handed Mabel a sheet of paper with a ballpoint pen clipped to the top. "See? We've all signed a petition."

Mabel glanced at the paper, a small smile tugging at the corner of her mouth, then handed it to Sarge. The night manager shrugged. "Humph. I'm overruled, no? City inspector might not like it, but tell you what . . ." Sarge grabbed the pen, laid the paper on the nearest end table, and signed it.

Now the residents did raise a cheer, laughing and slapping Sarge on the back. I saw Mabel turn her head toward the foyer as if listening to something, then slip out as Sarge passed the list of signatures to me.

I showed the paper to my mother, who had a fixed smile on her face, as if aware that something good was happening but not sure what it was. "Look at this, Mom! Everybody wants Dandy to stay here at the shelter as the official watchdog. Isn't that great?"

As I glanced over the list, I didn't see Lucy's name. But at the top, among the first few signatures, was a large, scrawled X.

My neck prickled. Was *that* why Lucy fussed about being asked to read Dandy's dog tag in the back of the squad car?

Lucy couldn't read!

A tap on my shoulder made me look up. "Gabby?" Mabel beckoned. "You've got a phone call. Take it in my office if you want to."

Strange. Who would be calling me? The boys? Maybe their granddad had told them they were staying in Virginia, and they wanted to talk to me. Or—

I picked up Mabel's phone. "Hello? Gabby Fairbanks speaking."

"*Gabrielle!*" My name was shouted in my ear like a cuss word. "What are you trying to do—ruin me?"

I recoiled from the phone in shock. *Philip!* But I took a deep breath and tried to collect my equilibrium. "What do you mean, ruin you? Why are you calling, Philip? This isn't exactly a good time. I've got a lot going on—"

"Yeah, I'll bet you do. Talking to reporters, splashing the Fairbanks name all over the news!"

I squeezed my eyes shut and pinched the bridge of my nose, trying to calm the voices shouting in my head. "Philip. I'm not—"

"Oh yeah? Turn on the TV! Of all the lowdown things to do,

neta jackson

making a spectacle of yourself. I'm supposed to play golf in an hour with one of our new clients today—now this!" He swore right in my ear. "Don't play innocent with me—I know what you're up to, Gabrielle. My mother always said you'd drag down the Fairbanks name someday!"

chapter 14

The phone went dead. Stunned, I stumbled through the multi-purpose room and into the TV room, turned on the set, and started flipping channels. *Cartoons . . . cartoons . . . home renovation . . . cooking show . . . news . . .*

There. Mabel Turner standing with the arched oak doors of the Manna House shelter at her back, camera lights bouncing off her maple-colored skin, finishing our carefully worded statement. *". . . grateful that no one was seriously hurt."*

Questions flew before she even had time to take a breath. *"Ms. Turner! Ms. Turner! You said the dog was treated by a vet—how badly was he hurt?" . . . "Who does the dog belong to?" . . . "Why was he at the shelter? Are you taking in homeless animals too?" . . . "Where's the dog now?" . . .*

"Oh brother," Mabel's voice breathed in my ear. I jumped. Where had Mabel come from? "The one time I'm on television and I look like I just fell out of bed."

". . . belongs to one of our staff," Mabel was saying on air, *"and just happened to be here last night. Fortunately."* She smiled into the cameras. *"Thank you. That's all."*

Aware that others were pushing into the small TV room and peering over our shoulders, I deliberately slowed my breathing. That was it? Mabel had been very careful not to give out any personal information. *What is Philip's problem?* But just then, the TV camera zoomed in on a perky blonde reporter with perfect makeup and a big microphone, saying, "Earlier this morning, a squad car brought back the shelter's hero, a mutt named Dandy . . ." The footage showed Officer Krakowski lifting Dandy out of the car, swathed in bandages, followed by Lucy Tucker in her pajama bottoms, sweatshirt, and purple knit hat—and me, running up the steps and leaning on the door buzzer, pulling it open until the trio got inside, then turning around while voices yelled, *"Mrs. Fairbanks! Mrs. Fairbanks! Can you—"*

Close-up of Gabby Fairbanks, bags under my eyes, snarly chestnut curls that hadn't seen a comb or brush (or a haircut) since who knew when, and chirping, *"Uh, hi folks. It's been a stressful night, as you can all imagine. I'm sure Manna House will issue a statement as soon as possible. Please be patient."*

Residents all around me babbled with excitement. "Hey, Lucy! You were on TV!" . . . "Didja hear that? They called Dandy a mutt! Stupid reporters." . . . "Me? On TV? Where?" . . .

But their chatter was drowned out by the TV voices echoing in my head—*"Mrs. Fairbanks! Mrs. Fairbanks!"*—and Philip's snarl on the phone: *". . . making a spectacle of yourself . . . always said you'd drag down the Fairbanks name someday!"*

I never did get a nap that morning. Jodi Baxter showed up to teach her class, along with Estelle, who flounced in like a mini tidal wave, muttering that leftovers—the usual fare for weekend lunches, I gathered—would not do after the trauma of such a night. She immediately set about banging pots and pans and cooking something that began to smell mighty good.

"We saw it on the news," Jodi told me. "Actually, Denny and I heard screeching upstairs, and the next thing we knew, Stu was pounding on our back door, telling us to turn on the TV."

It took me a few seconds to remember that "Stu" and Estelle were housemates, and they lived above Josh's parents in a two-flat. One day I'd get it figured out.

"But what's this Josh and Edesa are telling me?" Jodi reached out and rested her hand lightly on my arm. I was aware of her gentle touch, and for some reason I wanted to cry. "Your husband locked you out, and you and your mother moved into the shelter?" Her eyes were round with disbelief, as if saying the words aloud felt like telling a fib.

I gave a little nod, afraid my high water mark was ready to breach and I'd soon be a blubbery mess right then and there. "Yeah, well . . ." I grabbed a tissue from my jeans pocket and blew my nose. Wasn't sure how coherent I'd be on no sleep, but I really did want to talk to Jodi. "Um, if you don't have to run off right after your typing class, I'd . . . guess I would like to talk to you."

"Sure! Besides, I'd never hear the end of it if I left before Estelle's sacrificial lunch offering. Cooking and sewing—that's how she blesses people. Oh! Speaking of blessings! I need a few strong arms to carry in a couple of computers from our minivan. Software Symphony donated two more used computers to the schoolroom." Jodi eyed me slyly beneath the bangs of her shoulder-length brown bob. "Of course, I bugged Peter Douglass about it mercilessly when I realized more women signed up to learn word processing skills than Manna House had computers."

I couldn't help but grin. Jodi Baxter wouldn't exactly turn heads on the street, but she could turn a few hardheads into giving up what she needed. Sarge was gone, but I rounded up Carolyn and Tina to help Jodi and me bring in the computers, monitors, and keyboards. We made space for the equipment on the long table in the schoolroom that already held two computers, as Carolyn lifted the mass of wires and plugs out of a box. "Hm. Might be able to get these up and running for you," she murmured. "Not in time for today's class, though."

I raised my eyebrows. What other talents lay underneath Carolyn's scraggly ponytail?

Kim and Wanda showed up for Jodi's typing class, along with one of the new residents, named Althea, who seemed to be Mediterranean-something. Sicilian? Turkish? She spoke good English—easier to understand than Wanda's Jamaican patois. Jodi seemed comfortable, though, so I slipped down to my office to check on Dandy. Lucy was parked on my chair, leaning on the desk with her elbow, wrinkled hand holding up her head, which was still crowned in the purple knit hat, and snoring away.

"Lucy!" I shook her awake. "Go upstairs and get a nap. I'll take over."

"*Umph . . . gurkle . . .* huh? Whatchu want, Fuzz Top? I ain't sleepin'."

"It's okay. You had a short night." *Huh. Didn't we all.* "Besides, I need to use my office."

"Humph. Okay." The phone rang just as Lucy hauled herself up from my chair. "You want me ta get that?" Without waiting for an answer, she snatched up the desk phone. "Miz Gabby's office . . . Oh yeah? . . . Okay, I'll tell her." She hung it up. "You've got a visitor."

116

I stiffened. A visitor? Philip wouldn't . . . would he? "Did whoever's on the desk say who it is?"

Lucy shrugged. "Only one way ta find out. C'mon."

I followed meekly. If it was Philip, having Lucy pave the way wasn't a bad idea. She wouldn't take any guff from him. Or maybe it was just some reporter . . . Good grief. I'd almost rather talk to Philip. Didn't the media know they were stirring up a hornet's nest in my corner?

But my visitor was neither.

"Mr. Bentley!" I cried as Lucy and I came through the double doors into the foyer. The doorman from Richmond Towers— wearing slacks, a nice button-down shirt, and a tweed golf hat hiding his bald head, instead of his blue uniform and cap—stood holding a big bag of something. And next to him, carrying a couple of plastic store bags, stood his wide-eyed grandson. But the boy's name had slipped my mind. "Uh, hi, young man. What brings you guys here two days in a row?"

"We saw the story about your dog on TV!" the boy piped up. "Grandpa said it belongs to your mama."

Mr. Bentley looked a little embarrassed. "Yeah, DeShawn wanted us to bring something for the hero dog." He hefted the load in his arms—a twenty-five-pound bag of dog food. "DeShawn has some stuff too—rawhide bone, dog toy, you know."

"Yeah, but Grandpa! Who brought all that other stuff out there?" DeShawn tipped his head toward the front doors.

The boy had a beautiful face—large, dark eyes, smooth skin, an impish grin lurking beneath the surface. He looked up at Mr. Bentley with obvious respect. I stared, fascinated. Then what he said finally penetrated my brain. "Uh, what other stuff?"

Lucy was two beats ahead of me, already pushing the doors open. "Uh-oh."

"'Uh-oh' what?" I peered over her shoulder, then pushed the doors open wider.

The steps of the Manna House shelter were stacked with bags of dry dog food, towers of canned dog food, dog toys, dog chews, dog treats, and homemade posters in childish scrawls: *Dandy the Hero! Chicago loves Dandy! Get well, Dandy!*

And a plethora of stuffed toy dogs sat atop the doggy loot—big ones, little ones, yellow and brown and spotted ones, with cute faces and floppy ears—like a child's menagerie sprawled all over a lumpy bedspread.

chapter 15

I stared at the gifts piled high on the shelter steps, touched by the generosity of total strangers. But something felt out of whack. All this fuss over an injured dog—and I was grateful, I really was. But I felt embarrassed. Most homeless people in Chicago were invisible to the general population, except for the sleeping bodies here and there, dotting the parks or slumped in an out-of-the-way doorway. The *Streetwise* vendors were tolerated by most, even respected by some, but homeless families like Tanya and Sammy . . . who cared?

"Well, better get this stuff inside. Could rain this afternoon. C'mon, DeShawn." Mr. Bentley put his load down in the foyer, then started hauling bags of dog food and stuffed toys inside. I saw a couple of people with cameras lurking across the street, snapping pictures before the piles disappeared.

Lucy and I started picking up the toys. "Aw, this here dog is cute," Lucy said, holding up a floppy yellow dog with a big face and big paws.

"It's yours, Lucy," I said. "From Dandy. Next to my mom, you're his favorite person."

"Ya think so?" Lucy allowed a big grin, showing her missing teeth.

Once everything was inside the foyer, Mr. Bentley straightened, hand on his back. "Now, where do ya want this stuff, Mrs. Fairbanks? Seems like all I'm doin' lately is hauling your stuff around." He rolled his eyes—but then winked at me.

"You've done enough, Mr. B. I'll get some other volunteers to move this stuff once we figure out what to do with it . . . oh! There's the lunch bell. DeShawn, you and your grandpa are invited for lunch. Estelle showed up this morning, decided to wrap up our hair-raising experience with a good meal."

Mr. Bentley chuckled. "Sounds like Miss Estelle. Some woman."

I noticed I didn't have to ask him twice.

Estelle's lunch perked up everyone's spirits. She put Jodi to work after the typing class, and they served up teriyaki chicken, rice, fruit salad, and pineapple upside-down cake for dessert. A couple of the board members who'd seen the news clips showed up—Liz Handley and Peter Douglass with his wife, Avis—to make sure everyone was all right and to huddle with Mabel about how to deal with the media. Estelle must have anticipated extra mouths, because she made everyone eat and still had leftovers.

I tried to save a couple of seats for Mr. Bentley and his grandson at the table where I parked my mom, but when I looked up, they'd been hijacked to the table with the Douglasses. When Jodi finally got to eat, she and Avis got their heads together about something. Even Mr. B and Peter seemed to be talking like old times. Huh. I invite Mr. Bentley *one time* to our Fun Night here at the shelter, and suddenly he's everybody's best friend.

Still, Jodi did say she'd like to talk to me, so I tried to hurry my mother along, hoping to grab Jodi before she left. But Mom would not be hurried. "Mm, that upside-down cake is good. But I need coffee with something sweet. Gabby, would you—?"

I jumped up to get the coffee, thinking it was as good as any time to speak to Jodi. But Mabel got to me first. "Gabby, better ask for some volunteers to help you move the stuff in the foyer. Guess you can put it down here in the rec room for now. But you better keep checking the front steps—I don't think we've seen the end of it yet."

Oh brother. I'd almost forgotten about the glut of "dog stuff" upstairs. With a sigh, I got Mom's coffee, then caught Jodi Baxter on her way up to the counter with her dirty dishes.

"Jodi! I'd really like to talk to you, but I've got to do something about all the stuff total strangers have been leaving on the doorstep. And I don't want to keep you waiting . . ."

"Oh, that's okay. Let me help." She grinned. "Denny and Josh are doing some plumbing thing over at their apartment. The only thing waiting for me at home is a dirty kitchen floor and two baskets of laundry to fold. I'd rather play with those stuffed animals—oh." She dumped her dirty dishes and pulled me aside. "Actually, I'd really love to meet Dandy. Is he—?"

"In my office." I eyed the closed door. "But let's wait till the dining room clears out. I'll grab a few more people to help haul stuff, and maybe by that time—whoa! What's this?"

Tina clattered down the stairs, hefting a bag of dog food over her shoulder, followed by several of the other residents, arms loaded. "Where does this stuff go?" Tina demanded. "I got one more trip."

I pointed to the rec room. "Uh, Jodi, could you help organize stuff in there? I'll go upstairs and see what's going on."

Squeezing up the staircase past several of the kids coming down, arms full of stuffed animals and posters, I ran into Lucy at the top, who'd planted herself squarely in the way of anyone coming up from the dining room. "Two trips, missy. With as much as you can carry 'fore you go to the beauty shop or take a nap, whichever is gonna revive that fuzz top o' yours—hey! Hey, Sheila! Ever'body's gotta take two loads a' stuff outta the foyer and get it downstairs 'fore they do anything else! Means you, sister! You signed the official mascot petition, din'tcha? Well?"

I scurried to the foyer and got my first armload. "Thanks, Lucy," I said on my way back to the stairs.

"Huh. Don't thank *me*. Them that can run up an' down stairs get to carry stuff. Them that can't get to boss all the rest a' ya." But she allowed a grin for the second time that day—then hollered after me, "An' ya better check the front steps! Bunch more stuff showed up during lunch!"

Many hands did make light work, to prove the cliché, and Estelle was shutting down the kitchen as we deposited the last bag of dog food in the rec room. Jodi had done a great job, storing most of it out of the way under the Ping-Pong table, the rest in black plastic garbage bags in the corners behind the bean bag chairs. On the spur of the moment, I grabbed an armload of the cutest stuffed doggies and went hunting for young Sammy. "Here, buddy, I have a job for you. Give one to each of the kids here at Manna House, okay? And choose one for yourself."

I was rewarded with a high five.

"What are you going to do with all this?" Jodi asked as I unlocked my office.

I shook my head. "I dunno. Can't think yet. Well . . . there he is. The Manna House Hero."

Dandy lifted his head as I turned on the light. Jodi immediately got down on the floor beside him. "Hey there, Dandy, good boy." She spoke softly, crooning his name, gently stroking his matted neck hair. The dog licked her hand. "Aw, Gabby. He's so sweet." Dandy laid his head back down under her gentle petting. "We used to have a dog. A chocolate Lab. We named him Willie Wonka. He died a couple of years ago, just old age. I still really miss him . . ."

I sat quietly in my desk chair while she petted Dandy. Then she turned her head to me, still sitting on the floor. "Gabby, I still want to hear why you and your mom and Dandy here are staying at the shelter. But I've been thinking . . . would you like to come stay at our house for the weekend? We've got a couple of empty bedrooms right now—I mean, Amanda's home from college, but she went with the youth from our church on a mission trip and won't be back for another week."

"Oh, Jodi. That's so nice. But I can't leave Dandy right now. And my mom—"

"I meant all three of you! Actually, thinking about Dandy's injury gave me the idea. I mean, we've got a backyard, well, at least there's some grass, and it's only a few steps from the porch to the yard. We could make a bed for Dandy on the porch since the weather's decent, give him a few days to recover from his injury and a place to be outside when he's ready. Sheesh! Stay the whole week if you'd like."

I stared at her. The idea of sleeping in a room all to myself instead of a bunk room with four other people, one of whom snored like a chainsaw, sounded like an ad for a vacation in Tahiti. The media couldn't find me or Dandy . . . maybe they'd go away. *Huh.* Philip couldn't find me either—I needed another phone call like the one this morning like I needed a root canal. Mom wouldn't have to climb stairs . . . and what Jodi said about Dandy being able to recover away from hordes of admirers and curiosity seekers was downright brilliant.

"Oh, Jodi. Are you sure? I mean, I have to come to work Monday—"

"So?" She got to her feet and brushed dog hair off her slacks. "Take the El. Josh and Edesa do it all the time from Rogers Park. I'm off for the summer. Your mom and Dandy can stay with me."

Of course I could take the El. That's how I'd been getting to work before the fallout with Philip. I'd just have to allow a little more time. But leaving my mother with the Baxters during the day . . . that seemed like too much. Didn't Jodi have to check with her husband?

Still . . .

I grinned. "Okay . . . why not? At least for the weekend, I mean." I jumped up and gave Jodi a big hug. "Thanks, Jodi." I had to push the words past the lump in my throat. "Thanks so much. I can't begin to tell you what a gift this is."

It still took us a good hour to let Mabel know the plan and check out for the weekend, pack a bag for my mother and myself, gather up a garbage bag of laundry to do, and enlist Tina's help carrying Dandy out to the Baxters' minivan. We took him out the lower side door into the gangway and met Jodi and the minivan in the alley to avoid dozens of questions about why the official watchdog was suddenly leaving—making sure the door got locked again this time, of course. But I did make a point to let Lucy know what was happening.

She was not a happy camper.

"Why all a' sudden you think that other lady can take better care o' that dog than me, huh? Didn't you say next to Gramma Shep that I was his fav'rite people?" The scowl on her face was deep enough to hide a quarter in.

"That's not it at all, Lucy! It's just a quieter place for a few days. Fewer people. A yard where he can get up and walk around without attracting lots of attention—you know, out there." I pointed to the front doors. "And we'll be back in a few days."

Lucy turned and stomped off like Billy Goat Gruff across his wooden bridge. "Huh. Of all the dang-blasted . . ."

I didn't hear the rest of her muttering. Probably just as well.

My mother seemed bewildered by the sudden upset to her shelter routine, and I realized with a guilty stab that Martha Shepherd hadn't been outside the building the entire week—not since Mabel had agreed she qualified as "homeless" and could sign up on the bed list. But when Mom realized Dandy was coming along, she meekly submitted to me snapping her into the seat belt in the second seat of the Dodge Caravan.

"Wait!" I told Jodi as she started the engine. "Didn't Estelle come with you? Where is she? I didn't see—"

Jodi laughed. "Don't worry about Estelle. Harry Bentley and his grandson took her home."

Harry Bentley. Jodi and I looked at each other. "Ah. Young love," she said, and we both cracked up.

Jodi found a through street that took her to Lake Shore Drive and headed north. I leaned back against the headrest of the front passenger seat and watched the parkland next to the lake fly by, the paths full of joggers, people walking dogs, parents pushing strollers, and bikers in Spandex and helmets weaving in and out, somehow managing to avoid running over anyone. And beyond that, Lake Michigan, a peaceful, flat line against the far horizon.

The second wind that had kept me going so far that day started to fizzle, and I felt my eyelids getting heavy. *Oh God, thank You . . . It feels so good to just sit, to be taken care of just a little bit . . .*

chapter 16

"Gabby? We're here."

"What?" I opened my eyes. Jodi was pulling the minivan into a two-car garage, next to a candy-apple-red Hyundai. "Oh, I'm sorry! I must have fallen asleep." I glanced back into the second seat. "Good grief. We all slept like zombies—except you, I hope."

Jodi laughed. "Got you here, didn't I? Come on. I'll see if Denny's here to carry Dandy inside."

I shook my mom awake and helped her out of the car. "Nice car," I murmured as we threaded our way past the Hyundai. "Denny's?"

"Ha! Doesn't he wish. No, it belongs to Stu, our friend who lives upstairs. Estelle's housemate."

Denny Baxter, it turned out, was sprawled in a recliner in the living room, watching Saturday afternoon sports with two young cats parked on his chest, and he didn't seem the least bit fazed that his wife showed up with three extra warm bodies who were going to "stay the weekend," as she put it. "Hey, great," he said, dumping the cats. "And you brought Hero Dog? Ha! About time these two got dethroned." He jerked a playful thumb at the disgruntled cats. Two big dimples creased his cheeks.

Jodi got iced tea for Mom and me, while Denny brought up a large cushiony dog bed from their basement and put it on the back porch near the porch swing. "I knew we'd need this again someday," Jodi said. "Couldn't bear to throw it out after Wonka died."

Denny carried a whimpering Dandy from the backseat of the minivan and settled him gently on the dog bed while Jodi showed us to our "guest rooms." "Take your pick," she said. "Sorry about all of Amanda's stuff in here. Even Josh left some of his stuff here when he got married. Can't blame him, though—their apartment is no bigger than a postage stamp . . . Say, do you guys want to finish your naps? You've had a long day—hey! Patches! Peanuts! Get out of here." She snatched up the two cats—big kittens really, one calico and the other mostly black with white paws—and disappeared.

I was so tempted to crash. But it was already four o'clock. Told myself I should probably gut it out and just get a good night's sleep that night. But I encouraged Mom to lie down in Josh's old room—it had the least paraphernalia to trip over—with a light afghan over her, then made my way back through the Baxters' dining room and kitchen and out onto the back porch to check on Dandy.

Jodi was in the porch swing, husking corn on the cob. "I think the squeak of this old swing put Dandy to sleep." She grinned, stopped the swing, and patted the seat beside her. "Come sit. You okay?"

I sat. The Baxters' backyard was narrow, with straggly flower beds running along the fence on both sides. The neighboring buildings were a combination of similar two-flats—brick, tidy, their garages facing an alley running behind the houses—and three-story apartment buildings. Trees lining the next street over and the occasional backyard softened the cityscape. A bird feeder hung from the corner of the Baxters' garage, and flower boxes decorated the railings of the back porch.

A far cry from the Fairbanks' parklike suburban home in Virginia, the lush lawn spilling over with flowering bushes and flower beds. And yet this tiny urban yard felt like an oasis of peace. "Incredible," I murmured.

"Yeah, well, my family likes to pretend I have a green thumb. Denny made the flower boxes, and Amanda stenciled them—but the flowers would all be dead if Stu and Estelle didn't help me out."

I shook my head. "Didn't mean the flower boxes. You and your husband . . . I mean, you brought me *and* my mom *and* a sick dog home without even telling him, and he didn't bat an eye."

"Oh, Denny. He's pretty unflappable." She laughed—then stopped herself when she saw the tears sliding down my face. "Sheesh. I'm sorry, Gabby. Me and my big mouth . . . Do you want to talk about it?"

I mopped my eyes with a bedraggled tissue I pulled out of my jeans pocket and shrugged. "Don't even know where to start . . ."

Jodi laid a hand on my arm. "Try the beginning. When did you two meet?"

Jodi was a good listener, asking a question from time to time, but mostly just letting me talk. And once I started, I could hardly stop. Not sure how she put it all together, because I jumped all over the place. Even told her about getting jilted by Damien, my high-school Romeo who turned out to be Casanova instead. "But Philip was different. He never messed with other women. I thought he really loved me . . ." I bit my lip. "And I loved him. Still do, I guess. My heart used to do flip-flops every time he walked in the room. He used to hold me, whisper in my ear, tell me I added spice to his life . . ."

Jodi handed me a clean tissue and waited patiently through another torrent of tears.

"But then . . . I dunno. He and his dad didn't get along in the business. Philip started trying to prove himself or something. Now he . . . he's like a different person! Not overnight or any-thing—guess that's the problem. Not sure when things started to go south. I got used to feeling like I was in his way, started second-guessing everything I said or did, worried about how he might react. And then . . . then this move to Chicago. Suddenly I felt like I'd landed on Mars, gasping for air . . ."

It was hard telling Jodi about Philip refusing to let my mother stay with us, deliberately losing the dog, and then locking me out of my own home. Jodi with her "unflappable" husband. Kind Denny. Funny Denny. Easygoing Denny . . .

I blinked back the hot tears that seemed to lurk behind my eyeballs. *What did I do wrong to get treated like a dog?!*

I shook my head, trying to regain my composure. The *squeak, squeak* of the porch swing and birds flitting in the trees played like a simple melody against the far-off drone of traffic. I finally sighed. "Really, if I hadn't run into Lucy and ended up with the job at Manna House, I don't know what I would have done. Jumped off the roof or something."

"From what I've heard, Manna House considers you a blessing."

I looked sideways at Jodi. "Huh. Don't know about that. But . . . do you know what Mabel said to me when I applied for the job of program director? She said she believes God brought me to Chicago because He has a purpose for me at Manna House. Like that's the *real* reason God brought us here."

"Really?" Jodi's eyes went wide. "She said that?"

I nodded. "Sometimes that's the only thing I hold on to. That, and this note Edesa left for me the other night." I pulled the crumpled note out of my jeans pocket and handed it to her.

Jodi read it, absently tucking a strand of her shoulder-length brown hair behind one ear, a smile softening her pleasant features. She looked up. "Sounds like Edesa, all right. Isn't she something? She's older than Josh, you know—just a couple of years, but I think he fell in love with her while he was still in high school." She looked at the note again. "Hm. Isaiah 49. Yeah, I love that verse. 'See, I have engraved you on the palms of my hands . . .' Powerful stuff. Did you read the rest of the chapter?"

I nodded. "Like a dozen times. But I don't know what she meant by that." I pointed to the last line of the note.

Jodi read it aloud. "'Dear Gabrielle, your parents gave you the right name. Live it!'" Now her smile widened. "Well, let's find out!"

"Find out? What do you mean?"

She jumped up and pulled me off the swing. "Come on."

Two minutes later Jodi had booted up the computer in their dining room, which seemed to double as the family office, and was clicking through Web sites. I hunched over her shoulder, wondering what she was doing. "How do you spell your name?"

she murmured. "Gabrielle, not Gabby." She typed it into a search box as I spelled it out.

A moment later a page came up. *Feminine Names and Their Meanings*, it said. Jodi read it aloud: "'Gabrielle. Meaning: Strong woman of God.'"

She turned away from the computer and, to my surprise, took my face in her hands. "'Strong woman of God' . . . Yes, that's it, Gabby. Live your name."

A male voice sailed down the hall from the living room. "Jodi! When's supper?"

"When you fire up the grill so we can throw on some chicken!" Jodi yelled back. She looked at me sideways and snorted. "Men!"

I was glad for the interruption. *Strong woman of God?* Maybe somebody else. How was I supposed to "live my name" when right now I felt about as courageous as an overcooked noodle?

We had a pleasant evening, just hanging out on the Baxters' back porch. Denny donned a big apron and wielded a mean pair of tongs over the hot charcoal grill set a few feet from the porch. Stu and Estelle invited themselves for supper, thumping down the back outside stairs with a fresh fruit salad to go with the corn on the cob. My mom looked bright eyed, her cheeks pink after her nap, though she had a hard time keeping up with all the banter.

While we were eating, Dandy whined and struggled to get up, so Denny managed to get him into the yard, and the dog actually peed a little. Everyone on the porch clapped. "You go, Dandy!" Estelle yelled—and we all laughed at the pun.

And then I slept, curled up like a baby with one of Amanda Baxter's old teddy bears hugged against my chest . . . the first night I'd slept without nightmares or waking in panic since Philip locked me out of his life.

We went to church the next morning with Jodi and Denny. Estelle and Stu pulled out right behind us in the candy-apple-red Hyundai. As Denny drove into the parking lot of the shopping center that housed SouledOut Community Church, I felt as if I'd entered a time warp. Had it only been a *week* since Mom and I had come to church here while Philip took the boys on a sailing weekend with one of his clients? Only a week since he brought the boys home early, accusing me of losing that client over some dumb phone message I'd tried to deliver, and told me it was the last straw?

The longest week of my life.

I shook off the troubling thoughts. Didn't want to go there. Didn't want to lose the sense of peace that had surrounded me ever since Mom and I had walked through the Baxters' back door yesterday.

"Oh look, Gabby." Mom pointed shamelessly as we came into the "sanctuary" that had been created out of a large store-front. "That nice Mr. Bentley is here too. And he has his son with him. About Paul's age, isn't he?"

"Grandson, Mom. And he looks a little younger than Paul." Just the mention of my youngest wrapped coils of regret around my heart, but we smiled and waved at Mr. B, who was proudly introducing DeShawn to everyone who came within reach.

The music team started playing right then, and a young white man invited everyone to find a seat—"But don't sit down yet!"— and join in singing the first song.

"I thought Peter Douglass's wife was your worship leader," I whispered to Jodi.

"Avis? She's one of them. People take turns."

The young man did all right, I guess, but I'd kind of looked forward to the dignity and passion the middle-aged black woman had brought to the service the previous week. I had to smile as the keyboard, guitars, drums, and saxophone filled the room with music, inviting shoppers to peek in the glass windows along the large storefront. I'd been in Chicago for two and a half months, and in that time I'd gone to church more than I had in two and a half years—if I counted the Sunday Evening Praise at the shelter—and still hadn't stepped inside an actual church building.

Josh and Edesa Baxter came in late with Gracie in a back carrier as if they'd walked to church, and Edesa slipped me a hug before they found seats in the back.

The children up through middle school left for Sunday school classes before the sermon, but the African-American pastor—Pastor Cobbs, Jodi reminded me—asked Peter Douglass to come up and pray for the youth from the church who were in Mississippi with Habitat for Humanity, building houses for poor people. Then Pastor Cobbs announced that his copastor, Pastor Clark—an older white man, I remembered, tall and skinny—had been taken to the hospital last night, suffering from chest pains. Shock seemed to run through the congregation, and four or five different people prayed about that.

And then other people started to go up to the mike and mention things that needed prayer. Personal stuff. That surprised me. A nephew who'd been in a car accident. A daughter who had a miscarriage. A brother who was going to drink himself to death "if the Lord don't get hold of him." Pastor Cobbs reminded the congregation that Scripture says, "If two or three agree, we can ask anything in the name of Jesus, and He will answer!" A lot of people shouted "Amen!" After that somebody started praying, and then another. And another.

The pastor never did preach his sermon. And nobody seemed to mind.

But the impromptu prayer meeting made me squirm. Good grief, if anyone in that room needed prayer, it was me. But go up to that mike and ask for prayer? Admit that this college-educated mother of two had gone from luxury penthouse to a homeless shelter in one measly day? Admit that my life was screwed up big-time—and I didn't have a clue what to do about it?

Couldn't imagine it. It'd be like walking naked down Lake Shore Drive.

chapter 17

Never did open my mouth, but seemed like a lot of people at SouledOut must have seen the news clips about Hero Dog chasing off an intruder at the Manna House shelter. At least seven people came up to me and asked how Dandy was doing, and started in on the questions I was trying to avoid, like, "How did the dog happen to be at the shelter, anyway?"

Jodi had gone off to the ladies' room with my mother, leaving me standing by the coffeepot, holding on to my Styrofoam cup with a grip that threatened to splatter hot coffee in all directions. I was trying to decide what I could say—just enough to not be rude but not anything that might make its way into the media by accident—when Estelle swooped down on me like a brood hen, her dress of choice this morning being a billowy yellow number with black swirls. She wrapped me up like a chick under her yellow-and-black wing and hustled me off. "No questions! No questions!" she tossed back over her shoulder.

I didn't know whether to laugh or cry with relief. "How do

they even know it's me?" I complained when we were safely out
of the crowd around the coffeepot.

"The hair, honey. The hair." Estelle patted my head full of
frowsy corkscrew curls, which had sprung up like perky weeds
after my fifteen-minute shower that morning. "Just don't commit
no crimes, honey. You'll be caught within twenty-four hours—
Hey! Florida! C'mon over here." Estelle waved her arm at one of
the women I'd met last week. I remembered the interesting Zulu
knots all over her head, looking like little tortellini noodles.

"How ya feel, Estelle? And this is Gabby, right? Girl, you all
over the news—"

"Put a lid on it, Florida. Gabby's staying at the Baxters' for a
little R & R this weekend—an' maybe till Mandy gets back. I'm just
checkin' about Yada Yada tonight—we're s'posed to meet at your
house, right? Gabby's got a mountain needs to be moved, and I'm
thinkin' Yada Yada got some mountain-movin' experience."

I was totally bewildered. Mountains? What in the world was
Estelle talking about!

"Estelle Williams!" Florida put a hand on one hip. "You know
good an' well it ain't us that moves mountains. That's God's business. We just do our part 'bout gettin' two or three together an'
agreein' in the name of Jesus, an' He'll do the rest in His own way
an' His own time—Oh yeah! Glory! Mm!" And Florida danced a
little jig right there in front of us.

"Humph. I'm just sayin'. Are we meeting at your house or
not?"

Florida stopped her little dance long enough to say, "Uh-huh.
An' thanks for the reminder. Works better if I kick Carl and the
kids out during the meetin', so I better go give him a heads-up.
Where he at, anyway?" The thin, brown woman craned her neck

this way and that, scanning the room, then startled me by giving me a quick hug. "Lookin' forward to seein' you tonight, girl. If you got a mountain needs movin', Yada Yada's a good place to start." And she flounced off.

Estelle raised her eyebrows. "Like I said."

Which is how I found myself in the backseat of Leslie Stuart's candy-apple-red Hyundai with Jodi Baxter late that afternoon. Estelle sat in the front passenger seat, fussing about the big tin of chocolate-and-caramel turtles that Stu had insisted on bringing.

"Whatchu bringing that for? Sister who's hosting always provides the snacks—and if that was you, we wouldn't be drivin' now, would we?"

"Well . . . just in case she doesn't have something. I thought it might help."

"Now, why wouldn't she have somethin'? You show up with this fancy-smancy stuff, an' it's like you sayin' her food ain't good enough."

"Estelle! That's not fair. I just wanted to help out."

"That's the trouble with you, Leslie Stuart. You helpin' out people even when they don't need no help, didn't ask for no help, don't want no help."

"Is that so? Maybe *you* didn't need any help when the shelter burned down. Guess I should've kept my mouth shut about sharing the apartment since you didn't *ask* for my help."

"Humph. That's different."

"Hey, you two," Jodi piped up from the backseat. "Quit arguing. What's Gabby going to think? It's her first visit to Yada Yada."

"Arguing? We're not arguing, are we, Stu?"

"Who us? Nope." And they both laughed.

Jodi rolled her eyes at me. "Some people," she muttered, but couldn't help laughing too.

I started to relax. It felt good to be with people who could argue and then laugh about it.

My mother had elected to stay at the Baxters' with Dandy, who was more alert today. He'd eaten some food and was drinking more water, though he definitely needed help up and down the Baxters' back porch stairs to the yard. After making sure Jodi's husband would be there that evening, I agreed to go to this Yada Yada whatever with Jodi and the two single women upstairs.

They were definitely the Odd Couple. Stu was in her thirties, tall and slender, and still wore her dark-blonde hair long and tucked behind one ear, which boasted a long row of small, glittery earrings. Estelle, on the other hand, was as brown as Stu was white, fifty-something, big-boned and solid, her hair worn natural and streaked with gray, and caught up into a bun on top of her head. Every time I'd seen Stu, she was wearing pants, tall boots, and a jacket over a tank top. Estelle in pants? Couldn't imagine it. She made her clothes: big, loose-fitting caftans . . .

Which reminded me. Sometime this week I needed to get my sewing machine from the penthouse before Philip moved all our stuff to who-knew-where.

Stu found a parking spot on a street that boasted the occasional "Chicago bungalow"—little brick houses, mostly one story, or one and a half—scrunched in between three-story apartment buildings. We had to walk a block to Florida's brick bungalow, which actually had a front porch with two white wicker chairs. "A housewarming gift from one of our Yada Yada sisters," Jodi whispered to me. "Chanda won the lottery and rained gifts down on all of us until we told her to stop it."

Whoever Chanda was. I guessed I'd find out soon enough. The door opened just as Stu was about to punch the doorbell, and two kids came running out—a girl about twelve and a boy in his midteens—followed by Carl Hickman, whom I'd met once before when he came to the shelter to help with security at our Fun Night. Okay, so far I'd met three couples: Florida and Carl Hickman, Avis and Peter Douglass, Jodi and Denny Baxter. Hopefully this Yada Yada group wasn't just a bunch of happily married women. Wasn't sure I could take it—

"Oops, 'scuse me, ladies." Josh Baxter came hustling out the front door, little Gracie in a back carrier. "Hey, Carl, wait up!" he yelled and hustled out to the sidewalk.

Oh right. Edesa and Josh Baxter too. Young. In love.

Like I'd been. Once.

Wishing I'd stayed home, I meekly followed Jodi, Stu, and Estelle inside. The small living room area was already populated with women talking and laughing. To the left, Edesa was just coming down the stairs. I made a beeline for Josh's wife. "Ah, a familiar face!" I gave her a big hug.

"Gabby! *Hola!* I'm so glad you came to Yada Yada tonight. Josh told me his mom invited you and your mother to come for the weekend. We were late getting to SouledOut this morning. Gracie had one of those nights."

I peeked up the narrow stairs. "So this is where you guys live?"

She laughed. Even her dark eyes danced. "*Sí.* Only slightly bigger than your office at the shelter. Want to see?"

We slipped up the stairs, past two bedroom doors—"The

Hickman kids," she explained—then through a door that cut the hallway in half. She was right about the tiny apartment. One room served as kitchen and living space, plus a small bedroom and bathroom. But the bedroom held only a crib, three dressers, and a freestanding clothes rack.

"Where—?"

"—do we sleep?" Edesa pointed to the couch in the living area. "It folds out."

"Oh, Edesa." I gave her a sympathetic hug. "You do need a bigger apartment. No wonder you study down at the shelter!"

"You think?" She laughed. "We better get downstairs. They're starting to sing."

Oh great. Now I was going to walk in late.

But no one seemed to notice as we settled into a couple of folding chairs. They were singing a capella, many with their eyes closed, several with hands raised.

"Lord, prepare me . . . to be a sanctuary . . . pure and holy . . . tried and true . . ."

I glanced around the room, seeing a few I'd met before, and several I hadn't, all different shades of skin color. As the song drew to a close, Avis—who seemed to be leading the meeting—moved right into a prayer, asking the Holy Spirit to be present, thanking God for the privilege of coming together in the name of His Son, Jesus. "And thank You for our sister Gabby, who is visiting us tonight . . . Sisters, this is Gabrielle Fairbanks, the program director down at Manna House. We've prayed for her before—now here she is!"

I wasn't sure when Avis had stopped praying and just started talking—as if God was just another person in the room. But everyone turned to me with welcoming smiles.

"Hey there, Gabby!" said a twenty-something white girl with short, spiky hair, wearing baggy overall-shorts over a T shirt. "I'm Yo-Yo. And that's Adele"—she pointed to a large black woman with a short black natural and large hoop earrings—"who does hair an' stuff like that. An' that's Ruth"—pointing to a fiftyish white woman with rather frowsy brown hair—"who comes to Yada Yada because it's the only time she's not chasing her two-year-old twins . . ."

"Enough already, Yo-Yo," fussed the woman named Ruth. "A mouth we all have; we can introduce ourselves. I'm Ruth and my twins are adorable. One's going to be a lawyer and the other a doctor. Remember I told you so."

Everyone laughed, but then they did go around the room and introduce themselves.

Chanda, the lottery lady—she didn't say that, but I remembered the name—had a Jamaican accent like Wanda at the shelter. A lovely young Asian woman, tall and slender, spoke so softly I didn't catch her name—Moshee or Hershey or something. But the big surprise was a Hispanic woman who waggled her fingers at me and said, "*Hola,* Gabby! We've met. Delores Enriques . . . I'm the volunteer nurse who comes to the shelter on Wednesday."

"Oh, of course! I'm sorry, Delores. I'm used to seeing you in your hospital garb." I'm sure my ears were beet red, but I stumbled on. "Thank you all for letting me come tonight. Edesa has mentioned her prayer group. I didn't realize I'd already met so many of you at Manna House."

"It's all Josh and Edesa's fault," Jodi Baxter moaned. "They got involved first and kept bugging the rest of us to volunteer until we said yes. I tried to get out of it by burning the place down the first time I volunteered, but—"

This was met with more hoots of laughter. "Oh stop, Jodi," the beauty shop lady said. "Gabby's going to think you meant it."

"You mean she didn't?" I teased. The words were out of my mouth, complete with wide eyes and fake surprise, before I even realized what I was doing.

Yo-Yo snickered. "Ooo, Gabby, you all right."

Their laughter pulled me in, and I realized the friendly banter had found a chink in my armor. Like I could be the real Gabby again, just hanging out with my girlfriends, laughing and teasing and making jokes.

But a nasty little whisper in my head pulled me up short. Philip's voice, back in his office. *"Listen to yourself, Gabby . . . If you weren't so pathetic, this would be funny."*

chapter 18

I tried to shake Philip's voice out of my head. Why did I let stuff he said get to me? I tried to focus on the conversation going on around me as several of the "Yada Yada sisters" shared stuff they needed prayer for. Florida, our hostess, asked prayer for Cedric, her middle boy, who had started dressing like the gangbangers—baggy pants, crotch hanging to his knees, no shoelaces in his big, clunky gym shoes. "I know why he's doin' it, 'cause he's got that learnin' disability an' the other kids rag on him. He wants to fit in. But now, what kind of man he gonna be, all hobbled up in clothes like that. Help me, Jesus!"

Yo-Yo wagged her head. "I read ya. Pete use to dress like one o' them outlaw bikers, till he joined the army. Now they're sending him to Iraq, and gotta say, I feel guilty, all the fussin' I did over his stupid clothes." Whoever Pete was. Yo-Yo seemed way too young to have a kid old enough to join the army. "Guess I need y'all to pray for him," she went on, "'cause my kid brother still don't have much use for Jesus."

Well, that answered that.

More prayer requests. Chanda was looking for someplace to invest her lottery money. "Someting dat would help a lotta folks—an' get mi relatives off mi back!". . . Adele said her nail girl quit and would they pray she'd find someone who didn't gossip and snap gum all day? . . . Avis read an e-mail from someone named Nony in South Africa, and from the way the others got all excited, the writer must have been one of the Yada Yadas at one time . . . And Delores, the nurse, said her husband, Ricardo, had lost his job again. "He gets so discouraged. I think he may be drinking again. He needs a miracle, sisters!"

A miracle. That would be nice. A miracle to sort out the mess that was my life. I was half-hoping these women would pray for me and half-hoping they'd forget I was there. But Estelle wasn't about to forget. "Most of you probably heard about what happened at Manna House this weekend," she started.

"What mi want to know is," Chanda jumped in, "why dat dog at de shelter in de first place! Poor t'ing."

Estelle glared. "Zip your lip, would ya, Chanda? I'm tryin' to say somethin'. An' like Avis is always sayin', anything we say at Yada Yada stays at Yada Yada. No blabbin' to the kids or the neighbors."

"Humph. What you t'ink I got, loose lips?"

A chorus of "Uh-huhs" was accompanied by nodding heads.

Chanda folded her arms over the tight blouse stretched across her ample bosom. "Humph. Jus' wanting ta know 'bout dat poor dog."

Estelle sighed. "As I was sayin', Gabby could sure use some sister-prayer because, well . . ." She looked at me. "Maybe you should say, Gabby. That way I won't be talkin' out of school."

Jodi leaned toward me. "You don't have to go into a lot of detail, Gabby. Just enough so Yada Yada has some idea how we can pray."

I nodded, feeling my armpits start to sweat. "Well . . . like Estelle said, I'd appreciate your confidentiality, because, as you've probably seen, the media is fixated on my mother's dog chasing off that intruder the other night. Jodi was nice enough to give us a place to hide out this weekend, so hopefully—"

"But—" Chanda started, then clamped her hand over her mouth.

I couldn't think what to say next, and my lip started to tremble. "Um . . ."

"Take your time, take your time," Estelle soothed.

I swallowed a couple of times. "Um, well, things aren't too good with my marriage. My mom and I are actually staying at the shelter right now, and to be honest, my, uh, husband is pretty angry at the media attention, afraid our personal stuff will end up splashed all over the TV, ruining his business chances here in Chicago . . ."

"Ooo, girl. You do need some mountain-movin' prayer!" Florida wagged her head. "You have kids?"

I nodded. "Two boys . . . in Virginia . . ." But now the tears were dangerously close to the surface.

"That's all right, Gabby," Avis said. "We don't need all the details. Why don't we pray."

"Avis? Before we pray, can I say something?" Jodi waved her hand like a timid kid in school who was embarrassed to ask for a hall pass. "Gabby, do you mind if I share what Mabel said when you first took the job at the shelter as program director?"

I shrugged, not sure where she was going with it. "I guess."

"Well, most of you have met Mabel Turner, the director at

Manna House. She's no slouch. Doesn't mince words. Also a real woman of God. And she told Gabby that from the first time they met, she had the sense that it was God who brought her to Chicago because He has a purpose for her at Manna House."

Murmurs of "All right!" and "Mm-hm, Jesus!" popped around the room. "See?" Estelle murmured.

"Now, don't laugh," Jodi said, "'cause you all know I tend to be a little skeptical about 'prophetic words' and stuff like that . . ."

Yo-Yo snickered anyway.

". . . but I've been thinking about it all day today, and I think Mabel's words to Gabby really are prophetic, and that all this stuff that's been happening, as painful as it is, isn't by accident. I think God really did bring Gabby to the shelter, and He has a purpose for her, and He's going to use it all somehow . . ."

"All right, now. Preach it, girl!" Florida said.

Edesa was nearly jumping out of her chair. "Oh, *sí*! And I told Gabby her parents gave her the right name . . . Gabrielle." She grinned at me impishly. "It means 'strong woman of God.'"

"See?" Estelle said again.

I wanted to protest, to tell them they had it all wrong, that I was a wimp, that I'd lost my children and ruined my marriage, my own mother was in a homeless shelter, and I didn't have a clue why I was at Manna House . . . but suddenly I found myself surrounded as several of the women got out of their chairs and knelt beside me, taking hold of my shaking hands, while others laid gentle hands on my shoulders. "Oh God!" someone started to pray. "Thank You for telling us in Your Word that when we are weak, that's when You are strong!" . . . "And You promised in Your Word that *all* things work together for the good of those who love You!" . . .

The prayers poured over me, pulling the stopper from the tears I'd been holding back. Someone handed me a box of tissues.

"Give our sister Gabby strength to face tomorrow!" . . . "Open her eyes to see Your purpose in her life!" . . . "Give her wisdom to meet the challenges she's facing right now!" . . . "Protect her children, Jesus, when she can't be with them!" . . .

I don't know when it happened. But somewhere in the middle of those prayers going up to God and pouring down on my head, like a river flowing two ways at the same time, a peculiar calmness settled over my body from the inside out. My hands stopped shaking. The tears dried up. My muscles relaxed, and yet . . . I felt invigorated, as if blood was surging through my body, like the time I'd treated myself to a spa treatment after Paul was born. Even the slump in my spirit seemed to straighten. It was the strangest feeling.

And that night, stretched out in my borrowed bed at the Baxters' house, I slept a dreamless sleep.

Denny Baxter offered to drive the three of us back to Manna House the next morning if that's what we wanted to do. "But really, Gabby," Jodi said, "Dandy could use a few more days of rest. I'm home most of the day now that school's out. I'd be happy to stay with your mom and Dandy while you go to work . . . the rest of the week, too, if that'd be helpful. Amanda doesn't come back till next Saturday."

It was a no-brainer as far as I was concerned. "Mom? You okay about staying here with Dandy and Jodi today? I'll be back after work. But if you want to come to the shelter with me, that's okay too," I added, feeling a bit guilty at leaving my mother in the care of strangers.

My mother scooped some kibbles into Dandy's bowl next to his bed on the back porch. The dog nosed the food and took a polite bite, then laid his head down again on the borrowed dog bed. "Dandy says he doesn't feel too good. I better stay here with him. You don't mind, do you, Celeste?"

Noticing Jodi's odd look, I whispered, "My sister. She gets confused sometimes—oh. Can I use your phone? I've got a calling card."

Hoping that P. J. hadn't left for sports camp already, I dialed the Fairbanks' number . . . and got Philip's mother. I steeled myself. "Marlene, this is Gabby. May I speak to P. J. please?"

"Where are you? I didn't recognize the caller ID."

The nerve! What business was it of hers where I was? "Please, just put P. J. on the phone."

Fortunately, Marlene Fairbanks was too much of a Southern gentlewoman to be outright nasty. I had a short but happy talk with my oldest, who promised to tell me all about the first day of lacrosse when I called that evening.

The commute on the El took twice as long from the Rogers Park neighborhood as it had from Richmond Towers, but I didn't mind. It gave me time to think about what happened at the Yada Yada prayer meeting last night.

But . . . what exactly had happened? Those women took Mabel's words seriously, even took the meaning of my name seriously, as if it all meant something. And they'd prayed for purpose, wisdom, and courage . . . not exactly the prayers I'd been praying, which mostly consisted of "Help, God! Fix it! Do something!"

Frankly, all I knew was that this morning I almost felt like a normal person. Going to work. Not scared out of my mind. Thinking about what I needed to do today. Grateful that my mom and Dandy were safe and cared for. Wishing I'd brought my umbrella because it looked like rain.

Nothing had changed. I was still homeless. Still broke. My marriage was still in the toilet. My sons were still in another state, and I missed them terribly. And yet . . . *something* had changed. As if God had stood up inside me and whispered, "I've got your back."

I laughed and got funny looks from the mute bodies standing around me in the crowded aisle of the El. Oh well. Let them think I was one of those weirdos who talked to themselves. These days it was hard to tell the weirdos from the hands-free cell phone users.

I hustled off the El at the Sheridan station and stopped in at the Emerald City Coffee Shop to pick up a coffee-with-cream-to-go from the young barista behind the counter, who wore two little rings in the side of her nose. "Hey. Aren't you the lady with the dog we saw on TV? Is he okay?"

"He's fine. Thanks." I tossed two dollars on the counter and hurried out, kicking myself for the splurge. That's what I got for pretending my life was back to normal.

At least no reporters were lurking about the shelter as I buzzed the front door, signed in at the reception desk, and sailed into the multipurpose room. Each person I met on the way to my office said practically the same thing. "Hey, Miz Gabby! Where's Gramma Shep? How's Dandy? How come you didn't bring 'em back?"

Everyone, that is, except Lucy. So far I hadn't seen the older woman on the main floor or the lower level. I double-backed to the reception cubby in the foyer. "Angela, have you seen Lucy today?"

Angela shook her black tresses. "She didn't sign out since I've been here . . . wait." The young receptionist turned the book around and flipped a couple of pages. "Don't see her on the sign-outs over the weekend either. Did you try her bunk room?"

Might as well. I ran up the stairs to the bunk room we'd been sharing. My bed and my mother's bed were still made up, and it looked like we'd added another roommate besides Tanya and Sammy.

But Lucy's bunk had been stripped, and her cart was missing.

chapter 19

I flipped the light on in my broom-closet office, feeling annoyed. Why did Lucy just take off like that? She didn't even sign out. I *told* her we'd be back in a few days. What if I'd brought Dandy back today? Hadn't she promised to help take care of him?

I sighed. Or maybe it didn't have anything to do with us. Lucy always had been unpredictable.

An envelope was leaning against my computer. A two-week paycheck and a note from Mabel:

> Gabby,
> So sorry. You should have gotten this Friday, but the accountant was sick. Hope you made it through the weekend.
> Mabel
>
> P.S. I won't be here today. Call if you need to.

I held the envelope against my chest. *Thank You, Lord.* This was going straight into the bank. A few more paychecks and I might have enough for a deposit on an apartment. "Not to worry, Mabel," I murmured. "God picked up the tab for my weekend."

It was true. And I wasn't going to let my frustration with Lucy ruin the feeling of peace God had given to me as an extra bonus.

The morning seemed to fly. I worked on my activities calendar, one that could be posted on every floor of the shelter to remind residents of regular classes and activities offered, as well as special program events. So far, so good . . . but I still had ideas I needed to pursue. Halfway through the morning, I left a message for Lee Boyer at Legal Aid to call, hoping to set up our next meeting. Now that I'd made a temporary decision about the boys, I was eager to find out what I needed to do next to strengthen my custody case. What else was I supposed to do before our next meeting? Oh right, the power of attorney papers he'd given me. I hadn't even looked at them yet! Well, tonight then . . .

Estelle poked her head in my door when she came in at ten thirty to do lunch. "How you doin' this mornin', sugar?"

"Good. Those prayers last night . . . I really appreciated them."

"Well, just keep 'em goin', honey. Let God do the heavy lifting. Say, I brought a bunch of material for my sewing class today. Didn't you say you had a sewing machine we could use?"

I grimaced. "Well, yeah, sorta. I mean, I said it, but it's still behind lock and key at the penthouse. And to tell you the truth, after limping out of Philip's office last Friday, I'm not feeling especially brave about calling him, much less actually going there to pick it up." I winced. "I know you all prayed for courage last night, but—"

"Nope. That's wisdom, honey. You don't need to be talking to that man right now. Hmm . . . that's the building where Harry works, right?" She tapped her teeth with a carefully manicured nail. "E-mail. The man's got e-mail, right? Tell him to leave the sewing machine at the main desk of Royal Towers or whatever it's called and someone will pick it up."

E-mail. It hadn't occurred to me to e-mail Philip. But I liked the idea. I could be brave in a note. Of course, I ran the risk that he'd just hit Delete. But he *had* agreed to me picking up the sewing machine this week . . . it was worth a try. I kept the message short. "Philip, I need to get my sewing machine this week. Please leave it at the main desk with Mr. Bentley. Someone will pick it up for me. Thanks. Gabby."

Then I hesitated . . . what was I doing? *After fifteen-plus years of marriage, I'm going to settle for just my sewing machine?!*

"Argh!" I grabbed fistfuls of my hair to keep from punching the computer . . . but a moment later I took a big breath and let it out. *No.* This was just for now. If it . . . if it actually came down to divorce, Lee Boyer would tell me how to get my fair share of our community property. Until then, I didn't want to do anything that presumed we'd never work this out. Philip's tantrum had to wear out sometime, didn't it?

Oh God, please . . .

I'd just clicked Send when I heard another knock on my door. "It's open!"

A head full of tiny black braids poked in. "Hey, Miz Gabby. How ya doin'?"

"Precious!" I jumped up, pulled her in, and gave her a tight hug. "When did you get back? Are you okay? Is Sabrina all right?"

Precious shrugged out of my embrace and sat on the corner

of my desk. "Sabrina all right. Leastwise I didn't kill her. But she ain't talkin' to me. Still, she home now. We'll get through. 'Cept . . ." The young single mom looked away.

"Except what, Precious? What's wrong?"

A big sigh escaped from her thin body, like a tire deflating. "Lost my job. Humph. I been waitressin' at the Lucky Straw almost two years. Ya'd think they'd hold it for me when I had a 'mergency, wouldn't ya?" She shook her head, the ends of her skinny braids tickling her shoulders. "But without that job . . . me an' Sabrina gonna be right back here at the shelter, back where we started."

We talked a long time. Or rather, Precious chattered and I listened. One minute she was fussing about how hard it was raising a girl in today's world when all the role models on TV and the movies were rich, slutty brats, and the next minute she was cussing out the boys who couldn't keep their pants zipped. "What is *wrong* with these young people? They either smokin' they brains out with drugs, or act like havin' a little fun today is all that matters. An' we end up with all these babies ain't got no daddies and the mamas livin' off welfare. No wonder them abortion clinics do so much business. I tell you, Gabby, things gotta *stop* somewhere."

She finally sighed. "Know I shouldn't go off so hard on Sabrina. Didn't I make enough mistakes for the two of us? Just . . . makes me so mad she's not usin' the brain God gave her. What was she thinkin', runnin' off like that? That I wouldn't find out? Wouldn't come get her? Now she done cost me my job . . . Lord, I'm at my wit's end."

I reached out and took her hand. "I'm so sorry, Precious. Maybe it's not as bad as it seems. I mean, if you can find another job, maybe you won't lose your apartment."

She shook her head. "Already lost a week's pay. Even if I find a job in the next two or three weeks, it gonna be awhile till I get enough to pay for two months all in a hunk—even with Section 8. An' my landlord? Mm-mm, Lord have mercy. He got the patience of a jitterbug. What I need right now is one o' them subsidized apartments where they just take a certain percentage of your income, no matter what it is." She shook her head. "But the waitin' list for them places so long you could wrap it 'round the whole city. Maybe twice."

Precious slid off my desk. "Anyway, thanks for listenin', Miz Gabby. You wanna be my case manager if we end up back at the shelter again?" She laughed. "You'd have it easy. I know the drill. I just need someone I can yell at long enough to get the monkey off my back; then I'll get down to business . . . Okay, I'm outta here. Gonna see if Estelle needs some help with lunch."

The door closed behind her. I absently chewed on the end of a pen. That was the second time in less than a week a single mom here had talked about needing "second step" housing—a place of their own, to be a family, even before they had a job that could pay full rent. Had Manna House ever considered doing something like that? I'd have to ask Mabel. And I still hadn't told Precious that my mom and I had ended up here at the shelter ourselves . . . but that was okay. I hadn't even thought about it while Precious was unloading.

Huh. Might be the first time in a month of Sundays I hadn't been thinking about myself.

Hannah the Bored flagged me down at lunch. "So are you gonna let me do nails for the ladies or not? You *said* to give you activity ideas, an' I've axed you twice."

Had she really? Had to admit it was easy to ignore Hannah. She irritated me, just sitting around filing her nails. I made my voice light. "Hannah, you are free to do anyone's nails at any time. Go for it."

The young woman frowned. "But to do it right, I need lotsa diff'rent stuff. Cuticle cutters, nail strengthener, lots of different colors o' polish, clear coats. If you made it official, ladies could make appointments. Depends on what they want done, how long it takes. Full sets, gel overlays, French tips . . ." An excited grin lit up her face. "You should see the designs I can make— flowers an' starbursts, stuff like 'at. But it takes special brushes and paint."

I studied Hannah with new interest. Sounded like she knew what she was talking about. A crazy idea popped into my head. "Hannah, tell me, have you ever done nails professionally?"

"Ya mean like in a salon? Oh yeah. I started cosmetology school once, but my ol' man got busted an' . . . nah, never mind. Anyway, had to drop out after that. My aunt had this salon an' she gave me a job, but . . . I don't really know what happened, but she lost the salon, back taxes or somethin', an' I lost my job and ended up no place ta go. So"—the young black woman grinned flippantly—"here I am."

"But can't you get another job at a salon?"

She shrugged. "That's what I wanna do, but most of 'em want ya ta graduate cosmetology, but can't do that till I can pay for tuition, can't get a job till I get a state ID, but I'm still waiting ta get a copy of my birth certificate. Wasn't born in Chicago, so it's takin' awhile."

Whew. I never really knew Hannah's background. Who was her case manager? I knew Manna House worked on priorities and goals for each resident, and I didn't want to get the cart before the horse, but—

"Hey, Miz Fairbanks. Let me do your nails." Hannah grabbed one of my hands. "Oh, girl, they are in *bad* shape. I got a nice color, would look real good on you."

I pulled my hand back. "Oh, that's nice, Hannah, but I—"

"Aw, c'mon, Miz Fairbanks—"

"Call me Gabby, Hannah."

"Okay. Gabby. But jus' give me half an' hour, show ya what I can do."

Something Precious once said hovered at the edges of my memory. *"When you been living on the streets, a bit of pamperin' is pretty nice. Homeless women need ta feel like women, too, ya know."*

I relented. I would like to see what she could do.

By the time I left Manna House that evening, my nails glowed with a dark honey-peach nail color that did not clash with my hair. Hannah had soaked them—in a shampoo solution, but oh well—then she'd softened and rounded the cuticles, lotioned and massaged my hands, filed my nails, and painted them with an undercoat and a top coat. "My last couple bottles," she'd said. "That's why I need ta get put on the activity list, so you can get me some real supplies."

She had me convinced, but I told her I couldn't promise what the budget would be.

I had one errand to do on the way back to the Baxters'— deposit my paycheck. When I had a chance, I was going to move my household account to the branch bank near the Sheridan El. But for now, I had to get off at Berwyn and deposit it at the bank near Richmond Towers. Not likely that I'd run into Philip at this hour.

Lucy still hadn't shown up at Manna House by the time I'd left, even though there'd been brief thunderstorms off and on all day. Where did she go when she wasn't at the shelter? I'd run into her three times in the park near Richmond Towers. Should I walk over there on the off chance I'd run into her? I didn't have my umbrella, but when I came out of the bank, the sky was just overcast, so I took a chance.

No Lucy in the park. I even walked through the underpass to the beach. No sign of a purple knit hat. *Drat!* If I had my cell phone, I could call Mr. Bentley and tell him to keep a lookout when he was on the job, but . . . On a sudden impulse I headed straight for Richmond Towers and into the lobby. Mr. Bentley was holding the inside security door open for a resident whose arms were full of shopping bags from upscale stores, and his eyebrows went up like question marks when he saw me.

"Mrs. Fairbanks! Going upstairs to storm the fortress?"

I grimaced. "No, and I want to make this quick. Don't really want to run into you-know-who. Could you keep a lookout for Lucy—you know, my bag lady friend? She disappeared from the shelter this weekend, and I kind of want to find her. She wears a purple knit hat Estelle made for her—you've seen it, I'm sure. Second thing, my husband is supposed to bring my sewing machine down here to the desk for me to pick up. Either one, would you call me at the shelter and let me know? Or call Estelle, whatever's easier."

"Sure thing, Mrs. Fairbanks."

I felt a little bad at how brief I'd been with Mr. B, but at least I'd made an effort to find Lucy. Hopefully my mom wouldn't ask about her . . . but when I got to the Baxters' house, that was the first question out of her mouth. "Did Lucy send me a message? I know she's worried about Dandy. Did you tell her he's getting better and we'll be back tomorrow?"

I put her off as best I could—no, Lucy was out, but I was sure she'd be glad to see us as soon as Dandy was strong enough to go back—then collapsed on the stool in the Baxter kitchen with the glass of iced tea Jodi handed to me. "Hard day?" she asked.

I grinned at their cats, weaving in and out between her bare legs. "Actually, a good day. The prayers last night—they really made a difference, Jodi. Not sure I can explain it."

She just grinned and continued to chop vegetables for a stir fry. Patches, the calico, meowed pitifully. But Peanut, the black-and-white, hopped into my lap, knowing a sucker when he saw one.

I stroked the beautiful fur absently and was rewarded with a loud purr. "But I'm wondering if you have a phone number for the Yada Yada lady—I forget her name—who owns a beauty shop and needs a new nail girl?"

"You mean Adele Skuggs. Sure—I think her shop is open on Monday nights. You want to make an appointment? If she's got an opening, I could drive you over when Denny gets home."

I grimaced. "I should. I need a haircut. But actually, it's for somebody I know at the shelter who does nails and needs a job." I waggled my nails. "I brought home a sample. Not sure how long they'll look good, though. I'm hard on hands."

Jodi laughed. "Uh-huh. Sneaky way to get out of doing the dishes—oh, here's Denny. "

The back door banged open, and Jodi's husband came in. He pecked his wife on the cheek, then handed me a plastic bag. "Something I thought you could use."

"Me?" I was so flustered, I hardly knew what to do. I pushed Peanut off my lap, reached into the bag, and pulled out a box. A cell phone. "Oh, Denny, I can't accept this. It's too much!"

He chuckled, sending those cheek dimples into big crevices. "I don't think so. It's one of those pay-ahead phones—no bells or whistles. Just a phone, but it's got decent service. You need it so you can call your boys whenever you want, and . . . whatever."

I glanced at Jodi. Was she okay with her husband giving me a gift? But she was smiling at her husband with obvious approval.

Oh dear God, I do need my own phone . . . "I—I hardly know what to say." I opened the box and took out the phone. Petite. Ice blue. A mini lifeline. And I did just get a paycheck. "Thanks, Denny. I'll pay you back."

Denny laughed and shook his head. "Uh-uh. The phone's yours, Gabby. But you can pay the monthly—the paperwork's in there. It's already charged and activated." He clapped his hands together. "Okay, enough schmaltz. What's for dinner?"

I clutched the phone to my chest and slipped out to the back porch. Might as well try it out, find out how P. J.'s first day of lacrosse camp went.

chapter 20

After supper, I spent an hour on the Baxters' back porch swing, going over the power of attorney forms with my mother. "This is just in case something happens and you can't make these decisions yourself," I assured her. Dandy, bright-eyed, seemed to enjoy our company. He'd cleaned out his food bowl, and even though it was a struggle getting out of the cushiony dog bed, he limped over and licked my toe.

My mother beamed. "See, Gabby? He's better. We can go home now."

Home. Did she mean North Dakota? . . . or Manna House? I let it go.

Mom went to bed early, but I stayed on the porch, inputting phone numbers into my new phone from the list I'd made before my old one totally lost its juice. Jodi came out and handed me a slip of paper. "Here are a few more numbers you might need— the top one is ours, then Josh's and Edesa's cells, and that one is Adele's Hair and Nails. It's almost nine—I think that's when she closes on Monday. Might be a good time to call her about your nail girl. Oh—wait a minute." She disappeared inside, then re-appeared with their kitchen cordless. "Here, use our phone. Don't waste your minutes."

"Thanks, Jodi." I tapped in the number for Adele's Hair and Nails . . . but as the phone rang, I started to have second thoughts. Did I really know Hannah well enough to recommend her to—

"Jodi Baxter! Make it quick, girl. I'm trying to get out of here." The voice exploded in my ear with no introduction.

"Uh, is this Adele Skuggs? Sorry, it's not Jodi. Just using her phone. This is Gabby Fairbanks—I met you last night at your Yada prayer thing."

A deep chuckle on the other end was somewhat reassuring. "Oh, sure. I remember. What can I do for you, Gabby? Want me to do something with that white girl 'fro you've got?"

A white girl *what?* "Oh . . . my hair. Well, yeah, guess I do need a cut." Understatement. "But I was calling to ask if you still needed a nail girl."

"Why? You want the job?"

Jodi must have noticed the flustered look on my face. "Don't let her muddle you," she stage-whispered. "That's just her way."

Okay then. Two could play. "Oh, you wouldn't want me. You'd lose all your customers." I was rewarded by Adele's throaty laugh in my ear. "But actually," I hurried on, "there *is* a young woman at Manna House who's had experience in a nail salon, and she needs a job. I don't know if she's what you're looking for, but—"

"Really? Well, bring her in. I'll give her an interview. Can you . . . just a sec." I heard pages flipping. "I have a cancellation at two o'clock tomorrow. Can you bring her in? And might as well give you a cut while we're at it."

"Uh . . . sure. Two o'clock tomorrow."

I hung up and looked at Jodi, who was laughing. "You just got run over by a steamroller, didn't you? Well, that's Adele!"

Tuesday morning my mother told me Dandy was much better and she thought we all ought to go back to the shelter. "I think she's bored," Jodi murmured to me. "But I'm happy to have her stay as long as you want. She's no trouble. In fact, I'm keeping the car today and going to run some errands. Does she like to shop?"

I talked my mother into letting Dandy rest another day, privately hoping we could stay out the week until the Baxters' daughter came home. I was glad, because when I got to Manna House, a reporter and a cameraman accosted me at the front steps. "Mrs. Fairbanks! How is the Hero Dog doing? No one has seen Dandy for three days! Has he taken a turn for the worse?"

Oh good grief. "He's fine. He's resting out of the limelight and hoping all you good people will forget about him and let him return to doggy oblivion." I gave what I hoped was a friendly smile and hustled up the stairs.

"But Mrs. Fairbanks!" the reporter called after me. "What about all the donations people are sending to the shelter since Dandy caught the intruder and saved the life of one of your staff? What are you going to do with the money?"

I nearly tripped on the last step, but caught myself. I turned slowly. "I'm sorry. I don't know anything about that." I punched the buzzer, and the door clicked to let me in.

Angela Kwon looked up as I came in and waved a slip of paper at me. But I ignored the receptionist and headed straight

into Mabel's office. "Money?" I demanded, even before the director looked up. "People are giving the shelter money? Mabel, we
can't use Dandy to get contribu—"

"Whoa, whoa, whoa!" Mabel's face clouded. "Close the door,
Gabby, and sit down."

I obeyed, stifling a groan. Why didn't those reporters just go
away?

Mabel stood up behind her desk and leaned forward on her
knuckles. "First of all, Gabby Fairbanks, we are not *using* Dandy
to get contributions. Second, we *have* received a sudden flood of
donations in the mail—unsolicited, I might add. Third, I am calling a staff meeting this morning to bring everyone up to date.
What we do with the money will be a decision of the board." She
sat back down with a *whump*. "Satisfied?"

I cringed. "Sorry. It's just . . . I got accosted by a reporter and
a cameraman two minutes ago who were asking *me* what I was
going to do with all the donations Dandy had generated for the
shelter. If Philip hears about this on TV, he's going to be
furious."

Mabel's expression softened. "Apology accepted. I agree; it's
a bit startling. But we can talk about it at the staff meeting."

"How much—?"

"Staff meeting. Ten thirty. Now, go, Gabby." Mabel stuck on
a pair of reading glasses and turned back to her computer.

Angela waved the sticky note at me as I walked back into the
foyer. "Message for you, Gabby. And don't forget to sign in."

I took the note. *Lee Boyer at Legal Aid returned your call.* Oh
good. And when I got to my office and booted up my computer
a few minutes later, there was an e-mail reply from Philip. All it
said was, *OK.*

I stared at the e-mail a long time. He was agreeing to leave my sewing machine at the lobby desk of Richmond Towers, wasn't he? So why did that "OK" make me feel crummy? So brief. Dry. Impersonal. Like . . . like being offered a thimble of water when I was dying for a long, cool drink.

No, no. Couldn't go there. I eyed the Bible on my desk. I hadn't really followed through on my resolve to read it regularly. Then again, I hadn't expected my whole life to turn upside down, like that disaster movie where the huge ship *Poseidon* got flipped over by a monster wave and everything was total chaos. A little hard to find "quiet time." Still, when I was reading the gospel of Matthew every day during our vacation in North Dakota, God had used it to speak to me, hadn't He? Maybe I should—

But maybe I should call Lee Boyer first. Hopefully he had some good news. I dialed my office phone . . . and finally got through. "Mr. Boyer? Gabby Fairbanks. I was wondering what you've been able to find out."

"*The* Gabby Fairbanks?" The male voice on the other end chuckled. "When I saw you on Friday, I didn't know you were such a celebrity."

I felt my ears turning red, glad he couldn't see me blushing. "I didn't know it either. Yeah, we had a bit of excitement here at the shelter that night, but I think it's blowing over. Hope so, anyway. My husband was livid when he saw us on TV."

Now the laughter was outright. "I can just imagine." He took a few seconds to recover. "Anyway . . . I don't think it'll hurt your case—might even help. But it'd be best if we could go over our next steps in person rather than over the phone. And bring in those power of attorney papers I gave you, if possible. Can you come in tomorrow at eleven?"

Right. The papers. I still needed to get them signed and notarized. "Sure. I think eleven would work."

"All right. Are you doing okay?"

His question caught me off guard. "Uh, actually, yes, I am. Some friends of the shelter took us home with them for the weekend and are actually taking care of my mother and Dandy for a few days. I almost feel like a normal person this week." I didn't mention the Yada Yada group and the impact of their prayers. Might sound a little weird.

"Atta girl. You're going to be fine. And we're going to stick it to your husband with everything we've got. You just hang in there. See you tomorrow, Gabby." *Click.*

I almost said, *"Wait! I don't want to 'stick it to my husband.' I just want my life back!"* But he was gone. And I had to admit, it was nice of him, asking if I was okay, telling me to hang in there. Calling me by my familiar name.

The phone call had definitely perked up my spirit.

I looked at my watch. Ten fifteen. Still had a little time before the staff meeting. Maybe I could get in a few minutes of Bible reading . . . wait! I had to find Hannah and tell her about the appointment at Adele's Hair and Nails! *And* find out how to get there!

Hannah went berserk when I told her she had a job interview. She threw her arms around me and practically picked me up in her excitement. "Oh, Miz Fairbanks, thank you, thank you, thank you . . . oh! What should I wear? Is my hair okay?"

I looked at her critically. She was a big girl, but not fat. Medium-brown skin, smooth, not rough and scarred like some of the women who'd been out on the streets for years. Hair was braided tight to her head, without extensions. She probably did it herself, but it was neat. "Do you have a skirt? You don't have to be fancy. But dress as businesslike as possible. Iron whatever you've got. And don't chew gum. Never, never. This woman has a thing about gum." I grinned. "Now, go. We need to leave by twelve thirty." And *I* needed to get to the staff meeting.

Only five of us—Mabel, myself, Angela, Estelle, who blew in right at ten thirty, and Stephanie Cooper, the DCFS social worker who came on Tuesdays and Thursdays for case management meetings—gathered in the schoolroom on the main floor. I expected Mabel to plunge right into the matter at hand, but we spent the first ten minutes just praying. Well, mostly it was Mabel and Estelle, but the two of them praised God for all He was doing at Manna House, for the progress many of the residents were making toward their goals, and that none of the residents or staff had been injured during the break-in over the weekend. "An' we ask You to heal sweet Dandy," Estelle added, "who risked his own safety to protect the women here. An' Your Word tells us to pray for our enemies, so guess we oughta be prayin' for that perp who broke in here. Turn him around, Lord. Clean him up and set him on the right path. An' we give You thanks that Dandy didn't hurt him too bad."

The rest of us looked at each other self-consciously as the prayers ended. Praying for the "perp" wasn't exactly at the top of the prayer list for most of us.

Mabel told the staff what the rest of Chicago already seemed to know—that good-hearted people who'd seen the TV clips about Hero Dog stopping an intruder at a local women's shelter were sending donations to Manna House. "A few are earmarked to help with Dandy's medical expenses," she said, with a nod in my direction, "but most are coming in as general donations."

Angela waggled her hand. "Like, how much?"

I was glad someone else asked. Mabel shrugged. "Right now, about two thousand dollars. But my guess is there'll be more. The reason I'm telling you now is twofold. First, we are *not* 'using' what happened to generate contributions—an accusation you may hear from some people. All contributions have been spontaneous. Second, the board will need to decide whether this goes into our general operating fund—God knows we operate on a tight budget as it is—or whether it should be deposited in a special fund for a particular project or outreach."

"We need a van." That popped out before I even thought of it.

Mabel allowed a wry smile. "Well, two thousand dollars won't go very far for a van, but Gabby preempted my next point. I'm sure the board would be willing to entertain ideas for what to do with this money—but *please*, submit them in writing." She stood up. "Okay, that's it."

"Well, hallelujah!" Estelle jumped up and was practically out the door. "I still gotta do lunch, an' I'm half an hour behind already."

Stephanie Cooper was right on her heels. "Yeah, and I need to squeeze in two case management meetings *before* lunch."

"Stephanie! Wait up!" I needed to tell the case manager about the job interview for Hannah and get a CTA pass for her.

But Mabel caught me as I started to follow. "Gabby, just a minute. Speaking of contributions, don't forget there's an awful lot of dog food and dog stuff piled up in the rec room. I'm going to let you decide what to do with it—but I want it out of here by the end of the week. *Capisce?*" She strode out the door.

Good grief. Now Mabel was beginning to sound like Sarge.

chapter 21

I went online to get directions to Adele's Hair and Nails on Clark Street, and it didn't seem too complicated. Take the Red Line north to Howard Street—the border between Chicago and Evanston—walk a couple of blocks to Clark, turn south. Easy.

Stephanie Cooper, Hannah's case manager, had worried that it might be a wasted trip since the girl didn't have her state ID yet, but she gave her a CTA one-day pass since I was going with her. "Can't hurt to try," she agreed, pushing her long bangs out of her eyes. "Let me know how it goes. And hey, why don't we set up a time on Thursday to talk about you? You and your mom are still on the bed list, right?"

I hoped. Our stay at the Baxters' was temporary at best. Made me feel funny to be treated like the other residents, but I had to admit, Stephanie had a right as case manager to talk about our "case" since we were, in fact, homeless.

When Hannah and I got off the train at Howard Street, the newish shopping center between the El station and Clark Street looked awfully familiar. "Hey, Hannah. That's the church where Edesa and Estelle go. See? In the shopping center."

She squinted and frowned. "I don't see no church. Whatchu talkin' about?"

I laughed. "That large storefront over there. See on the awning? 'SouledOut Community Church.'"

"Humph. Weird. How many more blocks we gotta walk? These shoes hurt my feet."

"Not sure. Shouldn't be far."

Wrong. How had I misjudged so badly? At ten blocks—a healthy city mile—Hannah was talking mutiny. "I ain't gonna walk this far to work ever' day! Why I let you talk me into this, I don' know. I'm so beat, I'm 'bout ready to fall over. You got any money? Can we get somethin' to drink?"

We'd passed a fruit market a ways back, but now most of the shop windows displayed a jumble of ethnic languages. Spanish. Korean. Arabic . . . I looked at my watch. We still had ten minutes, and the store numbers were getting closer. But I wasn't about to drag a disgruntled Hannah into the beauty shop. Adele Skuggs didn't seem the type of person who put up with any nonsense.

I ducked into a corner "pantry" and bought two cans of cold Pepsi. Okay, I was hot and tired, too, not to mention mad at myself for not getting better directions. But I'd gone out on a limb asking for this interview, so it was my reputation on the line too. I dangled the sweating can in front of Hannah. "I'm sure there's a closer El stop, Hannah, and if you get this job, we'll figure out a better way to get here. But if you go in there whining like a spoiled brat, you can forget going on the activity list at the shelter, too, you understand?" I handed her the can. "Now, pull yourself together. We're almost there."

A bell tinkled when we finally pushed open the door of Adele's Hair and Nails.

I glared a warning at Hannah, and she muttered, "Okay, okay."

Three beauty shop chairs lined the mirrored wall to the left just beyond a tidy waiting area. Adele Skuggs, her own hair a short salt-and-pepper 'fro, was taking pink spongy curlers out of a woman's hair in the middle chair. The shop owner gave us a brief glance. "Be with you in a minute."

A beige corduroy couch against the window and a matching love seat against the wall made an inviting waiting area. Magazines—*O* and *Essence* and *Jet* and *Newsweek*—littered a coffee table. A coffeepot and a platter of sweet rolls sat on a corner table. "Ooo, my fave," Hannah said, helping herself to a frosted twist and a napkin. Oh great, sticky fingers for her interview. But too late now.

Posters of beautiful black women with sculptured and braided hairstyles decorated the shop walls. Three "beehive" hair dryers sat across from the chairs, hidden behind the front desk counter. I didn't see anything that looked like a nail salon.

"All right, Miss Lilly. This what you wanted?" Adele gave a hand mirror to the middle-aged African-American woman in the chair. I stared. I'd expected Adele to do a comb-out or style the hair somehow, but she'd left the springy curls just as they came off the curlers, looking like fat sausages all over the woman's head. "Miss Lilly" nodded and smiled at her reflection front, side, and back as Adele took off the plastic cape.

Adele glanced our way as if sizing up Hannah, who was licking crumbs off her fingers—good grief!—but she kept talking to her client. "You in a hurry, Miss Lilly? How would you like a free

manicure and pedicure while you're here?" Adele grinned, expos-
ing a small gap between her front teeth. "I've got a new nail girl
I'm trying out, and I need a victim."

Miss Lilly laughed. "Oh, why not?" She hefted herself out of
the chair and shuffled toward the back of the shop, disappearing
around a corner. Hannah swallowed her last bite and hastily
dabbed her full lips with the napkin, her eyes wide like the pro-
verbial deer caught in the headlights.

Adele grabbed a broom and swept up hair from around the
second chair. "Take that first chair, Gabby Fairbanks. Be with you
in a minute. Come here, girl—Hannah, is it? Mrs. Fairbanks says
you've got experience. Come on back with me . . . Wash your
hands in that sink there . . . What can you do? Full sets? French
tips?" Her voice faded as they disappeared around the corner.

By the time we left Adele's Hair and Nails at four o'clock,
Hannah had been offered a provisional job two days a week, a
four-day week if she proved responsible . . . and my wild curls had
been clipped, tamed, and freshened. "You color your hair?" Adele
had asked, blow-drying my wet tendrils.

"No. My natural color." I'd tried to keep the pride out of my
voice. "Used to be redder, but it has darkened quite a bit.
Chestnut, I guess."

"Mm. Just wondered. You don't have the freckles and green
eyes of most redheads." Adele finger-curled a few misbehaving
strands. "Hazel eyes are nice, though."

She'd charged me twenty bucks, which was certainly reasonable, though it was hard to hand over my debit card and see that
much disappear from my account. When I asked directions to the

closest El stop and Adele found out we'd walked all the way from Howard Street, her shoulders shook with silent laughter as she gave simple directions to the Loyola El station. "Six or seven blocks at most," she'd promised.

Hannah, pumped at the chance to show her stuff in a real salon, generously offered to get herself back to the shelter so I could walk to the Baxters' house from there instead of going all the way into the city and back so late in the afternoon.

By the time I dragged myself up the front porch steps of Jodi and Denny's two-flat, I was pooped. I rang the doorbell, eager to hide out in Josh's old bedroom and call my sons. And my aunt Mercy too. I needed to give her my new cell phone number and let her know where we were staying this week.

I rang the doorbell again. As I waited, it occurred to me that I hadn't talked to either one of my sisters since North Dakota, when I told them I was taking Mom back to Chicago with me "for a visit." I groaned, leaning against the doorpost. Celeste and Honor certainly had no idea Philip had kicked me out and that Mom and I were "guests" in a homeless shelter. But I needed to talk to them about the power of attorney forms the lawyer had given me for Mom. *One* of us had to do it.

Well, better late than never. I'd call tonight, maybe around nine. That would be seven o'clock in California and six in Alaska.

I frowned at the front door, still closed in my face. Strange. Finding my way around back, I found Dandy stretched out in a patch of sun in the tiny backyard. "Hey, boy. You home alone?" Mom's yellow dog jerked his head up, his mouth open in a doggy smile, pumped his tail, and struggled to get up. I squatted beside him instead. "Good boy. Easy, now . . . you doing okay? Where is everybody?"

I even climbed up the back stairs to the second-floor apartment to see if I could use the bathroom, but neither Estelle nor Stu was home either.

At about the time my bladder was threatening to burst, the Baxters' minivan pulled into the garage, and Jodi and my mother came into the yard, hauling groceries. I had to make a beeline for the bathroom the moment Jodi unlocked the back door. "Sorry!" she called after me. "I didn't know you'd be home so early!"

Back in the kitchen, much relieved, I offered to peel potatoes and carrots for the stew Jodi was making while she put groceries away. "How'd it go with my mom and Dandy today?"

"Fine. No problem . . . except your mom complained of a headache this morning. I gave her something for it and she slept, oh, a good three or four hours. That's why we ended up doing our errands late this afternoon—oh! Your hair!" Jodi reached out and pulled a curl, letting it spring back. "It looks nice, Gabby. Adele did a great job." She winked at me. "Okay, you gotta tell me about your first visit to Adele's Hair and Nails. And then I'll tell you about *my* first visit . . . when MaDear was still alive. Hoo boy, Adele's mother definitely kept things interesting!"

We had lots of time for "girl talk" that evening because Denny went to some guy meeting at Peter Douglass's house. Jodi's stories about MaDear left me bug-eyed—especially the time Adele's senile mother mistook Jodi's husband for the white man who'd lynched her older brother way back in the thirties, screaming at Denny to "Get out!" when he came to the beauty shop to pick up Jodi. I could hardly believe Jodi's husband actually asked forgiveness for the horrible deed someone else had committed just so the poor confused woman could experience some peace.

We talked so long it was ten o'clock before I remembered to make my calls, but I didn't get either sister, so I left my new cell phone number on their voice mail and told them to call me ASAP.

I was still thinking about Denny's amazing response as I was getting dressed for work the next morning. Jodi said the situation had put a real strain on their relationship with Adele, and Denny had gotten really depressed at being falsely accused. "MaDear had some kind of dementia. There was no way to make the old woman understand he didn't do it," Jodi had said. "But Denny kept reading the Bible and one day had a revelation—that Jesus had taken the death penalty for *our* sins so we could be free! That's what gave him the idea."

I grabbed my hairbrush to work on the snarls in my hair without the benefit of a mirror—didn't guys have mirrors in their bedrooms?—still chewing on what Jodi had said. *Good grief.* It was hard enough having to say I was sorry for something I *did* do wrong. Couldn't imagine asking forgiveness for something I *hadn't* done. Was sure I wasn't spiritual enough to—

I stopped brushing. A little voice niggled in my ear. *Yeah, but Gabby, aren't you always saying you're sorry for stuff Philip thinks you've done wrong when you haven't really done anything, just to keep the peace?*

chapter 22

My mind stewed on that one all the way to the shelter on the El. My mom had insisted on coming with me that morning. "It's Wednesday, isn't it, Celeste? Estelle needs me to help with the knitting club."

"I'm Gabby, Mom," I'd snapped. "Not Celeste. *Gabby*, remember?" I immediately felt bad about my snitty comeback. But good grief, why should I let her call me by the wrong name? I was tired of being at the wrong end of everything.

At least Estelle came with us that morning, since she not only had to put lunch together at the shelter but also supervise the knitting club during "nurse hours." She graciously sat with my mother on the El, leaving me holding on to a pole, alone with my garbled thoughts.

I barely noticed as the train stopped and started, picking up its morning glut of commuters, as I tried to grasp the difference between what Denny Baxter had done—and even Jesus, for that matter—and my own knee-jerk contrition. *They* had freely taken on the burden of sin to lift it off someone else. Me, I allowed myself to swallow Philip's accusations and innuendos because . . .

Because why?

Because I was afraid.

But why was I afraid? Philip had never hit me. But somehow . . .

I stared at the backs of brick buildings flitting by, windows with shades pulled, and skinny back porches with the occasional hopeful flower box as my mind tried to make sense of my failed marriage.

Somehow . . . somehow Philip had managed to whittle away at my self-confidence, at my ideas and dreams, until I barely knew who I was . . . and I lived in fear of the real me vanishing altogether. For some reason, I had clung to Philip's version of who I was, even his negative depictions, because at least it was *something*.

"Sheridan!" the intercom squawked as the train lurched around a sharp corner and slowed at our station. I shook off my disturbing thoughts and followed as Estelle helped my mother out the doors and onto the platform. When we came out on the sidewalk below the elevated station, I suddenly remembered the papers I was supposed to bring to the lawyer at eleven.

"Estelle, wait. Do you have a minute? Mom and I have to get these power of attorney papers notarized, and we need a witness. There's a bank just up the street . . ."

"Humph," she grumbled. "If lunch is late today, I'm gonna send all the complaints to you." But Estelle accompanied us to the bank, duly witnessed my mother's and my signatures on the various forms, and even murmured, "This is good. Real good," as the notary handed the forms back to my mother.

She seemed lost in thought as we walked arm in arm with my mother the few blocks to Manna House. "Mm-mm, I wonder . . ."

"Wonder what?" I said.

"Oh. Just thinking about Harry's mom, wondering if he's taken care of this power of attorney business with her."

"Mr. Bentley's mom? You know her?"

"Oh, sure, sure. He asked me to do an assessment for her when he found out I was licensed to do home care for seniors, an' I've dropped in on her from time to time, unofficial-like. Nice lady. Real nice lady. A bit odd, but . . . she likes me." Estelle glanced sideways at me as if she'd said too much as we rounded the corner toward Manna House.

"Estelle Williams!" I whopped my friend on the arm with the back of my hand. "This is getting serious. I mean, now Mr. B's taking you home to Mama . . . oh, good grief. There's that reporter again. Don't say anything."

We hustled up the steps as the female reporter called out, "Mrs. Fairbanks! Is Dandy back at the shelter yet? We hear the residents have made him their official watchdog. So why isn't he—?"

"No comment!" I sang out, and we disappeared inside.

Where in the world was that snoopy reporter getting her information? I was tempted to call the residents and staff together then and there and insist that nobody talk to any reporters, but I forgot my snit as a happy chorus greeted us when we walked into the multipurpose room. "Hiya, Gramma Shep!" . . . "Miz Martha! We been missing you!" . . . "Where's Dandy? Thought he was comin' back!" My mother's cheeks turned pink as everyone from Carolyn the Book Maven to eight-year-old Sammy gave her warm hugs.

"Dandy needs a few more days," I said. "Don't worry, he'll be back." So what if they thought I meant a few more days to heal—which was true. But my real motive for leaving Dandy at the Baxters' as long as possible was to hopefully starve any remaining media interest in Hero Dog.

"Gramma Shep!" Hannah hustled over. "Did Miss Gabby tell you I got me a job in a beauty salon? Ooo, can I do your nails, Gramma Shep? I need the practice!"

"But where's Lucy?" My mother's face fell as she looked around the room. "I told Lucy I'd be back in a few days. Maybe she's downstairs seeing the nurse."

Carolyn caught my eye and gave a quick shake of her head.

"Come on, Mom," I said, steering my mother to a comfortable armchair near an end table. "Let Hannah give you a manicure. You have some time before the knitting club starts."

I was grateful for Hannah's offer, because I wanted to get some work done before heading out the door to make my eleven o'clock at Legal Aid. By the time I signed out and caught the southbound El for my appointment, I had a proposal on Mabel's desk to purchase a list of basic supplies to give manicures and pedicures to the residents of Manna House, using the words of Precious McGill: "Homeless women need to *feel* like women too." It wouldn't be the spa treatment, but hey, we'd do what we could do.

I arrived at the Legal Aid office on Diversey, a storefront along a strip of stores and small businesses—a medical and dental clinic, a resale shop, a real estate office, a pizza joint—with two minutes to spare, but then had to wait fifteen minutes to be called. I smoothed the wrinkles out of my cream-colored slacks and picked some stray lint off my pale green cotton knit top with the crocheted scoop neck. Did I look all right? I should've repaired my makeup before I left the shelter. Maybe they had a restroom here—

A woman with pale bug-eyes and wispy hair dyed an odd burgundy stormed out of the doorway leading to the offices, throwing dagger glances at everyone in the waiting room as she passed. "Tell *me* I don't got a case," she muttered. "They're gonna be sorry. Yessir, they're gonna be sorry. That woman *owes* me—" She jerked the front door open and disappeared.

The African-American receptionist didn't even look up from her computer screen. "Fairbanks. You're next."

Down the hall, Lee Boyer's door was half-open. "Sorry about that," the lawyer said, running a hand through his brown, salty hair, then pulling off his wire rims and cleaning them with a man's handkerchief he pulled out of his desk drawer. "Please, sit down . . . May I call you Gabby?"

I sat. "Please. 'Mrs. Fairbanks' sounds like my mother-in-law, and I'm not too happy with her at the moment."

The man laughed. "Got it. Gabby it is."

Was Lee Boyer this good-looking the last time I was here? Not Philip's kind of suave, Double-O Seven good looks that turned heads when he walked into a room. But pleasant. Open. Warm. I watched as he threw the handkerchief back into the drawer and hooked the wire rims behind his ears. "Okay, Gabby, let's get started. Let's see . . ." He studied an open folder. "Do you have the power of attorney forms?"

I pulled a business envelope out of my shoulder bag and pushed it across the desk. "Signed, sealed, and delivered."

"Excellent." He pulled out the forms and skimmed them. "We'll make copies for your files and keep these here." He then handed me a set of papers he'd drawn up to file for unlawful eviction and to regain custody of my children, which needed my signature. My skin prickled as I read, "Plaintiff—Gabrielle Fairbanks . . . Defendant—Philip Fairbanks . . ." *Oh God, is this really happening?*

But I signed.

Lee Boyer clipped the affidavits to the file folder and leaned back. "Now, anything I should know on your end? Besides you turning up on the TV news." He grinned mischievously.

I told him about the phone call with my father-in-law and the difficult decision I'd made to leave the boys where they were until I found an apartment. I didn't tell him about my ill-fated visit to Philip's office. Did it matter? But I hated looking like a fool in front of this man.

". . . know that was a hard decision," he was saying. "But all the more reason to find an apartment so we can get the boys back here with you before school starts. Have you found anything yet?"

He said *we*. "Uh, apartment . . . no. I haven't had time to look. The break-in at the shelter kind of kicked dust in my eyes. We're staying with some, uh, friends till Saturday, and then we have to come back to the shelter. With taking care of Mom and her injured dog, it's been a bit hectic. But maybe this weekend . . ."

Lee Boyer leaned forward, hands clasped on his desk. "Gabby. I understand that things are tough on you right now. But I can't emphasize enough that you need to find an apartment so your sons can come live with you, or this case could very well be thrown out. No judge is going to take two young boys out of their grandparents' home and put them in a women's shelter."

He said it kindly, but tears sprang to my eyes. I reached for a tissue from the box on his desk. "I know," I croaked. "But how can I afford—"

"Don't worry about that. You find an apartment and let me know about it. Then we'll see about supplemental funding until all this gets straightened out." The lawyer leaned back in his desk chair and chewed on the end of a pen, as if thinking about something. But all he said was, "What's the best way to get hold of you if I need to? Between meetings, I mean."

"Oh." I dug in my bag. "I have a cell phone now. A gift from my hosts." I gave him the number.

"All right." Lee Boyer consulted the calendar on his computer. "Next week? Same time good for you?" The man stood up and extended his hand. "I'll call you if anything comes up, Gabby. You do the same."

I shook his hand. To my surprise, he covered it with his other hand and held it for a nanosecond longer. Startled, I looked into his eyes—those warm, brown eyes. "It's going to be all right, Gabby," he said.

Somehow I made it out of there without blubbering. Lee Boyer wasn't anything I expected from a Legal Aid lawyer. He actually seemed to care about what had happened to me, cared about getting my boys back . . . Was that normal for a lawyer? Didn't lawyers just want their money?

Except this was Legal Aid. They didn't do it for profit.

Well, whatever. Philip could sneer all he wanted that I'd gone to Legal Aid. I was lucky to get this lawyer.

And for some reason, as I settled into a seat on the next northbound El, almost empty at this time of day, that little "we" floated into my thoughts. *"So we can get the boys back here . . ."* Well, sure, as my lawyer.

But I tucked that little "we" into an empty corner of my heart.

chapter 23

Our stay at the Baxter household buoyed me up better than a week at a spa resort, a gentle oasis of ordinary family rhythms in the middle of the train wreck that was my actual life. Well, maybe not *ordinary* family rhythms, since we had no kid noses or bottoms needing to be wiped, though Dandy's "functions" and my mother's growing dependence came in a close second. Peanut—the black-and-white kitty—must have decided I was a member of the family, because he jumped into my lap whenever I sat down.

Jodi and I even played Scrabble on Thursday night after supper, just like normal people. Leslie Stuart, Estelle's housemate, came downstairs and beat us both. "And you're a teacher, Jodi!" she crowed, tossing that long, corn-silk hair back with glee.

"Yeah, but I teach third graders," Jodi protested. "My brain is stuck on third-grade spelling words, like *clean* and *could* and *cure*."

"And I'm a social worker, but you didn't see me winning with words like *caseworker* and *caseload* and *colleague*."

"No," I jumped in, "but changing *cop* to *copacetic* on a triple word score?! Who even knew that was a word?"

Stu chuckled. "Harry Bentley, that's who—my erstwhile client, your friend, and Estelle's *boyfriend*, if she'd ever admit it. He's been mourning the loss of his *copacetic* life ever since his grandson moved in with him." Which had left all three of us gasping with laughter.

But Saturday loomed when Mom and I would need to move back to the shelter. How Mabel had been able to hold beds for us, I wasn't sure. New faces appeared at the shelter every few days, and I knew our beds had been assigned temporarily to someone else Wednesday night when a major thunderstorm rolled through the city, drenching the normal haunts of the homeless. But when I checked my e-mail at work on Friday, I had two e-mails from Mabel—one an announcement to all staff and available volunteers regarding a staff meeting on Monday, the other to me saying she'd put our names back on the bed list, same room, same bunks, starting Saturday night. I stopped in at her office just before I left for the day to thank her.

"Glad you stopped in, Gabby. Shut the door and sit a minute." Mabel pulled out a file with my name on it. "Stephanie Cooper says she met with you yesterday about housing options."

I nodded, pursing my lips. That had been a little weird. The housing programs Stephanie usually worked with—Theresa's Place, Sanctuary Place, Deborah's Place, and others—typically targeted specific people groups: ex-cons trying to reenter society, addicts going through recovery, alcoholics doing AA, or the mentally challenged, though she'd also given me a list of shelters for victims of domestic violence, several out in the burbs and a couple in Wisconsin.

Mabel must have guessed my thoughts. "I know a case management meeting might feel a bit awkward, Gabby, since you're also on staff here. But neither you nor I want you here for long, right? If you and your mother are on the bed list, Stephanie needs to help you set priorities and goals for getting back on your feet. You've got a job. Now get yourself on some housing lists."

I sighed. "Yeah, I know. My lawyer is bugging me about getting an apartment, too, though he's talking about a regular apartment, not the housing programs Stephanie deals with. I don't even qualify for half of them, since I'm not an ex-con or a drug addict. And not that many take kids—just ask Tanya! The ones that do have lists from here to New York and back."

Mabel nodded, eyes sympathetic. "I know, Gabby. Look, all of us will do whatever we—"

"Why doesn't Manna House add an option like that for homeless single moms like Tanya—you know, a building with separate apartments, where women can make a real home for their kids, but with services that prepare them to make a go of it alone?" I stood up and started to pace. "Even Precious is about to lose her—"

"Gabby! Gabby." Mabel's tone pulled me up short. "That's a wonderful idea, and one of these days—years—we'd love to do something like that when some philanthropic billionaire floats us a nice fat donation. But right now, *your* reality is looking for an apartment, okay?" She came around her desk and softened her words with a quick hug.

I returned the hug. "Okay. Thanks again for putting us back on the bed list. Dandy too, right? Denny Baxter said he'd drive us down tomorrow morning, so getting Mom and Dandy squared away might take most of the day. But I'll hit the streets on Monday, I promise. *After* the staff meeting."

I left her office and almost made it out the front doors when I heard, "Oh, Gabby! One more thing." I turned, shaking my head and laughing.

Mabel was standing at her office door. "What?"

"Mabel. You always have 'one more thing.'"

"Oh. Well, I do have one more thing. All that dog food and doggy stuff, remember? It's got to go."

I had talked my mother into staying at the house with Jodi Baxter the last two days, due to a recurrence of that nasty headache during the knitting club on Wednesday. Since I was out, Estelle had helped her lie down in the multipurpose room, where she'd slept again for several hours. And when I got back to the house Friday evening, dragging from the rising humidity, Jodi said my mom had had another one that afternoon, so bad it made her cry. She was still asleep.

"When was the last time your mom saw a doctor?" Jodi asked, handing me a cold iced tea as I collapsed on their back porch swing, then settling herself on the top step leading down into the postage-stamp yard. I nudged Dandy on his dog bed with my toe, but he just flopped his tail a few times. Too hot for woman and beast alike.

"Mm . . . don't really know. She had a fall Mother's Day weekend, and my aunt Mercy took her to the hospital to get her checked out. And another fall when the boys and I were visiting her in North Dakota earlier this month. She tripped over Dandy,

and we had to ice a knot on her head, but she said she was fine."
I shrugged. "Have no idea when her last physical was."

"You might think about getting her checked out."

"Yeah, good idea, Jodi." I heard the slight sarcasm in my tone
but couldn't stop. "I don't even have a family doctor yet! And in
case you haven't noticed, my life has been a *little* crazy lately, what
with getting thrown out of my house by my own husband, losing
my sons overnight, and my mother and an injured dog dropped
in my lap!" I threw up my hands, sloshing my iced tea. "When
was I supposed to see a doctor?"

Jodi winced, but to her credit she didn't walk back into the
kitchen, leaving me to wallow in my own frustration. "I know.
Just . . . when you can."

We sat in silence for a long minute, with just the *squeak
squeak* of the swing and the drone of traffic several streets over as
background. Jodi picked up a stray nail and chipped at the loose
paint on one of the railing posts. Finally I said, "Sorry, Jodi. I
know you care. You and Denny have been super. Can't thank you
enough for hosting us this whole week and giving us a respite
from the shelter. Even dog-sitting! Not many people would do
that—especially when we were virtually strangers."

Jodi glanced up through her brown bangs, looking girlish in
her shoulder-length bob. "It's been fun, Gabby—really. It gets a
little lonely around here with the kids gone."

"Well, but Amanda will be back tomorrow, right? And she'll
be here the rest of the summer, till it's time to go back to college.
She sounds like a neat kid."

"Yeah, she is . . . when she's not driving me crazy." Jodi made
a face. "She's got this boyfriend, José, a really nice young man, but

'Manda can't decide if he's 'just a friend' or if she's in love . . . oh wait! You know his mother. Delores Enriques, the nurse at Manna House. And she's one of our Yada Yada sisters."

Delores's son? I grinned. It was fun getting "inside information" on the staff at Manna House. José and Amanda, *hmm* . . .

"Gabby." Jodi suddenly sounded serious. "I feel awful thinking about you and your mom going back to a homeless shelter. It doesn't feel . . . right. Don't get me wrong. I love Manna House, I think they do a terrific job, and I'm enjoying teaching the typing class—all two weeks of it so far. But . . . I'd hate to be living there—in a bunk room, no less. Sheesh!"

I shrugged. "It's better than some shelters I've heard about, where they've got one huge room housing thirty to sixty women, like Katrina victims wall to wall in the Superdome."

Jodi glanced at Dandy, snoring peacefully in the dog bed. "It's been nice having a dog around again. Dandy's a sweetheart—right, buddy?" She reached over and gave Dandy's ears a scratch. He rewarded her with a few more tail thumps. "Mm. Wish Amanda could meet him. She'd go bonkers! You'd have to sneak him away when she wasn't looking."

Still scratching the dog's ears, Jodi looked at me sideways. "It can't be easy having a dog at the shelter—no yard to romp in, all those stairs to climb—and he's still stiff from those stitches. What would you think about us keeping Dandy, at least until things settle down for you, you know, find a place of your own, get the boys back . . ."

I couldn't believe my ears. In a heartbeat! *Okay, God, where was this option when I really needed it, like* before *Philip got fed up with having Dandy underfoot? Don't You have Your timing a little screwed up?* But even now it would solve so many problems—like who was going to walk him if Lucy didn't come back. And the problem of getting him up and down two flights of stairs each day . . . not to mention those media hounds who were sure to sniff him out once we got back to Manna House.

The Baxters would be a perfect family for Dandy!

But I reluctantly shook my head. "My mom wouldn't hear of it. That dog means the world to her. She turned down a perfectly good retirement home I found here in Rogers Park because she couldn't keep Dandy with her."

Jodi's eyes brightened. "Well . . . your mom could stay here too! I mean, even when Amanda comes back, we still have Josh's old room. Really! She wouldn't be alone, because I'm off for the summer. And Estelle lives right upstairs. She could take her on like one of her in-home-care seniors."

I gaped at Jodi. "Are you serious?" I felt as if gold from heaven were pouring down into my lap. A safe place for my mom with people who like dogs . . . "Just until I find an apartment, though. Actually, she's got some money. We could pay, you know, for room and board."

"Oh, don't worry about that. She eats like a bird."

I was so excited, I could hardly think straight. "Oh, Jodi. This is wonderful. It's like the answers to all my prayers. Let me go talk to my mom. You think she's awake yet?"

Martha Shepherd was packing, and Martha Shepherd wouldn't budge. "No, Celeste. We have to go home. I promised Lucy that I'd be back."

"Mom! The Baxters are inviting you *and* Dandy to stay here for a while. Isn't that what you wanted? And it's just until I find an apartment for us—or until your name comes up for assisted living back in Minot. Then you can go home."

"The Baxters have been very nice, Celeste. But I promised Lu—"

"*Mom!* Lucy isn't *at* Manna House right now. She's been gone all week. Maybe she's not coming back." I hated to do it, but my mother was being totally unreasonable.

My mother calmly folded her nightgown and put it in the small suitcase. "She'll be back. She said she'd look after Dandy. And besides, I promised . . . Hand me those underthings, would you, Celeste?"

chapter 24

I tossed all night, snatching bits of sleep here and there, but waking every hour or so, wound up in the sheet. The fact that it was hot and muggy and the Baxters didn't have central air didn't help either. But mainly I was angry. The perfect solution for my mom and Dandy had been handed to me on a silver platter—and my mom said *no*?!

Argh! I mean, she "promised Lucy"? How did *that* weigh in on the grand scheme of things when I was trying to get my family back together and take care of her and Dandy too?! *Lucy* was totally unpredictable. Here today, gone tomorrow. Couldn't my mother understand that?

I kicked off the sheet, got up, and turned the fan in the window up another speed before flopping back onto the bed, my thoughts as wilted as the cotton camisole I'd worn to bed . . . Should I *make* my mother stay here? It made so much sense! She might pout a day or two, but she'd get over it, wouldn't she?

I reran my list of arguments. For one thing, there were all

those stairs. "I'm not dead yet," my mom had said, pooh-poohing my concern. "And Manna House has an elevator." Which she had yet to use.

Another thing: A homeless shelter was no place for a dog. True, they'd adopted him last weekend as their official "watchdog"— but who really cared? Lucy, maybe. Sure, she'd gotten attached to my mom and Dandy, and her disappearance was probably a royal snit because I'd whisked them away right under her nose. But I couldn't believe we'd let *Lucy*, of all people—a bag lady who'd been living on the street most of her life—determine what happened with *my* life!

I squeezed my eyes shut, remembering the day I'd first met her. Tripped over her was more like it—or rather, tripped over her cart sticking out from the bushes while I was running in the sudden rain shower, trying to get back to our penthouse before Philip showed up with his new business partner. This old bag lady came out from under the bush, hacking and coughing, with only a garbage bag for protection, fussing over *me* because I'd cut my bare foot.

I started to giggle in spite of myself just thinking about it now.

And then! The *look* on Philip's face when the two of us came in the front door of the penthouse, Lucy in her layers of mismatched clothes and smelling rather, er, stale, both of us dripping wet . . .

Ohhh! I stuffed my face into the pillow, shoulders shaking with laughter.

I finally threw off the pillow and wiped my soggy face with the sheet. Okay, Lucy had impacted my life big-time. If it wasn't for her, I never would have visited Manna House, never would have been offered a job as their program director. And I had to admit, in her own odd way, she'd been a real friend. She'd kept my mom company when I had to bring my mom to work . . . she'd taken Dandy for walks when I had to bring *him* to work . . . she'd gone hunting for Dandy when Philip "lost" the dog on purpose . . . and Lucy had found Dandy and found *me* when the tables turned and *I* was the one homeless with nowhere to go . . .

My anger slowly evaporated as the first morning light bathed the Baxters' guest bedroom in hazy blues in spite of the closed blinds and whirring fan in the window. A chest of drawers, a bookshelf, a desk—Josh Baxter's boyhood furnishings—gradually took shape in my vision.

Might as well get up. What time was it . . . five o'clock? If I could find my Bible, maybe I'd go out on the back porch, sit in the porch swing one last time, and get back to the Bible reading I'd started during my trip to North Dakota—before my life unraveled. Hadn't Jodi and the other Yada Yada sisters prayed that I'd begin to see God's purpose in my life? Prayed for wisdom to meet the challenges? That I'd have strength to face tomorrow?

Well, tomorrow was here, and I definitely needed some of that wisdom and strength. I'd already found some of it in the Matthew chapters I'd been reading a couple of weeks ago. Maybe there was more . . .

"Hey, Gabby! Wait!"

I turned to see Estelle waving at me from the upstairs porch midmorning just as we were loading up the Baxters' Dodge Caravan. The fifty-something black woman came schlepping down the outside stairs, her loose, multicolored caftan billowing in the stiff breeze off the lake, as I let Denny and Jodi walk my mother and Dandy into the garage to get them settled in the minivan.

"I'm not *leaving* leaving," I teased, setting down our suitcases. "See you Monday. Staff meeting at ten, right?"

She ignored me, gathering her pepper-and-salt, loose, kinky hair into a knot on top of her head, as if she'd been interrupted. "Humph. Harry just called. Said to tell you that your *husband*"— she dragged out the word with thinly disguised contempt—"left your sewing machine at the front desk of Richmond Towers. I say hallelujah!" She fluttered a hand at me. "You go on now. Might as well pick it up on your way. That'll come in real handy on Monday when I do my sewing class." Estelle turned away, muttering to herself as she hauled herself back up the steps. "*Mm-mm.* Maybe Mama sewed clothes by hand, but I ain't goin' back *there*. Uh-uh."

"Come on, Gabby!" Jodi yelled. "I'm teaching a typing class at eleven, remember?"

I looked at my watch. Only ten o'clock. We had plenty of time. But it was a good thing we'd left then, because traffic was heavy on Sheridan Road. "Taste of Chicago going on this weekend." Denny glanced in the mirror at me. "You ever been, Gabby?"

Jodi backhanded his arm from the passenger seat. "Don't you go getting any ideas, Denny Baxter. Last time we went, we lost a kid in that crowd, remember? And I said *never* . . ."

I was only half listening. Philip left the sewing machine as agreed. That was good. But the idea of picking up the machine *today* left a knot in the pit of my stomach. Philip said he was moving out by the end of June. Which was yesterday—Friday—but maybe he was moving out today since it was Saturday, even if it was July first. I didn't want to stop by there and risk running into him. Or maybe I did. I had Denny and Jodi Baxter and my mother with me . . . Wouldn't Philip feel like a rotten heel if we all walked in there while he was loading *our* stuff into a moving van?

"Denny, would you mind stopping by Richmond Towers a minute? There's a frontage road just off Sheridan. I need to pick up my sewing machine, and it'll be easier with a car."

I saw Jodi and Denny in the front seats glance at each other. But Denny said, "Sure. No problem."

Dandy was sitting on the floor behind the driver's seat, putting his paw in my mother's lap, trying to see out the window. As we turned onto the frontage road, I peered out the front windshield. No moving truck that I could see. Intent on the dog, my mother seemed oblivious to where we were until Denny pulled up in front of the luxury tower along the frontage road. She looked past me at the revolving door and stiffened. "This isn't Manna House." She shook her head vigorously. "No, no, won't go . . ."

"Mom, Mom. It's all right. Stay in the car. I just need to pick up something. Uh, Denny, would you mind going in with me?"

Jodi's husband turned on the hazards, got out, and we pushed through the revolving door into the lobby. Sure enough, Mr. Bentley was behind the desk, reading the newspaper, traffic through the lobby being lighter on a Saturday morning. I looked left and right. So far so good.

"Hey, Mr. B," I said. "What are you doing working the weekend?"

The doorman quickly folded the paper and jumped up, grabbing his uniform cap. "Mrs. Fairbanks! Denny, my man." He shook hands with Denny Baxter in a familiar way and grinned at me. "Oh, you know, we got a problem keepin' a weekend man on this job. So I end up with extra hours." He winked. "Don't mind the extra pay. Oh . . . here's the sewing machine Mr. Fairbanks left down here this mornin'."

Denny took the heavy case over the top of the counter. "Where's that grandson of yours today?"

Mr. Bentley chuckled. "Oh, my mama thinks she's takin' care of him, but it's actually the other way around. Just till I get off work. Then we're goin' down to the Taste. Mm-mm, can't wait to get some of Sweet Baby Ray's barbeque!" He laughed and gave Denny a high five.

Mr. B and Denny certainly seemed buddy-buddy. "You two know each other?" I wagged a finger from one to the other.

Denny grinned. "Harry's been coming to our men's group, meets on Tuesday nights. Small world." The two men laughed.

I shifted nervously, keeping an eye on the security door leading to the elevators. "Uh, Mr. B, my husband said he was moving out this weekend. Have you seen a moving truck or anything?"

Mr. Bentley shrugged. "Don't know anything about that, Mrs. Fairbanks. In fact, I'd be surprised if he's movin' out this weekend. When he brought that sewing machine down this morning, he had one of those overnight cases on wheels with him, and he headed for the parking garage. That was about . . . oh, I'd say, maybe an hour ago."

I stared. *Not moving out?* What did that mean? And if he wasn't moving out, where did he go? Had he gone to Virginia to visit the boys?

Mr. Bentley glanced about and then leaned close, as if wanting to be sure no one else heard him. "Thought you might be wantin' to go upstairs since management made him replace the original locks. I think they told him it was that or be sued for breach of contract." He straightened. "You didn't hear that from me, though. Understand?"

This news ricocheted in my head like a pinball trying to find the right hole to drop into. The locks had been changed *back*? As in, the key in my purse would actually open the door to the penthouse? I could go up the elevator, unlock the door, and—

"Denny. I—I'd like to go upstairs to our apartment for just a few minutes. Can you wait?" Was I out of my mind? What if Philip came back?

"I'll go with you." It wasn't a question. "Harry, we'll pick this up on our way out." Denny handed the sewing machine back over the counter and followed me through the security door.

Neither of us spoke as the elevator whirred its way to the thirty-second floor. The door *ping*ed open, and I stepped into the cool foyer with the beautiful ceramic floor tiles. The last time I'd been here, my clothes and personal things had been piled in a jumble of suitcases, boxes, and bags. Today the floor glistened.

Was Camila Sanchez still cleaning the penthouse on Fridays?

Quickly, before I lost my nerve, I stuck my house key into the lock and turned. The door opened noiselessly. I stepped into the cool dimness of the entryway—the "gallery," they called it—my heart beating so fast I could feel it in my chest.

The *tick-tock, tick-tock* of the old Fairbanks grandfather clock pulled me into the high-ceilinged living room with the floor-to-ceiling glass windows sweeping in a curve all along the far side. Across Lake Shore Drive, Lake Michigan sparkled under a cloudless blue sky. I felt lightheaded. I looked away.

"Wow," Denny said. Then, "Are you sure you want to be doing this, Gabby?"

I didn't answer, just started walking from room to room. Philip's den, his desk still cluttered, nothing packed . . . past the powder room on the way to the kitchen—everything fairly neat, except for a few dirty dishes in the sink . . . the dining room with its long, polished wood table, able to seat ten people . . . our Lenox wedding china—the Spring Vista pattern Marlene Fairbanks had picked out for us—still in the buffet . . .

Not a packing box in sight.

I stopped at the boys' bedrooms, side by side in the hallway leading toward the master bedroom, doors closed. Trembling, I reached out a hand and opened the door to Paul's room. The bunk bed was made up neat, but the desk and storage cubes held a jumble of CDs, action figures, games, the clothes in the closet askew . . .

The tightness in my chest squeezed so hard, I could hardly breathe. The last time I saw my sons, they'd been staying in this room together so my mother could sleep in P. J.'s room next door. When I left the house that day, I had no idea they'd be gone when I got home . . .

My breath started coming in big gulps, pain and anger rising from their hidden places like steel tendrils winding themselves around my heart. I was vaguely aware that Denny disappeared from my side, but the next minute he reappeared with a glass of water. "Gabby. Drink this. You need to sit down."

I took a couple of swallows. Then he led me to the breakfast nook in the kitchen and I sat down, my head in my hands. Jodi's husband sat opposite me. As my breath slowed, he said, "Gabby, you have every right to be here. In fact, if you want me to, I'll go get your mother and Dandy and you can move back in. But I think I should go . . . and Jodi's supposed to teach that class, remember?"

I heard the nervousness in his voice. Wasn't about Jodi's typing class either. Didn't blame him. If Philip came back right now, Denny's presence would be sorely misunderstood. Might even get ugly.

Stay? Oh, I was so tempted. I'd love for Philip to come back and find me and my mother and Dandy back in the penthouse, making ourselves at home, watching TV, soaking in the Jacuzzi, baking brownies . . .

Or would I be asking for the ugliness to start all over again? I couldn't do that to my mother—not to mention she'd flat-out refuse to come back to this house. My sweet mother could be as stubborn as a two-year-old.

Did I have the strength to face Philip alone? Mom and Dandy could stay at the shelter, and I could hunker down at the penthouse, demand my rights, lay claim to the furniture, the china, the family pictures—

"Gabby?" Denny's voice was gentle. "Your mom and Dandy are waiting in the car, and it's hot out there."

I stood up. I didn't have to make this decision right this second. I had the key. It opened the door.

But I left the water glass on the kitchen counter with my lipstick smudge.

chapter 25

Harry Bentley handed over the sewing machine on our way out of Richmond Towers but gave me a puzzled look. "What? No contraband?"

I offered a dry smile. "Not this time. But I left my calling card. Thanks, Mr. B."

When we came out of the revolving doors, we saw the mini-van had been moved to a visitor parking space. And the van was empty. "Jodi!" Denny yelled after loading the sewing machine in the back with our suitcases.

"Over here!" Jodi's voice shot back from somewhere in the park that lay between the frontage road and Lake Shore Drive in the distance, and a few moments later we saw Jodi, my mother, and Dandy making their way toward us along the jogging path—except that Jodi was having a hard time getting Dandy to cooperate. The dog kept pulling in the opposite direction, sometimes spinning her around. Denny belly laughed as the trio jerked their way toward us in stops and starts.

But we finally got my mom and Dandy in the car as Jodi collapsed in the front seat. "I don't know what happened!" she groaned. "The car was hot, so we got out and went looking for a bench . . . when all of a sudden Dandy went nuts! He darted off, and I had to run catch him; then he didn't want to come with me."

"It was Lucy," my mother announced.

I buckled her seat belt. "Uh-huh. Did you see her?"

My mother shook her head. "But it was Lucy."

"I don't know." Jodi shrugged as Denny pulled back out onto Sheridan Road. "*I* didn't see anybody."

I dropped it. Traffic was still heavy, but we finally drove under the Sheridan Road El station that crossed over the street a few blocks from Manna House. I glanced at my watch. "You're gonna make it, Jodi!" I sang out. "With a whole minute to spare!"

Denny rounded the corner by the Laundromat and slowed. "Uh-oh."

That pesky female reporter was hanging around the front steps of Manna House.

"Denny!" I hissed. "Back up and go around to the alley."

"Good idea—but if we back up now, she's going to guess we're the prey and run after us. I think it'd be best to just get it over with."

I was starting to panic. "But I don't want that reporter going after my mom. They don't know Dandy is her dog! But if they did, they'd start poking around and asking questions about why *she's* at the shelter—which could get messy for me real quick."

"Then you just go in with Dandy," Jodi said quickly. "We'll drive off, and nobody will follow us. We'll drive around the block and bring Martha and your stuff in the side door. Just make sure when you get inside to ask somebody to unlock it."

I hesitated only a nanosecond. "Okay. Come on, Dandy. Time to face the lions." I grabbed his leash as the car stopped. As quickly as I could, I opened the side door of the minivan, lifted Dandy to the ground, and walked him toward Manna House.

Immediately the reporter's voice began shouting at me. "Mrs. Fairbanks! Where has Dandy been?" The woman whipped out her cell phone. "Tony! Get your camera over here. Hero Dog is back . . . Mrs. Fairbanks! Will Dandy be staying at the shelter as official watchdog now? How did he happen to be at the shelter last weekend when—"

Even I didn't notice when the minivan pulled away.

"Girl, you too much! And I thought I had drama in my life!" Precious McGill tucked her beaded extensions under a white mesh hairnet and shook a bread knife at me from behind the kitchen counter. "When was you going to tell me about your mama's dog getting' sliced up last weekend—not to mention you an' she takin' up space on the bed list here, just like all the rest of us po' folks?" She stuck out her lip.

"Just give me a cup of coffee, Precious. Cream, no sugar. Please?"

"You go on, Drama Queen. I gotta brew a fresh pot."

Gratefully, I unlocked my office and sank into the desk chair. The plan had worked. Hoping to pacify the reporters, I'd smiled into the cameras and made pleasant, vague comments. Yes, Dandy was much better . . . Yes, he'd been voted the official Manna House watchdog, "but we'll see" . . . We were all grateful to Chicago citizens for the outpouring of sympathy, but getting back to normal would be the best thing for all concerned.

And then I'd ducked inside. Precious, who'd turned up to do Saturday lunch on Estelle's weekend off, had been standing in the foyer, and she ran downstairs to open the side door. "Gramma Shep" and Dandy had been immediately mobbed with a spontaneous "welcome back" celebration by the residents and taken to the multipurpose room to hold court.

Given all the hullabaloo, Jodi had given up on teaching her typing class, and she and Denny were on the verge of leaving when Josh and Edesa showed up with Gracie in a back carrier, offering to take a few of the older shelter kids to the Taste of Chicago. "Dad! Mom! Didn't know you'd be here," Josh crowed. "You wanna go to the Taste with us, help chaperone the kids? Let's see, who's going?" Sammy had jumped up and down, waving his hand, along with seven-year-old Trina and her six-year-old brother, Rufino, and Keisha, a bright-eyed girl of ten. "All riiight. That would make one kid per adult, plus Gracie." He'd beamed at his parents.

Even Edesa had laid it on thick. *"Por favor?* Like a family outing, *si?"*

Jodi knew the jig was up. Before they left, she'd given me a hug and murmured, "Invitation is still open. Think about it. And don't forget your name—'Strong Woman of God.' See you tomorrow for church?"

Now, waiting for Precious to deliver that much-needed shot of caffeine, I thought about Denny and Jodi . . . *Such nice folks.* And if Lucy didn't show up, I'd definitely lean on my mom to accept their hospitality for her and Dandy. But frankly, I was kind of relieved to leave the Baxter home. Their affectionate teasing dangled a working marriage in front of me but out of reach, like watching two lovers share a full-course meal in a fine restaurant while I stood outside the window by myself, stomach growling.

"Coffee!" Precious nudged my office door open and set down two cups of coffee, then plopped into the extra folding chair beside my desk. "Okay, no more stallin'. Whassup wit' you, girl? I want all the deets."

"Huh." I cradled the cup of hot, creamy coffee in two hands. "If I give you all the 'deets,' you'll never make lunch and we'll have a mutiny on our hands. How about the skinny version, and I'll fill you in later? Besides, I have a favor to ask you."

I'm sure Precious meant well as lunch volunteer. But bologna sandwiches on white bread—no lettuce—with mayo and mustard, potato chips, canned fruit cocktail, store-bought cookies, and a mysterious red juice that tasted like colored sugar water was definitely not in the tradition of Estelle Williams's yummy lunches. Funny thing, though. I heard no complaints from the residents, many of whom went back for seconds on those bald bologna sandwiches. Ugh.

Nutrition. I still needed to ask Edesa Baxter about doing a couple of workshops in nutrition. For everybody—not just the few in Estelle's cooking class on Thursdays. She'd be the perfect person since she was she getting her master's degree in public health.

On the pretext of taking my barely nibbled lunch into my office to work, I dumped it into the wastebasket and made a note to myself: *Ask Edesa—nutrition?*

Once the dish crew started cleanup, Precious joined me in the rec room since I'd asked her to help me decide what to do with all the dog food stacked under the Ping-Pong table, plus all the stuffed dogs, dog chews, and doggy toys we'd loaded into garbage bags last weekend. She surveyed the loot, hands on hips. "What's the problem? Keep some of the dog food for Dandy—whatchu need, three, four bags?—an' donate all the rest to the Humane Society or someplace like that. No, wait . . . I heard 'bout this group called Pet Supplies for Seniors. They give stuff free to old people who can't afford food for their pets. Call 'em up. I'm sure they'll send a truck or somethin'."

"Really? That's perfect." I held up a yellow stuffed dog with brown floppy ears. "But what about all these stuffed animals? I mean, we gave a few to the kids here at the shelter, but . . ." I swept my hand at all the garbage bags. "There must be at least a couple dozen more dogs here!"

"Keep 'em."

"What? I'm not *that* desperate for something to cuddle in my bed."

Precious cracked up. "Girl, I don't mean *you* keep 'em. I mean, store 'em someplace and give one to every kid who comes to the shelter with his or her mama, along with the basic kit. Somethin' of your own to love is lots more important than a new toothbrush to a kid who's been sleepin' in a car or just got evicted."

I liked her idea. But would Mabel? "Where in the world would we find room?"

"That, sister girl, is your problem. Look, I gotta go." Precious headed out the door of the rec room, and I followed. "Sabrina got an appointment at one o' them crisis pregnancy centers, an' I wanna make sure she goes. She kinda ridin' the fence about carryin' this baby. Pray for us, will ya, Miz Gabby?"

We paused just outside my office. Should I offer to pray with her now? Seemed like it might be the right thing to do, but—

"That your phone ringin'?" Precious darted inside my office, picked up the desk phone, listened, shrugged, and hung it up again.

"What? Oh, could be my cell." The ring was coming from a drawer in the file cabinet where I'd stored my shoulder bag. I still wasn't used to the ring on my new cell phone. My old one had the "William Tell Overture," which *always* got my attention. I finally found the phone and flipped it open, but the caller was gone.

And so was Precious.

Feeling a tad guilty that I'd let an opportunity to pray with Precious slip past me, I tapped my phone keys until I found Missed Calls. *Lee Boyer?* Why was he calling? I hit Call Back but realized I had no signal and didn't get one until I got outside on the front steps of Manna House. *Whew.* It was hot out here.

He answered on the first ring. "Lee Boyer."

Should I call him Lee? Still felt weird. I skipped it. "Hi! Gabby Fairbanks, returning your call. What's up?"

"Have you found an apartment yet?"

He was checking up on me? I tried to keep the irritation from my voice. "No. I—"

"Good. Because this real estate guy I know has an apartment for rent in a six-flat in the Wrigleyville area. Not too far from where you are now. Nice place, pretty nice area. Actually he's trying to sell the building, but that shouldn't be a problem. Buyers have to honor leases, and most are glad to keep current renters."

My irritation dissipated, replaced with . . . what? A warmth that somebody was looking out for me. "I need three bedrooms, you know." As long as my mother was with me, the boys would have to bunk up, but that's the way it was.

"That's what caught my attention. This building has both two- and three-bedroom apartments, but it's the three-bedroom on the first floor that's available. Plus it's only a couple of blocks from the Red Line—a real bonus if you don't have a car."

The first floor! No more dizzy moments just looking out the window from the thirty-second floor. As Lee Boyer spoke, I realized how overwhelmed I'd been feeling about trying to find a place to live. Where in the world would I start? I was still a Chicago tenderfoot. Could I find something big enough for me and the boys *and* my mom? And if I did, could I afford it? An actual apartment, recommended by someone who was in my corner . . . it felt almost too good to be true. "Sounds good. Could I take a look at it? Do I need to call somebody?"

"The old tenants are supposedly moving out today. But I think if I pushed, the owner would be willing to show it tomorrow, though it would still need cleaning, maybe some repairs. How about eleven? I could pick you up and take you there."

Pick me up? "Oh, Lee. You don't have to—"

"Don't mind at all. Not doing anything else. The sooner you get into an apartment, the sooner you can get your boys back. I think I've got the address of the shelter . . . See you at eleven, then."

Only after the call ended did I realize that tomorrow was Sunday. Eleven o'clock meant I couldn't take Mom to church at SouledOut.

chapter 26

My mom's face clouded when I told her the news. "But we have to go to church, Gabby. It's Sunday."

"Mom! It's just this once. My lawyer wants me to look at an apartment near here. It's important!" Did she just call me Gabby? Well, hallelujah.

"But does it have to be eleven? Couldn't you make an appointment in the afternoon?"

I tried not to roll my eyes. Actually, I'd thought of that myself after Lee hung up. Sounded like he'd just pulled eleven o'clock out of the air. But I was chicken to call him back and change the appointment. What would I tell him? *Oh, I forgot, can't do eleven; gotta go to church.* Which obviously wasn't on his agenda. Would he think I was some fundy chick?

"I'm sorry, Mom. Just this once. And they have church Sunday evenings here at Manna House, did you know that?" Couldn't remember what church group was scheduled for tomorrow, but I'd check it out.

Mom was slightly mollified by the idea that church would come to *her* . . . and by the time a youth group from Wheaton arrived at five o'clock with the makings for a taco salad supper and sides of beans and rice, I'd called the Pet Support for Seniors people and arranged for a pickup on Monday of the dog food, chews, and toys. The woman on the phone went all gaga when she realized Dandy, the "Hero Dog" of Manna House Women's Shelter, was making this donation. I barely got her off the phone.

I was antsy to call the boys. Still had time. Supper wasn't until six—but it was already six in Virginia. I had wanted to call all day but realized I'd been putting it off. Was Philip there visiting P. J. and Paul? The idea churned in my stomach. If he was, that was good . . . in a way. Would show he cared about them. They needed their dad. But they'd wonder why I hadn't come too. Would they think I didn't want to? Was too busy to make the trip? Should I tell them their father had put a lock on my finances?

Oh God, I don't want to put my boys in the middle of our mess . . .

I grabbed my cell, scurried to the main floor, and slipped outside into the warm, humid air. Several shelter guests were lounging on the front steps, having a smoke. I walked halfway down the block until I got a good, strong signal on my cell. So far, so good. No reporters lurking about.

Philip's mother answered the phone. Just my luck. "Hello, Marlene," I said evenly. "May I speak to P. J. or Paul? Actually, both."

"I'm sorry, Gabrielle. The boys are out."

And . . . ? Out where? With whom? My insides screamed, *Would it hurt to give me a little more information, mother-in-law dear?!*

I let a few beats go by while I calmed down. But I blatantly fished. "With their father?"

"With their fa— . . . with Philip? Why do you ask?"

A simple yes or no would've been nice. "He's out of town this weekend. I thought he might be visiting the boys." I loaded up my tone with sugar.

For a moment, her end of the line was silent. Then . . . "No, he's not here."

Philip isn't there? So where . . . ? The funny thing was, Marlene Fairbanks sounded startled. And offended. I wanted to laugh. The woman didn't *know* her precious Philip was out of town! Worse, he hadn't told her where he was going. Oh! I could almost hear her nose cracking out of joint over the phone.

I let Philip dangle. "So when will the boys be back? I'd like to talk to them."

"They'll be late tonight. Try tomorrow. Good-bye, Gabrielle." The line went dead.

I would've been more teed off at her rudeness, except I couldn't help but enjoy knowing Marlene didn't know any more than I did about Philip's whereabouts.

But I could take a good guess. The Horseshoe Casino in Indiana. With Henry and Mona Fenchel, who'd—

"Hey! What time ya got, Fuzz Top? Anybody take that dog out yet since ya been back this mornin'? No, 'course not. Don't know why I bother ta ask. Just wanna know if I got time 'fore supper."

I grinned as Lucy Tucker, purple knit hat perched on her head, wrestled her overloaded cart up the front steps of Manna House. "Hey yourself, Lucy. I know somebody inside who'll be mighty glad to see you."

I kicked off my sheet and sat up, careful not to bonk my head on the bunk above me. Odd. My watch already said six thirty. What happened to the usual six o'clock wake-up bell? Did they actually let the residents sleep in on Sunday morning?

I peered around the dimly lit room. The four bunks were full, top and bottom—me, my mom, Lucy, and Tanya on the bottom bunks, Tanya's boy, Sammy, above her, plus three more new lumps on the top bunks who'd been put on the bed list this past week. Must be the sweltering heat driving them in. Had hit ninety-plus yesterday.

Sliding off my bunk slowly to avoid the inevitable squeaks, I pulled on a pair of running shorts and a T-shirt, stuck my feet in my slippers, and fished under my bed for my jute carryall bag with the leather handles. Since I wasn't going to church this morning, maybe I could find someplace to read my Bible since I'd started reading the gospel of Matthew again yesterday. *Huh.* Was I just feeling guilty? Okay, maybe a little. But I really did want to find a quiet place to read and think and pray.

Dandy raised his head from the dog bed the Baxters had given him as I opened the bunk-room door, but laid it back down again as if saying, *Following you around is too much effort.* Poor dog. He still wasn't completely healed.

I slipped down the stairs to the main floor, wondering where to go. Could go to my office, but that felt too much like work . . . The chapel! Of course. It was easy to forget the small prayer room tucked behind the multipurpose room—especially since you had to pass the TV room, schoolroom, and toddler playroom first.

But this morning I peeked into the small room, with its several rows of padded folding chairs, a small lectern, and a kneeling prayer bench . . . *Drat.* Somebody was there already. I started to back out when the person turned—Liz Handley, the former director of Manna House, who'd shown up last night to do weekend night staff duty. "Gabby? Don't leave. I'm done here. Gotta go start breakfast now anyway. Wake-up bell's at seven thirty." The short woman with the mannish haircut gave me a friendly pat on the shoulder as she passed and shut the door behind her.

Well, okay. Guess I hadn't really chased her out.

I settled into a padded chair on the front row. The tiny prayer chapel didn't have the benefit of the stained-glass windows that graced the front of the building and spilled prisms of tinted light into the foyer. But warm lights of various colors embedded in the ceiling—yellow, green, rose—created a quiet mood. For several long moments, I just sat, not really thinking. Just soaking up the sense of peace.

"Come to Me . . ."

Whoa. There it was again. Jesus' words from the passage I'd read weeks ago in Matthew's gospel. The last time that Voice had tugged at my spirit with those words was the night I couldn't sleep and Dandy ended up foiling our would-be robber.

A week ago.

Okay, okay, I'm here, God. I opened my Bible and found the place I'd left off reading in Matthew's gospel, chapter 13. Oh yeah. The parable of the sower. I remembered this story from Sunday school days. Jesus telling a story about a farmer who sowed some seed. Some of it fell on the hard path, and the birds ate it . . . some seed fell on rocky ground, so it only had shallow roots . . . some seed fell among thorns and got choked when it came up . . . and some seed fell on good ground and produced a big crop.

Never really thought much about this parable. After all, people who believed in Jesus were the seed that fell on good ground, right? Been there, done that, end of story. But today I had the same question the disciples did. *What does this mean?*

I read and reread Jesus' answer. The seed was the Word of God. *Got that much.* The hard ground was like people who didn't understand it, so it never took root. *Okay, got that too.* The seed that fell on rocky places were like people who embraced God's Word at first, but when trouble came, it died, because their faith was shallow . . .

Ouch. Kinda like me when Damien dumped me, back when I was nineteen. I'd been a Christian up till then—thought I was, anyway. But at the first big bump in the road, my faith was too shallow to survive.

I kept reading. Thorns next . . . Jesus said the thorns were all the worries of this life, choking the Word of God. He said the "deceitfulness of wealth" did that too.

Oh brother. This parable had my name all over it. I'd let Fairbanks money cushion me from the pitfalls of life—until now. Huh. Always thought I didn't really care about money, but I'd let its comforts and expectations blind me to the way it'd been eating away at my marriage, numbing the person I was inside.

Or maybe, keeping me from knowing the person God wanted me to be. *Gabrielle, strong woman of God.*

I leaned forward, elbows on my knees, chin on my hands, and sat that way a long time . . .

Somewhere on the floor above, the wake-up bell was ringing. Seven thirty.

But I still didn't move. Funny that I'd found God again at a homeless shelter, of all places. Of course, if I really thought

215

about it, God was always showing up in unlikely places. Jesus, the long-awaited Messiah—the Son of God!—had been born in a drafty, smelly cow barn, which certainly didn't look good on *His* résumé. At least I got to sleep in a room with actual people.

Except . . . if I was honest with myself, my budding faith was still choking on all my worries. Even though the prayers of the Yada Yada sisters had buoyed me up last weekend, I hadn't taken much time to pray since then. Really pray, I mean. Or listen. Most of my prayers were still talking *at* God. I let my mind get so garbled, wrestling with all my problems, that God would prob-ably need a sledgehammer to get my attention—

Oh.

Okay, God, I get it! Back off, already!

Lucy had just snapped the leash on Dandy's collar for a morn-ing walk when Lee Boyer pulled up in front of Manna House in a black Prius. "Just a sec!" I called out, and turned back to Lucy. "Just . . . try to keep Dandy out of sight as much as possible. Alleys or whatever. Those reporters, you know."

The old lady gave me a look. "Don't ya think I know a thing or two 'bout keepin' outta sight?" She craned her neck to look into the car. "Who's that?" Her eyes narrowed. "Not that slime-ball husband o' yours, I hope."

"My lawyer, Lucy. We have an appointment." I decided not to say anything about looking for an apartment. She'd been mutter-ing not-so-subtle digs ever since she showed up yesterday about how we'd "up and left her" last weekend. "Thanks again for walk-ing Dandy."

I opened the car door and slid into the leather passenger seat.

"Ohh, nice." I glanced at Lee behind the wheel. His usual business attire of blue jeans and boots had given way to khaki shorts and sturdy sandals. "Don't know what I was expecting, but not such a high-tech car."

He let slip a shy grin. "Hey. When gas went over three bucks a gallon last year, I figured I'd get smart and get one of these hybrids. You all set?" He touched a button. No sound . . . until he stepped on the gas and pulled into the street.

For some reason, I was totally self-conscious of my black-and-white floral print skirt skimming my knees, freshly shaved legs—I had to sign up for the tub—and white wedgie sandals. Lee hadn't commented on what I was wearing, but was that an approving glance as I got in the car? I wished I could flip down the mirror on the visor and check my makeup once more. At least my mop head was behaving after my haircut last week.

Down, Gabby, down. Good grief. I was still a married woman. Should have worn slacks.

It seemed as if we'd only been driving for five minutes when Lee turned into a tree-lined two-way residential street and backed into a parking space. I got out and looked up and down the street. Mostly large U-shaped apartment buildings, three stories high, the kind with a courtyard with small plots of neatly cut grass and well-tended flower beds behind an iron fence. "This way," Lee said. He headed down the sidewalk and stopped in front of a narrower building—a three-story brick with a set of apartments running up either side of an entryway door. Six apartments. To my surprise, each one had an enclosed sunporch jutting out on either side of the steps leading up to the entryway door. A For Sale sign was posted in front of the six-flat next to the sidewalk.

I followed Lee up the short flight of steps, as he pulled open

217

the glass-paned door. We stepped into the tiled entryway, and Lee poked the doorbell for 1-B. A moment later the inside door buzzer bleated, allowing us access into a small foyer. Carpeted stairs rose in front of us with a door to the left and one to the right; 1-B must be the one on the right.

Sure enough, the right door opened and a thin man with an angular face waved us in. "How ya doin', Lee?" He ran a hand through his mousy hair. "Place is more of a mess than I figured, but . . . you insisted." He shrugged. "Look around. Give me two weeks and it'll be in a lot better shape."

We walked through the apartment. I could see what he meant. Trash had been left behind in some of the rooms. Walls needed painting. The wood floors were scuffed. The stove and refrigerator in the kitchen at the back needed a good scrubbing. But I was dazzled by the high ceilings and wooden beams in the living room and dining room. It felt so spacious! Doorways and windows were framed in dark wood. And the wraparound windows on the sunporch captured mottled sunlight coming through the trees along the parkway. I peeked out the windows. The postage-stamp front yard and the sidewalk were a comfortable six feet down.

And three bedrooms with decent closets. I closed my eyes, trying to imagine the apartment filled with the happy noises of my two sons. *Could this be—?*

"It's a classic." I opened my eyes. Lee was grinning. "Could look real nice."

I swallowed. "How much?"

"Thirteen hundred a month."

And just that fast, my hopes plunged in a nosedive.

chapter 27

I got in the Prius and slammed the car door. "Lee Boyer! What are you thinking! I can't afford thirteen hundred a month."

"Easy, Gabby. Let's talk about it over lunch—Kitsch'n makes omelets to die for." He started the car with that push-button thing and pulled out.

Lee must have taken my silence for assent, because he parked a few minutes later, and we walked to a small retro restaurant that had sidewalk seating. We picked a tiny table-for-two and ordered omelets from their "Kitsch'n Sunday Brunch" menu.

Time to launch my disappointment. "Okay, guess I'm gullible. Why I thought this apartment would be a slam-dunk, I don't know. Maybe because my *lawyer* suggested it? You know my situation, Lee, know I have next to nothing. So why get my hopes up?"

"Did you like it?"

"Yes, I liked it! I mean, as far as apartments go. I'd rather have a house out in the burbs, where my kids could ride their bikes in the street, but since my reality right now doesn't include a *house* . . ." I realized I was glaring at him. "But 'liking' is beside the point. I can't afford it."

Lee leaned forward, eyes serious behind those wire rims. "I know you can't afford it—right now, anyway. But once we take your husband to court, you'll have a nice hunk of change. Thirteen hundred a month? No sweat. What do you think he's paying for that penthouse?"

I shook my head. "Lee. You don't get it. You told me yourself that could take awhile. I need an apartment *now.* I need to get my boys back here by August so I can enroll them in school. If I don't, they'll start the school year at George Washington Prep in Virginia and . . ." I grabbed a napkin and pressed it to my eyes. I did *not* want to cry in front of Lee Boyer.

I felt his hand on my arm. "Gabby. Listen. I showed you that apartment because that's what you're going to need to bring your boys here. Family-size apartment. Decent neighborhood. Not upscale, but decent. You don't *want* to live in an apartment you can 'afford' right now, believe me. You need to be thinking long-term."

I took the napkin off my eyes and blew my nose with it. "So what do I do? What about that housing subsidy you mentioned in your office—oh."

Our omelets arrived. Lee busied himself buttering hot corn bread and digging into his spinach omelet. For some reason I missed thanking God for the food—even though I'd long lost the habit after I married Philip. But it always touched me at Manna House—women who had nothing were actually grateful they had some food on their plate. Wimp that I was, I sent up an unspoken *Thank You* and dug into my omelet too. *Mmm.* Rich, moist, and cheesy. Hadn't realized how hungry I was. Cold cereal that morning and day-old pastry donated by a local bakery hadn't stayed with me long.

After a few bites Lee pointed his fork at me. "Yes, you could apply for a housing subsidy. The Housing Choice Voucher Program—used to be called Section 8—is actually a wait-list lottery. Which means, even if you qualify, your name might get pulled or not—though thousands of names each year do get vouchers."

"Like how many 'thousands'?"

"Thirty-five . . . forty."

"Oh." That sounded hopeful.

"And there are some other subsidy programs. But there might be another option, Gabby—especially with time being an issue." Lee laid down the fork. "Have you asked your mother if she can help cover the rent?"

I stopped chewing. "My mother?" I quickly swallowed the bite I was working on.

He nodded. "Weren't you looking for a retirement home or assisted living for her here in the Chicago area a couple of weeks ago? How were you going to pay for that?"

"Well, her money, of course, but—"

"How is this different? She stays with you. She can keep her dog—something she couldn't do at the places you looked at. She pays her share of the rent." Lee lifted his eyebrows at me and smiled.

"Hey, Gabby. Wanna play some Scrabble?" Carolyn caught me as I came through the multipurpose room after Lee dropped me off. In spite of it being the weekend, the room was fairly full of women just sitting, a few sleeping, several playing cards—and Hannah doing Wanda's nails.

"Would love to, Carolyn—another time, though. Got something I have to do." I spied my mother dozing in a chair with Dandy at her feet. "Try my mom—but watch out. She might beat you."

I slipped downstairs to my office. I needed someplace quiet so I could think about Lee's idea. The apartment wasn't on the market yet, he said, so I had a few days to think about it. But it made sense . . . didn't it? Still, there were some things I needed to check out.

I booted up my computer and spent the next couple of hours surfing the Net for private schools in Chicago. I had tried calling several weeks ago—before my husband decided his life would be better "unencumbered" by me—and had gotten the usual answer. "Registration is closed" or "Would you like to be on the waiting list?" Philip hadn't seemed concerned, assuming the boys would just go back to Petersburg. But it wouldn't hurt to get on some of those waiting lists. And what about public schools? Some were college-prep and magnet schools. Did any of the high schools offer lacrosse? That would be a big draw for P. J.

By the time the supper bell rang, I had a long list of schools to call, including magnet schools with a variety of fine arts emphasis, language immersion, math and science specialties, classical education, global perspective, and interdisciplinary studies. I'd better add more minutes to my cell phone.

Lucy decided Dandy *had* to go out just as folks from New Hope Missionary Baptist Church showed up to lead Sunday Evening Praise. Well, resident participation was voluntary, so I didn't say anything. I introduced my mother to Pastor Clyde

Stevens—"One of our board members," I said, smiling and shaking his hand, wondering if Mabel had filled in the board on my "adverse" circumstances. It wasn't every day a staff member ended up on the bed list. But the pastor didn't say anything about it, just proudly introduced his hugely pregnant wife to my mother as "Lady Sarah." The attractive Mrs. Stevens—glowing brown skin, hair straightened and worn short like a black cap, large gold loop earrings—looked ready to pop, but she still managed to corral three young boys all dressed in pint-size suits and ties. "Joseph! Joshua! Come here now and shake hands with Mrs. Fairbanks and Mrs. Shepherd. You too, Jeremiah! Uh-huh. I'm talking to you, young man!"

My mother beamed. "That's sweet. All Bible names." *Right.* This from a lady who'd named her daughters Celeste, Honor, and Gabrielle.

Precious waved at me and tipped her chin in the direction of her daughter, Sabrina, who looked like she'd rather be having a root canal. Mabel breezed in, trailed by her nephew C. J. The boy hunched his slender shoulders inside a Bears hoodie sweatshirt, the hood up. My heart squeezed. Had I been praying for him since his suicide attempt? No. All caught up in my own "drama," as Precious would say.

Oh, God, forgive me for being so self-centered. Help me to—

"Sister Gabby!" Edesa Baxter snuck up behind me and gave me a one-armed hug, Gracie riding on her hip. "*Hola,* Gramma Shep." She hugged my mother too. Then she plonked the Hispanic baby in my arms. "Can you hold Gracie a few minutes? Josh needs help setting up more chairs." She bustled off to help her young husband. I couldn't help grinning. The three of them looked like chocolate, vanilla, and maple cream.

Maple Cream looked up at me soberly with her dark eyes as if trying to decide if I was safe . . . and then grabbed a handful of my chestnut curls. "Aha, I knew it, you rascal." I tried to untangle her fist from my hair as a trio of African-American young men opened up the meeting, one on an electronic keyboard, another mastering a set of large bongo drums, and the third bouncing back and forth at the front of the circle of chairs, encouraging us, "Come on, come on, people! We're here to praise the *Lord*!"

New Hope had brought overheads for the words to the worship songs this time, which helped me a lot. After a few lively rounds of "Shout to the Lord" and "We Bring a Sacrifice of Praise," my mother poked me. "Don't they sing any hymns?"

Maybe she thought she had to talk loudly over the music, but she happened to speak up just as the music faded, and her voice carried. Half the residents snickered. I hid my face behind Gracie in my arms. But the young man up front, mopping the sweat from his face with a small towel, called out with a wide grin. "What hymn would you like to sing, Mother? We'll sing it just for you."

My mother got flustered, but someone else piped up, "How 'bout ''Tis So Sweet to Trust in Jesus'?" Mom nodded and smiled as the electronic keyboard gently led into the old familiar words. "'Tis so sweet to trust in Jesus, just to take Him at His Word . . ." A few of the residents sniffled as the chorus finished with "Oh for grace to trust Him more."

The words niggled at me. Was I really trusting Jesus about that apartment? About getting my sons back? How did one get that "grace" to trust Him more?

As the notes of the chorus died away, I remembered it was this group that had introduced me to the gospel song "I Go to the

Rock." Josh Baxter had actually found a CD with the song on it and had given it to me. A CD that'd been missing for two weeks, I reminded myself. But if New Hope was taking requests, maybe they'd sing it—

Too late. Pastor Stevens got up and, to my surprise, introduced his wife as tonight's speaker. "My queen, the First Lady of New Hope Missionary Baptist, Lady Sarah." All the residents clapped. A few hooted, "All right! All right, now!"

The pastor had a twinkle in his eye. "I hope you're clapping because you're going to hear this anointed woman of God speak—and not because *I'm* not."

Everybody laughed.

Mrs. Stevens—it was a little hard thinking of her as "Lady Sarah"—seemed comfortable behind the music stand that served as a lectern. "Praise the Lord, church!"

Several of the residents hollered, "Praise the Lord!" right back at her.

"How many people want that old devil to get off your back?"

"Now you're talkin'!" . . . "Preach it, sister!" I recognized Precious.

"Now, you all know John 3, verse 16, right? 'For God so loved the world . . .'" Several people joined in and finished the familiar verse. "But, ladies, I want to talk about the next verse. 'For God did not come into the world to *condemn* the world . . .' *God* isn't looking to condemn us for how we've messed up. No, God wants to set us *free* from that mess! But how many of you know, that's exactly what Satan is busy doing all day, all night, whispering in our ears, 'You bad. You no good. Look at you! You're just one big failure.'"

The room got very quiet.

"Or maybe he's sayin', 'Girl, you've been givin' it out on the street so long, *nobody* gon' want *you*. You're just damaged goods.' That's condemnation, sisters. Oh, that first part might be true. You've sinned. *I've* sinned. We've all sinned. Scripture is clear about that. Sin is sin and needs to be cleaned up. But *conviction*, my sisters, is different than *condemnation*. The Holy Spirit says, 'Don't carry that sin around anymore. Let me wash you clean and set you free. I made you beautiful! Don't wallow in that muck anymore.' When the Holy Spirit convicts you of your sin, it's because God wants to free you from its clutches, pick you up, and set your feet dancing!"

The young man on the keyboard played a few notes, and shouts of "Thank You!" and "Praise Jesus!" filled the room.

"All right, all right, I'm almost done here," said Lady Sarah. "Let me read you one more verse from Romans, chapter 8. 'There is therefore now *no condemnation* to them which are in Christ Jesus, who walk not after the flesh, but after the Spirit. For the law of the Spirit of life in Christ Jesus has made me free from the law of sin and death.'" She looked up, tears spilling down her cheeks. "Oh, sisters. Don't let that old devil keep you down with his condemnation. Listen to the Holy Spirit, who wants you to let go of all that old baggage, be washed in the blood of Jesus, and be *free*! Oh, glory!"

Pastor Stevens jumped up and helped his pregnant wife into a chair as the praise leader led into a song, something about being "washed in the blood of the Lamb." But I didn't even hear the words. Because as Lady Sarah spoke, I realized she'd given me the answer to my riddle—what the difference was between what Denny Baxter had done, asking forgiveness for a sin he didn't commit, and the times I'd apologized and said I was sorry when Philip accused me of stuff.

Philip's blaming made me feel condemned.

While what Denny had done had set both him and his accuser free.

chapter 28

Pastor Stevens and his wife stayed afterward to pray for a few of the residents. I noticed Lady Sarah praying for Sabrina, who was sobbing into a paper towel someone had stuffed into her hand, while Precious sat close by, praying in agreement with what was going on.

Gracie had fallen asleep in my arms. "Pray for me," I whispered to Edesa as I handed her the sleeping child. "I think I found an apartment. Just can't afford it."

"Oh, *muy bien!*" Her eyes danced, then faded. "Pray that we find an apartment too. Same problem. No money."

"Did you guys apply for a housing subsidy? Section 8 or whatever?"

Edesa grimaced. "Josh is too proud. But I'm *this* close to wrapping his pride around his neck." She lifted her eyes heavenward. "*Lo siento, Señor Dios!*"

I still had to call my boys, so I sat out on the front steps with my cell phone. Lucy came down the sidewalk with Dandy as the last New Hope people were leaving. "Nice timing, Lucy," I teased, holding open the door for her.

"Humph. He walks slow, case ya haven't noticed."

Almost eight thirty. Mom was visibly tired and complaining of another headache. I talked her into using the service elevator to the bunk room floor rather than the stairs. "For Dandy's sake," I said. Should I ask about the apartment? Maybe tell her about it, give her time to think it over?

Tanya came into the bunk room to put Sammy to bed while I was tucking my mother in. "There'd be room for P. J. and Paul, *and* Dandy and me?" Mom said.

"Yes," I whispered, wishing we were still alone.

My mother sighed . . . or was that a groan? Her head must still be hurting. I tiptoed out of the room and used the bathroom. When I came out, Tanya was curled up in one of the chairs in the small second-floor lounge, arms covering her head.

"Tanya? Are you okay?"

Her answer was muffled, and I realized she was crying. I pulled up another chair. "What's wrong?"

The young mother just shook her braided head and rocked for a few minutes, then took the tissue I handed her and blew her nose. "Are you . . . are you an' . . . Gramma Shep movin' out? I mean, didja find a place ta live?"

So that was it. "Found a place. Not sure we can afford it, though."

The tears came fresh. "Oh, Miss Gabby. Don't know what I'm gonna do. You got a place, Carolyn's got a place—"

"Carolyn?" How did I not know that?

"Yeah, yeah. Over at Deborah's Place. One o' them studios. Her name came up—she been waitin' almost a year. But she ain't got no kids. But me an' Sammy . . ."

I wrapped my arms around the girl and just let her cry. What could I say? As bad as my situation was, I had more options than Tanya did. If my mom had the money to help with the rent, we'd be out of there faster than Lucy's disappearing act. And, Lee Boyer assured me, once my court case came up, I could soak Philip's assets. One way or the other, my homelessness—and hopefully, my financial straits—were temporary.

But what about Tanya? And Precious, about to lose *her* apartment?

I got up, got another paper towel, and wet it in the bathroom sink. My reflection nodded at me from the mirror, like we were having a conversation. *So, Gabby, you're having a staff meeting tomorrow. Why don't you suggest that Manna House get an apartment building and do subsidized housing for moms with kids? . . . Huh. I tried once. Mabel pretty much shot it down. Way too expensive . . . But would it hurt to explore the idea? There have to be buildings for sale in this neighborhood—like the building you looked at today. Wasn't it for sale—?*

I felt my skin prickle.

Yeah, right. How much would a building like that cost. Half a mil? More?

I stared at the woman with the curly chestnut "mop" in the bathroom mirror and sighed. Who was I to get on some bandwagon about affordable housing? For the past fifteen years I'd managed my monthly household allowance—period. I let Mr. Big handle everything else—and look where that got me. Nowhere. Just like Tanya.

Except . . . Tanya had one thing I didn't have. I took the damp paper towel back to the girl to wipe her face. "At least you've got Sammy with you," I murmured. "He's a great kid."

I was floating a couple of inches off the floor when I headed for the staff meeting the next morning, eager to share my news. Mom's headache seemed to be gone when she woke, so I'd put the question to her. Would she be willing to share the rent for an apartment with me and the boys? "And Dandy?" she'd said. "Of course, Celeste."

Hopefully getting my name mixed up with my older sister didn't negate her positive answer. I'd called Aunt Mercy to check on Mom's Social Security and monthly annuity to be sure our two incomes could float the rent for a while. What I'd do when Mom's name came up for the assisted-living retirement home back in Minot was another "if." I couldn't take her money then.

Well, we'd jump that fissure in the plan when we got to it.

Coming into the schoolroom, I was surprised to see Peter Douglass along with the usual staff—Stephanie Cooper, Angela Kwon, Estelle Williams, Liz Handley, and Sarge. Mabel said Peter was there as president of the board. Some of the long-term volunteers—Josh Baxter, Precious McGill, and Delores Enriques, the nurse—filed in too.

Mabel started the meeting with a prayer of thanks for all God was doing at Manna House, and a few others jumped in with their own thanksgivings. I still wasn't used to this conversational-type prayer, where people talked like God was sitting with the rest of us in the circle. Didn't mean I didn't like it. I added my own silent *Thanks*.

Then Mabel got down to business. "Peter, would you like to present our first update?" A small smile played around the corners of her mouth, softening her brisk demeanor.

The African-American businessman rubbed his hands together like a kid about to dive into a chocolate cake. "You bet! As all of you know, our little incident with the intruder and Mrs. Shepherd's dog got us quite a bit of media attention a week ago." He looked over at me. "By the way, how is Dandy doing, Gabby?"

"Coming along. A little stiff. Supposed to get the stitches out on Wednesday."

"That's good. Anyway, as most of you know, it also generated some unexpected contributions . . . which have continued to come in."

Murmurs went around the circle. Last Monday Mabel had said around two thousand. Had it doubled?

Peter was grinning. He wore middle age well. Touches of gray above his ears, always in a suit and tie. I'd always thought he and Avis, who'd led the Yada Yada Prayer Group when I was there, made a handsome couple. Somebody said they'd only been married a couple of years, a second marriage for her after her first husband died of cancer.

"We don't know what the final tally will be," he was saying. "These things tend to taper off pretty quickly when the story gets old. But right now, Dandy's Fund, as we're calling it, has a little over ten thousand dollars—"

"Ten thousand!" A cheer went up. "Hallelujah!" "Praise Jesus!"

I was stunned. Right away my mind started clicking.

". . . so the board decided to act on a request that came to our attention recently, to get a fifteen-passenger van to assist our program director in—"

"Wait!"

All eyes turned on me. "Yes, Gabby?" Mabel said.

"Uh . . . uh . . . I know I requisitioned a van. Didn't really think we'd *get* one, but—"

Laughter tripped around the room. "Know whatchu sayin'," Precious hooted. "Guess the age of miracles ain't past!"

I barreled on. "But can we talk about this a little more? I mean, ten thousand dollars?! Maybe we should use it on something more substantial, like buying another building, a six-flat or something, you know, to develop some second-stage housing for moms with kids—like Tanya and Sammy, who shouldn't be staying in emergency housing for months on end, or—"

"Whoa. Slow down, Gabby." Peter Douglass frowned. "Another *building*? It took us two years to raise the funds to rebuild this one!" He spread his hands out. "I can appreciate the idea, but these contributions don't constitute that kind of funding."

"But—"

Liz Handley, the former director, jumped in. "I like Gabby's vision. I think we'd all like to see more options for homeless moms with kids . . ."

Thank you, Rev. Handley.

". . . but Peter's right. Minimum down payment on property is at least 5 percent. With ten thousand down . . ." Liz squinted, as if mentally running numbers in her head. "Biggest mortgage we could get would be $200,000." She shrugged and shook her head. "Don't think we could find even a two-flat for that. And then there'd be monthly payments."

I pressed my lips together. For one skinny moment, I'd thought we could give Tanya some hope.

"Now a van . . ." Peter Douglass eased his grin back into the fray. "Ten thousand won't buy a brand-new one, but I'm sure we can find a good used one for that."

Heads nodded all around, and Mabel moved on to the next item on her agenda. I sighed. I should be grateful. Really I should. After all, I was the one who sent a requisition to the board. With a van, I could take residents to the museums, plan trips to special events in the city, like the Taste . . .

"Wait!"

Mabel rolled her eyes. "Gabby!"

Precious guffawed. Estelle covered her mouth.

"I'm sorry to interrupt, it's just . . . is there any chance we could get that van today? I mean, tomorrow's July Fourth, and it's the last day of the Taste of Chicago. With a van I could take some of the residents and . . . what?"

Polite chuckles had turned to outright laughter. "Now, that *would* be a miracle," Sarge snorted.

Josh Baxter came to my rescue. "Even if we had a van today, you don't want to drive to the Taste, Mrs. Fairbanks. It's a parking nightmare. Take the El."

"But on Saturday . . . didn't you—?"

"Nope. We took the kids on the El and picked up my folks' minivan later." The young man grinned. "That's okay. It takes awhile to get used to Chicago."

Mabel gave me the eye. "We appreciate your enthusiasm, Gabby. Sounds like a plan. But can we move on now?"

"Okay." My head jerked up at a familiar sound. "Wait . . ."

"Gabby!" Several voices chimed together.

I held up a hand. "No, I mean it. Listen."

The room quieted . . . and then we all heard it. Dandy barking. Angry voices. I sprang for the door, pulled it open, and ran down the hall and into the multipurpose room. A knot of resident women were clustered at the open doors leading into the foyer, fussing at the top of their lungs. Pushing through them, I saw two muscular police officers, one black, one white, with blue shirts and black bulletproof vests standing in the foyer. The black officer had Dandy's leash, while the white officer held Lucy's arm in a tight grip as the old woman struggled to pull her arm away, muttering every curse word she could think of. Dandy barked and growled, while several voices behind me complained, "Leave 'er alone" and "Dumb cops," in loud voices.

"What's going on?" I demanded, startling myself with my sharp tone.

The black cop stepped up. "You in charge here, lady?"

"No. But that's my dog. What's the problem?"

The man looked down at Dandy. "Is this the Hero Dog we've been hearing about on TV?"

"Some people call him that. Is there a problem?"

The two officers cast a quick glance at each other. "Depends. We saw this, uh, derelict person here with the dog, and she tried gettin' away from us. We thought maybe she was stealing the dog. We brought them here in the squad car to check it out."

Lucy jerked her arm from the officer's grip. "I *tol'* these uniforms I'm jus' walkin' the dog, but they treatin' me like some two-bit looter, hoofin' it with hot loot."

I took the leash from the officer and handed it to Lucy. "She's right. Lucy is Dandy's caregiver."

The two officers squirmed. "So why'd she run, then?"

Mabel, followed by Peter Douglass and several other staff, now pushed through the knot at the double doors. "I'm the director of Manna House. Is there a problem, Officer?"

Grateful to be let off the hook, I laid a comforting hand on Lucy's shoulder. The old lady angrily shrugged it off and marched toward the multipurpose room with Dandy at her heels. The crowd in the doorway parted like the Red Sea, then closed after them.

The front door buzzer blatted. Good grief, it was like a zoo in the foyer. I tried to duck out, but someone yelled, "Somebody askin' for Mrs. Fairbanks!"

What *now*? Two strangers stood on the front steps, looking bewildered as the two policemen passed them. Beyond them I could see a van that said Pet Support for Seniors on the side. "Oh! Come on in. This is great. Hope it all fits in your van."

Rounding up some of the residents to help, I showed the Pet Support people where the donated dog food was stored, and they set to work. As I went back through the multipurpose room, I saw Lucy refilling Dandy's food and water dishes, which had been moved temporarily so he wouldn't have to go up and down so many stairs.

I detoured to their corner. "Lucy? Are you all right?"

"Humph," she muttered. "You the one tol' me to avoid all them reporters and people makin' a fuss over Dandy."

"I know." I hadn't meant she should run from the police, but I bit my lip.

"Them cops always pickin' on homeless folks. 'Can't be here.' 'Can't go there either.' 'Don't bother people.' 'Just go 'way.'"

"I'm so sorry, Lucy. They don't know you like we do."

Dandy finished his water, then laid down on the floor with a *whumph*. Lucy looked sideways at me from under her purple knit hat. "That true what you said?"

"What I said?"

"Yeah. 'Bout me being Dandy's caregiver."

I grinned. "True. Don't know what my mom and I would do without you." And this time she didn't push me away when I gave her a hug.

chapter 29

I waved as the Pet Support people pulled away from the curb with their van full of dog food. If I hurried, I might catch the rest of the staff meeting. Just needed to put the donation receipt on Mabel's desk—

But Mabel was back in her office.

"Everybody gone? Yikes. Sorry. Guess I missed the rest of the meeting." I handed her the receipt. "But at least all that dog stuff got taken care of—except for the cuddle toys. Precious suggested we keep those for kids who end up at the shelter with their mothers."

Mabel rubbed her forehead. "Mm. And which bunk room have you filled up with Pluto and Snoopy?"

"Uh, well, right now they're in my office. Still looking for an extra closet . . . oh. Before I forget. Do you think we can use some of the Dandy Fund to give the ladies a bit of fun at the Taste of Chicago tomorrow? Ten bucks each? And CTA passes?"

"CTA passes are for trips to the doctor or public aid office—"

"And field trips! Field trips are in the program budget, you know."

Mabel wagged her head and sighed. "You do have a way of keeping things on the edge around here, Gabby Fairbanks."

"Well, good news, then. Instead of 24/7, I'll only be here day-times. I found an apartment." I flopped down in her extra chair.

"Really?" Now Mabel looked interested. "Tell me."

I ran through the details. "My lawyer at Legal Aid told me about it." I didn't say he'd taken me to see it and we had lunch afterward. "And if Mom and I put our money together, we ought to be able to make the rent."

Mabel raised an eyebrow. "What happens when your mother's name comes up on the assisted-living list back in North Dakota?"

Gee. Couldn't she say, "That's great!" or something? Why did she always get to the sticking point? "Well, uh, hopefully by then my court case against Philip will be far enough along, I'll be able to get my fair share of assets. Or something."

Angela stuck her head in the door. "Phone call for Gabby." Mabel started to reach for her desk phone, but Angela shook her head. "It's male," she hissed.

I hid a grin. "Probably my lawyer. I'll take it in my office, Angela. Tell him to hold." Scurrying downstairs, I flipped on the light in my office and reached for the phone. Why'd he call on the Manna House phone? Had Lee lost my cell number?

"Gabby speaking." *Silence.* "Hello?"

Then his voice. "Gabrielle."

Philip! I caught my breath. Why was *he* calling?

"I see you were in the penthouse while I was out." A statement. Not a question.

239

"Yes." I matched his tone—crisp, level, with a slight challenge—and pressed my lips together to keep from explaining or making an excuse.

"How did you get in?"

"I still have a key to our penthouse, Philip." I dropped "our" in there.

"Why? Did you want to see me? Get something?"

"I thought you were moving this weekend. But obviously not. Where were you?"

The pause lasted a full second. "That's my business. I don't have to explain anything to you."

"Nor to your mother or your sons, it seems. No one knew you were out of town." *Oops.* I wouldn't know either if Mr. Bentley hadn't said he'd seen him leave with a suitcase.

"Who said I was out of town?" Now his tone heated. "I don't like this spying, Gabrielle."

I kept my voice even. "I'm not spying, Philip. I thought you were moving. We need to talk about our household goods. I found an apartment, and I need to furnish it." Which was true, even though I'd visited the penthouse before I knew about the apartment.

"An apartment?" He sounded off step. "How—"

"Like you said, Philip. My business."

For the first time I could remember, Philip Fairbanks didn't shoot back. And I was still standing.

I caught Estelle alone in the kitchen after lunch cleanup, making potato salad for the next day's holiday, and told her about Philip's phone call.

"Good for you, honey. 'Bout time you stood up to that man!"

"But it was strange, Estelle. I couldn't figure out why he called. I mean, I thought he'd really yell at me when he found that glass with my lipstick on it. But he just asked why I'd been in the penthouse."

Estelle chuckled as she cracked and peeled hard-boiled eggs under cold running water. "Humph. Probably wondered why you didn't trash the place. *He* would've, if you'd tossed *him* out." She shuffled over to the fridge, stuck the egg bowl in it, and grabbed a bag of potatoes.

"Yeah, well, that would've been stupid of me, wouldn't it? Since it's my stuff too. I told him I'm going to need my things when I get my apartment."

She looked at me sharply. "What apartment? You know somethin' I don't know?"

"Yeah, well, I was going to tell the staff this morning, but we kind of got interrupted. My lawyer found it for me." I gave her a quick rundown of Lee Boyer's call and our Sunday rendezvous.

"Hm. Who's this Lee Boyer? Sounds a bit overzealous to me."

"Oh, come on, Estelle. He's been really helpful."

"Uh-huh. *Really* helpful." She shook a potato peeler at me. "You be careful, young lady. Don't you go runnin' after the first man who sweet-talks you. You gonna need some *time* to untangle yourself from this Philip mess 'fore you be thinkin' clearly."

"Good grief, Estelle. He's just my lawyer. He knows I have to get a place to live before I can get the boys back." Was he just my lawyer? When I talked with Lee, I always felt so . . . safe. But maybe that's how a good lawyer *should* make you feel.

241

The pile of peeled potatoes was growing.

"Uh, Estelle, how much food are you making for tomorrow? You know I'm trying to pull together a trip to the Taste. If Mabel agrees to spring some of that Dandy Fund for an outing, we'll be gone most of the day. And fireworks . . . maybe we'll even stay for the fireworks."

"No you won't."

"What? What do you mean, no we won't?"

Estelle started dicing the peeled potatoes and dumping them into a pot on the big, black stove. "'Cause Chicago does its fireworks thing on July third. And I was crazy enough to let Harry talk me into goin' with him an' his cutey-pie grandson tonight. Lord, help me." She rolled her eyes and started in on a second bag of potatoes.

I grinned. Sounded like Estelle and Mr. Bentley still had a thing going on. "Why don't you just take a holiday?"

"Humph. Taste or no Taste, I'm makin' Chicago dogs with all the trimmin's an' good ol' mustard potato salad an' apple pie for my ladies. You'll see. After all that fancy-smancy food-on-a-stick at the Taste, them ladies gonna come back here an' be beggin' for my leftovers." Estelle held up a bag of onions. "You gonna just be standin' around? 'Cause if so, you can start choppin' these onions."

"Whoa, I'm outta here. Sorry! I've got calls to make!" Which was the truth. I'd barely had time to start in on my list of schools before lunch. But as I made call after call, I either got a voice message saying the office was closed because of the Fourth of July holiday, instructions to leave name and address so they could send an application, or the dreaded answer: "Fall registration is closed. However, you may apply and we'll put your child on our waiting list."

My list was growing shorter. A tinge of panic dried out my throat. What if I couldn't find a good school for P. J. and Paul? What if—

My eyes fell on the note card Edesa had left for me the second night I'd been at the shelter. I'd taped it to my computer, but now I peeled it off. The words *"I will not forget you"* and *"your sons hasten back"* leaped out at me.

Edesa had written those verses from Isaiah 49 as God's promises to me. And last night at Sunday Evening Praise we'd sung, *"Oh for grace to trust Him more."*

I took a deep breath. *Okay.* I was going to go for broke. I'd fill out every application and put P. J. and Paul on every waiting list. After that, I'd have to trust God.

To my delight, when I got the notes from the staff meeting that afternoon, Mabel had included an addendum: *CTA passes and $10 per resident approved for Taste of Chicago outing.* Quickly making a sign-up sheet, I passed it around at supper and ended up with several I knew fairly well—Hannah, Tina, Aida, Wanda, Carolyn, and Diane. I recognized a few others like Althea, the Iranian woman. A couple of names were new.

I counted the list. Only thirteen? *Hmm.* Not as much interest as I'd expected. My mother had shaken her head. "Too much walking." Well, that was true. Probably just as well. She'd been needing a nap almost every day.

Lucy's name wasn't on the list either. Was she embarrassed to just put her X? I tried to let her off the hook. "Hey, Lucy, want me to put your name down for the Taste? You get ten bucks to spend."

"Huh. Ain't got time for no gallavantin'. Dandy's stitches need to come out, and I need to stay here with him. Doc said ten days. Ten comin' up tomorrow."

I'd forgotten Dandy's stitches. "But tomorrow's a holiday! I don't even know if the animal clinic will be open on July Fourth. We can wait one more day. Dandy will be fine. Come on. It'll be fun."

"Nah. Don't like them big crowds. Dandy an' me'll stay here with Miz Martha. 'Sides, Estelle's makin' apple pie."

Well, okay. Thirteen was a good number, probably better than a huge crowd. At least I didn't have to keep track of any kids—the Baxters had taken them to the Taste on Saturday. But should we try to keep together? No, that was stupid. These were adults. They'd want to go off, do their own thing. As I understood it, the festival had music stages and other entertainment in Grant Park, besides all the food vendors.

Still, I felt kind of responsible since it was a Manna House outing. I mused about this out loud when Sarge and her college-age assistant, Susan, showed up to cover the night shift. Sarge shrugged. "Not a problem." The ex-marine grabbed Susan, who was wearing a Manna House T-shirt. "See this? Orange. Best color to stand out in a crowd. Put 'em all in Manna House T-shirts."

I grinned. "Great idea!" I had another great idea. "Sarge? Would you like to go with us tomorrow? I sure could use another staff person."

"I can go too," Susan offered. "I don't have summer school tomorrow."

Which is how sixteen of us in bright orange T-shirts that said *Manna House Volunteer* in black letters pushed our way onto the crowded Red Line El train and rode to the Loop. Once off the El, it was only a couple of blocks to Columbus Drive and Grant Park, which was teeming with the holiday crowd. After getting our food tickets at one of the ticket booths—a strip of eleven for seven bucks—and agreeing to meet at Buckingham Fountain at three o'clock, the bright Manna House T-shirts melted into the crowd like so many orange Popsicles on a hot day. Even Sarge and Susan disappeared.

But no way did I want to go solo my first time at the Taste. I felt overwhelmed at the sheer number of booths and competing smells—Thai spices, sizzling pizzas, and grills spitting out BBQ chicken and ribs. Then I spied an orange T-shirt and a familiar brown-and-gray ponytail in the line waiting at Sweet Baby Ray's booth. "Hey, Carolyn! You decided to get some ribs?" I sidled up beside her, giving the person behind her in line a "we're together" smile.

Our resident bookworm, hands stuffed in the pocket of her jeans, nodded. "But one strip of tickets isn't going to go far around here."

"Yeah, I know. Best I could do from the budget, though." The line inched forward. "Say, I heard you're leaving us. Is it true?"

Carolyn grinned, softening the plain effect of always wearing her hair pulled back in that skimpy ponytail. "Yep. My name finally came up at Deborah's Place. Been waiting a long time."

I felt a real pang. "I'm going to miss you, Carolyn. Who's going to take care of our budding libr—Oh. We're next." I squinted at the menu board. "What are you going to get?"

Five minutes later we each walked away with a boneless rib sandwich dripping a pungent red sauce. But the crowd was so thick I felt like a salmon fighting to swim upstream against a strong current. We finally stopped for a breather to watch a clown twisting long, skinny balloons into wiener dogs and giraffes, to the delight of a dozen kids and perspiring parents.

"Meant to ask you 'bout the library thing." Carolyn headed for a patch of grass where we could sit. Between bites of her sandwich, she said, "I'd like to come back to the shelter and volunteer. Didn't we talk once about doing a book club?"

I sucked some sauce off my fingers. "Carolyn! That would be wonderful! Will you have time? Won't you be getting a job or something?" Carolyn was one of the smartest women I'd met at Manna House. Mabel said she had a master's degree in literature. Had no idea why she'd ended up in a shelter.

Carolyn shook her head. "Not for a while. I'm on disability." The word hung in the air for a long moment, my unspoken *Why?* hanging there with it. Then she shrugged. "Had a nervous breakdown on the job at the public library, got really abusive, and ended up doing time in a psychiatric facility. I'm still on meds and under a doctor's care."

I stared at her. "Never would have guessed it. To me, you're one of the solid rocks at Manna House! I'll never forget you taking my boys under your wing that day and playing board games with them." I touched her arm. "Not sure what we're going to do without you."

To my surprise, the stoic Carolyn suddenly wiped the back of her hand across her eyes. "Tell you the truth, Gabby, I'm kinda scared. I want this so bad, but . . . I'm not sure if I can make it on my own."

"Oh, Carolyn." I almost added, "Sure you will," but frankly, I had no idea. Why would a talented woman like Carolyn end up in a shelter? I wished I knew how to support her on her way back to a "normal life"—whatever that was.

But who was I to help someone else? I was having a hard enough time patching my own life back together.

chapter 30

For the next couple of hours, Carolyn and I wandered around the Taste of Chicago, running into some of our orange-shirted residents in twos and threes from time to time. Some of them had pooled their leftover dollars and bought more food tickets. Carolyn and I stood in line for fresh-squeezed lemonade and ended up thirty minutes early at Buckingham Fountain, one of Chicago's breathtaking landmarks. We sat on nearby benches, gawking at security personnel riding around on Segways—those funny two-wheeled vehicles that looked like motorized pogo sticks—and little knots of Japanese tourists taking pictures of each other in front of the fountain. A menagerie of dogs on leashes trotted past.

Carolyn poked me. "Ever notice how many owners look like their dogs?" A tall, thin woman with straw-colored hair floated by behind a long-legged Saluki. I giggled right into my lemonade, snorting it up my nose and splashing it onto my tan capris and sandals . . . so it was several seconds before I realized my cell phone was ringing.

"Oh! My phone!" I snatched it out of my shoulder bag and scurried away from the fountain so I could hear better. "Hello? Hello?"

I couldn't tell if the static in my ear was from the phone or the noises all around me. But I finally heard "Gabby? Gabby? Can't hear you!"

I stuck a finger in my other ear and hunched over the phone. "Celeste? Is that you? Oh! I'm so glad you called! You got my message?"

The connection from Alaska was a little erratic, but I caught the drift. "Mother's with you in Chicago? What did you mean, Philip kicked you out? Gabby! What's going on?"

At the sound of my sister's voice, sudden tears clouded my eyes, and I had to wipe them on my orange T-shirt. I tried to bring my older sister up to date on all that had happened the past month, but it was hard. She kept saying, "What? Slow down . . ." and I had to repeat myself.

When I finally stopped to gulp a breath, Celeste blistered my ear. "I can't believe you've got Mom in a homeless shelter, Gabby. She's got a perfectly good home in Minot! You've got to take her back there."

My hackles rose. "But she can't stay alone! That's why I brought her home with me in the first place. She's had a couple falls—and left the stove on."

I could all but hear Big Sister's practical brain wheels at work. "Well, since Philip's being a jerk and you don't have a place to stay right now, why don't you just go home to Minot with Mom? That way she wouldn't be alone! Honestly, Gabby!"

Go home with Mom? That option had never occurred to me. "Can't do that, Celeste! I'm trying to get my boys back, and I need to be *here* so I . . . Celeste?" The static went dead. "Celeste? Are you still there?"

Nothing.

I closed the phone and stood at the far edge of Buckingham Fountain, feeling as if I'd just been cut loose, adrift in space. Celeste was *family.* Didn't she know I needed her right now? But Denali National Forest wasn't exactly on the cell phone highway.

If I couldn't talk to my own sister, who *could* I talk to?

Three o'clock came and went as our crew with orange T-shirts drifted to the fountain. "Will we stay to watch the fireworks?" Althea said in her careful English. "That is what you do on Independence Day, yes?"

"I'm sorry, Althea," I said. "I think the fireworks were last night."

"Yeah, too bad we missed it," Carolyn offered. "They play music to go along with the show, an' shine colored lights on the fountain, water going up and down in time to the music . . ."

Fireworks . . . we'd never missed taking P. J. and Paul to watch the fireworks back in Petersburg. It was practically unpatriotic not to celebrate the Fourth of July in the heart of historical Virginia, and we'd always made it a huge family event—grilling hot dogs and hamburgers over at the Fairbanks' grandparents' with the other relatives early in the day, then joining the throngs at Fort Lee for music, food, and the nighttime show. Were the boys doing the same thing with Philip's parents today?

Diane shook her big Afro impatiently. "I'm tired. Let's go."

I ignored Diane's whining. Our people were still straggling in. *Next year,* I thought. Next year I'd take P. J. and Paul to the Taste of Chicago on July third, and we'd stay till it got dark to watch the fountain dance as the big-city fireworks burst overhead.

We waited an extra half hour but still only counted fourteen noses. "Who's missing?" I pulled the list out of my bag. "Anyone seen Chris and Alisha?" Both were newcomers to the shelter. Late twenties or so. Hard faces. I didn't know their stories.

Aida Menéndez piped up, "*Si.* I saw them talking to two men—tough hombres. Gold . . . *cómo se dice?*" She made necklace motions with her finger.

"Oh yeah. Loaded with gold jewelry." Sarge snorted. "You guys go on. I'll wait around and see what's going down. But those two know their way around. If they want to come back by curfew, fine. But if they came out here just to pick up some johns . . ." She drew a finger across her neck.

They'd better come back, or Mabel might dock my pay for their T-shirts. But now I was feeling impatient to get back to the shelter after my aborted call with Celeste. I still had minutes on my phone card. Maybe a land line would work better.

When we finally dragged ourselves in the front doors of Manna House, Precious McGill was at the front desk, covering for Angela, who had the day off. "You guys still hungry? Estelle left food for ya downstairs." I practically got run over in the stampede. Sure enough, the kitchen counter on the lower level was covered with a platter of watermelon, skinny slices of leftover apple pie, and a sign that said potato salad was in the fridge. I loaded my own paper plate and dug in.

Maybe we should have stuck around.

Celeste's comment about taking Mom home to Minot bugged me all night. Is that what I should do? On one hand, it made a lot of sense. I could just imagine how crazy it must sound to my sisters that Mom and I were staying in a homeless shelter. And I'd never wanted to come to Chicago in the first place!

But . . . that was before I got the job at Manna House, which was more than just a job. I really loved my work, felt as if I was doing something important for people who often got ignored. Even more important, my main priority was getting my sons back, and North Dakota seemed light-years away from Virginia. Philip *might* agree to the boys coming back to Chicago, near both of us, but he'd fight me tooth and nail if I took them to Minot.

I kicked the sheets off in the dark, stuffy bunk room. Should I pray about it? Something in me resisted. I didn't really want to ask God what He thought. What if He didn't agree with me? Besides, God gave me a brain. A mother's responsibility was to her children first . . . and Mom wasn't unhappy here. She even seemed to like it. And now we had a possibility to get a real apartment, so I could take care of my boys *and* my mom. Wasn't that God at work?

I pressed the button on my watch to make it glow . . . ten past one. Already Wednesday. I was supposed to have a meeting with Lee Boyer at Legal Aid this morning. I'd call and ask him if I could sign the contract for the apartment today.

Lucy, however, was all over me the next morning about getting Dandy back to the vet to get his stitches out. "He still ain't himself," she growled. "Lookit that; he's still all stiff. What if them cuts ain't healed right?"

"And how are we going to get him there?" I shot back at her. "I don't have a car—and I can't afford cab fare these days."

Lucy shrugged. "Call that nice cop 'at took Dandy in the first place. He gave you his card, didn't he?"

Yeah, right. I was pretty sure Chicago cops didn't do cab service.

I called Lee Boyer instead. "Lee, I have a huge favor to ask . . ."

To my surprise, Lee agreed to use my eleven o'clock appointment and his lunch hour to pick us up at Manna House and take Dandy to the vet. "And could we swing by the apartment you showed me? I'd like to bring my mom, too, see what she thinks. If she likes it, I think I'm ready to sign the rental contract."

"Great. I'll give him a call."

Lee showed up in that snazzy Prius of his, and my mom and Lucy climbed into the backseat, with Dandy between them. "Thanks, Lee. I really appreciate this."

"Hey, gotta treat my girls right . . . right, Lucy?" He tossed a grin into the back seat, then winked at me behind his wire rims.

"Humph," Lucy growled. "I ain't your girl. An' Gabby ain't your girl either. She's a married woman—even if her husband is a jerk. Humph."

My face burned, but Lee just laughed.

Dandy, as it turned out, was coming along just fine. He only whimpered a little as the stitches came out, then jumped up and licked the vet in the face. The vet laughed. "Not every day I get kissed by a celebrity." He handed me the bill. "We usually ask for payment in full at the time of service. But you can pay in installments if that'll help."

I looked at the total and winced. "Thanks. I'm going to need it." I felt a little disgruntled. All that money in the Dandy Fund, and Dandy could sure use some of it. Did I dare ask—

Lee plucked the bill out of my hand. "Let me take care of this."

"What? No, you can't do that! Give it back."

Lee held it out of my reach, dug a credit card out of his wallet, and handed both to the receptionist.

"Lee," I hissed on the way back to the car. "You can't do that. You're my *lawyer*. I'm sure it's illegal or something."

"Nothing in the rules says your lawyer can't be your friend." He looked at me sideways, that little shock of hair falling over his forehead. "I want to be your friend, Gabby."

I didn't know what to say. I felt confused. Lee *had* been more than a lawyer these last couple of weeks. When I talked with Lee, he listened. Made me feel like a real person, with valid concerns and feelings. He'd gone out of his way to go to bat for me.

Oh God, it feels so good that someone wants *to be there for me.*

But I wasn't ready to give up on my marriage yet, was I? What I really wanted was for Philip and me and the boys to be a family again. All of us. Together. That . . . that madman who'd thrown me out wasn't the man I'd married. If I didn't do anything rash, if I gave him some time, Philip would come to his senses, realize he'd made a big mistake, and maybe . . . maybe we could work it out.

Oh dear God! For the boys' sake, I hope so!

We rode in silence to the building with the For Sale sign in front of it. I turned to the backseat. "Mom? This is the apartment I told you about. Would you like to see it? You too, Lucy. Dandy can stay in the car."

"Nah. Don't wanna see no apartment. Leave those windows down," Lucy snapped. "Dog needs some air."

I pressed my lips together. The woman could be a real pain sometimes.

Workmen were in the apartment, scraping walls and painting, but we picked our way around the drop cloths. "See, Mom? Three bedrooms. One for you, one for the boys . . . and a nice sunroom. On the first floor too. What do you think?"

"My head hurts, Celeste."

I grimaced at Lee. "Must be the paint smell." I really did need to get my mom to a doctor and get those headaches checked out.

Fortunately, the owner hustled in, tie askew, with the contract in his briefcase. Lee had told me to bring a paycheck stub and proof of my mother's income or savings. I had a copy of her Social Security check and monthly annuity, plus her savings passbook. "We'll be sharing the apartment," I explained.

The man frowned. "Are you both signing the contract?"

I shook my head. "I'm her power of attorney. I handle her affairs."

He shrugged. "All right. But you won't be able to move in for another week and a half—maybe two weeks. Got a lot of work to do here."

"Fine with me." I needed time to work out something with Philip about household furnishings anyway.

I signed and wrote a check for the security deposit. *Ouch.*

Lee grinned and gave me a hug. "Congrats, Gabby! Now let's get those boys back to Chicago."

I hugged him back. "Thanks, Lee," I whispered. But the touch of his arms and the warm smell of his aftershave lingered as we got back in the car. I watched as he helped my mother into the backseat, buckled her seat belt, and then slid into the driver's seat in those down-home jeans and boots he always wore.

I turned my head away. *Stop it, Gabby. What do you think you're doing?* In all the years I'd been married to Philip, I had never looked at another man *that* way.

Until now.

chapter 31

I woke the next morning with Sarge's bell, realizing I'd slept the entire night without getting up once. The square of daylight framed in the one window tried to lift the dim interior, outlining the four bunks, one on each wall. Even as the other bunks creaked and feet hit the floor, I stretched and lay on my bunk a few more minutes—a disastrous decision, I knew, since the bathrooms, showers, and sinks would get more and more congested the longer I waited.

But something felt different. Different good. Like it was my birthday or something—which it wasn't.

And then I remembered . . .

I had an apartment. Or would, as soon as I delivered the deposit.

"Hallelujah!" I shouted—earning me a dirty look from Lucy, who covered her ears as she lumbered out the door with her toothbrush.

An apartment changed everything! I vaulted out of bed, my

mind spinning. If the painting and repairs to the apartment moved along, I might be able to move in by the fifteenth. That gave me a week and a half to figure out how to furnish the place—and I was going to start with Philip. He had to know that a divorce settlement would give me *at least* fifty-fifty rights to our "community property," as Lee called it—maybe more, if I got custody of the kids. Why not just divvy it up now without a big fight? Why make it difficult?

Because he can.

I shook off the little voice in my head. No! I wasn't going to go there. I would present my case in a rational way and presume we could work this out like two adults. If not . . . well, I'd cross that bridge later if I had to. In the meantime, I had a lot of work to do *besides* my Manna House workload. Filling out all those school applications for the boys, for one thing.

My mother was sitting on the edge of her bunk. "How're you doing, Mom? Come on. Let's go use the bathroom before you get dressed, okay? . . . You okay?"

My mother nodded, but she didn't really seem like herself this morning. *Rats.* The nurse had been here yesterday morning, but we were off getting Dandy's stitches out and looking at the new apartment. I really should've had Delores Enriques take a look at my mom. Next week was too far away.

I'd told myself I was going to keep up with my own Bible reading in the gospel of Matthew, but we barely got downstairs in time for group devotions at six forty-five. Susan McCall, the young night assistant, was reading short passages this week from the book of Proverbs—all those warnings about avoiding loose women and fools. Wasn't sure it really spoke to the women at

Manna House, some of whom *were* loose women and fools. But, oh well. Then Sarge read the chore list at breakfast . . . *groan.* Diane and I got assigned to clean the bathrooms and showers on the top floor. That always took more time, even with two of us. And Diane usually spent more time whining about ruining her nails than actually working.

But even scrubbing toilets couldn't dampen my spirits today. It felt like a new day. I'd turned a corner. I still had the pieces of my broken marriage to contend with. Was still separated from my children by a thousand miles. But it felt like the logjam had broken. Things could move forward.

"Thank You, Jesus," I murmured as I poured pine cleaner into the last toilet bowl. "I'm trusting You. Don't let me down now." I even started to whistle.

"What's that tune?" Diane called into the stall where I was working. "Didn't our girl Whitney sing that?"

"Yeah. It's called, 'I Go to the Rock.' I lost my CD . . . have you seen the soundtrack to *The Preacher's Wife* around anywhere?"

"Maybe. Whole buncha loose CDs kickin' around down in the multipurpose room without they covers . . . say, we got any more spray stuff for the mirrors? Then I gotta quit. Gotta meet with my case manager at ten."

Oh rats. That's right. It was Thursday again already. Last week Stephanie Cooper had said she wanted to meet with me again on Thursday, just to keep current on my goals. Well, we could make it short today. I'd found an apartment, and I planned to be off the bed list in less than two weeks.

On the way downstairs to my office, I checked on my mom,

who was sitting in the multipurpose room with an *Essence* magazine open on her lap, but not reading it. "Hi, Mom. Where's Dandy?"

She smiled up at me. "Dandy? Out in the yard, I think. Will you let him in?"

Oh dear. This wasn't good. "You mean Lucy took him for a walk?"

She nodded and smiled. "Yes, that's right."

"You okay? Or would you like to come down and sit in my office with me while I work?"

"No, no. You go on. I've got plenty to do." She patted the magazine in her lap.

I gave her a kiss, then remembered what Diane had said about "loose CDs." Sure enough, the boom box in the corner, sitting on top of the game cabinet, was surrounded with piles of CDs, half of which were out of their cases. I shuffled through them . . . and struck gold. *Aha.* My CD. Looking a little worse for wear, but maybe it would still play.

My CD player was sitting on top of the file cabinet in my office. I plugged it in, popped in the CD, booted up my computer, and started work updating the Manna House program calendar for July while the gospel songs filled the tiny room. Finally "my" song hit its groove. *"Where do I go . . . when there's no one else to turn to? . . . Who do I talk to . . . when nobody wants to listen? . . ."*

I stopped what I was doing. That was for sure. I still felt upset by my sister's phone call. She'd barely heard my story before she started jumping all over me! If we had more time to really talk or just be together, maybe she'd understand. But how *that* was supposed to happen between her log home in the middle of Denali National Forest and my broom-closet office in the basement of a homeless shelter in Chicago, I had no idea.

The song had launched into the chorus . . . *"I go to the Rock of my salvation, go to the Stone that the builders rejected . . ."* Huh. Had I heard that line before? The one about the Stone being rejected? It was talking about Jesus. Well, yeah, the Son of God had been rejected big-time. But I hadn't read that part of the gospel story since I quit church back in college. Maybe I should keep reading in Matthew until I came to the part where people turned on Jesus and killed Him. And maybe that's why I should be talking to Jesus, because He knew what it was like to be rejected . . . just like me.

I eyed my Bible and then my watch. Could I—?

No, I should get this calendar done and printed; then I had to see Stephanie. But lunchtime was coming up. I'd take a half hour then to read my Bible. And pray.

The next few days settled into an odd but not unpleasant routine. From 6 a.m. until 9, I was a Manna House resident. From 9 until 5, I was a Manna House employee. At 5, I turned into a resident again. But at least my world wasn't spinning.

Except . . . what about Philip? He was still my husband. But he had become a stranger. Was there any hope for our marriage? Didn't seem like it. Not when we weren't even talking. Maybe I should file for divorce—before he did.

Divorce. The word made me shudder. Ending up twice divorced and living single was *not* one of my life goals. And Philip and I had kids! Two beautiful boys. We were supposed to be a *family.* If we divorced, P. J. and Paul would have to choose between living with Mom or Dad. Or be split two ways during their teen years.

I shoved the question into the back of my mind. Couldn't think about that now or I might crawl back into my black hole. I had to keep moving forward. Get moved. Get the boys. Get my mother to a doctor . . .

Now, that was something I could do now. I called Delores Enriques at work on the pediatrics floor at Stroger Hospital, and she agreed it'd be good to get my mother checked out by a physician. "You could always bring her to the clinic here at County, Gabby," she said on the phone. With her Spanish accent, my name always came out *Gab-bee.* "But why don't you ask Mabel or some of the other staff who their doctor is? It's not easy to get an appointment on short notice, but if you explain that your mother's elderly, from out of town, has these symptoms, and needs to see a doctor, sometimes . . ."

Mabel agreed to call her primary doctor over at Thorek Professional Building on Mom's behalf. He was booked solid for three months, the secretary told us, but his associate, Dr. Palma, happened to have a cancellation on Friday afternoon.

I couldn't believe it! God must be listening to my prayers after all! Except, had I even prayed about getting an appointment? Well, if I did or didn't, I decided to thank God anyway. Wasn't there some verse in the Bible that said, "Before they call, I will answer"? I'd have to look it up.

Mom had another one of her headaches Friday, but she insisted on sitting in on Edesa Baxter's Bible study that morning. When Edesa heard I was borrowing Mabel's car to take Mom to the doctor after lunch, she offered to go along for moral support. "If you don't mind *la nena* too. The shelter keeps a couple of car seats for kid emergencies."

I was grateful for the company. It always helped to have

another pair of ears to hear what the doctor had to say. Lucy wanted to go, too, but frankly, I was glad I could tell her we didn't have room. As devoted as she seemed to be to my mother and Dandy, she'd been getting downright bossy when it came to either of them, and it'd been getting on my nerves.

We found the Thorek Memorial Professional Building on Irving Park Road without too much trouble, though filling out my mother's medical history for the nurse was problematic. My mother seemed confused by the questions and gave conflicting answers. And half the stuff I didn't know either. But I promised to call Mom's doctor in Minot and try to have her records sent on Monday. Hopefully Aunt Mercy could help me out.

Dr. Palma was Filipino, a pleasant young man with no trace of accent. He only had a half hour between patients, so he couldn't do a complete workup on my mother, but he seemed kind and conscientious. He listened to her heart and breathing, took a urine and blood sample, and asked gentle questions. After I helped her get dressed, I asked Edesa to take my mother into the waiting room while I talked with the doctor.

"Your mother seems reasonably healthy for her age, which is . . . what? Seventy-four? Her heart is steady—no history of heart disease?—and her lungs clear. We'll see if the urine or blood tests turn up anything unusual, but it's hard to say. She does have some early stages of dementia, but you say she's still fairly functional, though unable to live alone. As for the headaches . . ." Dr. Palma looked over the history we'd filled out. "It says here she's had several falls. Tell me about them."

I told him about Mom tripping over the dog and hitting her head. "But my aunt Mercy—she lives in the same town—said she's had a couple other falls when no one was around."

Dr. Palma frowned. "Falls are not uncommon in the elderly. I don't know if there's any relation between the falls and the headaches. But to be on the safe side, I'd like to schedule a CAT scan—the sooner the better. Hopefully early next week."

I gulped. A CAT scan? Those had to be expensive. Would Medicare cover it?

Dr. Palma shook my hand as he left the exam room. "I'll call you Monday to set up the CAT scan at Thorek Memorial—it's just next door. In the meantime, I'll give you a couple of sample bottles of a stronger headache medicine. Should give your mom some relief."

We left the office and drove back to the shelter with no real answers. In the back seat, Mom and Gracie seemed to be sharing giggles. "Well, one thing I know," I murmured to Edesa in the front seat, "staying at the shelter is better for Mom than living alone in that house of hers. She really thrives on being around people. And kids." I grinned. "Listen to those two."

My mom was doing her own version of "Creep Mousie," walking her fingers across the seat, up the side of Gracie's car seat, and tickling the eleven-month-old's neck or ear or nose. Gracie, it seemed, never got tired of it, though by the time we parked Mabel's car, I'd had enough "Creep Mousie" to last the rest of the year.

"What's that?" I said, as we came around the corner by the Laundromat. A long, white passenger van sat in front of Manna House.

Edesa giggled. "It's the van you ordered! Josh and Señor Douglass have been looking all week—and this is what they found! What do you think, *mi amiga*?"

chapter 32

Josh Baxter dangled a set of car keys as he came down the steps of the shelter. "So, Mrs. Fairbanks, what do you think of Manna House's new vehicle?" Edesa's husband kicked a tire. "All new tires, about seventy-five thousand miles on the engine, but it runs smooth enough, shocks are good, brakes ditto . . ." He slid open the side door. I peeked in. The flooring and seats were a bit worn, but all the seat belts seemed functional, and it was clean. I trusted Josh when he said everything checked out under the hood.

Josh held out the keys. "Here. Take it for a spin around the block. I'll see that Mrs. Shepherd gets safely inside." He took my mother's arm, and the little Baxter family escorted her inside as I climbed into the driver's seat. Once around the block . . . okay. But I had to admit, a fifteen-passenger van felt like driving a Mack truck as I lurched around corners, trying not to sideswipe any parked cars. Five minutes later, I pulled up to the curb in front of Manna House. So far, so good. But what if I had to parallel park the thing? I'd better practice before driving the monster on an actual outing.

At supper, which was provided by the Silver Sneakers from a Jewish senior center, I announced a contest: "Name the Van." Entries should be written on a piece of paper, I said, and given to me by supper tomorrow night, at which time we'd vote. I grinned. "Can't let our new baby go a whole weekend without a name."

Carolyn waved her hand. "I'm moving out tomorrow, so I won't be here to vote. But I have a name."

"That's great, Carolyn. Why don't you—"

"Moby Van. After Moby Dick, the big white whale in Herman Melville's novel."

"Oh, *yeah*," Diane sputtered. "That thing sure do look like a big white whale!"—which got snickers and guffaws even from women who'd probably never heard of Herman Melville.

Hannah waved her manicured hand. "No, no! Name it somethin' pretty, like Pearl or Frosty."

"Oh, be quiet," Lucy grunted. "Carolyn leavin'. Let 'er name the van."

Hannah stuck out her lip. "But Miss Gabby said we could vote."

"So? Let's vote on Carolyn's name," Lucy cut in. "Ever'body good with Moby Van?" A resounding chorus of yeahs bounced off the walls. "Nos?" Hannah just rolled her eyes.

And that was that. We even used "Moby Van" to help move Carolyn the next morning over to the apartment building sponsored by Deborah's Place on the west side. We picked up several boxes she'd stored at a friend's—dishes, a few pots and pans, a couple scatter rugs, several towels, sheets and blankets—plus two boxes of books and her clothes from the shelter. I was a bit taken aback at the tiny "studio" apartment—just one room with a refrigerator and hot plate in one corner, a single bed and dresser in another, a small table and chair by the window, and a door that led to a small bathroom with a shower stall, shared with the studio next door.

Carolyn flopped down on the narrow bed and stretched out. "Isn't this *great*? I love it! My own place!"

I was speechless, thinking about the three-bedroom apartment I'd just signed for. Could I be happy here? "Uh, well, guess it's a step up from a bunk room with roommates who snore."

"Ha!" Carolyn threw back her head and laughed. "And *that* was a step up from getting locked in my room at night up at the psychiatric facility." She rolled up to sit on the side of the bed. "I remember one of Edesa's Bible studies; she said Paul the apostle had learned to be grateful whether he had a lot of stuff or just a little. Guess I'm learning that too. The hard way."

A lot or a little . . . I qualified on that score. But had I reached grateful yet? *Huh.* I sure had a lot to learn about this business of being a Christian. Never thought my current role models would be people at a homeless shelter, though.

With a promise to come back to Manna House next week to talk about starting a book club, Carolyn gave me a hug and I headed back toward Manna House. I felt a little teary as I eased Moby Van onto the Eisenhower Expressway heading back into the Loop. People came and went from Manna House all the time. Why did Carolyn's leaving feel like such a loss?

Maybe because her story wasn't all that different from mine. Minus the husband, but still. Middle-class woman, educated, good job, whose life had suddenly spun out of control, nowhere to go. Except to God and God's people. Now she was taking her life back, one step at a time. But even Carolyn had admitted she was scared.

Me too.

As I drove through the Loop and turned onto Lake Shore Drive, I could see the huge Aon Center, which housed my husband's office, its white granite facade standing out from all the steel and glass buildings surrounding it. My last visit to Philip's office tasted like bile in my mouth. But . . . it was time to walk through my fear and get to the other side. I had a sudden urge to pull off the Drive, head for the Aon Center, and ride the elevator to the sixty-second floor. Philip and I needed to talk!

It's Saturday, nitwit. I kept driving.

As I approached the Irving Park exit, which would have taken me to Manna House within a few minutes, I drove past and took the next exit, turning right onto Montrose Harbor Drive. I parked and got out of the big van. A lot of sailboats, a few small yachts in the protected harbor. Rock wall out by the lake. Not much sand. But just being near the water felt good. Traffic noise along the Drive faded into the background as seagulls screeched overhead.

Mmm. If I missed anything about living in the penthouse at Richmond Towers, it was being able to walk through the pedestrian tunnel under Lake Shore Drive and magically be at the beach.

The penthouse . . . Why not call Philip right now and make arrangements to get some of our stuff for my apartment? I'd be able to fit quite a bit into Moby Van. Maybe I wouldn't even need to rent a truck. I sat on the rock wall, pulled my cell phone out of my shoulder bag, and punched in our "home" number.

Heard my chipper voice on the answering machine. *"Hi! You've reached the Fairbanks. Sorry we missed your call. Leave a message . . ."* Like a ghost out of my past, haunting my present. *The Fairbanks . . . we . . .* I flipped the phone closed, losing my nerve. I didn't want to leave a message on the home phone. Philip would just ignore it anyway.

Get a grip, Gabby. It was time to quit hiding from Philip. If he backed me into a corner on the phone, I could just hang up and wouldn't answer the next time. But we needed to start talking, the sooner the better. Taking a deep breath, I tried his cell. Got *his* voice mail. This time I left my new cell number and asked him to call.

But by Sunday evening I still hadn't heard back from Philip.

It had been a busy weekend. When I got back to Manna House with Moby Van after moving Carolyn, Angela was standing at the window of her cubicle, clipboard in her hand, talking testily with two women who looked vaguely familiar. "Do you want to be put on the wait list or not? As I said, the bed list is full right now."

"What about them other two, come in just 'fore us? Betcha put *them* on the bed list." The darker-skinned of the two women stabbed a finger in the direction of the multipurpose room as I tried to creep past.

"That's right." Angela was obviously trying to keep her cool. "We had two empty beds, but they came in first."

The lighter-brown-skinned woman, black hair pulled tight into a stubby ponytail, got in Angela's face. "Those beds 'sposed to be ours! Chris an' me was stayin' here just a few days ago. We left our stuff to hold our place!" The woman glowered at me. "Ain't that right? *You* 'member—we went to the Taste!"

I caught Angela's eye. *Uh-oh.* Chris and Alisha. The two who did a disappearing act at the Taste of Chicago.

"It doesn't work like that." Angela was losing patience. "You didn't come back, so we had to put your stuff in storage. I'll be *happy* to get it now." Angela came out of the cubicle and headed resolutely for the double swinging doors. "Gabby," she hissed at me, "stay with the phone."

"Yeah!" Alisha yelled after her. "You better get our stuff, Chingy Chong, an' nothin' better be missin' or I'll—" The street woman muttered a string of profanity as the doors swung closed behind Angela.

I sweated out the next five minutes, but finally the two women were gone with their "stuff" . . . without filling out the forms for the wait list. Angela blew out a breath as she took back the reception cubicle. "That was close. Look who got the last two beds." She jerked a thumb in the direction of the multipurpose room. "Thank God!"

Precious was getting herself a cup of coffee and loading it with powdered cream and sugar, surrounded by a couple of over-stuffed backpacks and a bulging black plastic bag.

"Precious! What happened? Did you get evicted?" I cried.

Precious shook her head. "Ain't gonna wait to get evicted. Uh-uh. Them sheriff's officers just dump your stuff in the street, rain or shine. I packed it up, storing some stuff at a friend's. Good timin', though. I think we got the last two beds." Precious pulled me aside. "Sabrina, though, she real upset. Don't wanna have her baby at a shelter. She threatenin' to run off again, live with the dawg who knocked her up." Precious practically spit.

"Humph. Over my dead body. She do that? Somebody's gonna die."

I followed her eyes to the black teenage girl across the room, slumped in one of the overstuffed chairs, arms folded over her voluptuous chest, her pretty features tight. How far along was Sabrina . . . three months? Four months? And now she and her mom were homeless again? She was right—a shelter was no place to have a baby! Huh. Maybe we should have taken advantage of all the media attention Dandy's "hero act" had created to raise money for another building, some second-stage apartments for homeless moms like Precious . . .

"Precious—" I wanted to say I'd do everything in my power to help them find a place to live before Sabrina's baby was born, but just then Lucy Tucker came into the multipurpose room with my mother's dog on a leash. Under the purple knit hat, the old woman's crafty eyes took in Precious, then swung across the room to Sabrina. With a shrug, she lumbered over to Sabrina's chair, unsnapped Dandy's leash, and ordered, "Sit. Stay." Dandy sat, his eyes following Lucy as she shuffled out of the room and down the stairs to the kitchen-dining area.

The whole time I was talking to Precious, Lucy didn't come back. Dandy sighed and lay down, right where he'd been put, head lying on top of Sabrina's feet. I took a step in their direction, afraid the sulking Sabrina might kick him away. But Precious grabbed my arm and turned us away, as if we weren't watching. But out of the corner of my eye, I saw Sabrina lean down and tentatively stroke Dandy's silky gold head.

"That crafty old airbag," Precious murmured. "She did that on purpose!"

Even though I felt badly for Precious and Sabrina, for some

reason my spirit lifted having Precious around. Next to Edesa and Josh Baxter—and Gracie, of course—Precious was one of the first people I'd met here at Manna House. She'd given me the official tour, with a lot of unofficial "facts" thrown in. The woman seemed to know everybody's story—and wasn't at all shy about sharing her own! "Girl," she'd told me, "somebody gonna write a book about me someday. Be a best seller! Oh Lord, what I been through."

Mom had another headache Saturday afternoon, but the new medicine Dr. Palma had given her seemed to help. After a short nap she wanted to play Scrabble and somehow talked Tina and Aida into playing with her after supper. "A good way to learn English," she scolded when Aida resisted. I wasn't so sure about that. The last time I'd played with Mom, she'd spelled several of her words backward.

But after getting the Scrabble board set up for them, I excused myself to call Aunt Mercy and bring her up to date. She totally agreed about getting the CAT scan and said she'd call Mom's doctor first thing Monday morning about getting her records sent to Dr. Palma. "But about the apartment you found, Gabrielle. Celeste called me . . ."

I knew what was coming. Now they were both going to get on my case to forget the apartment, bring Mom back to Minot, and stay with her at the house. "Aunt Mercy, look, it's more complicated than that. I'm trying to get my boys back with me, and I have to stay here in Chicago right now. But keep praying, okay? God's going to work it out somehow."

Somehow was right. I just wished He'd give me more than one clue at a time.

chapter 33

Mom insisted on going to church the next morning. "Don't want to spoil my perfect attendance," I heard her tell Precious. I decided I didn't need to remind her we'd both missed last week.

The SouledOut church service started at ten. Normally I'd allow an hour to take the Red Line up to Howard Street—especially with Mom—but at breakfast I had an inspiration. "Anybody want to go to Estelle's church this morning?" I announced. "Same church that comes here on third Sundays. If we get at least eight people, I'll drive Moby Van." Getting residents to church surely qualified as a program.

To my surprise, it wasn't hard. Precious was the first to shoot a hand up, and with Sabrina that made four. Tanya and Sammy made six. And after playing Scrabble with my mother last night, Tina and Aida had a hard time resisting when Mom sweetly asked them to go with her too. She even got a noncommittal grunt out of Lucy.

Tina, however, seemed anxious. "Señora Gabby," she hissed.

"Any Puerto Ricans at that church? Some people think we're Mexican or assume we're all *ilegal*. I get nasty comments sometimes. Don't usually go to places that are just black or white."

Big-boned Tina didn't seem the type to be intimidated, and her comment took me aback. SouledOut had seemed very multicultural to me—but come to think of it, I hadn't noticed any Latinos, though I wasn't sure. "It'll be all right, Tina. I promise." If one could promise something like that.

Lucy, however, managed to disappear with Dandy when it was time to leave. My mother wanted to wait, but I knew those two could stay out for hours. "Maybe next time, Mom. We need to go."

Driving Moby Van up to the Howard Street shopping center was easier than I'd thought—a straight shot up Sheridan Road. It was fun unloading my crew in front of SouledOut. Josh and Edesa Baxter came outside to greet us and laughed when I told them what Carolyn had named the van. "But so far I've been lucky," I confessed. "I haven't had to parallel park the Big White Whale."

A lot of people already seemed to know Precious and Sabrina, and they warmly welcomed the others. Jodi Baxter's face lit up when she saw us. "Gabby! I'm so glad you came! I want our daughter to meet you and your mom. I've told her so much about you both . . . Amanda! José! Come here a minute." In a sly undertone she murmured, "José is Delores Enriques's son . . . might be mine, too, one of these days."

Amanda Baxter had butterscotch-blonde hair caught back in a knot with an elastic hair band in that just-got-out-of-bed look of the young, and her daddy's easy smile. José's dark eyes drifted often to Amanda's face. Their fingers lightly intertwined. *Uh-huh.* I could see what Jodi meant, though neither one looked even twenty yet. "Oh, Mrs. Shepherd, I heard what happened to your dog," Amanda squealed, giving my mother a hug. "I wish I could meet Dandy. Is he all right now? Tell us about him . . ."

Across the room, I saw Mr. Bentley hovering near Estelle, so I left my mother with the young people and headed in their direction. I so badly wanted to ask my Richmond Towers doorman friend if he'd seen my husband at all that weekend, until I remembered Harry Bentley didn't usually work weekends.

"Mm-hm, what did I tell you, Harry? They just couldn't stay away from my cookin'!" Estelle lifted an eyebrow at me as I joined them. "You *are* staying for the potluck today, aren't you, Gabby girl?"

Potluck? Sure enough, right after the two-hour service, chairs were pushed back, tables set up, and food set out for a potluck meal. I felt a little anxious about staying, since we hadn't brought anything but appetites . . . but the rest of the Manna House crew obviously had no qualms, filling their plates and going back for seconds. Even Sabrina seemed to be having a good time, hanging out with Amanda, while José Enriques kept Tina and Aida laughing with his rapid Spanish.

By the time we finally climbed in the van and headed back down Sheridan Road, it was going on three o'clock, and I, for one, was peopled out.

I skipped Sunday Evening Praise that night. I saw Rev. Liz Handley come in—hers was some kind of liturgical church group, if I remembered right. But Mom seemed extra tired, barely touching her supper, so I took her upstairs early and helped her get ready for bed. Even Dandy seemed glad for an early night after staying out nearly all day with Lucy. He curled up in his borrowed dog bed and let out a long doggy sigh.

"You're a good girl, Celeste," my mom murmured, patting my hand as I tucked her into her lower bunk. "Isn't she, Dandy?" Dandy declined comment, probably thinking, *Who's Celeste?*

I kissed her cheek and gently brushed back her soft, gray hair as she fell asleep, thinking it was time for another trip to the beauty salon for a cut and set. I'd be so glad to get my mom into that apartment, to do right by her . . . maybe she wouldn't even need to go to assisted living.

One step at a time, Gabby.

By the time I turned out the light and went downstairs, the Sunday Evening Praise service was half-over. I slipped into the empty prayer chapel instead. I needed some time alone to think. And pray.

Even after the multipurpose room had cleared out and Sarge had locked the front door, I realized Philip still hadn't returned my call. I let myself out onto the front steps, making sure I had my key. The night was muggy and warm, and an almost full moon scuttled in and out of patchy clouds tinged orange from the city lights. Taking a deep breath, I tried calling the penthouse again.

Still no answer. Again I left a brief message. "Philip. This is Gabby. Please call this number. We need to talk." I bit my tongue before I said anything more. But I wanted to say, *"Are you all right? I'm worried about you."*

My cell phone rang at nine thirty the next morning . . . but the caller ID said *Palma, MD.* "Mrs. Fairbanks, can you get your mother to Thorek Memorial on Tuesday at two? Just bring her Medicare card. I've got her registered for the CAT scan."

I wrote it down. Maybe I could borrow Mabel's car again.

But still no call back from Philip. Mabel wanted to have regular staff meetings Monday mornings at ten . . . did I have enough time? I sucked up my courage and called his office. The sure place to get him. "Fairbanks and Fenchel," came the bright voice of the new secretary. "How may I direct your call?"

"Philip Fairbanks, please." I tried to sound businesslike. I didn't need to be afraid; I could live into my name, "Strong woman of God," as Jodi and Edesa had encouraged—

"I'm sorry. Mr. Fairbanks isn't in. Would you like to speak to Mr. Fenchel?"

Philip wasn't in? *What in the world*—? I hesitated. The last time I'd talked to Henry Fenchel, he'd backed off. Way off. But I heard myself say, "Yes."

A moment later a line picked up. "Fenchel speaking."

"Henry? It's Gabby."

"Gabby! Hey, are you all right? Mona and I have been worried about you."

I stifled a snort. Mona Fenchel worried about me? I doubted it. "I'm fine, Henry." Let him figure out what *fine* meant. "But I need to talk to Philip. I thought I could catch him at the office this morning, but—"

"Philip." Henry's voice got tight. "He's *supposed* to be here this morning. We've got a meeting with a key account at eleven, but I haven't seen him. He hasn't called either. If Prince Charming blows this off, I'll—"

"You mean you don't know where he is?" *Oh God, has something happened?* He hadn't gone to Virginia. At least the boys hadn't said anything about their dad when I called them on Sunday. So where—

"Humph. Didn't say I don't know where he is—or was. We did the Horseshoe Saturday night, but Mona got her, you know, female thing, and didn't feel too hot, so we came on home. But Philip decided he was on a roll, told me not to worry, he'd be here for the meeting Monday morning."

"Philip stayed at the casino by himself? Didn't you guys drive down together? He wouldn't still be there this morning, would he?"

"Huh. Meet the new Philip Fairbanks," Henry snapped. "Dashing casino man. Thinks he's got a lucky pinkie . . ." He stopped. There was an awkward pause on the other end.

"Henry?"

I heard a sigh. "Look, Gabby. Forget what I said. Buses run back and forth from Chicago to the casino all the time. He'll probably show up fresh as a daisy for the meeting, and he'd be livid if he knew I'd said anything about . . . you know."

"That's priceless, Henry. You and Mona were the ones who first took him to the Horseshoe when I was gone Mother's Day weekend, remember?"

"Yeah. Don't remind me. Didn't think he'd get so obsessed . . . But, hey, I gotta go. You sure you're okay, Gabby?"

I softened. Henry was basically a good egg, even if his wife and I had gotten along like two Brillo pads. "Yeah, Henry, I'm okay. Real good, in fact . . ." Someone was knocking at my door. "Look, Henry, I've got to go too. I'll try Philip later."

Carolyn stuck her head in and grinned. "Got time to talk about starting that book club?"

I glanced at my watch. "Uh-uh. Got a staff meeting from ten to eleven." But I grinned back at her. "It's good to see you, Carolyn. Let's talk at eleven, okay?"

Carolyn and Precious were both going through the donated books that comprised the start of our so-called library when I joined them in the multipurpose room after the staff meeting. Dandy was back from his morning walk with Lucy, bestowing wet kisses on my mom, who was supervising the activities from her usual overstuffed throne. Across the room Lucy poured out the dregs of that morning's coffee from the carafes, loading up her cup with big tablespoons of powdered cream and sugar.

"Who put all these dumb romances in here?" Carolyn frowned, waving a handful of paperbacks with similar bare-chested hunks clutching fainting damsels on the covers.

"Let me see dose!" Wanda appeared out of nowhere and snatched the paperbacks.

Precious snickered and waved her off. "At least the girl's readin'."

"Okay, ladies. Book club. Got any suggestions, Carolyn?" I sat down across from my mother, while Dandy wiggled his rump against my legs, begging for a scratch.

"Something classic—good literature. Hey, what about *Moby Dick*? You know, since we named the van and all."

I groaned. I'd barely made it through *Moby Dick* myself in school. "Might be a bit hefty to start with. What do we have already? Whatever we choose, we're going to have to get more copies." Did I have "books for book club" in my program budget?

My mother struggled up out of her chair and started rummaging through the books on the bookshelf with Precious.

"Man, what a mishmash," Precious murmured. "*Augustine's Confessions* . . . what is that? True confessions? Le's see . . . *The One*

Year Book of Hymns . . . huh. Never heard of some of these. Oh, what's this? *The Idiot's Guide to Grandparenting* an' *What Shall We Name the Baby?*" She pulled out the last two books and waved them in the air with a big grin. "Hey, maybe I can use these when Sabrina's baby gets here."

"This one," my mother said, pulling out a slim book. She turned and held it out to Carolyn. "I . . ." Her voice trailed off.

Carolyn tried to take the book. "Thanks, Miss Martha. Uh, I've got it; you can let go."

My mother stared at her, gripping the book. Her knuckles were turning white.

I started up off my chair. "Mom? You okay?" It was like my mother had gone into a trance. "Mom? . . . Mom!"

Dandy started barking. "Grab her before she falls!" Carolyn commanded. I leaped to her side, and the two of us lowered my mom into her chair. The dog was going nuts, barking and whining, trying to climb into the chair with my mother. Out of the corner of my eye, I saw Lucy heading this way like a runaway train.

"I think she's having a stroke!" Carolyn cried. "We need help!" She ran for the foyer.

A stroke! . . . A stroke . . . I'd learned ways to tell if it was happening. I crouched beside her, my heart racing. "Mom! Can you smile at me?" My mother just stared, still gripping the book. "Raise your arms! . . . What day is today?" No response, just my mother's wide eyes.

Lucy pushed her way in between us, grabbed my mother's shoulders, and shook her. "Miz Martha! Wake up, honey!" The frumpy old woman turned to me, her own eyes wide and frightened. "Do somethin', girl!"

The double doors to the multipurpose room swung open, and I saw Mabel, Angela, and Carolyn running toward us. I didn't wait. Snatching my cell phone out of my pants pocket, I flipped it open and punched 9-1-1.

chapter 34

The ambulance ride, siren wailing . . . my mother strapped to the gurney with an oxygen mask covering her face . . . the rush into the emergency room of Thorek Memorial . . . filling out forms about my mother's insurance . . . watching as they sent her frail form into the doughnut-shaped machine to do a CAT scan of her brain . . .

The last few hours blurred as I sat in the waiting room, riding a roller coaster of jumbled thoughts and emotions. *Oh God, Oh God, I don't want to lose her . . . not Mom . . . not now . . . Did I wait too long to check out those headaches? . . . I need to get hold of my sisters! . . . Should I call Aunt Mercy? . . . No, wait until I hear what the doctor has to say . . . Oh God, please don't take her . . . What if she's paralyzed? Strokes can do that . . . but didn't Dr. Palma say mom was basically healthy for her age? . . .*

Mabel, Carolyn, Precious, and Lucy had all shown up in the emergency room and waited for the doctor to come talk to me. Mabel sat beside me, her warm-brown face calm and concerned.

Carolyn paced, her pale hands nervously patting pockets, as if looking for a cigarette. Precious sat in a corner of the room, eyes closed, mouth moving, murmuring a constant stream of prayers. From time to time I heard "Jesus!" or "My Lord!" like little puffs shot into the air. Gray-haired Lucy sat slumped in the opposite corner, looking like she'd just been Dumpster diving in her sloppy pair of cropped pants, loose button-up flowered cotton shirt, purple hat jammed on her head, and ratty gym shoes, laces undone, no socks.

I was glad these new friends were here . . . but for some reason I felt terribly alone. The responsibility for my mom, the decisions to be made, felt like too much. Where was my family? Why did my sisters and I live so far apart? Even if I got hold of them today—a big "if"—there'd be no way they could get here quickly. Even if they could, what would we say to each other? It'd been years since we'd spent any time together. Since we'd really talked.

Family . . . Philip and the boys were my family. That was the biggest hole of all. Fifteen years ago, almost sixteen now, Philip and I had made vows to be there for each other through thick and thin. Times like this. I squeezed my eyes shut and tried to imagine my husband's arms around me, holding me, shielding me from the guilt and pain and what-ifs . . .

I couldn't. He'd cut me adrift. Left me alone. I didn't even know where he was.

And the boys! *They should be here! This is their grandmother!* Anger surged up through my gut and pushed hot tears down my cheeks. It was one thing for Philip to kick me out of his life. But to take my sons away—

"Mrs. Fairbanks?"

I looked up, startled. Dr. Palma stood in the doorway. For some odd reason I noticed the neat baby blue dress shirt and blue-and-black-striped tie he wore beneath his open white lab coat, a stethoscope stuffed in the coat pocket. The emergency room doctor must have called him. I quickly wiped the wetness off my cheeks and stood up. "Dr. Palma. I'm so glad to see you."

The Filipino doctor glanced at the other women, then back at me. "Would you like some privacy? We can go to a conference room." I was tempted to smile. Guess it didn't take rocket science to figure out that the other women in the room weren't exactly family members.

"We can talk here. They're with me." I sat back down and groped for Mabel's hand.

The doctor sat on the edge of the padded chair next to me and leaned forward. "Mrs. Fairbanks, your mother has suffered a massive brain hemorrhage—bleeding between the brain and the skull. Truth is, I've never seen such a large bleed."

"A hemorrhage? But why?"

"We can't be sure. Some patients have weak blood vessels that break and cause seepage into the brain. Or it can happen suddenly, without warning, as it appears to have done in your mother's case." The doctor's voice seemed to fade in and out of my head, like TV sound bites coming from another room as he listed possible causes. *High blood pressure . . . taking an anticoagulant over a long period . . . brain trauma . . . brain tumor . . . an aneurysm that burst . . .*

I forced myself to focus.

"—or possibly a combination of factors. Since I saw Mrs. Shepherd for the first time a few days ago, it's hard to tell."

I stared at him, stunned. Finally I managed, "How . . . how is she? I mean, what can you do?"

Dr. Palma shook his head. "With a smaller bleed, we might be able to do surgery, suction off the blood and try to repair the artery. But you have to understand, Mrs. Fairbanks, the hemorrhage is so massive, I'm afraid the damage has already been done."

My mouth went dry. "What does that mean?"

"It means you need to make a decision. She's in a coma now, not aware of any pain. If you want, we can put her on life support, keep her alive. Or we could make her comfortable and . . . let nature take its course."

I stared at him. "Life support? If we do that, is there a chance she'd get better?"

He shook his head. "The damage is extensive. She'd most likely be hooked to machines for the rest of her life."

"And if we don't?" My voice had dropped to a whisper.

His gray eyes were gentle, full of concern. "She might last anywhere from twelve to twenty-four hours."

My head sank into my hands. I felt Mabel's arm go around my shoulders and hold on tight. *No . . . no . . . no! Oh God, I don't want to have to make this decision alone.* I sensed Precious, Lucy, and Carolyn gathering around, like protective mother hens.

I raised my head and looked at the doctor. "Dr. Palma . . ." My voice cracked. "If she was your mother, what would you do?"

The doctor shook his head again. "I can't make this decision for you, Mrs. Fairbanks. As her family, it's yours to make. But if my mother was in this situation . . . I'd let her go naturally." He rose to his feet. "Please, think about it. Call other family if you need to. I'll come back within the hour."

He started to leave, but I ran to the door and caught him. "Dr. Palma . . ." I had to know. "The headaches. Did they have anything to do with it? If I'd brought her in sooner—?"

He shrugged slightly. "Possibly. But we're second-guessing now. As you said, the headaches only started less than two weeks ago. Not usually a cause for alarm without other symptoms. Please, don't blame yourself. You brought her in when they continued—no one could have done more."

The moment the door closed behind him, Lucy was in my face. "He sayin' jus' let 'er *die*? Ya can't do that!"

"So ya think she oughta play God?" Precious snapped. "Step in an' keep Gramma Shep goin' after her body give out? What about you? If you was in a coma, wouldja want some machine ta be doin' your breathin'? Not knowin' anything?"

"That's diff'rent."

"Why?"

"'Cause—"

"Both of you, shut up!" Carolyn grabbed Lucy's arm. "Come on, let's go get some coffee, leave Mabel and Gabby." Pushing both Lucy and Precious ahead of her, Carolyn cleared the room. The door wheezed shut after them.

I sank back into a chair, feeling as if blood was rushing through my ears. *Oh God, I should have brought Mom in sooner. But I didn't know! And everything's been so crazy. I'm trying, God, I really am. Doing the best I can, but I can't do this alone! I need You, God. I need help. Please—*

"Gabby?" Mabel's voice finally penetrated my brain. "Do you want to call your family? Your sisters?"

I started to nod—then shook my head. "Aunt Mercy first." I slowly dug out my cell phone, but just stared at it stupidly.

Mabel pried it out of my fingers, found my contact list, and a moment later she pushed the Call button, listened a brief moment, then handed the phone to me.

Aunt Mercy's voice reached across airwaves and wrapped around me like a hug. Yes, yes, she'd get on the phone right away and keep trying until she got Honor and Celeste. What hospital were we at? Did I have a medical power of attorney? Yes, it was a terrible decision to have to make. "If it was me, honey, I'd want you to let me go," she said. "But I think I have your dad and mom's living will in my files. I'll get it and fax it to you. Give me half an hour. Hang in there, Gabby."

While we waited, Mabel read the psalms to me. "'The Lord is my shepherd, I shall not be in want' . . ."

Shepherd. Funny. I'd never made that connection before. Shepherd was my maiden name and was still my mother's married name. A shepherd takes care of his sheep—feeding, protecting, comforting—like my daddy used to take care of us girls growing up. But now Daddy was gone. My sisters were gone—or might as well be. My husband was gone . . .

But Psalm 23 says God takes care of me just like a shepherd.

Mabel was still reading. "'Even though I walk through the valley of death, You are with me' . . ."

I was definitely walking through the valley of death. My marriage was dying . . . my mom was dying. But God was with me. That's what it said. Did I believe it?

As Mabel continued to read, the words of Dottie Rambo's

gospel song danced alongside the psalm in my spirit. *"Where do I go when there's nobody else to turn to? . . . Who do I talk to, when nobody wants to listen? . . . Who do I lean on, when there's no foundation stable? . . . I go to the Rock, I know He's able, I go to the Rock!"*

Tears rolled down my cheek. I wasn't alone. God was my family. After all, He had the same last name . . . *Shepherd.*

chapter 35

Martha Shepherd lay small and slight under the taut hospital sheet, her eyes closed, an oxygen mask still covering her nose and mouth, her gray hair splayed out on the pillow as her breath rose and fell. I sat in a chair beside the hospital bed, holding her left hand. My fingers played with her wedding ring, a simple gold band she'd been wearing for over fifty years. *Over fifty years . . .* Was my marriage going to end after only fifteen?

I felt so sad. As if I was treading water in a huge pool of loss.

And yet . . . I *was* treading water. I hadn't gone under. *"The Lord is my Shepherd" . . . Hold on, strong woman of God, hold on.*

Aunt Mercy had faxed my parents' living will to the hospital. No heroic measures that would simply prolong dying, it said. I felt a strange relief. My mother's decision, not mine. They moved my mother into a private room. No machines.

And now we wait . . .

Mabel had taken a distraught Lucy back to Manna House to

take care of Dandy, leaving Carolyn and Precious to sit with me and my comatose mother. But the word must have gotten around, because Josh and Edesa Baxter showed up midafternoon, and the sweet young couple held me and we cried.

I left the room long enough to call my sons. They should know. It was Monday . . . what were the boys doing at four in the afternoon? To my huge relief, Mike Fairbanks answered the phone. He swore softly under his breath when I gave him the news. "Sure am sorry to hear this, Gabby. She was a sweet lady. But, uh, the boys aren't here at the moment. Marlene went to pick up P. J. at lacrosse camp, and Paul's out riding his bike—Oh, wait. I think I hear them now. Hold on . . ."

In the background I heard muffled voices, then running feet. Paul got on the phone first. "Mom! Mom! Is Grandma Martha okay? She isn't gonna die, is she?" I heard the click of an extension pick up.

I don't know where I found the words. "It's a very bad stroke. The doctor says she won't live long . . . P. J., are you there? Would you boys like to say good-bye to Grandma? She's in a coma, so she won't be able to respond, but you'll know . . ."

Both boys were crying now. Trying to reassure them, I walked the phone back into the room and held it to my mother's ear. "Mom, it's Paul and P. J. . . ." I don't know what they said. My mother's fixed expression did not change. But when I took the phone back out into the hall, both boys were still crying.

"Mom! I wanna be with you," Paul wailed.

"Me too." P. J. sounded ten again. "I wanna say good-bye to Grandma for real."

I could barely contain the tears. "I know. I want to be with you too. I'll call you again real soon and let you know what's happening, okay? Now, let me talk to Granddad Mike again."

Mike Fairbanks must have been right there. "Gabby, have you called Philip yet?"

Philip. Was he even back in town? "No. I—I don't want him here right now."

"Humph. Don't blame you. Look, let me work it out with Philip about getting the boys there when . . . you know, the funeral and everything."

I closed the phone and leaned my forehead against the wall outside my mother's room. Odd. Philip's father was turning into my advocate—

"Gabby!" Estelle swept down the hall, wearing a bright turquoise caftan, her loose kinky hair in an untidy topknot. "Oh, baby," she murmured, folding me into a big hug. "I'm so sorry." She turned. "Harry, give that basket here. This girl needs something to eat."

Only then did I notice that a bare-domed Harry Bentley was behind her, carrying a basket that turned out to be stuffed with sandwiches and fruit. "Mr. Bentley!" I couldn't believe he'd come. I wrapped my arms around him. "Thank you for coming," I whispered. "You . . . you know you were my very first Chicago friend."

"And you, Firecracker, added some pizzazz to a very dull job." The middle-aged black man chuckled. "Not to mention that you introduced me to my lady, here."

"*Lady* is right." Estelle gave him the eye. "And don't you forget it, mister. Now, where's Lady Shepherd? She's the one we came to see." Once in the room, the large woman leaned over the bed and kissed my mother's wrinkled cheek, her glowing cinnamon face a warm contrast to my mother's pale skin against the stark-white pillow. "We're all here, Gramma Shep. Lot of people who love you. And Dandy sends his love."

Estelle straightened and shook her head at me. "If Lucy had her way, she'd be bringing that dog up in here, but Mabel put her foot down. They'll be here soon. Now . . ." She sat on the end of the hospital bed. "Tell us some stories about your mama, Gabby. You don't mind, do you, Martha?" She patted my mother's foot under the covers.

The heavy spirit in the room seemed to lift. I racked my brain for memories of my mother—but once I started, it was hard to stop. "Sundays . . . Mom always got up early to put a pot roast or chicken casserole in the oven so it'd be hot and ready after church. She usually invited someone on the spur of the moment to come home with us too."

Mr. Bentley chuckled. "Sounds like my mama. Except the guests invited themselves."

Estelle gave him a poke. "Hush. This ain't about your mama. Go on, Gabby. Tell us about Christmas."

"Oh yeah . . . One time my dad wrapped up only one new slipper for Mom's Christmas present, because only one of her old ones had a hole in it. Mom laughed so hard she got a stitch in her side! And *then* he made her hunt for its mate—can't remember where he hid it, but it took her two days to find it."

Now everyone was laughing.

"I was always bringing home pathetic stray cats and dogs—drove my dad nuts, but Mom usually stuck up for me. But seeing how much she dotes on Dandy, I realize she has a soft heart for four-legged creatures herself. Of course, that doesn't explain the snake she let me keep—"

"Snake? Whatchu talkin' 'bout snakes?" Lucy and Mabel had returned, and Lucy pushed herself in and parked herself in a chair on the other side of the bed. "Hey there, Miz Martha. It's me, Lucy. Just wantcha to know, Dandy's missin' ya real bad, so don't pay these people no mind. Just come on home."

"Lucy—" I started, but Estelle gave me a leave-it-be shake of the head. That's when I saw Jodi and Denny Baxter leaning in the doorway—Josh must have called his parents. When I started to get up to greet them, Jodi shook her head. "Go on, Gabby. We want to hear the stories."

Mom's breathing had slowed, each breath coming farther and farther apart. "Guess the thing I remember most about my mom," I murmured, stroking her hand, listening to the ragged breaths, "is all the books she read to us after supper, at bedtime, on car trips—even when we were older. I was the youngest, and one winter she read all the *Little House* books by Laura Ingalls Wilder—and Celeste and Honor would 'just happen' to hang around to hear them, too, even though they were teenagers."

Carolyn and Precious looked at each other. "That 'splains it," Precious said.

"Explains what?"

Carolyn pulled a dog-eared paperback from her backpack. "The book Miss Martha was trying to give me when she . . . you know . . ." The Manna House book maven choked up and couldn't say any more.

Precious took the book from Carolyn and held it up so we could all see the title. *Little House in the Big Woods.* My eyes watered. I'd read a lot to my boys when they were younger. That had stopped when Philip sent them to boarding school. But, I vowed, if I got them back under my roof, I'd make sure we read aloud together, even if I had to read a Harry Potter book or—

"Miz Martha!" Lucy's voice rose in alarm. "C'mon, now, breathe!"

I rose quickly and leaned close to my mother's face. A long silence—and then suddenly another long, slow breath.

"That's right. C'mon!" Lucy's wrinkled face under the purple knit hat twisted with anxiety.

The room hushed as the people who'd been family to both of us in the last few weeks seemed to hold their collective breaths. I leaned closer, my face on the pillow beside my mother's, tears sliding down my cheeks. "Mom," I whispered. "I love you. I love you so much . . ."

The silence grew . . . one minute . . . two . . .

But this time—nothing.

My mother had slipped away as gently as that last breath.

Midnight. The hospital waiting room was empty now except for Jodi Baxter and me. Bless them! Josh's parents had offered to wait with me while I finished necessary paperwork with the hospital and help make phone calls, so everyone else could go home and get some sleep. Denny had taken charge of making arrangements with a reputable funeral home to pick up my mother's body and hadn't come back.

I played with the gold wedding ring I'd gently slipped off my mother's hand. Even now, I could still hear the voices of our friends—our Chicago family—as they'd gathered around Mom's bedside, held hands, and recited the Lord's Prayer. Then Estelle began to sing "Amazing Grace." The impromptu chorus of male and female voices joining in had been tender and sweet. My mother would have loved it.

And then they'd left quietly—all except Lucy, who'd stormed out during the song, anger masking her grief.

My cell phone rang, and I snatched it. "Celeste? . . . Oh, thank God Aunt Mercy got through to you! . . . Yes, she's gone, about two hours ago . . . I'm still here at the hospital . . . I know, I know . . ." We cried together on the phone. I tried to imagine my sister, ten years older than me, whom I hadn't seen since our father's funeral two years ago. All three of us girls had cried together then, holding each other, united for the moment in our grief—Celeste's thick brunette hair pulled back, hazel eyes and freckled nose both red and running . . . Honor's bare-faced California tan under her bleached-blonde shag, looking forlorn . . . and me, the baby, feeling like Little Orphan Annie—and I don't mean the hair—once Daddy's funeral was over and we'd gone our separate ways.

Now it was our mom. After wiping my face with the back of my hand, I tried to answer Celeste's questions as best I could, but I felt on the defensive. After all, I was the one who was here, trying to handle everything by myself. I tried to make her understand it was a *massive* hemorrhage . . . The doctor had given no hope of recovery, even if they put her on life support . . . Yes, I had power of attorney, but Mom's living will was clear . . . Of *course* Celeste was the oldest, but it wasn't exactly easy getting in touch with her in the middle of Denali National Forest . . .

Finally we got to "what next." "Yes, I know there's a plot beside Daddy back in Minot, but . . . All right. Yes . . . Call me tomorrow, please? Maybe we can get on a three-way with Aunt Mercy to decide what to do. And try to get hold of Honor, okay? It's already after midnight here."

As I closed the phone, Jodi handed me a tissue and I blew my nose. I looked up at her through bleary eyes and sighed. "I don't know what to do, Jodi. I'm sure my mom would want to be buried beside my dad, and we already have a plot in Minot. But how do I get her there?" I ran my fingers through my tangled mop. "I *know* I can't afford to bury her in Chicago."

Jodi pulled a chair next to mine and took both my hands. "Gabby, you've done everything you can do tonight. Come home with us. Get some sleep. I'll take you back to Manna House in the morning. I'll keep the car, and we can do any running around you need to do. Okay?"

I nodded wearily and stood up. Suddenly I felt more exhausted than I'd ever felt in my life. Jodi took my arm and I let her lead me through the hallways and down the elevator until we found Denny, who said the funeral home would be there shortly. I could go tomorrow to pick out a casket and make arrangements.

Denny went for the car and picked us up at the main entrance of the hospital. Thankfully, Jodi and Denny didn't try to talk as he drove their minivan the half mile to Lake Shore Drive and turned north. I sat slumped in the seat behind Denny, gazing out the window in a half stupor. A full moon shone over the lake on the right, bathing the trees and parks along the Drive in silver gossamer, competing with the bright neon lights of the city on our left.

The lakeshore was beautiful, even at night. In spite of everything that had happened, Chicago was growing on me. Maybe when I got the apartment and the boys had settled in, we could explore the city and its wonders—

The apartment. I stiffened, coming wide awake like a jolt of caffeine as streetlights flashed by. Mom and I had been planning to share the apartment, pooling our money! That was the only way I could afford it. But now . . .

Oh God! What am I going to do now? New tears sprang to my eyes, and I started to weep silently, feeling hope drain out of my spirit. It wasn't just being homeless again, forced to stay longer at Manna House—which was about as good a place as an emergency shelter could be, even if I did have to sleep in a bunk room with four to six other women.

It was my sons.

Without an apartment where I could provide a home for them, my petition for guardianship would go down the toilet.

chapter 36

It took me a long time to fall asleep in Josh Baxter's old bedroom, but at least I wasn't awakened at six o'clock by Sarge's wake-up bell. The bedside clock said 8:36 when I finally opened my eyes, the whirring fan in the window the only noise. Reluctantly I dragged myself out of bed, clad only in the big Bulls T-shirt and pair of shorts Jodi had handed me to sleep in. Finger combing the snarls out of my hair, I wandered into the kitchen, where Amanda Baxter was perched on a tall kitchen stool wearing blue-and-orange-plaid pajama bottoms and a rumpled tank top, trying to keep the calico cat on her lap from getting into her cereal bowl.

"Oh. Mrs. Fairbanks!" she burbled, quickly swallowing her mouthful. "I'm so sorry to hear about your mom . . ." She dumped the cat and hopped off the stool to give me a hug. "I'm so glad I had a chance to meet Gramma Shep last Sunday. She reminded me of my grandma—the one in Des Moines, not New York. My dad's mom doesn't even want to be called 'Grandma,' go figure . . . Oh, Mom said to tell you she took Daddy to work, but she'll be back soon. Coffee's hot—you want some?"

I nodded, hiding a smile at Amanda's monologue as the girl poured a mug of coffee. I added milk from a jug sitting out on the counter and sipped. The hot liquid felt good going down, waking up body parts still sluggish from my five short hours of sleep.

Amanda took the elastic band out of her honey-blonde hair, shook her head, and regathered the tousled locks back into the band. She eyed me tentatively. "What's going to happen to your mom's doggy now?"

I shook my head. *Dandy* . . . just one more worry in the long list of decisions I had to make.

"Wish I could take him. Peanut and Patches are okay, but I miss having a dog. You would've liked Willie Wonka, our chocolate Lab—he was a sweetheart. But I'll be going back to U of I in August, my second year." Amanda eyed me cautiously. "But my folks might take him if you need a home."

I gave her a wan smile. "They already offered. Sweet of you to be concerned about him, Amanda. But speaking of Dandy, I need to get back to the shelter. He's probably really confused that my mom isn't—" A sudden lump in my throat cut off my words, and I scurried for the bathroom before I blubbered in front of Amanda.

Jodi was back when I reappeared in the same slacks and top that I'd worn yesterday, my hair damp and frizzled. I held up my cell phone and made a face. "Dead. I need to get back to Manna House and charge it before I can make any calls."

"Use our phone, Gabby! It's fine."

I waggled the cell. "Unfortunately, all my numbers are in here."

"Well, let's get going, then." She held up two travel cups. "Have coffee, will travel. Oh—grab that bagel and one of those bottles of juice, if you'd like."

True to her word, Jodi put both herself and their Dodge Caravan at my disposal for the day. But I wasn't really prepared for the grief-stricken faces of many of the shelter residents when we came into the multipurpose room. The women who weren't already out for the day gathered around, bombarding me with questions and comments. "What happened, Miss Gabby?" "But she wasn't sick!" "It's good, ain't it? I mean, that she didn't die of cancer or somethin' painful, right?" "Gonna miss her powerful." "Gramma Shep—can't believe she gone." "Hope I go that way—*bam*. Gone. *My* gramma got sick and was in the bed for months . . ."

Jodi finally rescued me and spirited me away to my office. She ran up to the bunk room and brought down my charger, and while the cell phone was recharging, we made a list of things I needed to do. Call Aunt Mercy. Decide what we should do about a funeral. Try to get on a conference call with my sisters. Go to the funeral home, choose a casket, make arrangements.

"What arrangements?" I wailed to Jodi. "I'm sure my sisters and Aunt Mercy want to have the funeral back home—and we have to bury her beside Daddy. But what's it going to cost to ship my mom's body all the way back to Minot? And how long would that take, Jodi?" I threw down my pen, grabbed a wad of tissues, and pressed them against my eyes to stem the tide of new tears rising to the surface.

Jodi scooted her chair close to mine. "Gabby . . . Gabby, let's stop a minute and just pray, okay? I've been trying to learn to pray first, before I get into a big stew . . . Wait. I think I hear Estelle in the kitchen. Let me get her, and the three of us can pray."

Sure enough, Estelle had come in to make lunch, but she crowded into my tiny office in her big, white apron and hairnet, shut the door, and the two of them laid hands on my head and started to pray. Jodi prayed for God-given wisdom and peace in the middle of this painful loss. Estelle prayed that God would pull everything together—all those decisions to be made, all the jagged pieces of my life—and "knit them together in a way that's *good* for Gabby and her family."

That's when I lost it. "But . . . but . . . but . . ." I tried to say, the tears coming harder. "With Mom gone, I . . . I . . . can't afford the apartment Lee—Mr. Boyer—found for me. And . . . and . . . if I don't have an apartment, I . . . I can't get my boys back!" The last words were swallowed up as my whole body shook with sobs.

The two women just held me, crooning and soothing as if I was a child. And finally my sobs quieted, and I mopped my face and blew my nose.

"Now, listen, Gabby Fairbanks," Estelle said, her voice soft but firm. "God hasn't brought you this far to leave you. If that plan for the apartment doesn't work out, it means God's got a better plan in mind. You hear? Trust Him, baby. Trust Him." She gave me another hug and slipped out of the room.

"She's right," Jodi said. "I'll call the Yada Yada sisters to pray about the apartment thing, but if you can put that aside, let it sit in Jesus' lap, let's work on the things that need to be done today." She stood up. "Why don't we go to the funeral home first and, you know, find out how it's done when somebody dies in one city but needs to be buried in another state."

I nodded, blew my nose again, and followed her out into the dining room. Then I stopped. "Wait . . . have you seen Dandy since we came in? Or Lucy?"

As it turned out, no one I asked had seen Lucy *or* Dandy all morning. At the reception desk, Angela shook her head. "But you know Lucy. Sometimes she takes the dog out and doesn't come back for hours. Just takes him along to do . . . whatever it is she does. I'm sure they'll be back eventually."

Jodi had already wandered outside. "Well," I said to Angela, pushing the front door open to follow, "if she brings Dandy in while I'm out, tell her to wait here for me. I want to spend some time with Dandy too."

Jodi was standing on the sidewalk beside the big Manna House van parked in front of the shelter, standing on tiptoe in her sandals, peeking inside. As I came up to her, she turned. "Gabby, this is going to sound funny, but . . . back there, when we were praying, I think God gave me an idea how to get your mom's body back to North Dakota."

"What do you mean?"

"Drive the casket there. Yourself. In Moby Van."

I stared at her. "In *that*? I mean, can you *do* that?"

She threw up her hands. "I don't know! But the idea just dropped into my head while we were praying about what to do, like God was giving an answer. I didn't say anything back there, because, yeah, it sounds crazy. But standing here looking at this big ol' van, I'm thinking, why not? We prayed for an answer, didn't we?" Jodi giggled nervously, as if she couldn't believe she was talking this way.

"But . . . but . . . I'm sure you'd need some special permit or something. Who in the world would we ask about something like that?" I made a face. "They'll think we're nuts."

"Probably. That's why *you're* going to ask." Jodi laughed and pulled me toward her minivan. "Come on. I'll drive you to the funeral home. Then it's up to you."

"Me! It's your idea."

"Hope not. If it works, we're gonna give God the credit."

We sat across the desk at Kirkland & Sons Funeral Home as the impeccably dressed man tapped his pen on the papers in front of him. He had sallow skin, thinning hair, and an annoying habit of pushing his horn-rims up his nose every few minutes. "I'm sorry, Mrs. Fairbanks; personal transport of a body is highly irregular. However, we *can* transport your mother's remains to . . ." He squinted at the paperwork. ". . . Minot, North Dakota, if we have the name and address of the appropriate funeral home for delivery."

"How much?"

"Well, that depends on the mode of transportation. We can arrange for air, train, or ground. When do you want the body to arrive?"

"Why, as soon as possible. A few days . . ." I glanced at the calendar on the wall. Today was Tuesday. Give a few days for my sisters to travel . . . "By this weekend?"

"Well then. We would probably need to send one of our hearses, which would run about . . ." He tapped some figures on his calculator. ". . . four thousand dollars."

I stared at the man. The "discount package" he'd already

offered added up to roughly five thousand, which included the casket—a moderately priced metal one in medium metallic blue with silver shade and a white crepe interior—and service fee for staff and facilities ("All paperwork, death and burial certificates, embalming, hairdresser, use of our chapel if you so desire, the hearse for transport . . .").

I blew out a slow breath. "Can we, uh, have someplace where my friend and I can talk in private?"

"Of course." The man politely showed us to a small "family room" with padded chairs, a coffeepot, and pitchers of ice water and closed the door behind him.

I looked at Jodi. "Jodi, I can't afford this! That's almost ten thousand dollars!"

She nodded. "I know. But the man said it was 'highly irregular.' He didn't say it was illegal. I think we ought to check it out. I'll . . . I don't know. Call the County Clerk's office or something. And maybe you should call your aunt Mercy and find out what the funeral home in Minot says."

I called Aunt Mercy at the library where she worked. She couldn't talk long, but she promised to call the funeral home that had handled everything when my dad died. "I think my brother had prepaid funeral costs here for both him and Martha. I'll call you back as soon as I find out anything . . . Oh, I finally got hold of Honor. She's pretty broken up. But she sounded like she would come for the funeral—drive, I think. I don't know about her boys. But I'll call her back as soon as we can make plans."

It was already past noon. I told the funeral director we had to talk with family and I'd be back soon. Jodi and I walked a few blocks until we found a tiny restaurant and ordered homemade vegetable soup. I wasn't sure my stomach could handle anything heavier.

My cell phone rang halfway through my soup. Aunt Mercy. She was almost laughing. "Mr. Jacobs said, 'Hogwash. Of course you can transport the body!' He said all you need is a permit from the county—which the funeral home there can get for you—and a vehicle that will hold the casket. Period."

"You're kidding!"

"I'm not, sweetheart. Here's the information you'll need to fill out the permit. And I was right; your father prepaid for a casket, embalming—everything. There might be a few extra expenses since two funeral homes are involved, but the big things are covered. Jacobs said to tell your funeral director to call him if he has any questions." I jotted down the information on a napkin, including Mr. Jacobs's phone number. "And Gabby, as soon as you decide when you can get here, let me know so I can make arrangements for a service on this end. Celeste and Honor need to know when to arrive. And there are a lot of people here who were very fond of your mom and dad."

Jodi was waiting impatiently for news, her soup getting cold. Even though she was in her forties, she whooped like a schoolkid when I told her what Aunt Mercy had said. "See? See what God can do, Gabby?" She shook her head in amazement. "To tell you the truth, I'm still surprised when God answers my prayers. Some faith, huh?"

"Well, don't stop praying yet. I haven't even asked Mabel—or the board—if I can use Moby Van for something personal like this. And that huge van must be a gas hog. Can't imagine what the gas would cost all the way to North Dakota and back."

Jodi pulled a stray strand of brown hair out of her mouth and chuckled. "A lot less than four thousand dollars, anyway!" She waved her soup spoon at me. "And I think we should go back and take apart Kirkland & Sons 'discount package' and see what it'd cost for just the things you actually need. You won't need to use their chapel, unless . . ." She stopped and looked at me funny. "Gabby? I know you're going to have a funeral service for your mom back in Minot, but there are a lot of people here who've come to know and love your mom. Especially at Manna House. Why don't we plan something here for the staff and residents? Josh and Edesa got married in the multipurpose room at Manna House. I'm sure we could do a funeral. A memorial service to celebrate Martha's life!"

I got a little teary. "I'd like that. I know Mom would like that too."

We ate our soup in silence for a minute; then I put my spoon down. "I can't do it. Can't imagine driving my mom's casket all the way to Minot by myself in that big ol' van. You gotta admit, Jodi, it's a little weird."

Jodi turned her head and gazed out the restaurant window at the misty rain that had started since we'd arrived, almost as if she hadn't heard me. Then, as if somebody had flipped her On button, she snatched up the bill for our soup and dug out a ten from her purse. She left both on the table. "You won't have to. Come on. Let's go."

I scooted out of the booth and followed her out of the restaurant. "What do you mean, I won't have to?"

She took my arm with a grin and started off down the sidewalk, ducking raindrops. "Because I'm going with you!"

chapter 37

Jodi Baxter and I came out of Mabel's office just as the supper bell was ringing. I'd reviewed with the Manna House director all the plans we were proposing. First, a celebration service for my mom's "homegoing" here at Manna House Thursday morning, open casket, everything. Followed by a repast supervised by Estelle. Then—if the board approved—loading the casket in Moby Van and driving to North Dakota, where I'd meet my sisters, have another funeral, and bury my mom beside my father in the Minot cemetery.

Mabel had been open to the idea of using the van but was noncommittal. But she was a hundred percent on board for hosting a memorial service for my mother at the shelter. "We'll all miss Martha," she'd said. "I think she fulfilled a grandmotherly role for a lot of the young women and kids the last few weeks."

I gave Jodi a tight hug in the foyer as she got ready to leave. "I don't know what I would've done without you today, Jodi. I mean, I can't believe you got the funeral home costs shaved off! That's a huge help."

She grinned. "Hey, it was fun seeing that funeral guy squirm. And don't you worry about the van, Gabby. If the board nixes the idea of using Moby, maybe we can take our Caravan if we take out all the seats. I've been wanting to go see my folks in Des Moines anyway. We could stop there the first night. It's on the way. Well . . . sorta." Jodi peeked into the multipurpose room. "So where's Dandy? I'd like to say good-bye to him. You know, Hero Dog worked his way into our hearts at the Baxter household that week you guys stayed with us."

Good question. Angela had already gone for the day, but Carolyn was babysitting the phone and the door buzzer in the reception cubicle for the evening shift. "Hey, Carolyn. Have you seen Dandy or Lucy?"

Carolyn shrugged. "Haven't seen either one."

Jodi and I looked at each other. "I'm worried," I said.

But when curfew rolled around, and Lucy still hadn't come back with my mother's dog, I started to get mad. That's when I discovered Dandy's food and water bowls, bag of kibbles, and Lucy's cart were gone too.

I wished I'd gone home with Jodi Baxter again. My mother's empty bunk—as well as Lucy's and the empty dog bed—weighed on my spirit in the night like heavy stones. I finally took my pillow and blanket, found Sarge, and asked if I could sack out on a couch in the multipurpose room, just for tonight.

Sarge shook her finger at me. "Gabby Fairbanks, you break more rules than the rest of the women on the bed list put together! I know it's tough losing your *madre*, so I'm gonna let you do it, but I'm waking you up *before* I ring the wake-up bell so nobody else gets a wise idea. *Capisce?*"

I curled up on a couch in the corner, but my mind was still spinning. I still needed to call Lee Boyer and tell him about my changed circumstances. My next appointment with him was scheduled for tomorrow at eleven, but with everything I had to do, there was no way! Hopefully we could talk by phone . . .

Celeste had called me twice that evening. I told her how things were working out on this end. Awhile later she called to say she'd gotten a flight from Juneau to Billings, Montana, would meet up with Honor flying in from Los Angeles, and the two of them would rent a car and drive to Minot, arriving sometime on Friday.

"I'm impressed you two were able to coordinate that," I'd said.

"Ha. Coordinate nothing. I bought her a ticket. *She* was talking about borrowing a car from a friend and driving straight through. I can just imagine some rattletrap with no muffler breaking down in the middle of the Mojave Desert, and we'd have to call in the state troopers to find her. Even if she didn't, she'd probably show up two days after the funeral."

That had made me laugh. Celeste wasn't that far wrong.

I'd also called Mike Fairbanks to tell him about the funeral on Thursday morning here in Chicago, and that I'd be driving my mom's body back to Minot, where we'd have a second funeral. "I wish the boys could come to the funeral in Minot, but I think they'd have to change planes, maybe even twice. I don't really feel good about that." And, I had to admit, it would probably cost more than going to Europe. Mike said okay, he'd call me back after checking flights to Chicago.

Now, as I lay staring at the ceiling fans slowing rotating over-head, I wished I'd asked if he'd spoken to Philip. I probably should call Philip myself, even if he had. *"I trust in God, why should I be afraid?"* the psalm said. Besides, shouldn't I treat Philip like I'd like to be treated? At least let him know that my mother had passed.

But I drew the line at him coming to the funeral. Not that he would. But after the way he'd treated my mother, if he tried it, I'd probably sic Dandy on him and send him to the hospital like that midnight burglar.

Sometime during the night I must've fallen asleep, because the next thing I knew, Sarge was shaking me awake and telling me to clear out of there before other residents started to come down-stairs. She also handed me the first cup of steaming coffee out of the pot, and I managed to get through that Wednesday morning on constant refills.

I called Lee Boyer first thing, told him what had happened and that I had to cancel my appointment that morning. "But this changes everything, Lee. I can't afford the apartment now . . ." I tried to steady my voice so I wouldn't break down again. "And I don't know what that means since I signed a contract. Can he sue me?"

"Now, Gabby, don't worry about the contract. I know this guy; we'll work something out. He owes me a few favors. But we do need to get you an address so we can file your custody petition with the court ASAP . . . Hey, look. Let's not try to deal with that today. You just lost your mother; that's enough to deal with. When you get back from Minot, we'll get right on it. Trust me, Gabby. I'm working this for you."

"*Trust me, Gabby . . .*" Why did that put a ruffle in my spirit? I felt confused about my feelings for this man. Lawyer? Friend? More than friend? But just then my call waiting beeped. The caller ID said Mike Fairbanks. "I'm sorry, Lee. Gotta take this. It's my father-in-law." I flipped over.

The call was short. Mike said he was bringing the boys to Chicago, they had a late flight that afternoon, and Philip was going to pick them up at O'Hare. "We'll be staying overnight with Philip. I'll get them to the funeral tomorrow morning, Gabby, and we'll be returning tomorrow night. That way P. J. will only have to miss one day of lacrosse."

I felt like screaming, *What does lacrosse have to do with anything?!* Even if I was leaving for North Dakota soon after the funeral, didn't Philip want the boys to stay through the weekend? They could go back to Virginia Sunday night, and P. J. would still only miss two days of camp. But I bit back my sharp retort. *Focus, Gabby, focus.* Mike was bringing the boys to their grandmother's funeral. I'd get to see my sons for those precious few hours, whether they stayed longer or not. That was all that mattered. "Thanks, Mike," I managed. "I appreciate that you're coming with them."

Blinking back tears, I hustled into Mabel's office, and we spent an hour roughing out a funeral service—Mom's favorite scriptures, music, who might participate. "Type up what you want for an obituary, Gabby," she told me, "and I'll contact Peter and Avis Douglass, see if they'd be willing to officiate. Any of the residents you'd like to include somehow in the service?"

I shrugged. "Well, Lucy—*if* she comes back, and if I don't kill her first for absconding with Dandy." I threw open my hands in helpless frustration. "Should I go look for her? Call the police? I mean, I really do want to find Dandy."

Mabel thought a moment, then fished her car keys out of her purse. "If you think you know where to look, be my guest."

I took the keys but realized it was probably a hopeless cause. Lucy could be anywhere! She was a street person, after all. It wasn't like she had a home and a workplace and a list of relatives and friends I could check out. But I did drive around the streets and through the alleys near Manna House, and even drove through Graceland Cemetery where I knew she often walked Dandy. Nothing.

Not sure why I found myself driving up Sheridan Road toward Richmond Towers, except that the park there along Lake Shore Drive was the place I'd first run into Lucy. Literally. Parking Mabel's car in the visitor parking spaces along the frontage road where Richmond Towers faced the park, I resisted the urge to peek into the lobby and say hi to Mr. Bentley. Another time.

Walking the jogging path, I veered off through the mown grass to check under some of the lush bushes. Was this the one where I'd tripped over Lucy's cart that day in the rain? I wasn't sure . . . but it was stupid anyway. Why would Lucy crawl under a bush on a breezy, warm day like today?

But I still scanned the park, following the path through the pedestrian tunnel under the Drive and coming out just north of Foster Avenue Beach. That's when I saw them . . . two familiar figures sitting on the two-tiered rock wall that led down to the strip of sand about a hundred yards to my left, a purple knit hat topping the dumpy body of Lucy Tucker, her arm draped around a yellow dog patiently sitting beside her.

I did not call to Dandy. Instead I quietly walked up beside them and sat down on the wall beside the dog. He immediately rose up, excited, licking me in the face and whimpering his greetings.

"Hey, Dandy," I said, scratching his rump. "Easy, now. How you doing, boy? . . . All right, all right, that's enough. Sit . . . sit! That's a good dog."

Dandy flopped between me and Lucy, his brow wrinkled, as if unsure what was going on or what he should do. Lucy said nothing. I, too, just sat on the wall, watching the waves stirred up by the strong breeze coming off Lake Michigan, the horizon dotted with slender, white sails. The warmth of the sun on my head and the breeze running fingers through my unruly curls swaddled me in an oddly comforting cocoon, a momentary respite from death and funerals and—

"I was goin' ta bring him back," Lucy finally muttered.

I didn't answer. Two seagulls fought over some tidbit in the shallows.

"We jus' needed some time, the two of us, what with Miz Martha dyin' off so sudden-like. Couldn't get no peace back there! Ever'body yappin' an' cryin' . . ."

Sitting there on that wall, my mad at Lucy sifted out of my spirit like so much dust. "I know. I got worried, though."

Lucy sniffled and wiped her nose with a big, faded blue handkerchief she pulled out of somewhere. "S'pose ya gotta take him back with you."

"Yeah. My boys are coming for their grandmother's funeral tomorrow, and I know they'll want to see Dandy. Paul, especially. He took care of Dandy for my mom when she was staying with us . . . kinda like you."

Lucy's head swiveled toward me. "What funeral?"

I told her our plans. A funeral at Manna House tomorrow morning, another in North Dakota, probably on Sunday. "My dad is buried there. We want to bury my mother beside him."

Lucy slid off the wall and shuffled two or three steps until she stood right in front of me, a kaleidoscope of mismatched tops and bottoms. "How you gettin' from here ta there?"

"Uh . . . driving. Mabel's asking the board if I can use Moby Van."

Lucy's rheumy eyes bored into mine. "Takin' Dandy?"

That brought me up short. I hadn't thought about what to do with Dandy. The Baxters would probably be glad to take care of him—or even Lucy—for the five or six days I'd be gone. But somehow that didn't seem right. Dandy was family, had been Mom's companion for the past ten years. And that only begged the bigger question. What was I going to do with Dandy *after* the funeral?

If I had my apartment, I'd keep him myself. That would be a big draw for the boys—well, Paul, anyway—in coming back to Chicago. His own dog.

But I didn't have an apartment. Didn't know when I would get one either.

"Well?" Lucy put her hands on her hips and stuck her face close to mine. "I *said*, are ya takin' Dandy back to Dakota ta bury your ma?"

"Yes!" I shot back. Well, why not, since we were driving.

"Okay then." Lucy hauled herself up the big step onto the grass and wrestled her cart out from under a nearby bush. "I'm goin' too."

chapter 38

Lucy would not be dissuaded. I almost hoped we'd have to take the Baxter minivan so I could honestly tell her there wouldn't be any extra seats—but when I got back to the shelter with Lucy and Dandy, Mabel had left a note for me on my desk:

Gabby—good news! The board is granting permission to use Moby Van to transport Martha Shepherd's casket, since she died while a resident of Manna House, and since there wouldn't BE a van except for Dandy. All they ask is that you cover gas and any out-of-pocket expenses. Have a safe trip!

My skin prickled. This *was* good news—so why did I feel a tinge of panic? The whole idea was crazy! Driving cross-country with a casket in the back of a van the size of a small bus. Paying for gas and expenses . . . certainly a reasonable request. But where was it going to come from? My credit cards were dead. I'd have to use my debit card, which would take money right out of my bank account. I'd just have to keep a close watch so that I didn't drain my account completely.

And now what excuse could I give to Lucy? Even if we took out enough seats to accommodate the casket, there'd still be enough room for me, Jodi, Dandy, *and* Lucy.

I grabbed the note and poked my head out the door. I'd ask Estelle what I should do. Lunch was over, but Delores Enriques was still packing up her portable medical clinic in a corner of the dining room. Two of the residents whose names I didn't know were wiping tables and sweeping the floor. Estelle was bustling around the kitchen with a larger-than-normal crew.

"*Hola*, Gabby." Delores paused her packing and scurried over to give me a hug. "I am so sorry to hear about your mother. My own mother lives in Mexico, but it's been five years since I have seen her. Now . . . I think I should go. One never knows how short life is."

I hugged her tight. "I know. Thanks, Delores. I hope you can go see your mom. The last few weeks I had with my mother were precious." I let her go, then turned back. "Say, I met your son, José, last Sunday. At SouledOut. Such a good-looking boy! He was with Amanda Bax—"

"*Sí, sí*, I know." She rolled her eyes heavenward. "Señor *Dios, por favor!* Just let him get through college before those two get any ideas . . ." The dark-eyed woman leaned close to me and lowered her voice. "José looks up to Amanda's brother, and *he* married Edesa Reyes when he'd barely turned twenty. But José is the first male in my family to even *go* to college. My Ricardo . . . oh." Delores put her hand up to her mouth. "*Perdone*. You go on, Gabby. I know you have a lot on your mind. We'll talk another time, all right?" She gave me a kiss on the cheek, then turned back to packing her stethoscope, swabs, and other instruments.

The kitchen was bustling. I leaned on the wide counter that opened into the kitchen, hoping I could get Estelle alone long enough to ask what I should do about Lucy. Althea, her hair hidden by her Middle Eastern head scarf, and Diane—took a moment for me to recognize her with that big Afro tucked into one of those ugly white hairnet caps—were both holding the big electric mixer as it went around and around, to keep it from rocking off the counter. Sammy's mom and several others from the Thursday cooking class were slicing cheese and ham, chopping vegetables, and arranging it all on a big, round tray.

"Hi, Estelle! What's happening? Your cooking class meeting early this week?"

Estelle looked up from the cutting board, where she was slicing lemons and limes. "Hey there, Gabby. You doin' okay? We just combined the knitting club and cooking class today to fix some food for the repast tomorrow after your mama's funeral. Least we can do for Gramma Shep."

"Uh-huh" . . . "That's right!" a few voices called out.

"Sheila, turn the heat down under them greens! S'posed to simmer, not boil . . . Diane! That cookie dough mixed yet? Turn that thing off! . . . Whatchu need, Tanya? Another tray?" Estelle bustled past me on the other side of the counter, giving me a quick glance. "You need somethin', honey? Can it wait a bit? We got a lot of pokers in the fire here."

I backed off with a wave. Didn't look like now was the time. Besides, I had a lot of last-minute details to wrap up for tomorrow—run to the funeral home to pick up the transport permit, call Aunt Mercy and ask how arrangements were shaping up on that end, ask some of the residents to act as ushers, call Denny Baxter and see if some of the guys from his men's group would act as pallbearers, wash a load of clothes and pack for the trip, pack up Mom's things to take back to North Dakota . . .

Everything was moving along until I got to the laundry room tucked away behind the kitchen. All four washing machines were busy. Good grief! I only had a load of underwear and a few necessities for my trip. Who—?

Just then Lucy lumbered in, dragging her cart. Her *empty* cart.

"Lucy! What are you doing? Are all these yours?" I pointed at the four machines.

"Yeah, what of it? Decided to dump it in, wash it all. Don't know what it's like in North Dakota. Might need my winter coat an' stuff."

"Oh, Lucy." I leaned against the wall, shaking my head.

In spite of Lucy's wash-a-thon—which, I had to admit, I'd been hoping she'd do for a long time—I managed to get almost everything done that afternoon and evening. Sinking into my office chair after supper, I turned on my computer and glanced at my watch. Almost eight . . . I had time to work a little more on the funeral program and still get to bed by lights-out.

Wait . . . Mike Fairbanks had said he and the boys were supposed to get in at O'Hare Airport around seven thirty. Philip was going to pick them up, take them back to the penthouse, and they'd see me tomorrow morning here at the funeral.

That meant P. J. and Paul were already here! In Chicago! How was I supposed to wait fourteen whole hours before I saw them tomorrow? I couldn't. I had to see them! Grabbing a pad of note-paper, I started jotting down times. Half an hour, give or take, to get their bags if they checked anything . . . maybe another sixty minutes to get to Philip's parked car and drive into the city. Add another half hour for good measure . . .

At nine thirty I got off the El at the Berwyn stop and walked briskly the two blocks to Sheridan Road and turned north. The warm night air was somewhere in the seventies, cooled by a nice breeze off the lake. I'd had to get an "emergency pass" from Sarge just to go out and come in past curfew, and she'd shaken her head when I wondered out loud whether I should take Dandy with me since it was dark. "Just *go*, Gabby Fairbanks. You want protection? Dandy and I'll walk ya to the El and you can give me a call when you want to come back. But give the poor dog a break. They don't let dogs on the El anyway."

Now Richmond Towers rose just a few blocks ahead of me, lighted windows hugging the curves of the building like a clingy dress. I hesitated as I reached the revolving doors that would take me into the lobby of the luxury high-rise, my knees suddenly going rubbery. What was I walking myself into? Philip would be there, and I hadn't been invited. *Oh God, I don't want a nasty confrontation in front of the boys . . .*

Through the glass doors I saw a familiar figure rise up from behind the semicircular desk. My rubbery knees toughened up. I pushed through the doors. "Mr. Bentley! What are you doing here at this time of night?"

The doorman's eyebrows lifted as I came up to the desk. "I could ask you the same thing, Mrs. Fairbanks. Let me guess . . . Awhile ago two young men who looked an awful lot like you went up the elevators in there"—he pointed to the glass security area that separated the lobby from the elevators—"accompanied by their father and somebody I'd guess was Mr. Granddaddy."

I nodded, relieved to hear they'd arrived safely. "Yeah. Couldn't wait until tomorrow to see them. But, well, kinda decided last minute."

Mr. Bentley pursed his lips. "In other words, they don't know you're coming." He leaned toward me over the counter. "Don't you worry, Firecracker. You've got a right to see those kids. Hold on to that. Go on. I'll buzz you in."

"Wait. Your turn. Why are you working the evening shift? Did you switch?"

Harry Bentley shook his head. "Just traded a few hours with Gomez, who covers the first night shift. So I, uh, you know . . . so I could come to your lady mother's funeral tomorrow morning."

"Oh, Mr. B." I ran around to the other side of the desk and gave the man a big hug. "You're the best. Okay, say a prayer for me. I'm going up."

Two minutes later the elevator dinged at the thirty-second floor and the door slid open. I stepped out onto the gleaming marble tile of the foyer. Ceramic urns full of silk flowers stood on either side of the penthouse door. And somewhere on the other side of the door I heard a TV going and the banter of youthful voices.

My heart thudded in my chest. But I raised my hand . . . and knocked.

An eternity passed. Then the door opened. There he stood—tall, tan, shirt collar open, a stray lock of dark hair falling over his forehead. His left eye twitched, betraying his outwardly detached demeanor.

"Hello, Philip."

"Gabrielle. What are you doing here?" My husband swiveled his head toward the front room and frowned. "Did my father—?"

"No. I knew he and the boys were flying in tonight, and . . . I just want to see P. J. and Paul for a few minutes, Philip. I don't plan to stay long."

He hesitated for a moment, then stepped aside. "Fine. They're in the front room." He disappeared in the direction of the kitchen.

I closed the door behind me and walked softly through the gallery. My heart was still tripping, and my skin prickled with excitement. P. J. and Paul were flopped on the long end of the wraparound couch, their backs to me, their grandfather Mike stationed at the other end, watching something on the plasma TV. I crept up behind them and laid one hand on P. J.'s dark-brown hair, falling over his forehead like his father's, and the other on Paul's lighter curls. "Hey."

Paul's head whirled. "Mom!" he screeched, hurling himself over the back of the couch and tangling me in an awkward hug. P. J. jumped up too, came around, and locked his arms around me. For thirty blissful seconds, I held both my big boys in my arms, laughing and crying and drinking in the familiar smell of their skin and hair.

To his credit, Mike Fairbanks shut off the TV. "Good to see you, Gabby," he said gruffly, and also disappeared toward the kitchen.

I sat on the couch, my boys snuggling on either side. Paul fired questions like a machine gun. "Why didn't you bring Dandy? Is he okay? What happened to Grandma? Grandpa Mike says you're going to bury her in North Dakota. Can we go with you?"

P. J. reached out and shoved his brother. "Can't, dork. I've still got a couple of weeks to go before lacrosse camp is over."

As best I could, I tried to fill the boys in on what had happened to their Grandmother Shepherd, assured Paul he'd get to see Dandy tomorrow, and told them I was working as hard as I could to find a place to live so we could be together again. "But P. J.'s right—you guys need to stay in Virginia until he finishes camp the end of July. Then . . . well, hopefully we'll get you back here with your dad and me as soon as possible."

Their faces had gone ashen. P. J.'s mouth tightened. "What do you mean, find a place to live? Does that mean you and Dad are getting a divorce?"

I'd dreaded this moment. But I shook my head. "Nobody's said anything about divorce. But . . . your dad and I are having some problems, and we need to be apart awhile to sort things out." *Sort things out* . . . I hoped Philip was listening.

Finally scooching off the couch, I stood up. "I better go. I still have things I need to do to get ready for Grandma's funeral tomorrow." I grabbed them both in another three-way hug. "I'm so glad you came," I murmured into their hair. "I've missed you so much." Untangling myself, I found my purse and headed for the front door.

Paul ran after me into the gallery. "Mom! Don't go!" He threw his arms around me. "Can't you stay? We can go to the funeral together tomorrow morning."

I gently pried off Paul's arms and opened the door, aware that Philip had appeared in the arched doorway on the left, wiping his hands on a terry towel. "No, I can't stay, honey. But I'll see you tomorrow morning, okay?"

Paul sniffed and wiped his eyes with the back of his hand. "Okay, Mom. We'll get there early—right, Dad?"

My breath caught. Philip had stopped in midwipe, but lifted his chin and stared at me as if daring me to answer Paul's question.

I am Gabrielle . . . strong woman of God.

I held Philip's gaze, unblinking. "Sure, Paul. You boys and Granddad Mike can come as early as you like. But your father isn't coming to the funeral. He'll be going to work tomorrow."

I stepped out and pulled the door shut behind me.

chapter 39

The multipurpose room began filling early the next morning with residents and guests for the ten o'clock funeral service. The Kirkland & Sons funeral director and three of his staff had arrived at eight in their long, black hearse, unloading my mother's metal blue casket onto a wheeled cart and setting it at the front of the circle of chairs. I was surprised at the number of flower arrangements that arrived. As the funeral staff opened the casket, I busied myself looking at the cards—a large spray of pink gladiolas from the Manna House board and staff . . . red and white carnations from SouledOut Community Church . . . a mixed flower arrangement of colorful mums and daisies from Mercy Shepherd . . . a spray of white lilies with a card that said, "With sympathy, the Fairbanks Family." Probably Marlene's doing. But nice.

Another flower arrangement arrived by messenger, a huge spray of bloodred roses, which the funeral staff set up on a large stand. It took me a few moments to find the card . . . and then I couldn't believe my eyes. "With sympathy, Fairbanks & Fenchel Commercial Development Corp."

Of all the nerve!

Estelle Williams, smelling like gardenias and dressed in a black-and-white tunic over wide, silky black trousers, leaned around me and read the card. "Humph. Want me to chuck 'em for you, honey?"

Ha. I could just see them sailing out the front door and landing in the gutter. "Yeah . . . later. After the service." I didn't want any drama—for my sons' sake. Not today. But I took the card and stuck it in my pocket. No sense letting Philip "look good."

"Well, I gotta tend to some last-minute food prep. You gonna spend some time with your mama?" Estelle tipped her head toward the open casket, and I followed her gaze. My mother's face—so like her, and yet unlike her too—peeked out from the soft crepe lining of the shiny blue metal casket.

"Um, maybe when P. J. and Paul get here. Think I'll go wait for them outside." On my way to the foyer, I greeted several board members and got warm hugs from Avis and Peter Douglass, who were consulting with the female keyboard player from SouledOut about the service. Precious and Sabrina stood at the double doors, handing out the simple program and helping to seat people. "Thanks for ushering, Sabrina," I said, giving the pregnant teenager a hug. "You look beautiful today."

But I had to hide a smile as I overheard Precious send two of the residents back upstairs to "get somethin' decent on—you look like some ho. This is a funeral for a grand lady, an' don't ya forget it!"

The foyer was a beehive. Slipping around the crowd, I pushed open the oak doors and stood on the steps, my black crepe skirt blowing in the stiff breeze of another warm Chicago day. Craning my head this way and that, I was relieved to see Lucy coming up the sidewalk with Dandy, wearing a bandanna around his neck like a doggy cowboy. I'd been half-afraid she'd disappear again, and Paul would be devastated.

"Hey there, buddy." I bent down to give the dog a scratch behind the ears, his golden coat freshly brushed except for the area where the hair had not yet grown over his scars, when a familiar black Lexus SUV pulled up in front of Manna House.

I stiffened. Philip was driving.

The doors on the passenger side opened, and Mike Fairbanks and the boys piled out. Paul, unmindful of his good slacks and summer dress shirt, dashed over to Dandy, who immediately started barking and leaping all over him. Philip's father slammed the car door and hustled up the steps after P. J. My father-in-law gave me a peck on the cheek.

"What is Philip doing here?" I hissed in his ear.

Mike Fairbanks turned and jerked his thumb in a *get-moving* motion. "He's not staying. I made it clear he's not invited . . . Boys! Let's go in." They trailed Lucy and Dandy into the cool foyer.

I could have hugged him. Strange, I'd never felt that close to Philip's father, but suddenly I found him in my corner. I started to follow them inside when I saw Lee Boyer crossing the street in the middle of the block, making him pass directly in front of Philip's car. He had shed his jeans and boots for slacks, dress shirt, and tie. Stepping up onto the sidewalk, Lee peered over his wire rims at the car and driver, then at me. He raised his eyebrows . . . then came on up the steps and gave me a hug. "I'm so sorry about your mother, Gabby. You doing okay?" He followed my eyes as I lingered just long enough to make sure the SUV drove off. "Is that him?"

I nodded, not trusting myself to speak.

As we came into the multipurpose room, the young black woman from SouledOut was already playing some background music—hymns and classical pieces. Lee found a seat toward the back. People were still talking but had quieted to a low murmur, and those standing by the casket moved aside to make room for the boys and me. Mike Fairbanks crossed himself—odd, since he wasn't Catholic—then quickly sat down in the front row.

I stood at the casket, my arms around both boys, as we looked at my mom's body. A stranger lay there, hands crossed on a familiar Sunday dress. Her gray hair was done neatly, her glasses perched on her nose, but the waxy expression didn't look anything like my mother, who could in turn be sweet or stubborn—sometimes both at the same time.

To my surprise, P. J. reached out a tentative finger and gently touched my mother's hand. But as he touched the waxy skin, he recoiled, his face crumpling, and he darted to a chair next to his paternal grandfather. Paul, on the other hand, pressed himself into my side, clinging to my waist. He didn't want to leave . . . until we heard a whine at our feet. Dandy had slunk up beside us, his doggy forehead wrinkled. He sniffed the casket, whining pitifully.

Paul lost it. And so did I. We cried and hugged Dandy and each other . . . and I heard other sobbing around the room as we finally found our chairs.

Once the casket was closed and the funeral started, Avis led us in a "celebration of life." She read one of my mother's favorite psalms, and we sang "Great Is Thy Faithfulness" and "O Love

That Will Not Let Me Go." Someone had thoughtfully printed out the words and included them in the simple program. Edesa Baxter read my mom's obituary, and as she read the words I'd written, I realized what an ordinary life my mother had led, nothing terribly exciting. And yet . . . she had been a faithful and loving wife, had raised three girls who had the same genes but were as different as rain, snow, and hail, had rolled with the uncertainties of the past few years since my dad died, and took comfort in the small, everyday joys of life—puttering in her flower garden, talking to her doggy companion, going to church, and making new friends . . . even in a homeless shelter.

How many so-called celebrities could say that?

Avis invited anyone who would like to share something about Martha Shepherd to come to the front. To my surprise, Hannah was the first one up. "Even though she white, we all called her Gramma Shep, 'cause she'd sit an' listen to ya, as if you was important—*and* she let me paint her nails!" Hannah jerked a thumb toward the casket, which the funeral home staff had closed before the service started. "Jus' look in there an' see! An' if ya want your nails done, I'll—"

A chuckle went around the room as Avis Douglass cut her off. "Uh, no commercials, Hannah. We need time for others."

Carolyn got up and said it was a joy to know someone who liked to talk books and play Scrabble, followed by several other residents, staff, and volunteers—all of them giving testimony to the smiling presence of this simple, older woman who brought a bit of sunshine into the Manna House homeless shelter.

Then Lucy got up and laid a hand on the closed casket. Her rheumy eyes glistened. Dandy, who'd been lying at Paul's feet, got up and went to her, sat on his haunches, and looked up at the old woman. Lucy, dressed for the occasion in a clean but rumpled flowered skirt, white blouse, blue sweater two sizes too small, ankle socks, and sandals, didn't address the people in the chairs. She spoke to the casket.

"Miz Martha, this is Lucy." Her voice was husky. "Me an' you, we was kinda unlikely to be friends, but that's what you was—my friend. Don't have too many friends. Got one less now that you're gone. But you an' Dandy here . . ." She reached down and patted Dandy, who seemed to be hanging on every word. "You was some of the best friends I ever had. An' I really don' know what I'm gonna do now that you gone, Miz Martha . . . but if you're in that happy place they talk about 'round here, I'm thinkin' I'd like to find out how to get there, too, so we could . . ." Her voice faltered. She stood there a moment, her shoulders sagging. But then she patted the casket. "Jus' wantchu ta know, Miz Martha, you trusted me ta take care of Hero Dog, here, an' that's what I wanna do"—the old bag lady turned and gave me the eye— "though ain't nobody tol' me yet who he's gonna live with. But if Dandy needs a guardian angel down here, that's me." And she shuffled back to her seat.

Avis beckoned to me. I saw both smiles and tears in the wake of Lucy's eulogy as I faced the people who had gathered to cele-brate my mother's life. I suddenly felt overwhelmed at seeing all the faces seated in the rows before me—black, white, tan . . . young, old . . . homeless women and board members . . . Mabel Turner, who'd hired me on faith and whose patience toward me was long on God's grace . . . Precious and Sabrina, Tanya and Sammy—two mothers like myself who only wanted to make a home for their children . . . Estelle Williams, who'd taken me under her wing like my own personal mother hen . . . Edesa and

Josh Baxter and baby Gracie . . . Josh's parents and sister Amanda, who'd taken in a couple of strangers . . . and even some of Jodi's Yada Yada Prayer Group sisters . . .

My mother had been in Chicago a mere four weeks—most of that spent here at Manna House—and yet the multipurpose room was full. I nodded and smiled at Harry Bentley, sitting beside Estelle, who had been *my* first friend here in Chicago. "Thank you, everyone . . . ," I started, but the lump in my throat was so big, nothing more came out.

"All right, now," Precious piped up. "Take your time, Gabby, take your time."

There was so much I wanted to say. But as I struggled for words, I saw the double doors to the foyer open—and Philip slipped in.

Mike Fairbanks must have seen the stunned look on my face, because he turned his head to follow my eyes . . . and the next minute he was out of his seat and making a beeline for the back of the room. Almost at the same moment, I saw Lee Boyer and Harry Bentley get up from different parts of the room, like a pair of white and black cops, and head for the doors as well. Seeing his father and the other two men heading for him like bouncers at a nightclub, Philip backed out of the room, followed by the three men, and the doors swung shut behind them.

I caught Avis's eye, shook my head, and fled to my chair. The pianist took her seat at the keyboard, and the next minute we were all standing and singing, "Some glad morning when this life is o'er . . . I'll fly away . . ." I turned my head and looked toward the closed doors. What was happening out there? Leaning over to my sons, I whispered, "Wait here for me, okay? I'll be right back." Hoping not to be noticed as I ducked through the standing congregation, I slipped into the foyer. Empty. I crossed to the heavy oak front doors, turned the handle of one, and pushed it open a few inches.

Through the crack I saw Philip standing down on the sidewalk, smoking a cigarette—*since when?!*—and looking off into the distance, while Mike Fairbanks, two inches shorter than my six-foot-two husband, jabbed a finger in his face. "—ashamed to call you my son! You know Gabby didn't want you here today—and I don't blame her. After what you did—"

This was my fight, and I was tired of running from it.

I stepped outside.

Mike stopped, finger in mid-jab, and all four men gaped at me.

I marched down the steps until I faced my husband. *Gabrielle . . . strong woman of God.* If that was my identity, I better start living into it—though I had to admit that the presence of my three benefactors cinched up my courage a few notches.

"You're not welcome here, Philip. You know why. You turned my mother away from your home. You treated us both like dirt. She wouldn't want you here today. I don't want you here today. The least you can do is respect that."

No hysterics, no name-calling . . . *Thank You, God, for giving me words.*

Philip took a drag on the cigarette, dropped it to the ground, and ground it out. "I'm sorry about you losing your mom, Gabby. I—" His left eye twitched, the way it always did when he was tense, and he turned his head, as if watching the El train crossing the street a couple of blocks down. "That's . . . all I wanted to say." He pushed past his father and started down the street toward his car.

Lee Boyer laid a comforting arm around my shoulder, but I was startled to hear him call out, "Fairbanks!" Philip stopped and half-turned his head. "*Sorry* isn't good enough." Lee's voice was low and tight. "We'll see you in court."

chapter 40

The repast after my mother's funeral celebration was a noisy affair, with more food than I'd seen in a long time lined up on the kitchen counter—greens, fried chicken, hot wings, sliced ham, corn bread, beans and rice, taquitos, a fruit tray, red punch, coffee . . . and three kinds of cookie bars. A regular multicultural fest. Estelle must have shanghaied her prayer group, too, because I'd seen her housemate, Stu, and several other Yada Yada sisters bringing in food as well.

The servers were all Manna House residents and volunteers, wearing clean white aprons and brightly patterned African head wraps instead of the usual ugly hairnets. Even Carolyn had her long, brownish-gray ponytail tucked up under a blue-and-gold head wrap, and her cheeks were flushed, animating her normally pale skin with a glow of color.

Dandy took advantage of the hubbub, moving from table to table, getting handouts. By popular request, Sarge retold the story of her rescue from the midnight intruder by Hero Dog and his subsequent rise to mascot and official watchdog status—omitting her ominous threats to banish him just days earlier.

P. J. and Paul remembered some of the residents from their earlier visit, and they ended up in the rec room, playing Ping-Pong with Sabrina and Hannah and some of shelter kids. But poor Mike Fairbanks seemed a little overwhelmed by it all.

It was almost one thirty by the time Jodi Baxter leaned over my shoulder and whispered, "We better get on the road before two if we want to miss traffic."

The pallbearers—Josh Baxter; his father, Denny; Harry Bentley; Peter Douglass; and the two pastors on the board—had already taken out the last three rows of seats from Moby Van and loaded my mother's casket into the back under the supervision of the funeral directors at the end of the service. Now Jodi and I added our suitcases, Dandy's bed, dishes, and a bag of dog food, and everything my mom had brought with her from North Dakota a month ago into the back alongside the casket.

"I wish I could go with you, Mom." Eleven-year-old Paul stood on the sidewalk, shoulders hunched, hands in his pants pockets, his short school haircut grown out into a mass of unruly coppery curls, not unlike my own. "Why can't I take care of Dandy till you get back?" His lip quivered. "You *are* going to bring him back, aren't you?"

"Yes. I promise." I gathered my youngest into my arms. "I wish you could go with me, too, kiddo. But . . ." My eyes blurred. "You need to stay with Granddad a little while longer. We'll be together soon. You'll see." I reached out toward P. J., who let me pull him into our good-bye hug too.

"Don't you worry about that dog none, sonny," Lucy interrupted, bouncing her overloaded wire cart down the front steps of the shelter. "I been takin' good care of him for your gramma, an' ain't gonna quit now, even though she gone."

I stared at the cart. "Lucy! You can't take that cart on this trip! I mean . . ." Frankly, I'd been hoping someone would pull Lucy aside and talk her out of going along. When was I going to learn that wishful thinking never got me anywhere?

Lucy peered into the open side door of the van, where Dandy was already sitting up on the second seat, panting in the heat. "Whatchu mean? They's plenty of room in this ol' bucket. I gotta take some clothes along. We goin' up north, ya know."

Mabel stepped in to the rescue. "Lucy, come on. We'll find you a suitcase. You can leave your cart in my office, and it'll be safe and sound till you get back. Deal?" She led Lucy back into the shelter, cart bumping behind them.

Denny Baxter hovered around the van like a regular grease monkey, checking the windshield wiper fluid, making sure oil and water were full, checking the tire pressure. "You got enough gas to get you to Des Moines? Jodi, you sure you and Gabby want to stay at your folks' place tonight? It's gotta add a couple hundred miles."

"We know." Jodi flipped her bangs back. "But it's cheap lodging. And dogs are allowed. Free breakfast too." She kissed Denny right on his dimples and climbed into the passenger seat. "Besides, if I see my folks on *this* trip, you're off the hook the rest of the summer."

I shrugged and grinned at her husband. "What can I do? I need a copilot."

Mabel and Lucy came back out, this time with an actual suitcase—the old-fashioned kind with no wheels. Still, Lucy looked embarrassed to be carrying it. "Don't feel natural," she grumbled, shoving it into the van and climbing in after it.

"Where's your hat, Lucy?" All summer she'd been wearing the purple knit hat Estelle had made for her. But now she was bareheaded, her gray hair clean but badly in need of a cut.

"Too hot. Whaddya think?"

I laughed and climbed into the van behind the wheel. "Glad you finally figured that out."

At the last minute, Estelle came rushing out with a shopping bag full of leftovers from the repast to eat on the way. Amid a chorus of good-byes from our friends and family on the sidewalk, I pulled the van away from the curb, and in five minutes we were heading south on Lake Shore Drive. I looked sideways at Jodi. "Can't believe we're doing this."

Jodi glanced over her shoulder into the second seat and then back at me, tipping her head slightly toward the rear. "Me either." In the rearview mirror I could see Dandy sitting sideways, his chin resting on the back of the seat, eyes on the blue metal casket.

Better keep your eyes straight ahead, Gabby . . .

Jodi Baxter was a good navigator. She got me off Lake Shore Drive, through the city and going west on the Eisenhower Expressway, until we picked up the I-88 toll road all the way to Iowa—a boring stretch of road if I ever saw one. Construction, cornfields, and more construction. We didn't talk much, and I was just as glad. It was the first time I'd had fifteen uninterrupted minutes since the previous Monday, when Mom had the stroke. *Only four days ago . . .*

But the images tumbling behind my eyes were less than four hours old. Philip coming into the shelter halfway through my mother's funeral. After I'd told him not to! Was he *trying* to upset me? Or—if I took what he said at face value—did he honestly feel sorry that I'd lost my mom? Was he having a crisis of conscience about what he'd done? And Lee! I hardly knew what to think about his reaction. His protective arm around me. His challenge to Philip. *"We'll see you in court!"* It felt so good to have a man stand up for me. And yet . . . why did I get this feeling Lee meant something more than lawyer-and-client by that shouted "we"? And why did I like it? Was it because I felt attracted to Lee? . . . or because I wanted to make Philip jealous?

Construction on the toll road slowed us down. I rolled down my window to save on air-conditioning as we crept along, thinking about P. J. and Paul. My time with them had been too short. Already, the memory-touch of their boyish hugs was starting to fade. P. J., in spite of his almost-fourteen stoicism, had looked so sad, as if on this trip he'd begun to understand, maybe for the first time, that his parents might actually get a divorce . . . and Paul, obviously homesick, needing his mom and dad . . . and I couldn't promise them a home to come home to.

A tear rolled down my cheek. Jodi touched my arm. "Want me to drive?"

I nodded and sniffed. "Soon as we get off this toll road."

We crossed into the Quad Cities on the Iowa-Illinois border around five o'clock, pulled into a gas station, topped off the gas tank with my debit card, and took a potty break. "Don't have to go," Lucy muttered, sliding out of the van and reaching for Dandy's leash. "I'll just walk the dog."

I snatched Dandy's leash. "Rule Number One on car trips, Lucy. You *go* every time we stop, whether you think you have to or not. Next stop might not be for another couple of hours."

Grumbling, Lucy followed Jodi into the station. But I hadn't counted on mutiny from Dandy. He wouldn't leave the van. I pulled on his leash, and he pulled back. I finally had to pick him up and carry him to a grassy area alongside the station. Even then he didn't go . . . until we got back to the van, and then he lifted his leg against a tire.

Jodi drove the rest of the way to Des Moines. The supper Estelle had packed for us—cold fried chicken, a bag of chips, fruit, and a ton of cookie bars—perked us up, and Jodi and I started singing some old camp songs to pass the time. "She'll be coming 'round the mountain when she comes, whoo! whoo!"—all the more ridiculous since the fields on either side of the road were flat as a hairbrush. I suggested "Row, row, row your boat"—no rivers or lakes in sight, either—but Jodi warbled the college prof version: "Propel, propel, propel your craft, placidly over the liquid solution . . ." By this time we were giggling like junior-high schoolgirls.

"You guys are nuts, know that?" Lucy hollered from the second seat.

It took us another three hours to drive halfway across Iowa, but it was still light when Jodi pulled Moby Van into her parents' driveway. A bald-headed man and a petite gray-haired woman who reminded me a lot of my mother came out of the house, beaming a welcome as we piled stiffly out of the vehicle. I stood back as Jodi gave her parents big hugs. "Mom, Dad . . . this is Gabby Fairbanks, the program director at Manna House. And this is Lucy, um, a friend of Gabby's mom. And this is Dandy, the Hero Dog I told you about—oh, Lucy! Don't let Dandy do that!"

Dandy was peeing on a rosebush.

"I'm so sorry," I said, flustered. "Lucy, where's his leash? . . . Oh dear, it's been awhile since we let him out."

Jodi's father chuckled. "I'm sure Dandy's not the first dog who's mistaken that bush for a fire hydrant." He held out his hand. "I'm Sidney Jennings, this is my wife, Clara, and—"

"—and I've got supper waiting for you on the table," Clara Jennings finished. "Come on, come on in."

"Oh good," Lucy muttered, stalking up the sidewalk. "Been least two hours since I last et." We trooped along after her, though I noticed that Sidney Jennings hung back and peeked in the windows of the van, as though he couldn't quite believe we were trucking my mother's casket all the way to North Dakota.

Even though I wasn't really hungry after Estelle's sack supper, the homemade chicken noodle soup was so good that I asked for seconds. Lucy had thirds. The Jenningses graciously retired at ten, knowing we needed to get to bed so we could get an early start the next morning. Lucy and a reluctant Dandy bedded down in Jodi's old bedroom, and Jodi and I got the bunk beds in her brothers' old room. "Good thing I've got lots of experience sleeping in a bunk bed," I yawned, crawling into the top bunk. "You don't snore, do you, Jodi?"

We settled down, an oscillating fan moving the night air a little in the stuffy bedroom. It had been a long day, and I was tired beyond belief . . . but I suddenly rolled over and hung my head over the side of the bunk. "Jodi?"

"Mmph . . . what?"

"I feel kinda funny."

"What do you mean?"

"I mean . . . it doesn't really feel right that we're in here together, all comfy and cozy, tucked into bed . . . and my mom is still out there in a box in the van."

Jodi stifled a screech. "No! You didn't say that . . . Oh, that's *awful.*" She grabbed her pillow and whopped my upside-down head with it, trying not to laugh, but her horrified giggles seemed to pull a plug out of the dike of pent-up emotions from the past few days, and the next thing I knew I had tumbled off the top bunk, and the two of us collapsed together on the lower bunk, pushing our faces into the covers, trying to stifle our hysterical laughter.

chapter 41

After our irrational bout of laughter had turned to tears, Jodi and I comforted each other with the reality that Mom was safe and warm in the arms of Jesus, and we fell asleep . . . and were on the road again by seven o'clock with a long twelve-hour day ahead of us. I skipped my shower—a decision I later regretted. Still in his bathrobe, Jodi's dad had insisted we eat the hot breakfast he'd prepared—bacon, scrambled eggs, wheat toast, and coffee—and her mom had packed sandwiches to take along. "I'm sorry to take Jodi away so soon, Mrs. Jennings," I said, taking the small cooler with the sandwiches she handed to me and giving her a hug, catching a whiff of lilac in her hair.

Like my mom . . .

"Never you mind," she whispered. "Her dad and I are planning a trip to Chicago for Jodi's birthday in September—but don't tell her. It's a surprise."

I almost blurted, "No, no surprises!" Parents showing up on the doorstep unannounced had had disastrous consequences in my case. But I held my tongue, realizing I had to stop seeing the world through the Fairbanks grid.

Lucy had taken Dandy for a short walk after breakfast and managed not to get lost in the unfamiliar suburb, and Jodi drove first, heading north on Route 35 toward Minnesota. From time to time, I tried to engage Lucy in conversation, but she usually answered my attempts with a grunt or one-word answer, seemingly content to hunker by the window behind the driver's seat, eyes locked on cornfields and small towns as they zipped past. And when she did talk, she talked to Dandy. "Hey, lookee there, Dandy. Ever see so many cows? Wonder who doin' all that milkin' . . ."

We'd been traveling an hour or so when I heard a familiar rumble and realized both Lucy and Dandy had zonked out, the dog's head in her lap. I shook my head, kicked off my sandals, and put my bare feet on the dash with a big sigh. "Don't know what to do about Dandy. Lucy's gotten so attached to him. Paul would really like to have a dog, which would be fine with me, once I have a place for me and the boys. But now . . ." The mental wall I'd been holding up between me and reality suddenly started to crumble.

"But now . . . what?" Jodi prodded.

It all came tumbling out, the whole fragile house of cards I'd been counting on—finding an apartment so I could get custody of my sons, getting excited about the apartment Lee Boyer had shown me, thinking I could afford it if Mom and I shared the expense. ". . . That's what!" I said between my teeth, trying not to wake up Lucy. "I can't afford that apartment by myself—and I can't shoehorn myself and two big boys into those shoeboxes that the Chicago Housing Authority subsidizes for the homeless, even if I was number one on their waiting list, which I'm not." I banged a fist on the passenger door. "Now I know how Tanya and Precious feel, stuck in a homeless shelter, dangling between nothing and nothing. And all they want is to make a home for their kid, get a job, be a family!"

Jodi nodded but said nothing, concentrating on passing a big hog transport tying up traffic in the right lane.

"Huh," I muttered. "Maybe I should play the lottery like your friend what's-her-name—"

"Chanda." Jodi pumped the speed up to seventy, glancing anxiously back at the big semi before finally pulling the van back into the right lane. "Sheesh, I keep forgetting how long this van is."

"Yeah, Chanda. If I had *her* luck, I could buy that whole building and we could all move in."

Jodi settled back against her seat, finally glancing over at me. "You don't need luck, Gabby. Remember when you came to Yada Yada a couple of Sundays ago? That was some powerful prayer we had for you—you said so yourself."

I shrugged. "Yeah, I thought so too. I've really been trying to trust God, trying to pray—and for a while, I thought God was answering my prayers. Especially when Lee Boyer said he'd found an apartment for me. But now . . . I don't know. Seems like everything's back at square one."

"Must be that God's got a better plan."

I stared at her. "*What* better plan?!"

Jodi shrugged, keeping her eyes on the road. "Don't ask me. But that's what Avis Douglass always says when one of us Yada Yadas is fussing and fuming about something not working out like we wanted it to. And believe me, Gabby, it's happened often enough—when I get enough courage to pry my fingers off my plans and ideas long enough to ask God to take over, that is—that I'm beginning to think she's right."

Lucy woke up when we pulled into a gas station outside Minneapolis about eleven. "I know, I know," she muttered, climbing stiffly out of the van. "Rule Number One. But ya fergot the rule 'afore that 'un—take care of your animals first. That's what my daddy useta say, back when we had us a farm." And she marched off to a tiny strip of grass beside the gas station with Dandy in tow, her gray hair standing up like she'd stuck her finger in a socket.

I blew a limp curl out of my eyes in the climbing heat, trying not to watch as the little numbers whirled upward on the gas pump. Like Jodi said, at least it was cheaper than shipping my mom's casket, and a *lot* cheaper than buying a cemetery plot in Chicago. *Guess I should be thanking You about that,* I prayed silently as I hung up the gas hose and screwed the gas cap back on. *But, Jesus, if You've got a better plan for what happens next, I'd sure like to know what it is.*

Lucy and Jodi were coming out of the restroom as I came in. I took one look in the mirror over the sink and grimaced. My curly hair hung limp, the color dull, my face bare of makeup. *Ouch. Should've gotten up fifteen minutes earlier for a shower.*

I splashed my face and freshened up as best I could, and when I got back to the van, Jodi and Lucy had the back doors of the van open. "Them flowers is wiltin'," Lucy announced as she hauled herself awkwardly into the van and inspected the casket in the back. "Here." She handed two flower arrangements out to Jodi and me. "Go find some water."

Jodi stifled a grin. "Bossy, isn't she?" she murmured as we found a water hose and wet the green floral foam and containers holding the flower sprays.

Behind us, Dandy suddenly starting barking furiously. I whirled and saw a couple of lanky teenage boys pointing and laughing at the open doors of the van. Before Jodi and I could get the flower arrangements back to the van, a larger crowd had gathered—a mother and half a dozen kids from a minivan gassing up at the next pump, a couple of hefty, bearded guys who'd driven up in a dirty pickup, and one of the gas station attendants who came out to see what the ruckus was about.

I sucked in my breath. "Uh-oh . . . look at Dandy."

My mother's yellow dog was standing on top of the metal-blue casket, facing the open doors, barking and showing his teeth. Lucy stood at the back of the van, arms crossed, eyes narrowed as if daring anybody to get within punching range.

"You got a real dead body in there?" one of the teenagers snickered.

"Whatcha do, steal it from a graveyard?" The two boys thought that was real funny, slapping each other on the back. Even the pickup truck guys chuckled.

Sudden rage burned behind my eyes. *How dare they!* "Okay, show's over, you meatheads!" I yelled as Jodi and I pushed past Lucy and set our armload of flowers into the van. "Lucy!" I hissed in her ear. "Close the doors and get in the van. Now!"

I'd never seen Lucy move so fast. Slamming the back doors, the old lady hustled to the side of the van, climbed in, and slammed that door shut too. I got in the driver's seat, turned the ignition, and started the van while Jodi was still pulling her door shut. "Gabby!" she screeched. I slowed for a nanosecond, but

Dandy was still on top of the casket, barking and snapping at the windows as we lurched past the finger-pointing gawkers.

A glance in the rearview mirror as I took the on ramp for Route 94 heading west caught Lucy climbing over suitcases, boxes, and bags to get to the back doors. She punched the lock; then I heard her coaxing Dandy down from the casket. "Come 'ere, Dandy, it's okay . . . They was just jerks . . . Good dog . . . Miz Martha would be proud of you." Another glance in the rearview, and I realized Lucy and Dandy must be sitting on the floor with the casket and the luggage, because I could no longer see them.

It took me a good half hour to calm down, and Jodi had to point out that I was riding the accelerator ten miles over the speed limit. She finally coaxed Lucy back into the second-row seat and made her put on her seat belt, passed out the sandwiches her mother had packed, all the while cheerfully pointing out the picturesque farms, lush fields, and little lakes tucked into the rolling hills as we sailed down the highway.

I finally grinned at her. "You'd make a good Jewish mother, Jodi."

She laughed. "Well, I've got a good role model. Remember Ruth in my prayer group—the one who had twins at fifty? . . ." Pretty soon she had me laughing about the escapades of the two-year-old Garfield twins, running circles around their midlife-plus parents. Then she dug out some music CDs and filled the van with some good gospel, singing along and clapping and waving at other drivers who looked at us funny.

"If there's one thing I've been learning, Gabby," Jodi said, grinning at me, "it's that praise is *not* Satan's working conditions.

When the enemy throws something at you like what happened back there?—it's *praise* that changes the battle lines."

I wanted to hug her, but I kept my hands on the wheel. How long had it been since I'd had a friend who'd talk to me like that?

We traded drivers at Sauk Center, Minnesota, and again at Fargo as we crossed into North Dakota about midafternoon. We tanked up on Cokes to keep us awake, but my butt was beginning to hurt from the long hours driving. And we still had 250 miles to go!

"Hey!" Lucy called out. "What happened to all the trees and green stuff?"

It was true. The topography had drastically changed to grazing land and sagebrush country, with the occasional wheat field stretching clear to the horizon. I grinned in the rearview. "This is where I grew up, Lucy."

I saw her roll her eyes. "Humph. Look like this place never pulled through the Dust Bowl."

Jodi had just taken over the driving again when my cell phone rang. I scrambled to find my purse and snatched out the phone. "Probably one of the boys . . . Hello? Hello? . . . Oh! Hi, Lee . . ." I felt my face flush, and I turned toward the window.

Several minutes later I flipped the phone closed and dropped it back into my purse. "Uh, just my lawyer."

"Uh-huh. Does your face always get red when you talk to your lawyer?"

"He's sweet on her!" Lucy hollered from the backseat.

"Oh, stop it, Lucy. We're just friends. He's concerned, that's all." I assumed a nonchalant slouch as Jodi drove straight toward the sun slipping down the western sky, grateful for the wrap-around sunglasses hiding the telltale confusion in my eyes.

Familiar fast-food icons were harder to find once we left the main highway and headed north on a two-lane toward Minot, but we finally spied a Hiway Drive-In just as we turned onto Route 52. We ordered hamburgers, fries, and milk shakes to go—and to my surprise, Lucy shoved some crumpled dollar bills into my hand to pay for hers.

Once we'd finished eating, we all fell silent, opening the windows and enjoying the cooling air as the sun slipped toward the horizon. I couldn't help thinking about the last time I'd driven this road with Paul and P. J., going to visit my mom a mere month and a half ago. So much had happened since then . . .

I called Aunt Mercy when we were about an hour out and asked if she'd heard from Celeste and Honor. "They should be at the house by the time you get here," she said. "I'll meet you there too."

The setting sun had streaked the western sky with golden, orange, and brilliant red clouds when I finally pulled Moby Van into the parking lot of Minot's family-owned funeral home. Jodi and Lucy waited in the van while I went inside, signed the necessary papers to transfer my mother's casket, and walked out with the director and a couple of his staff pushing a rolling cart. Dandy whined as my mother's casket was loaded onto the cart and wheeled inside, but Lucy kept a tight hold on his collar.

The funeral director handed me a folder with my copies of all the papers. "I believe your aunt, Mercy Shepherd, suggested a family viewing tomorrow afternoon at four, and then a service in

our chapel on Sunday at two, with the burial immediately following. Does that sound right to you, Mrs. Fairbanks?"

I nodded, shook his hand, and climbed back into the van, not
really thinking about what he'd said. I was thinking about meeting my sisters after two years, showing up in my mother's
driveway with a monster van that said "Manna House Shelter for
Women" along the side, our mother's dog with still-visible scars
on his shoulder, and two strangers, one of whom was a crusty old
bag lady in a rumpled flower skirt and ankle socks.

chapter 42

I pulled Moby Van into the driveway of my mother's house, right behind a silver Chevy compact with a rental car sticker. *Home.* The yard had been mowed—Aunt Mercy must have hired a neighborhood kid—but my mother's beloved flower garden across the front was thick with weeds.

No, no, can't let the weeds take over! Heading straight for the flower bed, I started yanking weeds right and left.

Dandy tumbled out of the driver's side door I'd left open and ran all around the yard, sniffing and whining. "He knows he's home," Jodi murmured, climbing rather stiffly out of the front seat and sliding the side door open so Lucy could get out.

The front door opened. "You made it!" Aunt Mercy beamed. Her silver-rinsed hair was cut in its usual youthful pixie cut. "Quit pulling those weeds, Gabby Fairbanks, and come give me a hug . . . Oh, oh, Dandy, yes, yes, you can come in too . . ." She turned and called into the house. "Celeste! Honor! Gabby is here!"

My oldest sister appeared two seconds later, suntanned and

freckled, wavy brunette hair caught at the back of her neck with a wooden barrette, wearing a black tank top and khaki cargo pants cropped at the knee. She gave me a quick hug. "Hey there, Gabby. Talk about timing. We just got here thirty minutes ago . . . Oh! Who's this?" Celeste's hazel eyes looked over my shoulder, and I realized Jodi and Lucy were still standing on the front walk.

Uh-oh. Didn't I tell my sisters I wasn't driving alone? "Come on up here, you guys. Celeste, this is Jodi Baxter, my friend who graciously offered to help me drive the van from Chicago . . . and, uh, Lucy Tucker, a friend of Mom's who's been taking care of Dandy—kind of a long story. Jodi and Lucy, this is my dad's baby sister, Aunt Mercy, and my sister Celeste . . . Say, where's Honor?"

Celeste nodded a mute greeting to my guests and jerked a thumb inward. "Living room. Kinda broken up."

Aunt Mercy, bless her, rose to the occasion. "Well, come in, come in, girls. We've got the air on; it's cooler inside. Did you all eat? Because I've got a pasta salad in the refrigerator and garlic bread in the oven. Would you all like some iced tea?"

"Oh, good," I heard Lucy mumble, as we trailed my aunt inside. "Been a couple hours since I et."

I let Aunt Mercy herd Jodi and Lucy into the kitchen at the back of the house, while I detoured into the living room. My sister Honor was curled up on the couch, her face a blotchy red, a pile of tissues in her lap. Her screaming blonde hair, complete with green and red streaks, was even longer than the last time I'd seen her. She'd added skinny braids hanging down in front of her ears with tiny feathers and beads tied at the ends. A graceful blue dolphin tattoo dove from the top of her shoulder halfway down her bare upper arm. Probably had some mystical meaning. I wanted to shake my head. She looked like a cross between an aging hippie and a runaway kid on Rush Street in Chicago.

"Oh, Gabby," Honor wailed, throwing both arms around my neck as I bent down. "Can you bear it, coming home, and Mama not being here?"

I endured Honor's awkward hug for half a minute, then untangled myself. I could hear Dandy's nails clicking on the wood floors, going from room to room, whining, then scrambling upstairs to the second floor. At that moment, I felt worse for Dandy's loss than I did for me and my sisters.

"We've got company," Celeste informed Honor, raising an eyebrow at me reproachfully.

Honor's red-rimmed eyes flew open. "Who?"

I tipped my chin up defensively. "I couldn't drive Mom's casket all the way from Chicago by myself."

Celeste flopped in an easy chair, frowning. "But who's the old lady? I mean, she looks like something you found on the street."

I almost laughed. *Bingo.* "It's a long story. But please, be kind—"

We heard the dog scrambling back down the stairs, and then he appeared in the living room, staring up at me, brow wrinkled, whimpering. "Oh!" Honor gasped. "What happened to Dandy? Where'd those long scars come from?"

I sighed, settled down on the carpet with my back against Celeste's easy chair, and pulled Dandy down beside me. "Like I said, it's a really long story."

We talked until midnight, my sisters and I—me doing most of the talking as I tried to tell my far-flung siblings what had happened since I'd realized Mom couldn't stay alone any longer and had taken her back to Chicago with me for an indefinite visit.

Aunt Mercy graciously entertained Jodi and Lucy while we talked, put Lucy in the small "summer bedroom" off the back porch, made up the pull-out couch in my dad's study upstairs for Jodi, leaving the two bedrooms we girls had shared growing up for Celeste, Honor, and me. "I'll be back in the morning," she'd whispered, poking her head into the living room to explain the sleeping arrangements. I heard Lucy calling Dandy, and the dog disappeared. I wondered if he'd sleep in my mom's bedroom, as he'd always done before, or with Lucy.

I bet on Lucy tonight.

"Wish you had let us know what was going on." Celeste's scowl was in danger of becoming a permanent fixture. "It's bad enough that Philip threw you out, but *Mom* . . . !" She cocked an imaginary rifle and "aimed" it at a picture on the wall. "I think I want to kill him."

I gaped at her. "Let you know?! Not like I didn't try. Neither of you guys is very good at returning phone calls. Or living within reach of a cell phone signal."

"Mom was really staying in a homeless shelter?" Honor said it like she'd just driven out of the fog. "That's . . . that's *awful*. You should have sent her to live with me, or . . . or something."

I grabbed a throw pillow and smacked my California-dreaming sister with it. "Hey! I tried to get both of you out here in June for a family reunion. If you'd made half an effort, we could have made a decision about Mom together. But that didn't work out, did it? So quit blaming me. I did what I had to do." I folded my arms tight across my chest. Both my sisters stared at me. The wall clock ticked in the silence that followed. Finally I let my arms fall to my lap, along with the tears I'd been pushing down all evening. "Didn't know my whole life was going to unravel."

Our emotions spent, we finally flicked off lights and crept upstairs to our bedrooms—Celeste to her old room with the double bed that she'd earned as the "eldest" child, Honor and me to our old bedroom with the single beds and matching faded bedspreads. It had been a really, really long day . . . but somehow all the frayed and frazzled ends of my life felt tucked in for the moment, like the loose ends of yarn my mother used to tuck into her knitting.

Aunt Mercy showed up at ten the next morning with a manila folder tucked under her arm. "Hope you girls got a chance to sleep in." She poured herself a cup of coffee, pulled out a chair at the kitchen table where Honor, Celeste, and I sat in the rumpled T-shirts and shorts we'd slept in, and pushed the folder toward us. "Your parents' will. Your dad left a copy with me, and I suppose the lawyer has the original. I made an appointment for you girls at his office on Monday at ten." She looked from one to the other of us. "Hope no one has to leave before then."

Honor groaned. "My plane leaves from Billings late Tuesday afternoon, and it took us eight hours to drive from the airport— right, Celeste?"

Celeste nodded and picked up the manila envelope. "Yeah, but we can leave early Tuesday. Monday's fine."

"Oh, brother," I muttered, rolling my eyes. "It's going to take longer than that to deal with"—I waved my hand in a big circle that took in the whole house—"all this stuff."

"It's only Saturday, Gabby. That's practically three days."
Celeste frowned. "Where are your city buddies? They could help,
you know."

"They *are* helping! Who do you think made the coffee before
we came down? And they've taken Dandy . . . somewhere.
Probably to stay out of our way."

"Girls." Aunt Mercy eyed us. "You should look at the will.
You will have some decisions to make."

Celeste slid the will out of the folder. "Okay, they named me
executor when Mom died—but I understand you've got power of
attorney, Gabby?" She frowned at me. "How does that work?"

"Don't worry, Celeste. That was just because of Mom's
dementia." I sighed. "Just read the will. The lawyer can figure it
out."

The will held no surprises. Divide everything equally three
ways after paying any outstanding bills and funeral expenses.
That sounded hopeful. Maybe my account could get reimbursed
for the trip after all. I could sure use that.

Celeste stuffed the simple form back in the envelope. "Mom
had . . . what? An annuity she was living on? Maybe some savings
. . ." Her eyes roved around the house. "The big thing will be
selling the house. Can't do *that* in a day."

Honor stuck out her lip. "Wish I could buy it. Seems like it
oughta stay in the family."

Celeste and I both stared at her. "You buy it? Would you
really move back to Minot?"

Honor shrugged. "Maybe. River and Ryan . . . I dunno.
They've been hanging with a pretty fast crowd—River especially.
He'll be a junior next year, Ryan a sophomore. Maybe they could
finish high school here. But . . ." She shrugged again.

It was hard to imagine my tattooed middle sister, with her green-and-red-streaked hair and feather-and-beads, skinny braids, fitting back into small-town life in North Dakota. But it was a moot point. She couldn't afford the house anyway. Me either. And Celeste wasn't about to trade her log cabin outpost and park ranger husband in Denali National Forest for an old, two-story frame house in sagebrush country.

We spent the rest of the day making an inventory of furniture and household stuff. It felt weird, trying to decide what to leave with the house—we could sell it furnished—and what to divide between us. As long as Mom and Dad were alive, it had been sweet to come home to this house full of childhood memories. But, no, I didn't want to move back to Minot. I'd been gone too long. Besides, we *had* to sell it. Closest thing to an inheritance we three girls had.

I felt a tad guilty wishing we could sell it tomorrow. But, I told Jodi later, as she helped me count the china, glassware, and ironed tablecloths in the dining room hutch, I could sure use my third to help me rent that apartment in Wrigleyville and get back on my feet. My ticket to getting an actual address to prop up my custody petition.

Lucy shut herself into the downstairs bathroom and scrubbed it until floor, sink, tub, and wall tiles sparkled, then repeated the process in the second-floor bathroom—which seemed odd to me, since the Lucy I first met had been living under a bush, and housekeeping wasn't exactly a necessity. But it knocked the chips off my sisters' shoulders, and they started warming up to Lucy in little ways—a smile, a nod, an invitation to "come sit down, we're making some lemonade . . . want some?"

Four o'clock rolled around much too soon, when we were

supposed to go to the funeral home for the family viewing. "You go on," Jodi said, when Aunt Mercy invited her and Lucy to go along. "This is your time." I wished I could stay home too. I'd been through this once before at the funeral at Manna House. The memory was bittersweet, sad but satisfying, too, and I didn't really want to go through it again. But this was the first time for Celeste and Honor, so I climbed into Aunt Mercy's car.

The viewing room at the funeral home felt like a different planet from the multipurpose room at Manna House. Piped-in organ music instead of SouledOut's electronic keyboard. The funeral home staff talking in discreet, low tones instead of Precious loudly scolding the girls wearing low-cut tops and tight skirts. Tomorrow at the funeral, church folks and former patrons of Dad's carpet store would come to pay their respects, their faces pale or sunburned instead of the black, brown, and tan skin tones that populated Manna House. And we'd all speak North Dakota's flat, Midwestern English, instead of the street slang peppering most conversations at the shelter, with bits of Spanish, Italian, Asian, and Jamaican patois thrown in.

Still, standing with Aunt Mercy and my sisters beside the open casket, looking at the still, peaceful form that was our mother, we melded, sharing tissues and hugs. The tears came, fresh and cleansing. I was glad I came for this sacred moment . . . just us. Celeste and Honor and I had been apart too long—not just in distance and lifestyles, but letting our everyday lives and thoughts and care for one another drift further and further apart, like flotsam at sea.

I wanted my sisters back. I needed all the family I could get. I didn't know how to tell them, but I reached out my arms and slid one around each sister's waist as I made a silent vow. *Mom, I'm going to do whatever I can to keep our family together, I promise—*

"What is *that*?" Honor suddenly spluttered, pulling away from my embrace. She reached into the casket under the folds of my mother's pastel flower-print Sunday dress and pulled out a wadded-up purple knit hat with a crocheted flower bobbing on the brim.

Lucy's hat.

Her final gift to her friend.

I collapsed in a chair and laughed. And then I cried. And then I made my sisters put the hat back in the casket again, tucked beneath the folds of Mom's dress.

chapter 43

We picked up some Chinese takeout on the way back to the house, only to find out that Jodi had found a package of frozen chicken in Mom's basement freezer and had a pan of honey-baked chicken in the oven. "Told you you'd make a good Jewish mother," I teased, giving her a hug. I pulled her aside and told her about the purple knit hat, making her promise not to tell Lucy we'd discovered it.

All of us were too beat to do any more sorting or packing up of Mom's things, and we actually ended up playing a ruthless game of Monopoly all evening—well, we three sisters and Jodi, that is. Lucy and Dandy disappeared outside for their evening walk, and Aunt Mercy announced that her Monopoly days were long gone, and she'd see us tomorrow for church.

I looked at my sisters. They looked at me. I cleared my throat. "I think we'll take a pass, Aunt Mercy. The funeral and burial are tomorrow afternoon. I think we need the morning to keep sorting Mom's stuff. We don't have that much time."

Which turned out to be true. The next morning Jodi packed most of Mom's clothes in large plastic bags to take to Goodwill—none of us sisters could bear to do it—though she asked permission to let Lucy pick out some things as a keepsake. I knew Mom's dresses, skirts, and slacks would never fit Lucy's ample behind, but the old lady almost reverently picked out some silky head scarves and took all of Mom's socks.

The day seemed to pass in a blur. At one point, Lucy asked where she could find a shovel, and I sent her to the garage, too distracted to wonder what she wanted a shovel for. Outside, the sky was clear and the heat index hovered somewhere up in the nineties. "Thought it was s'posed ta be cold up here in the North," Lucy grumbled as the five of us climbed into Moby Van to meet Aunt Mercy for the two o'clock funeral. None of us answered, willing the AC in the van to hurry up before we all sweated our good clothes. Jodi had ironed Lucy's flower print skirt that she'd worn to Mom's funeral at Manna House and even tried to style her choppy hair a little, but to little avail. The old lady had been wearing the purple knit hat for so long, I hadn't realized what a squirrel's nest had grown underneath.

I could only imagine what the good folks of Minot were thinking when Lucy plonked herself down in a front-row seat at the funeral home.

Aunt Mercy had printed a nice program with a picture of Mom on the front and the obituary I'd written on the inside. Several new flower arrangements from my parents' church and some of Dad's old employees flanked the casket, open once again for a half hour before the service, then closed for the last time.

But the funeral service had almost no meaning for me. It lacked the life and celebration of the service we had at Manna

House, though people were kind, said how good it was to see the three Shepherd girls home again, what wonderful people Noble and Martha Shepherd were, the town was going to miss them . . .

The burial, however, was a different story. The white-haired pastor of the little stone church my parents had attended in recent years read the Twenty-third Psalm as we three girls and Aunt Mercy sat in folding chairs by the open graveside, which had been dug right beside my father's grave. A final prayer, and then several people pulled flowers out of the arrangements standing nearby, placed them on top of the casket poised over the open grave, and turned to go.

"Wait a minnit!"

I winced at Lucy's gravelly voice behind me. Heads turned. The old lady pushed her way through the small crowd until she stood right beside the grave. She was carrying the shovel, which she must have put in the van. "We ain't done yet! Look at that— they even got the pile o' dirt all covered up with that fake grassy stuff . . . whatchu call it? That sure ain't how it's done back where I come from."

Celeste started to rise up out of her seat, but I put out an arm to stop her. "It's all right," I said, loud enough for the others to hear. "This is Lucy, my mother's friend from Chicago." I got up and stood beside her. "Do you want to say something, Lucy?"

"Yeah. I ain't got any fancy words, but ever since we brought Miz Martha back home here, it's been eatin' at me. I met this lady here"—she patted the casket—"at a homeless shelter back in Chicago, where we was both stayin' . . ."

Celeste and Honor squirmed, and glances passed between folks in the crowd.

". . . an' then I come here and see that Miz Martha has a real nice house, just like a picture in a magazine. Not big an' fancy, but comfortable, nice place ta raise a family, nice place ta grow old in. *Lot* better than a homeless shelter, even if Manna House is one o' the better ones 'round Chicago."

Jodi slipped up and stood on the other side of Lucy, as if owning what Lucy was trying to say. A smile passed between us.

"An' yet she came to Chicago and stayed in a shelter, and ever'body called her Gramma Shep . . ." That got a chuckle from a few folks in the crowd. "An' she loved on the little 'uns 'at didn't have no home, an' read 'em stories, an' let Hannah paint her nails, an' let me take care o' her dog, when I ain't never had no dog of my own . . ."

Now tears were spilling down Lucy's cheeks. I saw a few other tears on the faces around the grave, too, before my own eyes blurred up.

"Just gotta say . . . kinda reminds me of all that Jesus talk I hear at the shelter, 'bout how He left heaven and came down to earth to live with all us riffraff." She sniffed and wiped her wet face with a big handkerchief she pulled out of somewhere. "That's all I wanna say. 'Cept"—she waved the shovel—"I don't plan on walkin' off till I see this good woman to her final restin' place. Now, you there . . ." She pointed at the funeral home staff. "Get that fake grass stuff off that pile of dirt, put the casket in the ground, and let's finish this up right."

Later that night I sat on the foldout couch with Jodi, and we laughed and cried, remembering the stunned looks on my sisters' faces as Lucy shoveled dirt on top of my mom's casket and then handed the shovel to me. But in the end Celeste and Honor had shoveled, too, and not a soul left without taking a turn shoveling that good, brown earth on top of the metal-blue casket. Someone even started to sing a hymn, as if decorum was being buried, and we'd all relaxed, witnesses to the natural cycle of life.

"And I'll bet your mom was looking down from heaven, enjoying the whole thing," Jodi murmured, pulling her knees up under Denny's extra-large Bulls T-shirt she usually slept in.

I giggled. "Yeah. Who ever thought we'd hear Lucy, of all people, preaching about the Incarnation!" Which set both of us off once more, laughing and crying.

But in fact, Lucy's little homily stayed with me all that night and into the next day, making me realize something I'd never really thought about before . . . just how much Jesus really *did* know about how I felt, because it all happened to Him—being rejected, scoffed at, homeless, no money, unappreciated . . .

For some reason I just wanted to sing and praise God the next morning, so while Jodi was making us all some breakfast, I got her gospel CDs out of the van and riffled through them. To my delight, I discovered she had the same CD her son, Josh, had given to me, the one with "my" song on it. I dusted off my mom's CD player—had she ever used the thing?—and turned up the volume.

Where do I go . . . when there's no one else to turn to?

Who do I talk to . . . when nobody wants to listen? . . .

I stood in the middle of Mom's living room, letting the words flow over me. *Yeah, that's why I can talk to God, because Jesus understands what I'm going through—*

"Hey!" Lucy poked her head into the living room. "Howza

body s'posed ta sleep when you makin' such a racket? 'Sides, Miz Jodi says it's time ta eat."

My sisters and I barely had time to eat Jodi's breakfast, get dressed, and pile into their rental car for our appointment with Mom's lawyer. Aunt Mercy, who'd taken the day off from work, threw up her hands in relief when we walked in at two minutes past ten. "This man charges by the *minute*," she hissed at us. "Get in there."

We made Aunt Mercy come in too—she was family, after all—and we all sat across the table from the lean man with hawk-like eyes. He peered at us over a pair of reading glasses perched on his nose, as if uncertain we were all related. "I'm Frank Putnam, senior partner of Putnam, Fields, and Pederson. Which one of you is Celeste? . . . Ah, all right. You've been named executor of the estate, as you probably know."

In a rather perfunctory manner, Mr. Putnam read through the will, which, he said, was fairly routine. "Bottom line, all assets should be divided equally between you three siblings, *after* paying any remaining costs surrounding Mrs. Shepherd's last illness, outstanding bills, and funeral expenses. Which are . . . ?"

Aunt Mercy handed over statements from Mom's bank and a handful of bills that had come in the mail since Mom had been in Chicago. I had brought the death certificate and receipts from the funeral home in Chicago. "I don't have the doctor and hospital bills yet from the past two weeks."

"All right . . ." The lawyer paged through a number of papers. "Your mother had Social Security and an annuity, both of which, of course, are cancelled at her death. But according to her bank statements, her checking and savings account amount to . . ." He punched numbers on his calculator. ". . . a few thousand dollars, which I recommend you leave in her account to cover any outstanding bills. As for the rest of her assets, there is, of course, the house—"

"How much do you think it's worth?" Celeste interrupted.

"Well, good news there. Your mother paid off the rest of the mortgage with your father's life insurance policy when he passed, which means you'll realize the full value of the house when it sells—minus any taxes and insurance due, of course. However, the real—"

"How much?" Honor's skinny, multicolored braids fell over her shoulders as she leaned forward. "Like, how much do houses sell for around here?"

Putnam shrugged. "I haven't seen your mother's home, but—"

"Your mother had it assessed not long ago," Aunt Mercy broke in. "Similar houses in this area are going for anywhere from one-twenty-five to a hundred seventy-five thousand."

The three of us sisters looked at one another with probably the same thought. We might realize a hundred fifty thousand from the house—fifty thousand each. My heart started to trip double-time. *That* would be a nice nest egg to enable me to start over again. Even rent that nice apartment in the Wrigleyville area. Except . . . how long would it take the house to sell? My heart started to sink again. Probably not soon enough to rent that apartment—or *any* apartment—before school started for my sons.

I was so engrossed in my thoughts, I didn't catch what the lawyer was saying until Honor gasped, *"What?!"*

The lawyer did all but roll his eyes. "I *said*, after paying off the house, your mother used the rest of the money from your father's life insurance policy to buy a simple term life insurance policy—which, I told her at the time, wasn't the wisest thing. A cash value policy would have also given her cash to invest or use to enjoy her retirement, go on a cruise, visit the grandchildren whenever she wanted, but"—he shrugged—"she insisted. Small premiums for her, its only value a benefit to her survivors."

Mr. Putnam handed a fat business envelope to Celeste. "Here it is—a term life insurance policy worth six hundred thousand dollars, to be divided equally between the three of you. With the death certificate, you should be able to cash it in fairly quickly. If you want, I can handle that for you and mail you each a check."

Our mouths hung open. Six hundred thousand dollars? Six. Hundred. Thousand. Dollars. Divided three ways? I couldn't breathe. That was two hundred thousand each . . .

No one spoke . . . until Honor screeched. "I—I could buy the house! With my share! And—and still have fifty grand left over!"

"Plus your third of the house sale," the lawyer said. "If that's what you want to do."

Celeste turned to her. "Do you want to? I mean really, Honor?"

"Yes! . . . I think." Her forehead scrunched. She chewed on one of her skinny decorative braids. "Or maybe not. I mean, it's cold here in the winter. River and Ryan would probably refuse to leave California . . . oh, I don't know!"

Mr. Putnam cleared his throat. "Uh, ladies. I have some papers here I need you to sign. You no doubt have some decisions to make, but I think we're done here. If you have any further questions, feel free to call my office. And, Ms. Shepherd"—he gave a short nod at Honor—"Putnam, Fields, and Pederson would be happy to handle the real estate transaction, if that's your decision." He stood up and shook hands all around.

I walked out the office door with my stupefied sisters, my mouth dry. I could hardly think what this meant. Except I kept hearing Jodi Baxter's off-the-cuff remark as we were driving here in the van: *"God must have a better plan . . ."*

I wanted to scream. Dance a jig and shout hallelujah! With two hundred fifty grand, I could afford an apartment! Get a real address! Bring my boys home! Maybe afford private school for them if I needed to!

Except . . . my heart twisted at the same time. *God, did my mother have to die for me to get back on my feet? Wish there'd been some other way.*

chapter 44

Aunt Mercy had said little during our visit to the lawyer's office, but when we got out to the parking lot, she asked me to ride with her to the house. "Gabby, I want to tell you something, but I don't want Honor to know . . . yet, anyway. Let her make her decision about whether to buy the house. If she wants to buy it, fine, don't say anything about this. But . . ." She glanced at me as we followed my sister's compact Chevy rental back to the house. "Noble and I grew up in that house. It has sweet memories for me too. If Honor decides not to buy it, I'd like to. I'm only sixty-two; I've got a few years before I have to pack it in." She grinned and turned her eyes back to the street.

"Oh, Aunt Mercy," I breathed. "Could you do that?"

She nodded. "What else am I going to do with my money, an old maid like me! I've been doing the research. A hundred-fifty thousand would be a fair price. Actually, I was going to say something to you girls, once your mom's name came up on the list for assisted living. But now . . ." She reached out and patted my knee.

"I'm so sorry you've lost your mom, Gabby. Sorry for everything that's happened to you the past few months. Please, I . . . I hope you'll let me be mama to you, whenever you need me. You and your sisters. You're all the family I've got."

Both of us were blubbering by the time we got back to the house. I grabbed her arm before she got out of the car. "Aunt Mercy, I think you ought to tell Celeste and Honor that you'd be willing to buy the house if Honor chooses not to. Frankly, I don't think Honor really wants to move back to Minot. I just think she's grasping at something to hold on to, now that Mom is gone. But if we had a home to come home to sometimes, a place to be together . . ."

Which turned out to be exactly the case. We sat around the kitchen table, eating a chicken Caesar salad we'd picked up at Marketplace Foods and downing copious amounts of iced tea as we sorted out "what's next." Honor was giddy with relief that the house could stay in the family, but that she didn't have to actually *buy* it and move back here. "Maybe in twenty years I'll be sick of California—or California will be sick of me—and I could buy it then," she giggled . . . and then realized what she'd said. "Oh! Aunt Mercy, I didn't mean I want you to *die* or anything in twenty years. But if you want to move into a retirement home or something . . ." She actually turned red under that California tan of hers.

Aunt Mercy laughed. "Hey, missy, you'll be *my* age in twenty years . . ." She put her silver pixie-cut alongside Honor's long tresses. "What do you think, girls? Can you imagine Honor at sixty-two?"

Celeste and I cracked up. "Yeah, sure," I gasped. "Spitting image—except she'll be sixty-two with that permanent dolphin tattoo."

"Yeah, yeah. You laugh. But believe me, there are already a lot of sixty-somethings in California walking around with tattoos. But hey—what about Mom's Galaxy? I could use a car. Could drive it back now."

As a matter of fact, I'd been thinking the same thing. I needed a car now, didn't I?

Celeste frowned. "What about your plane ticket? We got round-trip."

"Goose. So I lose a few hundred. That's cheap for a car. Or . . . should I pay you guys for it or something?"

We all decided Honor should take the car. I had the van to drive back anyway. Aunt Mercy said she'd see Putnam about the title change.

A load seemed to have lifted off the pressure to get everything done that Monday afternoon. With Aunt Mercy buying the house, we decided to leave most of the furniture, since Aunt Mercy's condo was a lot smaller and wouldn't fill this house. "But if any of you girls want something down the road, and have a way to get it, just tell me," Aunt Mercy said.

Celeste reached out a hand and gently untangled a few of my unruly curls. "What about you, Gabby? Aren't you going to need something to put in that apartment when you get it? Might as well take some of the family stuff now since you got that empty monster van out there in the driveway. *We* don't really need anything"—she nailed Honor with a look—"do we, Honor?"

"Ah . . . nope." Honor shook her head. "Couldn't take it on the plane anyway. I'd like some of Mom's jewelry, though. That old-fashioned stuff is funky right now."

I looked at my sisters—these virtual strangers Mom's death had catapulted back into my life. My oldest sister's gentle touch

370

as she untangled my rebellious curls had conveyed more affection than I'd experienced from her in a long time. And their encouragement to take what I needed from our family home to fill an empty apartment somehow seemed so much more than that—a step toward filling my empty life with a promise to care for one another once again . . .

I started to weep. And suddenly Celeste and Honor and I were in each other's arms. Grief and loss, love and hope all mixed up in our tears.

A last round of hugs with promises to call at least once a week—Honor still didn't have e-mail—and my sisters set out early Tuesday morning, driving in caravan to Billings, Montana, where Celeste would catch her plane for Anchorage, and Honor would just keep going, driving the Galaxy to Los Angeles. It had cooled off during the night but promised to be another sky-blue scorcher.

All six of us had spent the previous afternoon loading Moby Van with my old single bed, which we'd taken apart, and several boxes of dishes, silverware, pots and pans, blankets, sheets, and towels—most of which had seen better days, but hey, at this point in my life, something was better than nothing. We even squeezed in Mom's favorite wingback upholstered rocker and the Oriental rug from the dining room. "You need *something* to sit on in your new apartment," Aunt Mercy had insisted.

Celeste had had the brilliant idea of making Aunt Mercy the power of attorney for Mom's estate, even though she—Celeste— was still technically the executor, so we stopped packing long enough to drive back over to Mr. Putnam's law office to fill out the necessary forms, sign our names, and get them notarized. The man's secretary got a bit flustered when we piled into the law office with no appointment, but given the circumstances, Mr. Putnam agreed to stay an extra hour to squeeze us in.

"Huh. Probably charged us extra too," Honor grumbled on our way out.

Aunt Mercy had come over early Tuesday morning to say good-bye to all of us before going to work at the library. "I'll move this real estate transaction along as quickly as possible, Gabby," she whispered in my ear just before I climbed into the driver's seat. "I know you need the money to get on your feet and get your boys back. Now go before my mascara runs and I look like a raccoon when I show up for work." I felt a pang as I backed Moby Van out of the driveway and waved wildly to my aunt out the window, yelling good-bye, which got Dandy all excited, barking until the house and Aunt Mercy disappeared from sight.

With the van loaded to the gills, we left Minot behind and headed down the two-lane highway, intent on taking I-94 all the way back to Chicago. Jodi and I decided we'd split the cost of a motel room somewhere around Minneapolis—if we could find one that allowed pets—and get back at a decent time the next day. "You sure?" I asked. "That was an awful short visit with your parents. We could go back through Des Moines, same way we came."

Jodi shook her head. "Uh-uh. Right now I'd rather get home to Denny." She looked at me a little doe-eyed. "This is the longest we've been apart since Denny and the kids drove to New York to see *his* folks a couple of years ago. I had to stay home because I'd been sick all spring, and cases of SARS were cropping up everywhere . . ."

We talked a lot, Jodi and I, on the way back to Chicago. But I steered away from saying anything about the breakdown between Philip and me until I heard Lucy snoring in the backseat after we ate the sack lunch Aunt Mercy had packed for us. Jodi had taken over the driving, her shoulder-length brown hair caught back with an elastic band to keep it off her neck. She was a few years older than I, but somehow managed to look younger. Her face was relaxed, her eyes alive. The look of a woman who knows she's loved.

"I'm jealous, you know."

Jodi glanced at me, startled, then looked back at the highway. "What do you mean?"

"You and Denny. You guys ought to clone your relationship, sell it on eBay. You'd make a ton."

She slipped a small grin. "Yeah, well, we have our moments. Me, I'm a terrible nag. And Denny can be *so* dense."

I shrugged. "Maybe. But it's obvious you guys love each other. Philip and I were that way once. Crazy about each other. Gosh, Jodi, the man's so gorgeous I used to melt like chocolate on a hot day whenever he came in the room. We laughed at his mother's objections to our 'mismatch'—almost like marrying me was his rebellion against their snooty conventions. He was going to be the rising star in the commercial development business, and I . . ." I grabbed my T-shirt and dabbed at my eyes. "I tried, Jodi, I really tried to be the good corporate wife. But somewhere along the way, I lost myself. Lost Philip too . . ."

I leaned against the passenger-side window, watching the Minnesota hills rolling past. "It's like I don't even recognize him anymore . . . couldn't relax and be myself when he was around . . . everything I did was wrong. But"—I felt heat in my chest—"I still can't believe he just kicked me out, kicked my mother out, even kicked the dog out! I mean, who *is* that man?!"

My voice had risen, and I glanced into the backseat to be sure Lucy was still sleeping. "He even started gambling," I muttered darkly. "Practically every weekend! Last time I talked to Henry Fenchel, it sounded like Philip's new love affair with the dice was starting to affect their business partnership."

We rode in silence for a few minutes. Then Jodi glanced at me. "Do you pray for Philip, Gabby?"

I gaped at her. Pray for *Philip*? I'd certainly done a lot of praying *about* Philip. Or ranting at God about Philip. But pray *for* him? "Not really," I said slowly. "I've been too mad."

"Maybe you should. He sounds lost."

We found a motel just across the Minnesota-Wisconsin state line that allowed pets for a ten-dollar fee. Lucy complained about stopping, said she could sleep in the car just as well. "Maybe *you* can," I muttered. "*We* need a bed." The room had two queen beds, and Lucy claimed the one farthest from the door—after double-locking the door and jamming the desk chair under the handle. She didn't bother to undress either. I shrugged at Jodi. *Go figure.*

I was used to sleeping with Lucy's snores back in the bunk room at Manna House, but I don't know if Jodi got very much sleep. At one point, I got up and rolled Lucy over onto her side, and we managed to fall asleep before she moved again.

In the morning we treated ourselves to breakfast at a nearby pancake house before hitting the road again. Couldn't believe how many pancakes Lucy was able to put away. I asked if she'd like to sit up front for a while, but the old lady shook her head. "Nah, me an' Dandy is all settled back here. 'Sides, can't keep up with all that chitchattin' you two doin'. Ain't got no kids to talk about, ain't got no husband, ain't been anywhere, ain't got nuthin' to say."

I laughed and glanced in the rearview, still not used to seeing Lucy without her purple hat. "Okay, just one question, Lucy," I said over my shoulder, "and then we'll leave you out of the chit-chatting. Where did you learn how to clean a bathroom like you did at my mom's house? You even folded the ends of the toilet paper in that cute little hotel style too. I think you've been living a secret life."

"Humph. Ain't got no secret life. Got this job as a hotel maid when I first come to Chicago, but . . ." Her voice drifted off. "Let's jus' say, cleanin' bathrooms wasn't the only thing I learned on that job. All sorts o' people gonna take advantage of ya any way they can, 'specially if they think you ignorant. Decided it was safer out on the streets. Been makin' my own way ever since. Just . . . lonely sometimes." A long pause. "Gonna miss Miz Martha."

Jodi and I looked at each other. That might explain the triple door-locking last night. Still, there was a lot of story left out of that two-bit summary. But at least it was more than she'd ever given up before. "Thanks, Lucy."

"Yeah? Thanks fer what?"

"For being a good friend. I think you were the best friend my mother ever had."

Lucy made a funny noise. "Just . . . shut up an' drive, will ya?"

We laughed and settled down for the final day of our trip. Jodi studied the road atlas. "Gee, it's not that far. We oughta be home in six hours or so."

Home . . . For the first time in weeks, I let myself think about what that meant. I was still pretty broke, but within a few days or weeks, I'd have real money in my bank account. "Can't believe my mom actually left us an inheritance," I murmured. "Paid off the house when my dad died, bought that term life insurance . . ." The reality of it all was beginning to sink in. I might even have enough to buy a house one of these days—but that would have to wait. I had more immediate goals. "Can you believe it, Jodi? I'm going to be able to rent that apartment, get my boys back here in time for school—"

"Buy the whole building if ya want!" Lucy quipped from the backseat.

A big semi thundered past us, making the van shudder. I gripped the steering wheel, wondering if I'd heard right. I looked over at Jodi. She was staring at me. "Gabby! What Lucy just said."

"Buy the—?" Now a shudder did ripple through my insides. I shook my head. "Oh, no, no, I don't think so. I don't have *that* much . . ."

"How much? I mean, how much are they selling it for? You might have enough for a down payment."

"Yeah, buy the building," Lucy growled. "I might even move in. Or visit ya."

I kept shaking my head. "You guys are crazy, you know that?"

Jodi laughed. "Yeah, I know. God is crazy too—look at how He answered our prayer about how to get your mom's body back to North Dakota for burial! But Gabby, think about it! Josh and Edesa told me you wanted Manna House to use the Dandy Fund to buy a building for second-stage housing for mothers with children, but—"

My ears got red. "Yeah, what did I know? We're riding in the Dandy Fund."

Jodi was practically bouncing in her seat. "Gabby! Listen to me! What did Mabel Turner say to you when you applied for the job at Manna House? You told me yourself! *She* believes God brought you to Chicago because He has a purpose for you at Manna House."

My mind was tumbling even as she spoke. *A six-flat . . . not far from Manna House . . . up for sale . . . Precious and Sabrina . . . Tanya and Sammy . . .*

Jodi punched me on the shoulder. "Maybe this is it."

chapter 45

The idea of buying that six-flat was flat-out crazy, probably impossible . . . but it grew on me like a second skin. Dozens of questions tumbled through my thoughts, and I jabbered at Jodi like a set of wind-up chatty teeth all the way back to Chicago. Was a building for second-stage housing a good idea? Mabel had thought so, just not yet. Did I even want to live in Chicago? Well, yeah, because I loved my job—more than that, if Mabel was right, God had called me to it—and it made sense to live close by. Would my boys want to live there? Moot point. *I* was going to live there, even if I just rented the first-floor apartment, and they were going to live with me, because Lee Boyer said I had a slam-dunk custody case. But what about Philip? What if we got back together? There was always that possibility, wasn't there? Buying a building was a really big leap to take by myself. What would he think? Was it a smart thing to do with my money? Good question. Probably should invest it. But what about investing in the lives of women like Precious and Tanya? How would buying a building work with Manna House? I had no idea. Would my inheritance even make a dent in the asking price for the building? Probably not . . .

"Well, *duh!*" Jodi said. "Pull over. Let me drive, and you can call your lawyer friend and ask what they're asking! That'd be a start anyway. Look, there's an exit up there with a Wendy's. Time for lunch anyway."

We made a pit stop for hamburgers and fries, fed and watered Dandy, filled the gas-guzzler on my debit card, stretched our road-weary muscles, and climbed back in the van for the last leg of our trip, with Jodi behind the wheel.

"Step on it," Lucy grumbled. "I'm tired. Me an' Dandy 'bout ready to get out an' walk."

"Just a few more hours, Lucy," I said, twisting in my seat. "Don't blame you. But you and Dandy have been good travelers. I'm glad you came."

"The phone, Gabby," Jodi reminded me as she pulled onto the interstate. "Call the lawyer guy."

"You *are* a nag, you know that?" But I dutifully dug out my cell phone, found Lee's number, and pushed the Call button. "He's going to think I'm nuts . . . Lee? Hi, it's Gabby."

"Gabby!" Lee Boyer's voice crackled in my ear. "I was hoping to hear from you. Where are you? How'd it go driving the casket back to, uh, North Dakota, right?"

"Yeah. Minot. Real good. We're still on the road, almost to the Illinois border, though. But, hey, today's Wednesday, I think I missed my eleven o'clock appointment, so thought I'd check in."

He chuckled in my ear. "Yeah, I bill double for missed appointments."

Jodi was making *hurry-up* signs. I waved her off. "Well, just wanted to let you know it's going to work out for me to rent that apartment after all. You didn't call the guy to cancel my contract or anything, did you?"

"No, no, I said we'd deal with that when you got back. But that's good, real good! What happened?"

"Just . . . well, I got some inheritance money I didn't expect. I'll explain more when I see you. But I have another question." I held my hand up to stop Jodi's impatient gestures. "Do you happen to know the asking price for the whole building?"

There was a brief hesitation at the other end of the phone. "The *building*? I think he's asking six hundred. Why, are you—"

"Six hundred thousand?" I repeated for Jodi's sake. "Really? I thought it'd be even more."

"Are you thinking of buying? That must be some inheritance."

I laughed, feeling a bit giddy. "Not that much. But I might have enough for a down payment. Manna House needs a six-flat for homeless mothers with children, and I thought—"

"Gabby. Gabby! Whoa, slow down. Don't go making any rash decisions! Hey, promise me? One thing at a time. You need to be smart about this."

I felt a prickle of irritation. But what did I expect? It was a wild idea. "Well, don't worry. I don't even have the money yet. What I do have is a van full of furniture and household stuff for my new apartment. Can I get in yet? Is Mr. What's-his-name done with the refurbishing?"

Lee said he'd check it out and let me know when I could get the key. "Glad you're back, Gabby. Glad the apartment is working out for you too. Now we can move on the custody petition ASAP. As for the other . . . well, let's talk."

"Okay. Thanks, Lee." I closed the phone. "He thinks it's crazy."

Jodi grinned. "It *is* crazy. The question is, is it *God's* crazy idea? If it is, it doesn't matter what Mr. Lawyer thinks."

As we came into the city on the expressway, Lee called back on my cell and said I could get the key the next day—Thursday—and move in any time after that. "Well, at least we won't have to unload the van tonight," I told Jodi. "Hope no one needs it before tomorrow night."

"Denny and I'll come down and help you unload," Jodi said as she turned off the expressway and headed for her Rogers Park neighborhood on city streets.

"You don't have to do that, Jodi."

She grinned. "Oh yes I do. I want to see this building you're moving into, want to see just how crazy this idea of yours is, and"—her grin widened—"maybe even pray over the building too. You know, claim it for God." Now she laughed. "That's what the Yada Yada sisters would do, anyway."

I sighed. "I like that. Hope some of their faith rubs off on me."

We dropped Jodi off at her two-flat in Rogers Park, our good-bye hugs wrapped with the realization that our week together on the road had deepened our new friendship for both of us. Lucy even let Jodi give her a hug—not her usual MO. Back in the driver's seat, I drove south on Sheridan Road, under the Red Line El tracks that crossed over just north of Wrigleyville, and pulled up a few blocks later in front of Manna House.

"Home again . . . more or less," I told Lucy, shutting off the motor. I closed my eyes a weary moment, my heart full. *God, thank You for keeping us safe, for . . . for everything You've done the past few—*

"My butt's sore," Lucy grumbled. "Can you unlock these doors or what?"

So much for prayers. We straggled in the front doors of the shelter—even Dandy was limping, stiff from lack of exercise—and got a welcome screech from Angela Kwon in the receptionist cubicle. Mabel came out of her office to see what all the noise was about, and Lucy immediately insisted on trading in the borrowed suitcase for her wire cart. I left her busily rearranging her belongings in the foyer. Dandy and I tried to navigate our way through the multipurpose room but were cornered by a handful of shelter kids who fell on Dandy with hugs and kisses, which Dandy was happy to return.

I snuck off to unpack and clean up before supper, which was brought in that night by a service group from a local Kiwanis Club. The men, mostly middle-aged, looked pretty funny in the white hairnets required of all food workers, but they took the kidding with good humor. All the residents hooted and clapped when Mabel announced that Hero Dog was back. "Oh yes, and Lucy and Gabby too," the director teased. "If you two don't mind, why don't we have coffee and dessert up in the multipurpose room after supper to hear about your trip and Grandma Shep's burial? Estelle baked brownies to celebrate your return and said to give you both a hug."

Lucy shrugged off Mabel's attempt to pass on Estelle's hug. "Aw, c'mon, none o' that mushy stuff. But them brownies sound good."

"I'll take two hugs then," I grinned, holding my arms open.

Mabel gave me a warm hug, using the occasion to whisper in my ear, "And how about a meeting in my office tomorrow morning? Ten o'clock good?"

I woke the next morning in the bunk room before Sarge's wake-up bell and lay there a few moments as my new reality sunk in. *This could be my last time waking up here in the shelter* . . . I propped myself up on my elbow. Dandy's bed had been moved alongside Lucy's bunk. The bunk my mother had occupied had been filled with a new resident, a scrawny white woman with several missing teeth who'd raised a ruckus when she learned she'd be sharing a room with a dog.

"Tough," Sarge had sniffed. "It's a warm night. You can sleep here in *Dandy's room,* or outside. Your choice." The new woman stayed, turning her back on all of us.

I lay down again and closed my eyes. Maybe I should stay a day or two and move on Saturday. I still didn't know what to do about Dandy. Take him with me? Paul would be happy . . . but what about Lucy? Maybe I should leave him here at the shelter, since they'd dubbed him their official watchdog. But who would be responsible for him—Lucy? This was an emergency shelter, not a permanent residence . . .

I hadn't told anyone I was moving out yet. I wanted to bring Mabel up to date first. And I felt a bit guilty, having everything work out for me, while Precious and Tanya felt stuck here at the shelter with their kids. Should I tell them my hope? Or was it too soon to talk about a House of Hope—

My eyes flew open. That's what we would call it! The House of Hope.

I wanted to bounce out of bed and call Jodi. Tell *somebody*. But it wasn't even 6 a.m. yet. I squeezed my eyes shut again. *Oh God, is this idea for the House of Hope really from You? Or am I going out on a limb here? Show me the path, Lord! And I could use some patience too. But I do want to thank You, Jesus! Thank You for helping me get an apartment so I can bring my sons back. Thank You for my mother, for her sacrificial love, her sacrificial gift . . .* My heart was so full, my prayers poured out in the silence, praying for Celeste and Honor, for Aunt Mercy, for P. J. and Paul having to deal with their parents' separation . . .

Suddenly remembering what Jodi had said, I added, *Guess I ought to pray for Philip too. That's kinda hard, God, 'cause . . . 'cause he's hurt me so much . . . I don't even know what to pray for him. Shake him up! Do something! But . . . I guess You know better than I do—*

Sarge's wake-up bell and familiar bark shattered the silence. Bodies rolled off the bunks, and the morning routine started. Jostling for space at the sinks in the bathroom . . . trying to pay attention during the obligatory morning devotions . . . breakfast of cold cereal, bananas, toast and jam, hot coffee . . . getting chore assignments for that day . . .

Dandy didn't seem like his usual lively self—missing Mom, no doubt—so I let him curl up in my office while I tried to re-orient myself by reading staff meeting minutes and a board report I'd missed while I was away. And I took him with me to the main floor when ten o'clock rolled around—bumping into a perspiring Estelle in the foyer as she came bustling in with her usual haul of bulging grocery bags for that day's lunch.

I was immediately swallowed up in her sweaty hug. "Oh, baby, baby . . . Jodi told me you're going to be able to get your apartment. Ain't that just like God? Making a way out of no way!

Mm-mm, praise Jesus!" And then she was gone through the swinging doors as suddenly as she'd appeared, but not before she tossed over her shoulder, "Harry and I'll come help you unload that van tonight. I want to see the apartment!"

Whew. I needed to tell the residents I was moving before Estelle did all my announcing for me. But at least Jodi had been circumspect and didn't say anything about our crazy idea about buying the whole building.

But after bringing Mabel Turner up to date on everything that had happened since my mom's funeral at Manna House, including the inheritance that made it possible for me to get an apartment and bring my sons back from Virginia, I leaned forward in my chair, resting my forearms on my side of Mabel's desk. "And . . . there's something else. Don't laugh, and just hear me out, okay? I don't know how to make this happen, and I don't have a proposal to present to the Manna House Board yet. I—I just want you to pray about this with me." And in a big rush, I spilled out the crazy idea of using my inheritance money to put a down payment on the six-flat I was moving into, to create a House of Hope for moms like Precious and Tanya.

To Mabel's credit, she didn't laugh—though she did smile and wag her head. "So you've already got a name for this housing project of yours, hm? Well, it certainly won't hurt to pray about it. I'm happy to do that much." And she did, reaching across the desk, taking my hands, and praying in that wise and winsome way that was Mabel's special gift. "God, if this is just a wacky scheme percolating under the cap of curls sitting in front of me, protect Gabby from making a big mistake. But if this wild and wonderful idea belongs to You, we know nothing is going to stop it, and help us to know how to get on board."

I was stunned by Mabel's prayer. I even wrote it down as soon as I got back to my office so I could pray the same way. She'd called it a "wild and wonderful idea" . . . along with that "if," of course. But she was right. I didn't want this to be just my idea. Huh! If it was, it'd fall flat faster than it took me to trip over Lucy's cart. If it was from God, I had to give it back to God, because it was going to take God's help to pull it together.

But my heart was tripping a little that evening as I pulled Moby Van up in front of the six-flat, which turned out to be a mere five minutes from Manna House—I timed it. Lee Boyer was there with the keys, his light-brown eyes twinkling behind those wire rims of his. A few minutes later Jodi and Denny Baxter pulled up in their Dodge Caravan with Edesa and Josh, minus little Gracie this time, followed by Mr. Bentley's RAV4 with Harry Bentley, Estelle, and that cute grandson of Harry's, DeShawn.

Looking at all my friends, I wasn't sure if I was going to laugh or cry. "With all this help, it'll take us about ten minutes." Which was almost true, though once the van was unloaded, Estelle dragged me into the kitchen and insisted on opening the boxes of kitchen stuff and putting them into the newly refinished maple cupboards.

"Know you got a lot on your mind," Estelle murmured as she unwrapped a box of glasses stuffed with newspaper and handed them to me. "But want you to keep Harry in your prayers."

I looked at her sharply. "What's wrong with Mr. B?"

"Don't think he knows. But he been complaining about a blind spot in one of his eyes. I keep tellin' him ta see a good eye doctor, but you know Harry. Too busy with DeShawn these days. An' just between you an' me, I actually think he's scared. But don't say anything. Just pray."

"Sure." My heart squeezed a little. "Harry the doorman" had been my first real friend here in Chicago—and now he was so much more. But had I actually ever prayed for him? A blind spot in his eye! What did that mean? *God,* I prayed silently as I lined up the assorted odd glasses in a cupboard near the sink, *don't let me be so consumed with my own problems that I forget to pray for Harry . . . and Precious, and Tanya, and all my other friends who need You too.*

When Estelle and I had emptied the last box and wandered back to the others, Denny and Josh had already put my old single bed together, and Jodi had made it up, while Mr. Bentley and DeShawn had rolled out the Oriental rug in the living room and brought in the wingback rocker. We had all worked up a sweat in the muggy July heat, and I made a mental note to buy some fans and at least one window air conditioner.

I was about to thank everybody when Jodi whispered something to Estelle and Edesa, and the next thing I knew they were gathering everybody into the living room to pray over my new apartment—"and the whole building," Jodi slipped in. Everybody except Lee Boyer, that is. He disappeared, saying something about an evening appointment and he'd be in touch. The rest of us joined hands, even Harry's nine-year-old grandson, and several took turns praying for God's provision and protection, and that God would make this a true home for me and my sons . . . "and everyone else who takes up residence here," Jodi added, squeezing my hand.

Oh, Jodi was good.

As people climbed back into their cars and pulled away, calling out congratulations and waving good-bye, Jodi and I still stood on the sidewalk, arm in arm, looking at the front of the brick building. I pointed out the wide stone lintel above the doorway. "Don't you think 'House of Hope' would look good up there?"

Jodi grinned and squeezed my arm as I told her about the name that had popped into my head early that morning, and then about Mabel's prayer. Then I sighed. "But I can't think about that right now. Even with all the stuff we brought back from my mother's house, the apartment is still pretty empty. I'm going to need beds for the boys, a TV, more furniture . . . what?"

Jodi had pulled away and looked me in the eye, her face scrunched into a puzzled frown. "Gabby Fairbanks. I don't get it. You have all that good furniture sitting up there unused in that penthouse. It's *yours too*, Gabby. Didn't you tell me Philip had to put the original locks back? You still have a key. Just go get it, for goodness' sake! Why should Philip get it all? A judge will make you divide it up anyway."

I stared at Jodi. *Just go get it?*

Jodi blew her bangs off her damp forehead and grinned. "Want me to round up another moving crew?"

chapter 46

The rented U-Haul truck driven by Josh Baxter backed into the service lane of the parking garage at Richmond Towers and lined up with the wide doors leading into the security area. Mr. Bentley wasn't on duty on Saturday, but he showed up to make sure everything went smoothly getting the truck into the garage, letting the moving crew into the security area, and up the elevators to the thirty-second floor.

Penthouse.

I had arrived an hour earlier, let myself into the penthouse that had been my home for a mere two and a half months, and marked the furniture and items to be moved with large, lime-green sticky notes. I felt uncomfortable being there without Philip's knowledge and permission, but God knew I had tried.

I'd called his office Friday morning and asked to speak to Philip Fairbanks. I had planned to tell him—not ask his permission—that I was coming Saturday with a moving crew and taking enough stuff to make my apartment functional. I had no plans to rob him blind, just take a fair share.

But it was Henry Fenchel who came on the line. "He's out of town, Gabby," his partner said flatly. "Didn't tell me where, just said he was taking Friday off, and he'd be back in the office Monday morning. But I can guess. He—"

"But it's very important that I get hold of him, Henry," I interrupted, not really wanting to hear another rant from Henry Fenchel.

Henry snorted in my ear. "Well, you can try his cell phone, but I've tried that on weekends, and he usually turns it off when he's gaming. I tell you, Gabby, something's not right. First he dumps you, dumps his own kids, and spends nearly every week-end in Indiana at the Horseshoe. The accounts aren't adding up here in the office either. I'm calling in an accountant to—"

I'd hurriedly said good-bye and hung up. Philip siphoning business monies to support his gambling? Did he have debts he couldn't cover? No, no, I wasn't going to believe that about Philip . . . though there were a lot of things that had happened recently I never would have believed about Philip.

I did try his cell phone, got his voice mail, and left my message.

I never got a call back.

Now the volunteer moving crew—Denny and Jodi Baxter, Josh and Edesa Baxter, Estelle Williams and her housemate, Leslie Stuart, and Carl and Florida Hickman and their two husky boys—hauled in boxes, packed up the boys' rooms, and moved out the things I had marked. Everything from the boys' bed-rooms, including their small TV. My bedroom dresser and mirror and an upholstered reading chair. Some scatter rugs. I left the master bath as it was, but I cleaned out the powder room and the second bath—towels, cleaning supplies, shampoo, and lotions. I put neon-lime *Take Me* notes on the square kitchen table and its four chairs, leaving the expensive dining room set and the bar stools in the kitchen for Philip. I'd brought a lot of kitchen stuff from my mom's house already. The only piece I took from the living room was another upholstered chair—now the boys and I all had a place to sit. I left Philip's office untouched, except for the family photo albums and children's books I'd collected over the years. Those went in a box and out to the truck.

Mr. Bentley stayed out of the penthouse, doing no more than directing traffic on the lower floor. Maybe that eye was bothering him more than he let on. Still, it was for the best. I didn't want Philip or anybody else to make him lose his job over "conflict of interest" with a resident. But his grandson DeShawn wanted to be where the action was, especially since the older Hickman teens, Chris and Cedric, were doing a man's job hauling chairs and boxes, and kept saying, "Hey, DeShawn, you take that end" or "Get that box, will ya?" The youngster beamed.

"What about the big bed, Gabby?" Denny Baxter asked, standing in the master bedroom.

I shook my head. That was my marriage bed . . . and right now I didn't have a marriage. Sleeping in it alone would be too painful.

My throat tightened. Would Philip and I ever sleep together in that bed again—husband and wife . . . lovers . . . friends? Or was it really over?

Denny must have seen me brush tears from my eyes because he quickly left the room, but I lingered a few moments longer, picking up a framed photo from the top of Philip's dresser. The four of us two years ago in a candid snapshot, arms around each other, wide grins. Philip's dark head was next to my "mop top," as he often called it, the boys laughing as if they were being tickled.

The way we were . . .

I slipped the framed photo into my backpack.

"All done?" Jodi said as I came into the kitchen, where Estelle had managed to produce lemonade and paper cups. "Should we swing back by the shelter to pick up Dandy?"

I shook my head. "I, um, gave him to Lucy yesterday. Just couldn't bring myself to separate them. There are enough bags of dog food left at Manna House to last her at least six months. I made her promise that she'd take shelter in the winter—Manna House is probably the only shelter that's going to let her come back with a dog. And if she couldn't take care of him, I'd take him back." I grimaced. "Don't know if it was the right thing to do. She and Dandy disappeared last night. Her bunk was empty and her cart was gone. Dandy's bed too."

"Oh, Gabby." Jodi gave me a hug. "What about Paul?"

I shrugged. "I'll get him another dog, maybe a puppy. It'll be okay. But speaking of Paul, could you excuse me a minute? I'll meet you downstairs. I have a call to make."

The moving crew tromped through the gallery and out into the foyer, chatting with each other as they waited for the elevator. And then all was quiet.

I stood a few feet back from the wraparound floor-to-ceiling windows, looking out—not down—at Lake Michigan sparkling a deep azure blue in the midday July sun. Lake Shore Drive was bustling and alive . . . but silent up here behind the thick windows. To the south, Chicago's skyline rose into the air, a thousand stories walking the streets. And now, my story was one of them.

Strange. I would not miss this penthouse. Most of the memories here had been painful ones. But Chicago . . .

I pulled out my cell phone, made the call, and waited until I heard the voices of both my sons on the phone. "P. J.? Paul? It's Mom. It's time to come home."

Reading Group Guide

A note from the author . . .

Okay, okay! I've heard from enough faithful readers who were disappointed that *Where Do I Go?* (Book #1 in the **Yada Yada House of Hope** series) ended on a "cliff-hanger" without a clear resolution, that I feel compelled to share some background . . .

After including the Manna House Women's Shelter in the last two books of the **Yada Yada Prayer Group** series, I realized I knew zilch about homeless shelters or why people become homeless, so I began volunteering once a week at Breakthrough Urban Ministries women's shelter here in Chicago (www.breakthroughministries.com). I learned there are numerous reasons people end up homeless, and I began to feel a burden to tell some of these stories—and the fictional Manna House was the perfect segue.

But Gabby Fairbank's story got so deep, I found it impossible to wrap everything up nice and tidy by the end of the first book. I don't blame you if you were distressed over the ending. But my primary purpose was to bring Gabby to a place where she realized that when her whole life felt as if it were falling apart, she could turn to "the Rock" of her salvation, just as the song says—*even without the promise that life would turn out rosy.*

But I share your pain! I'm a person who wants hope and redemption in my stories—which is why Gabby's story picks up right where it left off in this second installment. I'm delighted that you've hung in there with the **House of Hope** series and read Book 2, *Who Do I Talk To?* So let's dig in and talk about it!

1. Even though Gabby Fairbanks' situation might seem extreme, what kind of life situations/experiences/circumstances can create that "end of the world" feeling? Even though your circumstances might not be the same, have you or someone in your family experienced a life-altering event where it seemed that nothing would ever be the same? What were the initial feelings you had to cope with?

2. What were the seeds of hope that Gabby clung to as this book opened, even though everything looked hopeless? What are the seeds of hope you or your family clung to when faced with a seemingly hopeless situation?

3. In Gabby's case, her anguish was exacerbated because someone deliberately "did something" that caused her pain (as opposed to an accident or natural disaster). **Read Psalm 37:1–17.** What phrases stand out to you that might give *comfort* in such a situation? What *guidance* does the psalmist give to help deal with hurts caused by other people?

4. A number of people come alongside Gabby during this crisis, but in different ways. What role does each of

the following play in helping Gabby to stand up and be strong? *Edesa . . . Mabel . . . Estelle . . . Harry Bentley . . . Lee Boyer . . . Lucy . . . Sarge . . . Mike Fairbanks . . . Jodi Baxter.* (Anyone else?) What (or who) do you think was most helpful to Gabby in changing her perspective?

5. How does Dandy the Hero Dog impact this story—and the various people in the story—beyond just stopping a nighttime burglar? *(Gabby? Her mom? Lucy? The shelter women? Any others?)* Why do you think dogs or other pets often play an important role in times of emotional stress and difficulty?

6. How do you feel about Gabby's difficult decision to leave her boys in Virginia (chapter 12)? Can you think of any other alternative? What does this show about Gabby's character?

7. In Book 1, Mabel Turner said she thought God had brought Gabby to Chicago and to Manna House "for a purpose." How does that "prophetic word" continue to impact Gabby in Book 2? What do you think that purpose is? How does knowing (discovering) God's purpose for our lives impact how we deal with our particular life situation and the people around us?

8. In what ways do you see Gabby growing and changing in this book? In what areas do you still want to shake her and tell her _____ ?

9. The death of Gabby's mother—Martha Shepherd— seemed to also be the death of Gabby's patchwork plan to get an apartment and get her boys back. First Estelle, then Jodi says, "God must have a better plan." Has anyone ever said that to you when things fell apart with

your own plans? How did it make you feel? Was it true? Or did it seem like "spiritual mumbo-jumbo"?

10. Philip Fairbanks . . . we all hate him. (At least you've told me you do!) Why do you think he showed up at Martha Shepherd's funeral? How did you feel about that? What do you think is going on with Philip? Is he redeemable? What do *you* think is going to happen with Philip? Why? How?

11. How realistic is Gabby's dream to create a "House of Hope"? She's well-meaning but . . . is she equipped? Is this the right time? What problems do you foresee? How do *we* know when to let go of our unrealistic dreams, and when it's important to hold onto those dreams?

12. Gabby muses at the end Book 2, "There are thousands of stories walking the streets of Chicago—and mine is one of them." Why is it important to realize that every person we meet "has a story"—even the homeless person or panhandler we meet on the street? How might that change how we relate to that person?

P.S. To my readers . . .

Wish I could be a fly on the wall to hear your discussion! Thanks for being such faithful readers of the **Yada Yada House of Hope** *series. I appreciate each one of you! Hang on for the next episode in Book 3,* Who Do I Lean On? *coming out in June 2010.*

Until then . . . be blessed!

Sometimes you find hope
in the last place you look.

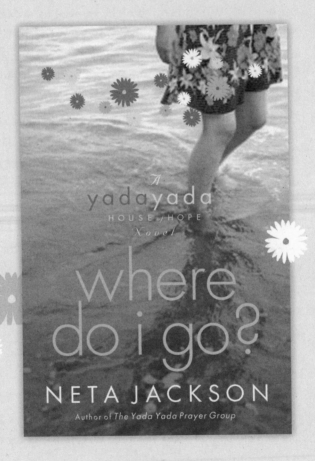

BOOK 1 *in the* HOUSE *of* HOPE SERIES

THOMAS NELSON
Since 1798

Who Do I Lean On?

For the latest on the
House of Hope Series,
please visit www.daveneta.com

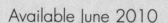

Available June 2010

BOOK 3 *in the* HOUSE *of* HOPE SERIES

THOMAS NELSON
Since 1798

Party With the
Yada Yada Prayer Group!

Each novel
includes
numerous pages
of celebration
ideas and recipes
that *flow from*
the story

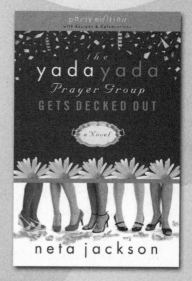

Available
Everywhere

An Excerpt from
The Yada Yada Prayer Group

CHICAGO, ILLINOIS—2002

I didn't really want to go to the "women's conference" the first weekend of May. Spending two hundred bucks to stay in a *hotel* for two nights only forty-five minutes from home? Totally out of our budget, even if it did include "two continental breakfasts, Saturday night banquet, and all conference materials."

Now if it had been just Denny and me, that'd be different. A romantic getaway, a second honeymoon . . . no teenagers tying up the phone, no dog poop to clean up in the yard, no third grade lesson plans, no driving around and around the block trying to find a parking place. Just Denny and me sleeping late, ordering croissants, fruit plates, and hot coffee for breakfast, letting someone else make the bed (hallelujah!), swimming in the pool . . . now *that* would be worth two hundred bucks, no question.

I'm not generally a conference-type person. I don't like big crowds. We've lived in the Chicago area for almost twenty years now, and I still haven't seen Venetian Nights at the lakefront, even though Denny takes Josh and Amanda almost every year. Wall-to-wall people . . . and standing in line for those pukey Port-a-Potties? Ugh.

Give me a small moms group or a women's Bible study any day—like Moms in Touch, which met at our church in Downers Grove all those years the kids were growing up. We had some retreats, too, but I knew most of the folks from church, and they were held at a camp and retreat center out in the country where you could wear jeans to all the sessions and walk in the woods during free time.

But listening to the cars on I-90 roaring past the hotel's manicured lawn? Laughing like a sound track at jokes told by high-powered speakers in tailored suits and matching heels? Having to take "after five attire" for a banquet on Saturday night? (Why would a bunch of women *do* that with no men around to admire how gorgeous we look?)

Uh-uh. Was not looking forward to it.

Still, Avis Johnson, my boss—she's the principal at the Chicago public school where I teach third grade this year—asked if I'd like to go with her, and that counts for something. Maybe everything. I've admired Avis ever since I first met her at Uptown Community Church but never thought we'd be pals or anything. Not just because she's African American and I'm white, either. She's so calm and poised—a classy lady. Her skin is a smooth, rich, milk-chocolate color, and she gets her hair done every week at a salon. Couldn't believe it when I found out she was fifty and a *grandmother*. (I should be so lucky to look like that when Josh and Amanda have kids.) I feel like a country bumpkin when I'm around her. My nondescript dark brown hair never could hold a "style," so I just wear it at shoulder level with bangs and hope for the best.

Not only that, but when we moved from suburban Downers Grove into the city last summer, I applied to teach in one of the public schools in the Rogers Park neighborhood of Chicago, where we live now, and ended up at Mary McLeod Bethune Elementary, where Avis Johnson just happened to be the *principal*. Weird calling her "Avis" on Sunday and "Ms. Johnson" on Monday.

Avis is one of Uptown Community's worship leaders and has tried to wean its motley congregation of former Presbyterians, Baptists, "Evee-Frees," Methodists, Brethren, and No-Churchers from the hymnbook and "order of service" to actually participating in *worship*. I love the way she quotes Scripture, too, not only from the New Testament, but also from those mysterious Minor Prophets, and Job, and the Pentateuch. I mean, I know a lot of Scripture, but for some reason I have a hard time remembering those pesky references, even though I've been in Sunday school since singing "Climb, Climb Up Sunshine Mountain" in the toddler class.

People at Uptown want to be "relevant" in an urban setting, which means cultivating a diverse congregation, but most of us, including yours truly, aren't too comfortable shouting in church and start to fidget when the service goes past twelve o'clock—both of which seem par for Sunday morning in black churches. Don't know why Avis stays at Uptown sometimes. Pastor Clark, bless him, has a vision, but for most of us transplants, our good intentions come with all the presumptions we brought from suburbia. But she says God called her to Uptown, and Pastor Clark preaches the Word. She'll stay until God tells her to go.

Denny and me—we've only been at the church since last summer. That's when Honorable Husband decided it was time white folks—meaning us, as it turned out—moved back into the city rather than doing good deeds from our safe little enclaves in the suburbs. Denny had been volunteering with Uptown's "outreach" program for over ten years, ever since the kids were little, driving into the city about once a month from Downers Grove. It was so hard for me to leave the church and people we've known most of our married life. But Denny said we couldn't hide forever in our comfort zone. So . . . we packed up the dog, the teenagers, and the Plymouth Voyager, exchanged our big yard for a postage stamp, and shoehorned ourselves into a two-flat—Chicago's version of a duplex—on Chicago's north side.

But frankly? I don't really know what we're doing here. Uptown Community Church has a few black members and one old Chinese lady who comes from time to time . . . but we're still mostly white in one of the most diverse neighborhoods in the U.S.—Rogers Park, Chicago. Josh says at his high school cafeteria, the black kids sit with the black kids, Latino kids sit with Latinos, nerds sit with nerds, whites with whites, Asians with Asians.

Not exactly a melting pot. And the churches aren't much better. Maybe worse.

In Des Moines, Iowa, where my family lives, I grew up on missionary stories from around the world—the drumbeats of Africa . . . the rickshaws of China . . . the forests of Ecuador.

Somehow it was so easy to imagine myself one day sitting on a stool in the African veld, surrounded by eager black faces, telling Bible stories with flannel-graph figures. Once, when I told Denny about my fantasy, he snorted and said we better learn how to relate across cultures in our own city before winging across the ocean to "save the natives."

He's right, of course. But it's not so easy. Most of the people I've met in the neighborhood are friendly—friendly, but not friends. Not the kick-back, laugh-with-your-girlfriends, be-crazy, cry-when-you're-sad, talk-on-the-phone-five-times-a-week kind of friends I had in Downers Grove. And the black couple who lived upstairs? (DINKS, Josh called them: Double-Income-No Kids.) They barely give us the time of day unless something goes wrong with the furnace.

So when Avis asked if I'd like to go to this women's conference sponsored by a coalition of Chicago area churches, I said yes. I felt flattered that she thought I'd fit in, since I generally felt like sport socks with high heels. I determined to go. At worst I'd waste a weekend (and two hundred bucks). At best, I might make a friend—or at least get to know Avis better.